THE SWEETWATER TRAIL

N. L. CAMPBELL

Text copyright 2013 by N. L. Campbell

Cover Art: Elise Ertel

All rights reserved. Without limiting the rights under copyright reserved above, no part of this publication may be reproduced, storied in or introduced into a retrieval system, or transmitted, in any form, or by any means (electronic, mechanical, photocopying, recording, or otherwise) without the prior written permission of both the copyright owner and the above publisher of this book.

This is a work of fiction. Names, characters, locations, brands, media and incidents are either the product of the author's imagination or are used fictitiously.

*For my family, and
EM, a survivor and an inspiration*

PREFACE

The Sweetwater Trail
August 18, 1851

"That's her. Brown dress."

Cade Braedon passed the spyglass to the New Yorker who laid down gold for two season's worth of trapping for a guide from Fort Hall to the Snake River.

Edmund Ormond wiped the sweat from the eyepiece on a square of silk and raised the spyglass to his right eye, pulling the focus on eighteen canvas covered wagons.

A cracked wheel. Metal band on the ground. A chisel.

Diapers on a line.

Hobbled oxen.

The emigrants, heads bowed, gathered around a pile of rock. A weathered hand tucked a gauge, perhaps a thermometer, against a cross.

A grave, not a food cache. Not the first seen since the trail head in Missouri.

His fingers adjusted, then lost the focus. He did not leave a Senate seat to stand at Felicity Sinclair's grave in the desert. She could not be lost to him, forever beyond this world.

Cade flipped the strap on his holster. "They couldn't have the strength to do more than scrape out a hole. Poor sods."

Edmund adjusted the spyglass, picking out a bonnet. The dusty hair did not match the braided wisp in his watch case.

Brown folds of a dress filled Edmund's vision. Home spun. Not the gown a young lady of society allowed in an armoire in

New York.

Not when he proposed marriage to her at Almstead House. Not when she blushed and accepted his ring, his token of esteem. Edmund slipped a finger into his vest pocket and rubbed his nail across the prongs of the Tiffany, Young and Ellis setting. A ring carried over miles of prairie grass and river crossings on the trail to the Oregon Territory.

"Done looking, Mr. Ormond? Mules need to get to water, and the only water's down there."

"Patience." She must be there, among the mourners.

"Glad I'm not the marrying kind." Cade yanked his revolver out of the holster and raised the gun over his head.

Edmund grabbed Cade's wrist. "Make another move like that and you'll be keeping company with the soul they're burying." The glare off the boulders above the slot canyon lit up the face of the New Yorker, making the parlor bred blue eyes shine from deep set sockets, while below the clean shaven chin gritted into a firm line. A man bending Fate, no matter the cost to his soul.

"I'm not gonna shoot her. That wagon master's a good shot and he's not expecting company out here."

"If that is the woman you've been paid to find, I do not want her alarmed." Edmund twisted Cade's arm, but the guide's arm did not move.

Cade pulled away and holstered the revolver.

"There's no 'if'. These folks are the only ones to make it this far. I'm telling you, she's your wife."

PART I

City of New York

1850

CHAPTER 1

Almstead House
May 1, 1850

"Do not breathe."

The white box embossed with *Maison Gagelin* in gold letters lay open on the floor of Felicity Sinclair's dressing room, gilt tissue thrust aside. French lace bordered tiers of ruffles of the finest wedding dress stock earnings from the Garrety-Brown Railroad ever purchased.

A wedding dress Felicity suspected belonged to a bride her father duly compensated for making a different choice of gown.

The dress lifted over Felicity's head and settled about her hips by her mother was not just a wedding dress. This dress was freedom.

Freedom from her mother's house. Escape to her own fashionable establishment, a home run according to her wishes.

All to be accomplished by accepting the part of dutiful daughter, binding herself in marriage to Edmund Ormond, the lean, blue eyed young man who rode to the hunt after others returned to the stables, who inspired Felicity to pray for the day she placed a change order at the stationer for her calling cards to read Mrs. Edmund Ormond.

A glow started in her chest and spread in a blush across her neck and face. And, if her prayers were answered by their first wedding anniversary, a son or daughter to be loved and cherished and spoiled out of the sight of nannies.

"I told you to put on your smallest corset." Faith Sinclair, mother of the bride to be, yanked at the waist of the dress.

"I'm wearing it," Felicity stepped out from behind the dressing screen and twisted to look in the mirror.

The back of the dress gaped open a hand's width at the waist.

"It fit you just weeks ago." Faith pulled her daughter behind the screen and unbuttoned the pearl fastenings. Grabbing the skirt, she peeled the satin and lace over Felicity's head and dropped the dress on top of the white box.

Felicity wished she looked like Maragon Ormond, her future mother-in-law, with slender powdered shoulders and hands a sculptor begged to carve in marble when she was sixteen. Or to look like Faith Sinclair, a green eyed porcelain doll of a woman with sweet bow lips and a nipped in waist.

"Try harder. Breathe out."

Felicity exhaled and Faith pulled the corset strings. The corset dug into her waist. Sweat started beneath the layers of petticoats and pantalets.

Tighter. Almost there.

Felicity whispered a prayer. Please, please fit.

The string broke and the corset edges flew apart.

"It's not yer girl's fault she's an easy keeper." Agnes Sinclair clamped her lips and studied the garlands in the plaster medallion on the ceiling of the dressing room, the floral wallpaper at odds with her stark blue dress. Black hair tarnished with silver and straight as a carriage whip, Aunt Agnes reminded Felicity of a raven.

The raven found in Poe's verses.

Faith unlaced the corset. "Stay out of this, Agnes."

"Maybe yer dressmaker made a mistake."

"It's not the dress." Faith pushed Felicity from the dressing screen. Felicity spread her hands across her bosom and snatched a dressing robe to cover her undergarments. "Look at her. She is larger than Hannah."

"I could take her back with us and put her to work on the farm 'til the weddin'. A little fresh air would do her some good."

Exile to the family farm did not factor in Felicity's dreams of preparing for the wedding. Exile to the farm meant staring out the window at milk cows, visiting the neighbors' farms and staring at their cattle, or sheep, or pigs, or carriage stock and capping off the adventure by sitting on blocks of burlap wrapped cheese in Uncle Jasper's cart on market day.

"Father set the date." Felicity picked up the wedding gown and smoothed the lace on the ruffles.

"You could meet someone like Cousin Hannah's husband. Someone more ... fitting for you. You would like that, wouldn't you?"

Thomas Clemms.

A plain Thomas, a cabinetmaker by trade. A nobody.

Felicity bent her head over the satin, careful not to let her tears well over and stain the creamy perfection.

"She must have somethin' to her if the Ormonds want her."

"Don't you want to wait until you know Mr. Ormond better?"

"She'll know him right quick after the 'I do's' are done and over."

Where is Mother's pride in marrying a daughter into the Ormond clan? Felicity's stomach rumbled. She laced her fingers together to keep from plucking her eyebrows.

Perhaps a small chunk of raisin cake is all I need to settle my nerves.

Faith grabbed her daughter's fingers and held them up for inspection. The orange tint under Felicity's fingernails betrayed a snack of cheddar and crackers. The salty crunch and smooth cheese soothed a bride's nerves. And scones. And the wafers in the tin box with "Chocolat de Vouvrais" on the label. And raisin cake.

"Hiding food again?" Faith opened drawers in the armoire, pawing through stacks of gloves and handkerchiefs. "You can eat all you want after the wedding. You'll be your mother-in-law's problem, not mine. I did what I could with you. If I catch you eating anything more than the biscuits you are allowed, I will –"

"Send me off to a bridegroom with bruises?" I can afford to be brave in front of Aunt Agnes. No chance Mother will take a hairbrush to the backs of my thighs, not in front of family.

"I'd a figured a blushin' bride was more in style. Can't that fancy doctor of yers prescribe somethin' fer yer temper?"

"Oh, go back to your dairy farm." Faith dumped a stack of nightgowns onto the floor.

"Soon as this little miss says, 'I do', I'm all for jumpin' in the wagon and headin' up the Hudson."

Faith slammed a drawer and held up a raisin cake wrapped in a napkin.

"That's where I left it," Agnes took the bundle from Faith's hand and bit into a chunk of cake. "I had a hankerin' for some of that cake last night."

Felicity could not look at her aunt. The last Aunt Agnes saw of the cake, the cake was on a silver tray yesterday afternoon in the east parlor.

"You're going outside. I don't care if it is raining. I'm locking you into the garden until you wear off some of that fat."

Felicity shuddered. Not the garden, where garter snakes skittered across the pathways and hid in the tulip bed. Not the garden, where she stepped on a snake playing hoops and sticks with Cousin Hannah. The mark of her slipper a sharp outline on the smooth scales.

Her mother's "cure" for a fear of snakes? Force a child to

stand in the nest of garter snakes. She remembered the smell of urine and the cling of wet linen, the apologetic face of the gardener who had a daughter of his own.

This is the life marriage to Edmund Ormond will free me from. Miss Sinclair, confirmed spinster, squirreling away food in cupboards and drawers. Saved from being like Mother, never leaving the house, hiding from callers and peering at them through the shutters until the back of their carriages could not be seen from the house.

"Please, Mama, not the garden. I'll be good. I promise. Whatever you want me to do, I'll do."

CHAPTER 2

An Engagement
May 2, 1850

Left foot on the black tile, turn, right foot on the white tile. Turn. Left foot on the black tile, turn, right foot on the white tile.

Felicity inhaled to the constriction point of her corset. She smoothed the folds of her gown, arranging the pleats into a march of printed blossoms in the apricot striped silk. The dress was her best dress because it was the one dress that buttoned from waist to collar.

At one end of the hallway lined with prints of locomotives and rail cars in place of family portraits, the drawing room and at the other end, Gerald Sinclair's library, the linen fold paneling covered by landscape paintings of wilderness scenes. Before her, the Sinclairs and Ormonds waited. Behind her, a sanctuary.

The library. In the fall, she sharpened pencils for her father and checked citations in his law books. The drapes over the diamond panes of the bay window proved a hiding place from her mother in the spring and summer. On winter days, Felicity sat in her father's chair before the fireplace, making up stories about the portrait of her father and Uncle Jasper Sinclair.

"The *sans souci* portrait" she called the piece, for the two ruddy faced young men were painted with hunting dogs and quail and without life's cares.

While Jasper Sinclair lost his hair but retained his spark for telling stories his niece shouldn't hear, Gerald Sinclair's hair silvered and his soul soured in the years since moving to Almstead House. The house drew the life from the man, season by season.

"The investment is still closed," Gerald's harsh voice carrying into the hallway, not the measured tone she loved to listen read *The Postumous Papers of the Pickwick Club*.

"Closed to everyone or just closed to me and my family?"

"It is closed to anyone foolish enough to homestead in the Oregon Territory. Put your money to work on establishing a land claim."

"Handling the farm sale doesn't give you the right to tell me what to do with the proceeds."

Aunt Agnes moved to her husband's side and nudged him. "Come on, Jasper. The answer ain't changin' any time soon. We'll make do like we always have."

Felicity cringed at the Tennessee twang, hoping Aunt Agnes left off using the spittoon for an evening.

Thunder rumbled. Felicity looked up at the skylight, listening to the hail.

"Would you like to compare notes?" Edmund Ormond's voice, so much warmer than the voice of her day dreams, caught her mid-turn on the marble tiles. The perfection of the man stood out more against the foil of an imperfect girl. The comb marks in his hair to the lacing on his shoes showed containment, an orderliness not to be disturbed.

Black for the right foot and white for the left foot? Or left for the black?

"I'm not sure I … ah … know what you mean."

"You're plotting an escape, aren't you? I would, if in your position."

"You are in my position." She whispered, not allowing her voice to warble.

"The difference is that I am a willing participant."

"And I am not?"
"I sense that you are reluctant to marry."
"Aren't you?"
"No."

Risking a glance, she studied his dark blue eyes. Marriage is an escape from this house for me, but what does Edmund get from the arrangement? Connection to the Sinclair family, so far beneath the matches available to him, how does that profit the man who has everything? A man so superior to a girl unmarried five years after her debut.

Felicity scuffed her slipper on a rough join between marble tiles. Why, we are as different as black and white.

"Aren't you longing to ask why ever not? The question is hanging between us."

Best to change the subject, she reasoned. "Did you know the Almsteads?"

"They were friends of my father's."

"Like my father." Felicity thought it odd Gerald kept the name on the Tudor house above 35th Street. The house reproduced so faithfully Felicity expected Henry VIII to ride across the lawn with Anne Boleyn riding pillion behind him.

"Why are we talking about them? Shouldn't we be talking about Paris? Or perhaps you would prefer London."

"You're planning to travel?"

"I believe tradition allows us a honeymoon tour."

"There is nothing traditional about this wedding." No proposal with Edmund on bended knee for me. No months of wooing. No stolen kisses. The wedding date set before the engagement was sealed. Just a civil arrangement brokered by Father between the Sinclair and the Ormond families.

"I assure you that we have taken care to be above reproach. My father approached your father and shortly I will, in front of witnesses, present you with a ring and ask you a very important question."

"Did you mean family?"

"Pardon?"

"You said witnesses."

Edmund smiled with the surety of a suitor certain of the response. "How will you answer?"

Felicity hesitated, her face reddened under his scrutiny.

"Do you always blush so becomingly?"

"I believe it to be the traditional state for brides."

"You see? Tradition. We're observing it."

"If I may ask …"

"Anything."

"Why the haste?" Her one friend from boarding school in Basel, now Victoria Van der Ploon, endured two years of engagement before her wedding. Cecilia Berger, three years. Cousin Hannah's engagement started in the spring and the wedding came after the harvest.

I will be married in that cream satin confection of a wedding dress come June 1st and the fact the dress doesn't fit will not matter to Father.

"Your father would say I'm to blame," Edmund straightened the left sleeve of his coat so the margin of shirt cuff matched the cuff exposed by the right sleeve. "It is the campaign. Timing is tight. Your father told you that you could expect to be the wife of a Senator?"

"I hope to be an asset."

"I can assure you that I am not after your fortune, if that is a concern."

"I never presumed –"

"Your mother's estate will be settled upon any daughters we may have."

"No one could mistake you for a hunter of fortunes." Faith Sinclair's inheritance, bound up in land near the proposed Central Park and in a woolen mill on the Hudson, provided for the family before her father's law practice yielded a profit. "Isn't there someone else, someone in your circle of acquaintances you prefer –"

"In my mind, the prospect of our marriage was formed at the initial Garrety-Brown investor dinner. Do you remember? At the Fairview Hotel? You played hostess for your mother. You encouraged me to enjoy the hot springs. They were most refreshing, you said."

Blood rushed to Felicity's face. She willed herself to remember bits of the dinner conversation for weeks, to recall Edmund's voice, his measured way of speaking to her. He was inspiration for a fit of awful poetry in her journal.

"You do remember."

"The blushing bride to be."

"Only if you say yes." Taking her hand in his, Edmund traced an intricate pattern on the back of her hand with his finger, the touch cool, light.

Words failed. She was a mongoose charmed before a swaying cobra.

Gerald cleared his throat from the entrance to the drawing room. "I have it on good authority that there is a question to be asked and answered this evening."

"Indeed, there is." Edmund took a firm hold of Felicity's elbow and led her into the drawing room.

"I yield the floor to the young Senator from New York."

"Do not put a hex on my efforts, Mr. Sinclair."

The faces in the room blurred and the voices buzzed. Felicity focused on the Meissen porcelain blue eyes above her and the young man's cool, confident grip.

"Miss Sinclair, will you do me the honor of becoming my wife?"

A question asked, but the answer stuck in her throat.

Can it be that this creature, so close in beauty to the vengeful angel painted in the drawing room's ceiling, is to be mine?

Is my marriage to be a marriage of equals, like my Aunt's, or a miserable affair like Mother's? Will we only speak to each other when necessary?

The rose patterned wallpaper pasted from cornice to baseboard on the wallpaper blurred and she swore the roses shifted.

Her father studied the whiskey in his glass.

No help there.

Her mother wiped away tears.

Sad to lose a daughter or sad to lose a target for her foul moods?

"Yes. Yes, I will." The words came out louder than she meant them to be.

"Then take this ring as a token of my esteem and affection."

The diamond Tiffany, Young and Ellis ring stuck fast above her knuckle, rolls of fat preventing it to settle into the correct place. Felicity forced the ring onto her dimpled knuckle where it stopped.

"May I?" Edmund kissed her damp palm and with a tug removed the ring.

He said nothing of love, perhaps he changed his mind?

Edmund smiled, following her thoughts and slipped the ring onto her little finger.

The wedding and courtship may not be traditional, but there is a chance the marriage will be bearable. Perhaps there was a harmony in contrast, like colors opposite each other on the color wheel.

The tea cakes on a side table caught Felicity's attention. Delicate white iris petals blossomed in buttercream frosting. Pansies and some unknown blooms filled out the pastry Eden.

Faith Sinclair stepped in front of the side table.

"Pardon me, mother." Felicity stepped to the side and took a tea cake.

Maragon Ormond slid her slender arm around Felicity's waist. "Welcome to our family, Felicity. With a wedding in a few weeks, there is much to discuss."

"Thank y-you," Felicity whispered, not daring to add the

words "Mother Ormond." Maragon Ormond, with her reputation for always choosing well whether a gown for the theater or a new carriage, was a mother figure to model herself after. "I understand the wedding will be at St. Paul's. My parents were married there."

"Hasn't your father informed you?" Edmund's mother tucked a strand of Felicity's hair into place. "The ceremony is to be performed here to accommodate your Mother. I understand she is ... indisposed to a gathering outside of your home."

Indisposed. A glossy word for does-not-wish-to-be-disturbed-to-make-plans.

"Would my father's library be acceptable?" Her sanctuary against the world, the one place of peace and order in the house.

"We will make it acceptable. It is not a matter of where the marriage takes place, but that the marriage takes place at all."

Mrs. Ormond kept her arm on Felicity's waist and studied the features of the younger woman with dark blue eyes like her son's. "I understand Sally Munston will be your matron of honor?"

Felicity pressed her fingers together. She had to have some eyebrow left. "There is a change. My cousin Hannah will stand up for me."

"Surely someone from our circle will stand up with you. One of the Nantes sisters, perhaps?"

Her cousin Hannah lapped a shawl over her stomach, but Felicity guessed Hannah was in an unmentionable breeding way. With friends travelling or with or other sudden obligations, Hannah became her only option.

"I wanted my family beside me on such an important day."

"But we are to be family, my dear. Once you are living with us, I know you will learn to consult with me in the future, to rely on me to guide you."

Perhaps her definition of family is different from mine.

Hannah rode in Uncle Jasper's market cart from upstate New York to be at a thrown together engagement party. She vomited most of the way to our front door. That is my definition of family.

And living with the Ormonds? No household of our own?

At least it gives me the time until Edmund purchases a suitable residence to study Maragon Ormond's perfection.

It will be just like when I studied Greek.

"Both Nantes sisters are travelling. And Mrs. Van Der Ploon is truly indisposed. If the wedding were to be delayed six months …"

"There is no delaying. The wedding will be as agreed. My son feels it is best this way."

"Yes, Mother Ormond."

Maragon Ormond withdrew her arm from Felicity and signaled to a footman to remove the tray of tea cakes.

"I am Mrs. Ormond, before the wedding, and after."

CHAPTER 3

A Betrayal
May 4, 1850

Two days after Felicity wore the ring from Edmund, the farm sale went through and Uncle Jasper decided his family would return home to finish preparations to depart on the trail to the Oregon Territory. While Uncle Jasper worried over the late start on the trail, Aunt Agnes's dark eyes followed her daughter. Felicity noted Hannah ate no food, for she heaved it up, and slept through the morning into late afternoon.

The family would not return for the wedding. Maragon Ormond had her pick of matrons of honor.

Hannah's calls of "goodbye" stayed with Felicity long after the family's cart left the driveway and gates. She did not want to forget the warmth of Hannah's last embrace or her cousin's face. Unless she traveled to the Territory, or Hannah travelled to New York, Felicity would never see her cousin or meet her children.

When Felicity thought of her cousin, she worried, but Felicity lost her sadness in the flurry to visit friends and relations of the Ormonds with Edmund and his mother.

Edmund, so kind, his hands ready to steady her in and out of carriages. Taking the reins of her white carriage he called "the Meringue." Not forcing her to ride with him and his racing stud Zeus in the park. Escorting Felicity and his mother to services at St. Paul's Chapel.

Events passed before she wrote them down in her journal.

"Is Mrs. Grayden at home?"

"No Miss Sinclair, she is out. As is Miss Grayden and her sister Miss Anne."

"May I leave my card?"

At the Langstons, she left her card. And at the Van Der Hoffs.

At the Van Gelder home, one of the Ormond carriages waited in the drive.

"Mrs. Van Gelder is away."

"Is Mrs. Ormond visiting?"

"I am afraid you are mistaken. Mrs. Ormond is not in the residence."

"Is that not the Ormond's carriage?"

"Yes, miss."

Perhaps the Ormond's housekeeper or some domestic used the front entrance when they should have used the servants' entrance. Mrs. Ormond's note "recommended" Felicity engage James Weir to produce the wedding arch and to her meet at his greenhouse at 1:00 p.m.

"May I wait for Miss Van Gelder?"

"Waiting for the Van Gelders would be … inconvenient, I'm afraid, today."

But Mrs. Ormond did not appear at the greenhouse and Mr. Weir did not have the appointment in his book.

Felicity clutched a drawing of a floral arch for the wedding, a perfect curve of cream roses to match the cream in her gown and directed the driver to return to Almstead House.

She flipped to the page in her journal. "J. Weir, 1:00 p.m."

Today's date.

"Where are you going?" Gerald Sinclair met her at the turn of the staircase. He walked up the stairs like he spent the night at his desk, jerky movements, feeling for each stair before putting his weight on it.

"Out, Papa. To meet Mrs. Ormond."

"I need you at home."

Felicity tucked her hair into a shirred bonnet and tied the taffeta ribbons. "I'll only be gone for an hour."

"I need you to stay at home with your mother and I for a few days."

"Why ever for? I'm meeting Mrs. Ormond and the florist did not have the – "

"Do as you are told –" Gerald drew a shaky breath. "I just want a little quiet time with my family right now. You can go to the greenhouse another day."

"But why, Papa?"

"Don't ask questions, girl."

Felicity removed her bonnet. "But she's expecting me. We are choosing roses for the arch."

"I'm sure she will manage on her own."

OBEYING HER FATHER'S wish to remain at home, Felicity spent the afternoon in her bedroom reading when she was not sulking. Bored, she wandered into the kitchen to find it empty.

Pots on the stove without a fire in the box below, breakfast dishes unwashed on the sideboard, pastry dough drying on the Carrera marble slab.

Preparations should be underway for dinner.

"Hello?"

No answer.

Felicity stepped into the pantry and found the canister of crackers. She crunched through three crackers and stopped, mouth full. She listened for the ordinary sounds of the house; the creak of the back stairs, the tinkle of the bell in the servants' hall. Voices.

Swallowing the wad of crackers in her mouth, she licked her fingers and went above stairs.

"Hello?"

She peered out the windows in the entry. The front gates, closed at midday. Why lock the gates in the afternoon?

The tray in the entry was empty. No cards from visitors.

Perhaps her father was full of his family and willing to let her out.

Gerald Sinclair slumped in his chair, the New York Post spread out before him at his desk.

Hoping for no crumbs on her lips or seeds between her teeth, she put her hands behind her back, twisting her fingers. "Did you give the kitchen staff the afternoon off? No one is tending to dinner."

"There is no hope of keeping this from you." Gerald slid the newspaper to Felicity.

"What is it?" She flipped through the pages. "Please do not tell me they posted the wedding announcement?"

How embarrassing.

The ceremony is weeks away.

What must the Ormonds think?

"Turn it over. On the front page."

Felicity flipped to the front page. The headline swirled into a mash of names.

"Papa?"

"I can explain."

"This paper is lying." Felicity tossed the paper onto Gerald's desk. "Will you be suing? Is that what you are worried about? I'm sure the Ormond's will understand if –"

"There is to be no further contact with Edmund or his family."

"I'm sorry, what?"

"Did you read more than the headline?"

Felicity laid the newspaper on her father's desk and smoothed out the crinkles in the newsprint.

The Garrety-Brown railroad, for which her father provided legal services and oversaw the accounting, laid all of five miles of track to nowhere.

Saplings sprouted between the rusting rails and ties.

A false corporate enterprise bilked investors and the government by charging inflated prices for construction expenses. Millions of dollars spent over years of supposed construction.

Cash bribes.

Worthless bonds.

Shares of stock offered to members of Congress at sub-par value. Stock that could be sold for an enormous profit in the open market to unknowing investors who wanted to own a part of the "high performing" railroad.

Congressional members who approved government funding for the railroad.

Gerald pressed his palms on the desk. "The reporter stated the facts correctly. I know because I gave him the story."

"I don't ... I don't quite understand."

"I wanted to be honest, to be clean so that people would know the truth. It is important to me that you know that even though I took money that wasn't mine to take, that I did not deny the action."

"Do you understand what this means?" Faith prodded. When her mother entered the library, Felicity did not know. She moved like a ghost, haunting the halls.

Felicity studied the carpet. No help in the neat rows of knotted fringe.

Her father was part of a fraudulent enterprise. According to the article, it meant he took money from modest people like her Uncle Jasper, and handed it over to cronies.

No wonder Father locked the gates. Not to keep me in, but to keep investors with questions out.

Papa is not the man I always thought him to be.

Felicity recognized the stiff white embossed envelope on her father's desk. A note, from the Ormond family. Perhaps from Edmund's own hand.

"Is that from Mrs. Ormond?"

"No."

"Edmund?"

"It is about business, another board that I sit on."

She pressed ice cold hands to her cheeks. "Do the Ormonds know?"

"Yes."

"Were they involved?" When the Ormond family invested, others followed. The investments chosen by the Ormonds exceeded expectations. There were a few disappointments, but always a new chance to invest and recover.

"That isn't important now."

"Did Edmund know? Is this why there was such an almighty rush to marry me off?"

"I thought I had time to get you settled –"

"Before what? Before you ruined my life? The lives of who knows how many people?" Felicity turned on her mother. "How long have you known this?"

"Don't blame your mother. She did nothing wrong. This is my entire fault."

Felicity dropped into a chair, stomach churning. She regretted the crackers. "No wonder you've been working so hard."

"I decided not to take any more money. I couldn't hide what I was doing any longer from you or your mother. All this money is owed to investors, and there isn't enough to cover it."

"How much?"

"More than what we have."

"How much?"

"No one knows for sure. There's been little to no record-keeping. The accounts are in disarray, at best. I can't pay it back."

"You have to ... if we are going to have any sort of life after this."

"It is impossible."

"How could you have done this? To me?"

"I know how you feel."

"You have no idea how I feel."

"My father's law practice failed when I was not much older than you. I watched him lose everything but our farm. What has been Jasper's farm."

"That's why you wouldn't take his money."

Gerald pulled open the desk drawer. Envelopes lay in rows. On the envelopes were names written in his copperplate script. Edgerton. Van der Ploon. Mill. Cavanaugh. Berger. "I told you I couldn't take any more money. This will all be returned. I couldn't do it to Jasper."

"What you did to the others ..." The servants. Most took stock instead of cash for wages.

"It wasn't just me. There was the board."

"You're a monster."

Faith jerked Felicity around to face her. "He's still your father. Don't ever speak to your father like – "

"Faith, let her go." Gerald rubbed his face, fingers digging into his scalp. "I went along with it. Greed overtook me. I'm not excusing myself or trying to blame everyone else. I wanted you and your mother to have the life a lawyer from up the Hudson couldn't give you."

"So all of this ... the house... clothing ... none of this really is ours. It belongs to the people you cheated."

"Yes."

"You have to give it back. All of it."

"I'm trying to. I want to make amends."

Felicity pulled a hair from her eyebrow. Then another.

"If it is any comfort, Edmund sincerely wanted to marry you."

No escape, now. No one, certainly not Edmund Ormond, would marry her. The name Sinclair would be a curse for generations. And changing her name would not put out the shame or the guilt of living on the backs of people who trusted her father with their money.

"How much ... how much did the Ormonds lose?"

"Nothing more than what they could afford to lose."

Felicity hauled herself up from her chair. "I have to call on the Ormonds."

Faith grabbed the fleshy part of her daughter's arm. "You'll do no such thing."

Felicity twisted her arm and broke her mother's grip, rubbing the reddened patch of skin. "You were against this marriage from the beginning."

"I didn't believe you to be a suitable wife for someone like Edmund. Not with his background, his standing in society – "

"Enough, Faith.

Felicity sniffed, patting the pockets of her gown for a handkerchief. "Is there nothing to be done?"

Gerald picked up the pages of the newspaper and put them into order. He folded the paper along the crease line, then folded it in half, pressing his palm on the corners. "I want you to leave New York. You should be in a safe place, far from the mess I've made. You and your mother will go on an extended holiday."

"I can't leave you here, alone. Where will you stay? How can we afford –"

Faith cupped Felicity's chin. "Your father is right. You've suffered enough. Europe will give us the buffer we need. Remember? You liked Paris."

Where did this version of her mother hide during the day? The sweet, concerned smile and dewy eyes. The gentle set of her mouth. This, the public copy of her mother appearing in private. Felicity expected the darker face, the one with cutting words and slapping hands.

Faith smiled. "You'll see. All will be well."

AN HOUR. AN afternoon. A night. Morning, again, behind the locked gates. She tried praying in the long days after her father's confession, but her mind raced, quiet thoughts impossible.

Why would God let Father cheat hundreds of people? Hard working people. Our friends. People who dined with us … went to church with us.

A former maid stood at the gates, and a footman. A carpenter beat on the lock with a hammer. More investors. Shouting, milling, trying to climb the walls to get to the front door. Pinkerton agents hired by her father kept the mob in check.

Felicity slept in her dressing room but the inside shutters pulled from their pockets in the wall could not block out the chanting at night and the cat calls during the day. She did not possess the daring to stand on the balcony.

Nowhere to go.

No one to see.

She gnawed another chunk of stale biscuit from the plate on her lap. The woman in the plaid cape stood at the gates. The same dirty plaid cape as the days before. The guards said she slept under the hedge. And the man in the suit with the frayed cuffs. Did he not have a shop to tend? Was it gone, caught up in the collapse of the stock?

How many of you lost everything?

Where were these people going to stay when the snows came? The hedge could not be much shelter in the spring rains.

All because of Gerald Sinclair.

Her father. How she wanted to be a lawyer like him. A lady of the law, defending the innocent. But he told her to study place settings and learn to direct the household staff. Oh, he taught her Greek and Latin and French and philosophy, but more out of amusement than for anything practical.

Setting the plate of biscuits on a side table, Felicity picked up her jewel case and dumped the rings and ear bobs onto the bed. The rope of pink pearls should buy the lady in plaid shelter for a good while. Her father paid a large sum for them in London.

The roar of the crowd startled Felicity when she eased the front door open. She stood under the carriage porch, the rain dripping down from the gutters. Should she go back, hide in her room?

What would that solve? Nothing.

Walking down the driveway to the front gates, a rock bounced off her shoulder. Felicity focused on the woman in plaid, keeping to the center of the driveway.

A Pinkerton agent stood between her and the fence. "I wouldn't be out here, Miss."

"Then will you please hand these to that woman in the cape?" She held the pearls out to the agent.

"I don't advise it."

Felicity stepped around the agent.

Up close, the breath and unwashed body of the woman caught Felicity by surprise. Of course, the woman had no place to bathe, much less relieve herself.

And the red plaid cape, cleaner when viewed from a third floor window, was grass stained at the knees. Has she been praying for the return of her pension? A pension never to be redeemed?

The woman held onto the bars and coughed up a wad of saliva. She spat at Felicity.

Ignoring the spittle on the bodice of her dress, Felicity reached between the iron fence rails and gripped the woman's grimy hand. "Take this," and she thrust the pearls between the spokes of the fence.

The woman hunched over the pearls. Hands reached out, grabbing at the rope, snapping the knotted silk. Pearls bounced once, twice and were scooped into pockets and bonnets and purses.

At last. Something she could do. If the pearls helped, there was more.

Picking up her skirts, Felicity ran up the wide steps to the entry hall.

The library. Of course. The landscape paintings can go. They belong to us, not the Almsteads.

She took two of the paintings off the library wall and holding them by the hanging wire on the back of the frames, carried them out the front door and down the driveway to the hands reaching through the fence.

"Thank ye, Miss. God bless you." A lightness in Felicity's chest began to build.

Felicity, gasping for breath, ran back to the house.

"What are you doing, girl?" Faith stood in the hallway in her dressing gown.

"Helping."

Felicity pulled the nails out of the wall taking down the painting of the Appalachian Mountains. A New England whaling scene followed.

The crowd at the gates shouted, but not for Felicity.

Faith reached between the bars of the fence to grab at one of the paintings, but the new owner held it just out of reach, taunting her to come to the other side of the gates to take it back.

"Mother, let it go."

Faith snatched the seascape from Felicity. "We need these. We can get money for them, you fool."

Felicity twisted the painting from her mother's grip on the frame and shoved the storm tossed whalers into the first hand to reach between the bars. A clerk, perhaps, with ink stained fingers. The mountain scene she pushed to the Van Gelder's butler, the neck of his white shirt grubby.

Out of breath, she caught Faith to her. "Come, come into the house."

"Felicity! Miss Sinclair!" Above her mother's head, above

the crowd, Edmund Ormond, perched high on a thoroughbred, beat at the head and shoulders of the crowd with his crop.

The man of her day dreams, whipping the victims of her father. She froze.

A man in overalls reached up to pull Edmund from his horse.

"Edmund!"

Jerking away from the hands yanking on the bridle and reins, the horse reared, twisting and lunging. Edmund whipped the horse, but it spun, knocking an old man in grey flannel to the cobblestones.

Hiding her face from Edmund, she grabbed the sleeve of the Pinkerton agent, the one who warned her to stay inside the house. "Help me. Get her into the house."

The agent wrapped his arms around Faith and half dragged, half carried her mother into the house.

Pressing her forehead to the bars, Felicity saw a hatless man, a woman with four children at her skirts help the elder man in flannel sit up on the cobblestones.

No Edmund.

No sign of horse or rider.

She looked for him again from the front steps, but saw only the backs of the Pinkerton agents. No one allowed to enter the gates and no one with the name Sinclair safe to be on the other side.

Faith wept, a puddle of silk on the black and white marble tiles, arms wrapped around her torso.

Felicity panted, hands on her knees, sweat rolling from her hairline to drip from her chin.

I've been wrong.

I've always believed her to be stronger than me. I see now I was wrong.

Wrong about so many things.

She caught herself on the sideboard, the tiles swirling. The dizziness passed. Perhaps the lightheadedness did not come from the trips up and back along the driveway, but at her escape from facing Edmund.

No one had enough to lose in her father's scheme. How badly damaged were the Ormond affairs?

Bang, bang, bang.

A knocking, a hammering, a pounding came from the rear of the house. The servants entrance door, perhaps.

Her heart thumped out the rhythm of the beating on the door. "Can I leave you for a moment? Tell me you will you stay here."

Faith turned away from her daughter.

Felicity ran through the hall to the back of the house, the heels of her slippers clacking on the stone floor.

The hinges on the servants' entrance rattled under a thumping fist.

He's here.

He's come for me. To save me.

"Wait, Edmund … I've almost got the bolt …"

She took a deep breath to steady herself and slid the bolt on the door.

CHAPTER 4

An Offer
May 31, 1850

"Uncle Jasper? How did you ... shouldn't you be on your way to Missouri? Is Hannah with you? What did you do with Aunt Agnes?"

"News travels, lass. I understand the name Sinclair isn't particularly popular."

Felicity held the door open for her travel worn uncle. "No, it isn't. Come in, come in, before you are tarred and feathered."

"What's that smell?" Her uncle sniffed, put a hand to his nose.

"The living conditions aren't the best. Papa let the staff go, that is, the ones that did not run from us. We've tried to keep up with the necessary things, but frankly Mother doesn't care about the niceties and Father is too morose to do much beyond thumb through his law books. I can promise you a bed ... I just can't promise clean sheets."

In the drawing room, Gerald picked at the stubble on his chin with black rimmed nails.

When did he last take a razor to his chin and cheeks? She was sure he stopped bathing.

"Thought you were somewhere headed west. What are you doing still in New York?"

"Seems to me it's what family does. Protects their own."

Jasper took a long drink from his glass of bourbon. "I've got an offer for you."

"What kind of offer?"

"We've put off the Territory this season. The farm sale stalled out and our Hannah ... our girl is doing poorly. She lost –"

Gerald held up a hand and flicked a glance towards Felicity. She looked up from sweeping ashes back into the fireplace.

"Is she sick?" With everything else, had her cousin lost her baby?

Jasper looked her square in the eye. "She needs time to heal before we make for the trail. We're late enough in the season, I'm afraid we'll end up like the Donner group, caught between the snows and a hard place."

"What's your offer?" Gerald grunted.

"Come with us. In the spring. I'm hoping by then to find a new buyer who isn't too fainthearted to work Sinclair lands."

"Thank you for your kindness, but we have to refuse."

"Papa!"

Jasper tapped his empty glass on the desk. "This would give you a chance to start a new life in a place that doesn't hate the name Sinclair."

"Faith will never consent, and I'm too old. It's one thing to read about Indian fights and shootouts in a novel, it's another thing to have to live through it. That's a young man's folly."

"Think about Felicity, then. Send her with us. Give her a chance."

"I can't leave Father. It wouldn't be right."

Faith stood in the doorway of the library. "I'm not living where there are no roads ... no sanitation and theater ... with naked savages and backwoodsmen."

Felicity laid her hand on her uncle's sleeve. "What does Aunt Agnes think?"

"I refuse to go anywhere with that woman," Faith crossed her arms.

This was the mother Felicity recognized. The one with the private face. "Mother, please."

"It was your aunt's idea. Hannah, too. I'm mostly the messenger."

Gerald shoved his chair back. "Tell Agnes we thank her for thinking of us, but it is not the life for Felicity or her mother."

Felicity pleated the fabric of her skirt between her fingers.

Papa sees me as a weak soul. Too weak for a life in a new land.

"Papa, what are you planning to do?"

"Why, clear my name."

The fabric between her fingers shredded. She pushed the frayed edges together. Fabric never to be made whole.

Just like us.

He can't be thinking we have a chance to rebuild. He's burnt it to the ground. There is no foundation to support us in this city. There is no household that will open a door to us. He turned the bricks to powder and the mortar is rotten.

Perhaps, this is the time for truth.

The back of the chair hit her shoulder blades. "I am quite certain there is nothing you ... or Mother, or even the Ormonds ... can do to repair this family's reputation. Whatever we chance we had ... why, they will put you in jail."

"No one is going to jail, pet. Not me, at least. It's been taken care of."

"Just like you took care of the investors?" The tone in her voice when addressing her father was new to her. "We need to go with Uncle Jasper. Aunt Agnes is right." She turned to her uncle, "Would we stay with you?"

"There's a boarding house not far from us, run by a Mrs. Clarke. You'll have to use another name ... just in case."

"Just in case Mrs. Clarke refuses us?"

"Yes."

"We're staying here, Felicity. You'll do as you're told." Her father slumped in his chair, out of breath, out of authority.

Faith tightened the sash on her dressing gown. "Plan all you want. I'm not going with you."

"Mother, use reason —"

"I'm staying in this house. Force me to go and I will burn it down around me."

"This isn't our house." Gerald ran his fingertips along the edge of his desk. "Don't you realize we're as homeless as the poor souls on the other side of the gates? It was only on loan to us, while I was on the board. This house goes back to the Ormonds. Sooner the better, I say."

Faith's head snapped up. "The Ormonds will take us in."

"No!" Felicity said before she could check herself.

"The Ormonds will not help us, Faith. We're on our own."

"I've made my position clear. I'm staying. I don't care what you do. Or her." Faith pulled her dressing robe up to her chin and drifted into the hallway.

"Uncle Jasper, what do we need to do? To prepare, that is, for the Territory?"

"Pack what you can. Practical things. Something to cook with. I've got some pamphlets about life on the trail in my bags that will help explain what you'll be needing." Jasper kissed Felicity's forehead. "I'll just leave them in the hall while you two talk things over."

Gerald rested his elbows on the desk.

"Papa."

No response. He rubbed his knuckles into his eyes, the heels of his palms digging in to wipe away tears.

Felicity's capacity for empathy, a silken thread, strong and fine and thin under pressure, held the seams of her patience and caring together. But the thread broke.

"You must tell me the truth from now on. No more lies. I can't bear it."

CHAPTER 5

Ashes, Ashes
June 2, 1850

Felicity drew a line through "sturdy clothing" on the pamphlet's "Suggested Packing List." Sitting back on her heels in front of a trunk, she considered the white box with *Maison Gagelin* embossed on the lid. It lay on the floor of her dressing room, gilt tissue tucked around the folds of cream satin. Rising on crackling knees, she closed the box and placed it in the bottom of the trunk.

The gold letters glowed.

Will I ever have a need for a wedding dress? What suitor, in good conscience, would dare to marry the daughter of Gerald Sinclair? No one I could ever meet in New York polite society.

But I can't leave the dress in the armoire. And I can't bear to see its perfection in the window at a second hand clothier's shop.

If the wedding dress went, something else must stay behind. Her belongings, reduced to one trunk in the back of a wagon, limited her wardrobe. Pantalets, corsets, stockings, yes; morning dress, no. She consulted the pamphlet. These items were not on the list, but she considered them to be necessities.

Felicity removed a muslin dress from the stack of clothing to be packed. There were more cooking implements on the list than clothing. Utensils she did not know the use for, nor how or when to use them.

Cooking made her think of food, and food made Felicity think of cake.

Wedding cake.

I should be sitting down to a frosted wonder of culinary style, not learning how to bake a cake.

I should be watching a ship's steward unload my trunks in a stateroom, not packing a trunk for a wagon.

I should be dressing for dinner, not deciding which dress to pack for a life in the back of a wagon.

I should be with Edmund.

Felicity opened the drawer of her secretary to take out a sheet of stationery. No paper. Blotting paper, gone. The tray with her collection of pens and tips, empty.

Mother must have visited my room.

The desk in the library contained pens and paper aplenty, she reasoned, and walked down the stairs to the library.

The nail head on the wall marked where *sans souci* painting of her father and uncle hung on the wall above the fireplace. It was a roll of canvas by the door, tied with twine, ready to be loaded into the carriage. A carriage to be driven to a dealer and sold to raise funds for tolls and ferry crossings on the trip to the west.

Gerald slid a volume into a packing crate on the floor next to the desk.

I'm not certain which of us is more practical. Myself, for packing a wedding dress, or Papa for packing law books for life in the Territory.

Gerald turned over the papers on his desk, knocking aside a jar of paste. "Packed?" Clean shaven cheeks and a wrinkled shirt testified to bathing.

"Not yet. Almost."

"Well, finish up so we can get on the road."

"There's something I need to do, and I'd like your blessing."

"Give away more paintings?"

~ 34 ~

Felicity tried to smile at her father's joke. "No, Papa. I want to send a letter to Edmund. I at least owe him some sort of explanation and a formal release of our engagement."

Gerald tucked another book into the crate and wiped his hands on his trousers. "I can't let you do that. Promise me that you'll have no further contact with the Ormonds. It is for the best, for you ... and Edmund. Go finish your packing."

"It's hardly polite to leave without some word from me."

"It's too late for good manners."

"All right, no letter. I'll go to them ... and explain ..."

"This is the last time I will speak to you on this subject. You will not write, you will not visit Edmund or his parents. You will take your good intentions and pack them in your trunk upstairs. Do I make myself clear? Do I?" Gerald barked.

"Yes, Papa." Tears started, blurring the text on the spines of the books in the crate. The one person who understood her, no longer cared to listen.

Sliding the lid on to the crate of books, Gerald paused. He took a deep breath. "I'm not trying to punish you. I'm protecting you ... from as much pain as possible. Trust me in this ... even though I haven't been worthy of that trust."

"I'm trying, I really am."

Gerald picked up the crate. "This one is ready to go. I'll be back for your trunk. Hurry."

She rubbed her fingertips on a rough spot on the corner of her father's desk. The library, once a refuge, was a room in a house no longer her home.

No comfort here.

She opened a drawer. Paper.

She opened the center drawer. Pencils.

Her father drafted documents in pencil for ease of corrections. He liked the smooth feel of graphite on paper.

She folded four squares of foolscap and tucked them into the pocket of her gown.

"Where's your father?"

Felicity startled, blush rising from her collarbones to her ears. Uncle Jasper wiped the sweat from his forehead with the back of his hand.

"He … ah … took a crate out to the carriage." *I can't very well tell him that his brother packed a crate of books any more than I can tell him about the wedding dress. He'd laugh and leave it in the driveway.*

"I just came from there."

"Maybe he's trying to get Mother to pack."

Jasper snorted. "Good luck with that enterprise."

Felicity smiled.

Jasper winked at her. "You ready?"

"Almost."

"Good girl. Get finished and give me a holler when you're ready with your trunk."

"I will."

Felicity tucked the pencil in the folds of her dress.

PULLING UP A stool in the kitchen, Felicity took out the folded paper and flattened the white pages on the marble pastry slab.

"Dear …," The pencil wavered. Did she address him as Mr. Ormond? "My dear Edmund" she whispered.

What to write? She bit the end of the pencil.

The truth.

The copperplate script flowing evenly through words and lines and paragraphs of explanation and apology.

"Thought you were going upstairs."

The lead of the pencil ripped a hole in the paper. "Uncle Jasper … I … ah … I thought you were Father …"

"I'm still looking for your Pa. Horse cast a shoe and it'll take time to get it back on. Can't find any tools of much use in the carriage house. Must have walked off with your driver."

Guilt washed through Felicity like dirty rinse water. "How much time?"

"More than I care to spend with those folks out front."

"Can you give me time to run an errand?"

"What kind of errand is so all fired needed?"

Felicity's cheeks flushed red.

"Whenever your cousin Hannah does that, I know she's up to no good."

Felicity folded the paper on the slab and tucked the pages in her pocket. "I need to go to the Ormonds."

"That a note for young Edmund you're working on?"

"Yes."

"Your father approve of this idea of yours?"

Felicity looked down at the marble. She picked at a flattened piece of dried dough. It flaked into stale crumbs. "No."

"My advice is to do what your father tells you to do. Obey your Pa. He knows what's good for you."

"But –"

"Burn it." Jasper took a lifter and took the lid off one of the burners of the wood stove. "Right now."

Felicity withdrew a sheet of paper and balled it up, tossing it into the fire box. Jasper picked up a box of matches.

No help from Uncle Jasper. He passed the box of matches to her.

"No more letters."

Felicity struck a match and dropped it onto the wad of paper.

Jasper replaced the lid on the stove. "I won't tell on you, but I'm expecting you to honor your Pa's wishes."

Felicity turned the box of matches over in her hands. "I understand."

Jasper took the box and placed it on the shelf over the stove. "After I get your folks organized, I need you to be ready to go."

He kissed her forehead. "You're up against a new life, a better one than the one you've been made to live in. Trust me that this will be a time that you look back on with pride. Not many folks have the backbone to start over from scratch."

Felicity nodded, throat too tight to speak.

After her uncle left to find her father, Felicity pulled the note with the copperplate script from her pocket and signed it "Felicity Sinclair". Slipping the Tiffany, Young and Ellis ring from her little finger, she kissed the smooth prongs and set it in the center of the page of explanations and apologies and folded the paper around the ring. A length of kitchen string served in place of sealing wax.

The distaste for not obeying her father weighing on her, Felicity took the passage leading into the butler's pantry and took the side stairs to the garden.

The water dripped from the gutters. The wet lawn, overgrown to her kneecaps, spilled into the flower beds. The roses, black spotted and overblown, leaked petals across the walkway. The marble benches, mildewed.

A rustle under the elm. She jumped, squeaked.

A squirrel. Not a snake.

Keeping to the side of the house, Felicity prayed to avoid garter snakes and the Pinkerton agents.

She opened the side gate under the wall of ivy covering the carriage house.

Felicity ran across rain slick cobblestones, the wet hem of her dress slapping her shins. Fast out of breath, she ran, walked, and trotted the six blocks until the knocker to the Ormonds' front entrance was in her hand.

The door opened wide.

"Miss Sinclair to see –" she panted.

The door closed.

She thumped her fist on the front door.

The door opened a hand's breadth.

"I cannot admit you, Miss."

She shoved her letter into the doorway.

"Will you give this to Mr. Ormond? Mr. Edmund, please?"

The Ormond's butler looked down at the letter tied with twine. "Miss Sinclair ... I regret to inform you that I cannot accept your letter."

"I've been through so much. Can you please, please help me?"

"As a Garrety-Brown stockholder ... no, to be accurate, a former stockholder, I cannot in good conscience go against the wishes of this house." He shoved her hand and the letter from the doorway.

The door slammed. The lock clicked into place.

Felicity stared at the door panels.

What to do? What to do?

If Uncle Jasper used the servants' entrance at Almstead House, I'm not above using the same strategy at the Ormond mansion.

She tapped on the door to the servants' entrance.

Silence.

She fed the envelope through the gap between the threshold and the door until the ring butted against the door. The ring, too large to slide under the door, was too small for her finger.

I can't leave the letter without the ring and the letter cannot be delivered without the ring.

She knocked on the door.

The clack of rapid steps sounded.

"Please, God, do not let the housekeeper be a stockholder, too."

The door flung open.

Felicity gasped and stepped back. Maragon Ormond was the last person she wanted to greet. Maragon Ormond and her controlled perfection, a painful reminder to Felicity with wet hem and dirty stockings.

"Let me be clear. You and your family are not welcome

here. The harm you have caused this family —"

"I am so sorry … Mrs. Ormond, my father never intended —"

"To let such a posting run is highly irresponsible."

"Posting?"

What posting? Posting for what? The editorials, bad enough, but …

The announcement.

Papa forgot to pull the wedding announcement for Mr. and Mrs. Edmund Ormond from the New York Post.

"I beg your forgiveness, but under the circumstances —"

Maragon Ormond slammed the door.

Staring at the painted panels and the brass door knob, Felicity's mind went blank.

Think, think, think.

What to do? What now?

She propped her letter with the ring tucked inside against the door and stumbled back.

Whatever punishment Father settles on for disobeying his wishes will never hurt me as much as this.

Two blocks from Almstead House, Felicity slipped and jammed her toe on a cobblestone. She bent to hold her toe to delay the rush of pain.

The evening sky glowed with a blood orange sunset.

She stood.

A sunset, in the rain. To the east, not the west.

She picked up her skirts and ran. Ran without regard for her aching lungs and thin slippers. Not caring what she stepped in or stepped on. Rushing past carriages, not stopping to let them pass. Ignoring the shouts from the drivers. Knocking against carts. Running.

The woman in the plaid cape hooted and danced in the smoke. The Pinkerton agents formed a bucket brigade from the stable to the carriage porch.

Her mother did what she swore to do.

Flames licked up from the attic of Almstead House.
Burn Almstead House to the ground.

PART II

The Trail

1851

CHAPTER 6

Lone Elm Grove
April 10, 1851

Tugging on her taffeta bonnet to shield her face from the morning sun, Felicity watched for movement along the trail, east towards Independence, Missouri.

No sign of rescue.

It was early in the year for wagon trains to be on the trail. The strip of spring grass in the middle of the track was not ground down by hooves or weathered by the sun. It was early for some emigrants, but not for Rye Jones, the scout hired in St. Joseph on the banks of the Upper Independence landing.

The stench of breakfast in the Dutch oven on the campfire coals made her stomach lurch. She shifted aching hips on the crate of tin dishes and reached beneath the hem of her skirts to pluck the pantalets away from her chafed thighs.

A groan and the splash of vomit in the relieving bowl came from the back of the canvas covered wagon.

Felicity gagged, saliva filling her mouth.

Gerald Sinclair vomited again, before settling back onto the feather bed laid over the barrels of flour and bacon.

Pouring tea into the gold rimmed cup beside her on the crate, Felicity hoped the Earl Grey brew would settle her nerves and picked up a pamphlet.

What I need is a medical journal, not a dissertation on choosing mules over oxen.

The campfire billowed at a change of the wind and sparks and ash flew upwards. She closed her eyes against the sting of the smoke and searched for the pocket of her apricot striped gown to find the remains of her lace handkerchief.

"You little fool!" The gravel-edged voice of Rye Jones sent a shiver down her spine buried beneath the layers of chemise, corset, under-petticoat, hoop petticoat, over-petticoat, and silk dress.

She slid off the crate and onto her blistered feet. Here was her personal vision of Kit Carson, hero of her father's blood and thunder ten cent novels.

Will I ever be accustomed to seeing a gentleman dressed in buckskins and fringe?

"What are you doing? Trying to set the whole prairie on fire?" Rye's grey eyes were cold as the Kansas River at the last crossing.

She bit the inside of her cheek, tasting blood rather than replying.

Rye limped over to stamp out the burning stubble outside the fire ring.

"Are you going to do something about your dress?"

"What's wrong with my dress?" It wasn't as if she packed many wardrobe options.

Rye glared at her and grabbed the tea pot from the rock beside the fire, dumping the lid and contents onto the ruffled hem of Felicity's dress.

She snatched back her skirt. A clump of wet tea leaves splatted on the grass.

"What are you doing? That's my tea!"

Rye held up the singed silk hem for her inspection. "I was trying to save your life. Although for the life of me I'm not sure why."

She slapped the fabric from his hand and smoothed down her skirt. "Where did you come from? I didn't hear you."

"Hunting."

Helmut Schneider, who also provided fresh meat for the wagon train, tugged the brim of his hat and nodded before he tied the reins of Rye's mare next to his rawboned gelding. The carcass of a doe lay over the mare's hindquarters.

"Why haven't you broken camp this time? The tea too cold for your taste? Or maybe the servants did not wake milady on time?"

She gritted her teeth. Tempted to kick his shins, the leaking bandage wrapped around his thigh stopped her. "The others voted. They thought it best to push on and wait for us at the next campsite."

"You're lucky we found you or you'd be out here on your own. Was it the smell of your cooking that drove them away?"

Cooking, not a talent she possessed. But a failure he didn't have to point out. "I didn't have a choice. There is illness among my family members."

"What kind of illness?"

Felicity waved the pamphlet in her hand. "I'm reading this to try to figure that out."

Rye nudged the Dutch oven with his boot. "Are you sure it isn't food poisoning?" Rye's hunting dog sniffed at a plate of biscuits near the coals. Dodge, a hound not known for passing up a meal, backed away.

"Quite certain."

"What are the symptoms?"

Felicity blushed to the roots of her blond curls beneath the bonnet. "It would not be proper for me to say."

"Pardon?"

"To relate the nature of bodily … indelicacies, as one would say, to a gentleman … why that is never done."

Her father groaned. Vomit splashed into the basin. Felicity pressed the ridges of her crocheted gloves to her lips.

"Didn't anyone tell you that the trail is no place for young ladies and their indelicacies? Get out of my way." Rye limped to the back of the wagon. He stepped onto the crate of her father's law books and lifted his bandaged leg over the tailboard. "When I'm finished with your father, I expect you to be packed up and ready to load this wagon or I will leave you here to rot."

The canvas flap whipped shut behind him.

"Do you have laudanum in your supplies?"

Helmut Schneider. She forgot the hunter with the deep laugh lines around his mouth bore witness to her weak stomach and weaker resolve.

"Why, no. I don't know." She scuffed the toe of her dusty satin slipper in the grass. "My Aunt, that is, Mrs. Jasper Sinclair, is at the creek. They're trying to refresh Mr. Clemms in the water. He is taken with the same fever."

"I'll speak with your Aunt. I'm sure she has a well-stocked medicine box."

She nodded towards the wagon flap. "Does he know what he's doing?"

"More so than you or me, meaning no disrespect, Miss. I'll be back in a flash."

Crumpling the pamphlet in her hand, Felicity perched on the crate of tin plates to wait for Rye to emerge with his verdict. She could not follow Rye's low voice and Gerald's response.

Felicity cradled the cooling cup of tea and read that the author of "Advice and Consolation for The Prairie Emigrant" considered their campsite at Lone Elm to be in the midst of a picturesque grove.

She sniffed.

Not so much as one spindly tree attempted the pretense of a grove. A grove by her definition was ornamental shrubbery and graveled walkways meandering around ancient trees and lichen covered benches placed just so as to give one rest between vistas. A grove was restrained, yet wild in a civilized manner.

Lone Elm was wild, and not in a civilized manner. Not a

trellis to be found. Nor an elm tree. The grove was likely burned in the campfires of earlier trappers or emigrants.

She dug the toe of her satin slipper under a clump of wildflowers but their roots held fast. Their practical petals and sturdy stems were nothing like the hothouse flowers she preferred. Their colors were riotous, not the blush tones of the paper roses and cotton leaves on her bonnet.

So this is the glory of my new life, Felicity mused. My life, limited to a space four feet wide and twelve feet long covered by oiled canvas. My life, crammed into boxes and barrels. She tossed a spindle from Aunt Agnes' broken rocking chair on the fire. The beeswax polish bubbled and smoked.

Will I ever get the stench of smoke and sweat out of my clothes? Will I never have clean clothes again?

She sipped the tea and laid the pamphlet atop the others.

Papa should be in New York where Dr. Foster could be summoned.

Surely after this episode Papa will heed my pleas to leave the wagon train and head east to civilization.

A boarding house could be tolerable.

It possessed a roof.

Of course, they would have to leave the wagon and all the supplies behind as it belonged to Uncle Jasper and Aunt Agnes. Hopefully the family would spare enough supplies for the walk back to Independence. And once they reached Independence, would her father have enough funds to wait for Edmund Ormond to respond to her letters?

Perhaps we could hire Mr. Schneider to guide them back to the trailhead.

Perhaps he had a legal issue that Father could tend to.

Perhaps a labor trade could be bartered for as Mr. Schneider sorely needs a Last Will and Testament if he pursues the madness of settling in the Oregon Territory.

And then Felicity saw it. Coiled on the ground behind the front wheel of the wagon.

It was surely a rattlesnake.

Sweat drenched her armpits.

Rye shot a four foot long rattlesnake in camp the day before.

Snakes terrified her. Garter snakes skittering in the leaves on the path in the Almstead House gardens made her heart pound. Rattlesnakes featured regularly in her nightmares on the trail surpassing any fears of Indian attack or stampeding cattle.

"Mr. Jones," she croaked.

Pamphlets alluded to children perishing from a strike. Adults maimed.

"I say, Mr. Jones!"

"I'm busy, here, Miss Sinclair."

"But Mr. Jones, there is a snake."

"Well, do something about it."

"A rattlesnake, Mr. Jones."

While "Advice and Consolation for The Prairie Emigrant" provided a remedy for snake bite, the pamphlet itself was not effective for preventing snake bite. Immediate removal to New York was the best prevention.

"And what do you propose I do about it?"

"Shoot it, if you have to."

"But I do not possess a gun."

"I suggest that you feed the snake whatever it is you are cooking. That should kill it."

Which utensil to use when eating an oyster was practical knowledge; but the preparation of a stew, a dish served to downstairs staff, was not one of her accomplishments. Yes, the Dutch oven contained a vile concoction.

But she hadn't killed anyone. Yet.

Felicity folded "Advice and Consolation for The Prairie Emigrant" into a tight packet. If she threw it just right, the snake might withdraw.

Preferably where Rye Jones might step on it.

Felicity squared her shoulders, closed her eyes and lobbed the pamphlet at the snake.

No telltale rattling.

Felicity peeked through her lashes. Perhaps it was asleep.

"Mr. Jones?"

Rye's horse shifted under the weight of the deer carcass. The wagon master's rifle was in a scabbard on the saddle.

Felicity tapped her fingers against her lips. Rye didn't tell her not to shoot the snake with his gun. Was the rifle loaded? It made sense that a man like Rye carried a loaded weapon.

"Your father wants to know if you have survived your snake ordeal."

Felicity lifted Rye's rifle from the scabbard like a cup from her mother's Sevres tea service.

Inhaling until her corset squeaked, Felicity pointed the rifle at the snake. She closed her eyes.

"Well?" Rye spoke as if a snake in the campsite was commonplace.

Felicity jerked the trigger.

The rifle cracked and the gunstock smashed into her shoulder.

Her eyes flew open at a sharp metallic clang and a whinny. Rye's mare shied, but remained tied to the wagon. Helmut's horse bucked like a fiend and galloped away.

The Dutch oven's lid was in the campfire on its back, dented. The vile contents, safe.

The canvas flap ripped open. Rye jumped down from the tailgate and snatched the rifle from Felicity's numb hands. He didn't move like a man with a leg injury.

"You fool. You could have hit the livestock."

Twice. He'd called her a fool twice. Felicity pulled her bonnet into place, struggling to tie the grosgrain ribbons. "It was only the lid ... you told me to shoot it."

Helmut arrived at a run. "I heard a shot."

"Miss Sinclair here put a Dutch oven out of its misery."

Rye slapped his gloves against his bandaged thigh. Felicity wagered he wanted to use them on her.

"Just what are you inferring?"

"That you are kinder to your cooking utensils than you are to your family."

Helmut struggled to keep his lips in a straight line as he pressed the vial of laudanum into Felicity's shaking hands. "This will help with your father."

"Thank you, Mr. Schneider. You are a gentleman."

"I'm off before my horse beats me to the Pacific." Helmut tipped the brim of his hat and jogged away.

Rye shoved his hands into his gloves. "Where's this snake of yours?"

"Over there. Behind the left wheel."

Rye limped away to kick the grass by the wheel.

She bit the crocheted ridges of her gloves expecting to see the snake strike at Rye's fringed leggings.

Rye snorted. "Here's your trophy, Miss Sinclair," tossing the snake at her feet.

She jumped back, skirt raised above her ribbon wrapped ankles.

It was a bullwhip.

Felicity wished the prairie to part and swallow her. Staring up at grass roots and dirt and letting the worms eat her must be better than facing Rye Jones.

He tipped his hat back. "Save the laudanum. Using it will just be a waste. Who else is ill?"

"My Uncle Jasper. Aunt Agnes is tending him and my cousin's husband, Tom, as Hannah is … indisposed. Please sir, my father is less than hearty. Will you send for doctor? Surely there is one in Independence."

"That's more than a day's hard ride from here. Your father will be dead before then. So will the rest of them."

"Dead? What do you mean, dead? My father can't die. Not here, not in this wilderness."

~ 49 ~

"If he is like the rest of humanity, he will meet his Maker despite what you or I might wish."

"But what's wrong with him?"

"Cholera."

Did she detect a grim satisfaction in his tone? "How do you know?"

"Vomiting, milky stool, gut pains, thirst." Rye ticked off symptoms with his fingers. "Did I miss anything?"

"But how do you know?" Her gut twisted.

"I've seen cholera before. Up close."

"And the laudanum?"

"Keep it for the living." Rye stared long and hard at the vial in her gloved palm, biting his lip before backing away.

Felicity grabbed the back of his vest. "Please don't leave us behind. Surely there is a cure. You have to do something."

"I don't have to do anything. There's nothing to be done. There's no cure."

"I read that peppermint leaves mixed with camphor are a cure."

"Where did you get that fool notion?"

"Here, in this pamphlet. The writer states peppermint leaves steeped in creek water will restore –"

"You can't find all your answers in a pamphlet. Where on the prairie do you think you will find mint leaves?"

"That's not fair." Her tears crested.

"Life isn't fair, or haven't you learned that? He has cholera, Miss Sinclair. You can't cure him. The best you can do is to make your father comfortable."

Tears dripped off Felicity's chin.

Rye rubbed his thigh, loosening the bandage.

"Give him a few drops of laudanum in whatever is left of your tea. It will make it easier for him. You can make tea, can't you?"

"Make what easier for him?"

"Death."

CHAPTER 7

Parting of the Trails
April 11, 1851

The morning blurred into afternoon and into twilight. Humidity wrapped around Felicity like a sodden wool blanket and should have warmed her. But she was cold inside, cold with dread and fear, cold from dipping and wringing flannel in the bucket of creek water.

Her hands registered the heat in the cloths she took from her father's forehead.

"Felicity?" Gerald Sinclair's voice, so treasured, so weak.

She lifted his sweat soaked head and pressed a cup to his mouth. "Drink this. It's tea."

"Tastes funny."

She smoothed the pillow and lowered his head. Brushing back the silver hair, she kissed his forehead.

"It is the laudanum."

"I have to tell you ... promise me ..."

"Yes, Papa, anything." Anything, anything at all to bring her father comfort. Felicity licked her lips, tasting the bitter residue of the leaves she sampled during the trips to the creek for fresh water. No refreshing bite of mint.

"Pray for me."

"Rest, Papa, rest. Save your strength." She waved away the mosquitoes. The candle flame flickered. This was not the time to confess her faith in God failed.

"Forgive me. Not the life I planned for you."

"Finish the tea, Papa." She settled him on the feather bed, the ticking stained yellow from his sweat.

"Keep th' law ..." his words slid, voice cracking.

"I don't understand."

"My law books ..."

"Do you want me to read to you?"

"No, child. Don't let anyone take 'em from you ... ish yer future. Laudanum's makin' my head spin."

She cradled his hand. His hand with the spidery veins taught her to write a legible script. His hand with the age spots wore a gold wedding band from a marriage in ashes.

"It's just your words slurring. You'll be better in the morning, you'll see."

"Promish' ..."

"I promise."

The canvas flap was thrown back and the candle flame blew out.

Felicity startled, but sank back on the crate of books when Rye lifted his stiff leg over the tailgate. She lit a match, restoring the candle flame. Blowing out the match, she flipped the burnt stick to the floor.

Rye picked it up and spit on the end.

"Going after the wagon next?"

He braced himself against a barrel and leaned over Gerald, watching her father's chest rise and fall. She clasped her father's hand, feeling an urge to protect.

Rye reminded Felicity of a predator. Like a mezzotint version of George Stubbs' lion. But this predator was conflicted. Like a lion with a conscience regretting a kill.

Clasping his dirt caked hands, Rye gritted his teeth and bowed his head.

Felicity didn't expect Rye to be spiritual.

How I wish I could pray. But it isn't in me.

The faith that drove her from childhood was dried up and

twisted.

Her father's hand fluttered, an injured bird in her palm. "The booksh' ... th' only legacy."

"We'll be in the Oregon Territory, you'll see, and we will have a fine set of shelves built for them."

"Faith ..."

Was he telling her to have faith, or did he think he spoke to her mother?

"Stay wit' Uncle Jasper and Aunt Aggie. Knows what to do ... alwaysh' did. Do everythin' Aggie tells you ..." Her aunt intimidated Felicity. But he didn't need to know that.

Felicity kissed her father's hand and tucked it under the wool blanket to keep it from the mosquitoes.

Listening to Gerald's labored breathing for a pace, Rye shifted his weight to his good leg. "This the first deathbed you've attended?"

"Yes."

"Frightened?"

The dirt on Rye's hands meant a grave was ready. The back of her neck prickled. Beyond the tailgate, quilts spread on the ground held squares of sod.

"He is all I have left."

Rye wrapped an arm around his ribcage, holding himself together. "I have to see to the others. Call me when there's a change."

Felicity dozed off before dawn, the sunrise masked by a grey drizzle. The drip, drip, dripping of the runoff splashing on the tailboard woke her.

"Papa?"

She laid her hand on his chest. A breath, shallow.

"Papa!"

"I'se here, chil' ..."

The burning terror in her chest spilled out. "Don't leave me, don't leave me, please, oh please, don't leave me."

"Love you, chil'."

Sometime after the drizzle turned to rain she closed her father's eyes and shut his sagging mouth.

Rye gave Felicity time to tuck the *sans souci* portrait beside her father's body before replacing the sod squares. Gerald Sinclair was not alone beneath the roots of the wildflowers. Uncle Jasper and Hannah's husband, Tom Clemms, joined him.

Uncle Jasper, the visionary for the crossing of the prairie, the kind man who sheltered his brother's family when he did not have to provide for them. The one man she and the others looked to for direction. How could Aunt Agnes bear the loss?

And Tom, sweet Tom who would never see his firstborn, never feel the softness of his child's cheek.

The agony of their losses filled Felicity's chest with a heaviness, a weight which pulled her down, down into misery.

Aunt Agnes and Felicity's cousin Hannah survived as the remnants of her family. A brief prayer for the dead muttered by Rye and it was done. No mausoleum or headstone marked the place of her great loss.

No one will dig up the grave to spit on Father's remains.

Her knees pressed into the dirty quilt beside her father's grave. Tears blurred the prairie grass on the sod squares. The wildflowers, bruised, sprang upwards to face the sun.

"Get up." Rye's voice failed to stir her.

"Thank you for the verses you chose. You know the bible." She slid a hand into the pocket of her gown, fingers rolling and unrolling the corner of a lace handkerchief.

"I had plenty of reasons to study it as of late."

"And did you find comfort?"

Rye grabbed her elbow and hauled Felicity up from the dirt.

Her knees, sore from the trail, locked and she sagged against him. He caught Felicity around her corseted waist.

She stared up at his rugged features. Felicity expected the customary condolences, not open disdain. Like she was offal to be scraped off his boots. She planted her hands on his chest and shoved him away.

Rye brushed her hand prints from the front of his suede vest. "The company can't spare anyone to take you east so you'll have to wait till we reach Pappin's Ferry to hire a guide. I reckon you can make it back to Independence before your cousin gives birth."

Her skin flushed from neck to hairline. Gentlemen never alluded to a blessed event.

"You don't know the first thing about life on the trail and I don't have the time or the will to teach you. All the pamphlet reading in the world is not going to help you survive. You're just going to drag the rest of the group down with you."

"I gave my word of honor to my father that I would stay with my Aunt Agnes. I cannot go back unless she decides to go back. But I thought to ask Mr. Schneider if he would consider acting as our guide."

"His family can't spare him."

"Do you not think that he should make that decision? Perhaps we could wait until he has a chance to consider the proposal."

"We can't stay here, Miss Sinclair. We have to keep moving. Of course, you can start walking if you prefer. I don't mind turning my back if that makes it easier for you."

A white hot streak of anger stiffened her spine. "If you hadn't pushed us to leave Independence my father would still be with us. And Hannah wouldn't have to endure her confinement in the wilderness. You can rush all you want about getting to the Oregon Territory, but what good will that do – "

"Ever hear of the Donner party? Ever read their account? Ever get caught outdoors in the open with snow up to your waist? I'm not making the mistakes they made. We need to be making at least twenty miles a day and we're only at the Lone Elm. We should be past Pappin's Ferry. We're days behind. As for your father, he was a weak man and cholera feeds on the frail."

"What's stopping you from getting on your horse and riding off to join the rest of the wagons?"

"I can't in good conscience leave your aunt and cousin by the side of the trail. I'm too tired to be digging more graves."

"The only hole you need to dig is one for yourself to go jump into. I hope that you –"

"I hope to disappoint you. I just don't want to have to go to the effort of digging a hole for you."

"Leave me to rot on the prairie as it will surely take up too much of your precious time to see to the niceties," Felicity folded her arms to keep from hitting him.

Rye glared at her.

Felicity glared back. She wasn't about to let him know how desperately she wanted to leave, to follow the rippling green strip of grass in the middle of the track towards civilization.

"If ya two are gonna shout like that in public, I'm gonna figure I can jump into the argument as a member of the public."

"Now, far as I can see, Felicity here doesn't have much ground to stand on when it comes to childbirth, her bein' unmarried and all. But I do. Hannah's a healthy girl and that baby will help her focus on gettin' over poor Tom layin' there in his grave. They weren't married all that long, but long enough for her to be attached to him."

Aunt Agnes spat a stream of tobacco juice. Felicity winced at her aunt's practiced aim.

"Now I started this wild goose chase with the aim to seein' this Promised Land or die tryin' so quit yer arguin' and get the wagons movin' so we can catch up with the others. As far as I can tell, God ain't creatin' anymore sunlight today."

Felicity uncrossed her arms and brushed by Rye. "Pardon me, but I have a wagon to pack."

AND SO THEY moved on, Rye leading the company beyond the parting of the Santa Fe and Oregon trails towards Blue Mound. Aunt Agnes drove the cattle while Hannah lay on the feather bed, pale hands supporting her belly against the jarring ride. Felicity lagged behind the wagon, hating every step she took west from the direction of Independence.

Felicity's return to the wagon company was greeted with surprise because she rejoined the company, not compassion for her loss. She distributed her father's clothing to the men in neighboring wagons. Grady Cavanagh wore the embroidered vest her father wore to services on Sunday and Lane Crandall had room to spare in her father's best linen shirt.

Rye refused to touch the coat she offered him.

The women in the company avoided her. When she joined a group of women knitting, the talk died. When she left, the talk resumed.

Did they know the name Sinclair?

On the prairie, I could use any name, be anyone one I wanted to be. But I left New York with the name Felicity Sinclair and I refuse to leave my identity behind with everything else.

And she did not dare to mourn for her father in front of Aunt Agnes.

She was hungry all the time, snitching food when her aunt visited with folks at other wagons. To pass the time, she planned dinner parties.

Dishes served a la Russe. Julienne soup. Filet de Soles. Canards a la Rouennaise. Madeira wine.

When Felicity curled up in a quilt at night under the wagon, she hoped not to be buried in the patched together cloth the next day. She feared Rye, shoveling dirt on her before she was truly dead. Wagons rolling over her, leaving her behind. And when she couldn't fall asleep under the wagon for fear of snakes and vermin, she watched her cousin stand at the edge of the evening campfire, swaying in the moonlight and staring out over the silver tipped grass.

As if Hannah waited for someone.

WITH THE LOSS of her father and the other menfolk, packing and unpacking the wagon fell to Felicity as did firewood collection and water. Hannah prepared the meals and did the light chores, the ones that did not demand heavy lifting. Aunt Agnes directed them, her words sharper and stronger than her thin body.

It was the same day, every day. Find a level campsite, but one without roots or rocks to sleep on. Wait for a family to repair a cracked the box bolster on their wagon. Listen to the rain and fret over the shoes she left beside the campfire. Hurry to pass graves along the trail. Dig a trench for the campfire on windy days. Remember to put the cork back on the bottle of matches. Not cry when her aunt chided her for keeping the prairie out after Felicity swept the wagon with a broom.

Felicity feared the oxen. She feared her aunt more and learned to hitch the team without as much as a downcast look.

At a campsite near Blue Mound, Felicity hurried to hitch the team. The morning breeze teased the ties on her bonnet. She stopped to tighten the ribbons and her billowing sleeve caught on an ox horn. Apricot striped silk ripped from wrist to elbow.

She stumbled backwards, tripping on her dress hem.

The yoke pin flew from Felicity's hand, settling in the crushed grass between the massive hooves.

Her jaw clenched. With one ox yoked, and one ox yet to be yoked, the wagon could not be moved into line.

Running late, again. My fault, again.

The yoke creaked as the massive brutes swung their horns

and bawled.

Felicity grabbed her father's ebony walking stick from drover's seat. With the tip of the stick, she rolled the pin towards her. The yoked ox swung a hind leg up and kicked out.

The pin snapped under his cleft hoof.

Felicity flung the walking stick into the prairie grass. She did not have another oxbow pin. Did they have spare pins? Did she have to make one? How?

"No, Felicity, that's wrong." Supporting her belly with one hand, Hannah slumped against the wagon wheel.

At least it wasn't Rye showing up to goad her.

"But this is how you showed me to yoke them."

"You got the yoke right, but you have the cattle in the wrong place."

"I don't understand. Oxen belong in front of the wagon."

Hannah grinned. A rare sight since the burials at Lone Elm. "You have 'em on the wrong side, silly. Right should go here, Left goes there. Like their names."

"Which one is Right?" The landrace oxen with their red splotched white hide were identical to Felicity. Large.

"See the notches? In their horns?" Hannah blanched and pressed her belly.

Two nights ago, Hannah pressed Felicity's hand to her stomach and the unborn infant's elbow or foot moved under her cousin's shift.

"Doesn't that hurt them? The notches?"

"Not as much as they'll hurt you if you get the cattle mixed up. They have a particular likin' to the side they work on. The horns are notched so you can tell which one is which in the mornin' when you're so tired you keep one eye closed to rest it."

"They know I'm afraid of them."

"You'll get used to handlin' them. They'll be your constant companions. But you need to pay attention. Left just about set off a revolution when he jumped at a bullwhip layin' on the dirt back home. Right's the steady one. You can depend on him to keep Left from mischief."

Felicity patted Left's dusty ribs, understanding his aversion to bullwhips. He swung his tail and it thumped against her skirts, brushing her away like a fly.

"And when you get the lead, don't walk in front of the oxen or you'll get run over if they spook."

Felicity didn't want the lead. Her fellow travelers would laugh to see her beat the grass with the walking stick to scare off snakes. She was happiest at the back of the wagon train, eyes red and dry from dust. At least the wagons ahead of her shooed the snakes away.

"You fetch your snake stick and I'll look for another pin."

"Late again, Miss Sinclair?" Rye's sarcastic tone bit.

The man confused Felicity. He'd bring a brace of dressed rabbits to their campfire and stay to talk with Aunt Agnes. He studied Felicity over the flames of the campfire, as if trying to make up his mind. And when the smoke blew in his direction, he moved to sit next to her, silent as the stack of kindling. Observing her.

Perhaps the gossips speculated on the Sinclair name within his hearing and the man wanted to satisfy his curiosity.

"My cousin was about to hitch the team." Hannah pressed an oxbow pin into Felicity's hand.

Twisting away from the ox's horns, Felicity shifted the bow around Right's neck.

Rye lurched to her side. "No, like this," and with a sure movement, set the pin into the yoke.

She breathed in Rye's scent. Masculine, earthy. Unlike the pomades of the dandies in New York.

He glanced down at Felicity for a moment, then away, brows drawn together.

Was he angry with himself for helping her?

Pushing back the brim of his hat, Rye hobbled towards the

Radnor's wagon. Felicity released her breath between clenched teeth.

That flirt Ulna Radnor should be happy enough to see him. The girl is half in love with him.

Maybe there is something to the man I'm not seeing.

TEAM HITCHED AND wagon packed, Hannah wrapped a quilt around her girth and settled onto the feather bed spread across the crates and barrels. Aunt Agnes settled onto the drover's bench up high on the wagon. Felicity took the place beside the oxen and waited for Rye's order to move out along the trail.

Flies buzzed around the eyes of the oxen. Felicity brushed them away.

She waited. The oxen dozed in the morning sun.

She counted the flies.

Named them.

Felicity's morning tea consumption made her shift from side to side. She kept liquid consumption to a minimum to avoid walking away from the campsite on her own.

Aunt Agnes' eyes were closed and her chin pressed down into the loose folds of her neck. The purple smudges under her eyes matched the smudges under Hannah's eyes. She coughed, a rib jarring hack Felicity heard before leaving the boarding house in New York.

Hannah did not stir in the back of the wagon.

Ulna Radnor swung her red trimmed boots against the tailgate of her family's wagon, nodding when Felicity waved to her. The girl's blouse, buttoned for a change. At fifteen, she discovered that a little flash of bosom made some men just lose their good sense. They gave her things. Pretty things.

"Watch the team for me, will you?"

Not waiting to follow someone through the grass, Felicity beat the knee high grass beyond the trail with the ebony walking stick, until she found a place away from the sight of Ulna and the others to relieve herself.

The ties on her pantalets snapped. She stared at the broken ends. Tempted to leave the threadbare linen in the tall grass to avoid making another repair, she wasn't ready to dress like a savage.

One has to have standards.

That means undergarments.

All the undergarments.

When I stitch the tear in my sleeve, I will reinforce the ties.

The line of twenty schooners straggled along the track. Uncle Jasper voted to travel with the second group of the original company of forty-four wagons that split to allow for adequate feed and water for the livestock, praying that Hannah delivered her child at the jumping off point in Missouri. The first group led by Joe Larkin left messages at campsites telling of water or Indians sighted. At night, the Larkin company's campfires twinkled miles away in the west.

The last wagon's wheel lay in the trail. The McHenry outfit. Until the wheel was repaired, they waited.

Away from the glare of Aunt Agnes, Felicity hid in the grass. She sobbed with the gulping breaths of a child. She wanted her old life. One that didn't require sleeping without a roof or eating out of cast iron. A life where her father still lived.

Felicity rolled onto her back and flung her forearm across her forehead. The corset did not move with her and she shifted it into place. The handful of silk on each side of her dress was evidence of the plumpness of New York living eroding and an unfamiliar tautness from walking across the prairie taking its place.

Something hard whacked the soft sole of Felicity's slipper.

She snorted and shot up, grinding her hip into the grass and lurched for the walking stick. Her breath came in short gasps.

It was Rye Jones, leaning on his rifle.

"Oh, it's you." She rubbed her foot through the slipper. Felicity was a fool for being caught alone away from the wagons. "That hurt."

"This is no time to be napping. Your cousin's labor has started."

CHAPTER 8

Blue Mound
April 15, 1851

Felicity stepped where Rye limped through the grass to the wagons. Hampered by the injury to his thigh, his long legged strides were too far apart for her tired legs to keep pace with.

"I've never so much as seen a kitten being born. What do I do?"

"Doesn't one of your pamphlets address childbirth?"

"I do not believe the authors thought it a fit subject for young ladies of society."

"It is an especially fit topic and you need to get over your ignorance if you're going to survive out here."

"What must I do?"

"Where's Helmut?"

"Mr. Schneider is over there, with his boy."

Rye whistled. Helmut turned in his saddle and waved.

"Are you leaving us behind?"

"Don't be foolish. I'm not about to leave anyone behind if it can be helped."

"With all your rush and fury over beating the snow, you can't be surprised at my question."

"Not much you could do that would surprise me at this point."

Helmut trotted up, his youngest before him on the saddle. Flicking the brim of his hat, he grinned down at Felicity. "Miss

Sinclair."

Rye squinted up at Helmut and the child. "Hey there, Samuel. Helmut, I need you to take the company on ahead. Hannah Clemms is in labor."

"You want Marta to stay behind?" Helmet offered.

"Nope. Miss Sinclair will be on hand."

"We'll wait for you at Pappin's Ferry."

"Rest the livestock for one day before pushing on. I can't imagine that we will be more than a day behind you. And take Dodge with you. I don't need a dog underfoot."

Felicity lowered the tailgate on the wagon, pulling out the crate of cooking utensils. That was her lot in life; pack the wagon, unpack the wagon.

"Why aren't we moving along with the others?" Hannah grunted, body twisting.

Felicity dropped the crate. How did one survive such pain?

Rye brushed Felicity aside to lift Hannah down from the wagon. "Between the dust from the trail and the lack of springs on this rig, you're likely to be more comfortable if we hang back a bit. Helmut knows what to do with the others. He doesn't know much about childbirth and I wasn't about to leave you to the mercy of Miss Sinclair's nursing talents. How far apart are the pains?"

Felicity glared at Rye and snatched the feather bed and quilts.

"Ma's delivered just about everyone back home."

"She's frail from her brush with the fever. Then I would have two patients under my care. And Miss Sinclair assures me that this is the first birth event she has attended."

Sending an engraved rattle from a fashionable silversmith and cooing over a lace wrapped bundle in the arms of a Van Der Ploon's nursery maid was the limit of Felicity's experiences in childbearing among her acquaintances.

"Is this your first child?" Rye's tone light, as if asking after the weather.

"First one that's has made it this far. We've had ... disappointments in the past."

"There's a bag that I need out of the Schneider's wagon. Rest easy and don't let Miss Sinclair near my rifle in case she goes snake hunting again."

Hannah laughed. She gasped and grabbed her belly.

Felicity smiled through her fear. "See what happens when you make fun of me? That is the first laugh ..."

"Since Lone Elm ... since Pa and Tom died."

"Sorry to bring that up."

"Shhhh. No worries. You didn't mean any harm. We both lost a chunk of ourselves that day. Can't lose someone you love without a part of you goin' missin'."

"I just think about how Tom ... that he should be here ..."

"But I feel like he's with me today, and if I was quick enough, I could see him just around the corner of the wagon. Watchin' over us, me and this baby of ours. Sometimes I see him out on the prairie ... smilin' at me ... kind of like he's waitin' for me."

Felicity spread the feather bed and quilt beside the fire ring from the night before. "At least you have a child to remember him by. Here, come lay down."

"I don't think he's the first baby to be born on the trail, do you?"

"He or she will have the distinction of being the first baby born on their head if you don't get onto that feather bed."

"Need you to promise me somethin' ... Ma and I talked it over. This wagon, and all the supplies, belongs to my baby after I'm gone. If anythin' happens to me, promise me to take care of him. Raise him ... up among your own."

"You're not going anywhere, missy, aside from catching up with the others when you're fit to move."

"Do you swear?"

"Only when Left steps on my hem."

Hannah grabbed Felicity's wrist. "Be serious. Promise me

... you will take my child and raise him as your own?"

"I swear. But it might be a girl and you know what a fuss they are. Especially when they are born on their head." It was an easy promise for Felicity to make. Hannah was a healthy girl. Heartbroken, but otherwise healthy.

Aunt Agnes said so, and Aunt Agnes's word was bankable.

"Here, take this." Rye shoved a leather satchel into Felicity's arms. "Don't drop it." The initials "P.R.D.J." were embossed in faded gold on the cracked leather.

"Don't just stand there, Miss Sinclair. Help her get comfortable while I stoke up the fire."

BATS DOVE AND fluttered in the twilight beyond the campfire. Supper should have been on the coals hours ago. Trying to see into a pot of beans leftover from noon, Felicity tipped the candle in her hand. Hot wax dripped over her fingers and into the pot.

"Ouch!"

At Rye's glare, she stirred the wax into the beans.

"Light the lantern." Rye's voice was clipped.

Struggling with the bottle of matches, Felicity tried pushing the cork in further to get a match out. The cork stuck. She took a slim blade from the box of kitchen tools and pried the cork out. Match in hand, she scraped the tip on a rock. And scraped.

No spark.

Rye snatched the matches and lit the lantern, turning the wick up. He thrust the match bottle at Felicity, but she dropped it.

Rye picked up the bottle and pressed her trembling hands around it. "Calm yourself, Miss Sinclair."

"What's wrong? Why hasn't the baby come?"

"My guess is that the baby is either early or your cousin did not correctly estimate her due date. What's she been like since we left Lone Elm? She been moody? Quiet?"

Felicity pulled away from his broad palms and stowed the match bottle in the wagon. Rye's hands, rough and warm, so unlike Edmund's cool touch. Why did his touch ease her shaking? She stared up into his silver grey eyes. And why did he care to console her?

"She hasn't been herself since we buried Thomas ... Mr. Clemms. We should have waited for her to have the child in Independence." Felicity's promise to Hannah flicked like the tip of a whip.

Hannah's baby won't last a week in my care.

"Who's to say the outcome would be any different? If you'd waited you'd have delayed your start on the trail and died in the mountains."

"Instead we are dying on the plains, one by one."

"When yer called to Heaven, you're called." Aunt Agnes glared at Felicity from her place beside Hannah. "A reason for it that we mere mortals don't always understand."

Rye blew out the flame in the lantern towards dawn. A soft rain fell, drops hissing in the campfire.

"Can you see him?" Hannah whispered, blue lips parting with each breath.

"We're nearly there. One big push. I know you're tired, but do it for me." Rye's voice was soft, soothing. "We want this child to see the Territory. Float on the wide rivers, and nap in the meadows. Swim in the cool lakes, with trout tickling at his toes."

Hannah, groaning, bore down.

"Catch him!" Rye commanded.

Hannah's son was long, with a tiny bottom and thin legs.

"Good catch, Mr. Jones!" Aunt Agnes crowed.

"He's slippery. I almost dropped him."

The babe was blotchy and squalling. So Felicity made the best of it for Hannah's sake. "He's a beautiful baby boy. What are you going to name him?"

"He's right there … can't you see him?"

"What you talking about, sweetling?" Aunt Agnes wiped the blood and birth from Hannah with quick swipes of a rag dipped in creek water.

"In the grass."

No one approached the circle of lamplight. And Rye was beside her, washing his arms in the basin.

"Indians?" Agnes whispered to Rye.

Felicity cleared her throat. "She told me that she's seen Tom out on the prairie waiting for her."

Rye took Aunt Agnes's wrinkled hand in his. "It's not Indians she's seeing."

"Tom …" Hannah murmured.

Felicity shivered, wrapping her shawl close around her neck.

Hannah died in her mother's arms before the rain passed the campsite.

FELICITY PICKED UP her aunt's bible, flipping to lines of family names and birth dates on the end pages. She wrote April 16, 1851 in pencil, the copperplate script dipping when her hand wavered.

Hannah never told her what to name the child. She ran a fingertip up the list of names. Francis was a family name. So was Erasmus. Neither appealed.

She tapped the pencil against her lips. She stared at the hickory bows that held up the canvas top on the wagon. Pulled at the ties that held the canvas top in place.

I'll think of one, tomorrow or the day after.

Care of the boy was an immediate concern. Having worn a diaper once in her life did not mean that in later years she recalled how to apply one. This meant the boy must be fed.

But with what?

Stew?

Neither Aunt Agnes nor Felicity were in a position to offer the child breast milk.

Bathing. It must bathe on occasion. Certainly not in a creek. Perhaps the wash tub. Hot water or cold water?

Clothing. Hannah showed me the basket of clothes. At least it comes with a wardrobe.

Education. That I can offer. But it has to learn to talk. And probably walk.

How best to protect the child in her care? The pamphlets did not help. The further she walked on the trail, Felicity identified which writer experienced the journey versus the writer with a romantic notions. The majority of Uncle Jasper's pamphlets were written as an advertisement to get people on the trail. The least useful pamphlets became fire starter.

The prairie is a place anything can happen. I can't control what will happen any more than I can control the wind or make the grass march in time.

It is out of the question to leave the child on the trail or give him to some charitable family. Aunt Agnes will skin me alive just for admitting to the thought.

Should I take Rye's advice and sell the equipment at Pappin's Ferry? I might get ten or fifteen dollars for the wagon. The provisions aren't worth much.

Or should I soldier through and make a life for Aunt Agnes and the child in the Oregon Territory?

She plucked an eyebrow hair, looking at it like it was a divining rod. Plucked another. And another.

Thump, thump, thump on the side of the wagon.

That was the sign.

She poked her head out of the canvas opening.

"Your presence is requested, Miss Sinclair." Rye limped away from the wagon, shovel swinging at his side.

Staying with Hannah, helping to bring her son into the

world sparked something in Felicity. It wasn't envy; it was a wonder at what her cousin experienced. A moment she couldn't ever see herself experiencing..

I may not have birthed the baby, but I made a promise to Hannah.

I will survive this ordeal to spite the man.

Aunt Agnes cradled her grandson in her bony arms near the fire.

"Do you feel any different about travelling to the Territory?" Felicity whispered.

"Nope." Aunt Agnes kissed the top of the baby's head.

"How soon can we pack the wagon?"

"Soon as ya come down and start packin'."

"How are we going to feed it?"

"Sugar tit will tide him over 'til we can meet up with the wagon train."

"What do you think of a goat?"

"Not much."

"I imagine they're less expensive than a dairy cow. Where are we going to get one?"

"The Lord will provide, just you wait and see."

CHAPTER 9

Pappin's Ferry
April 18, 1851

Felicity blew air into her cupped hands. She wouldn't want cold hands grabbing her in the morning. Wedging the bucket between her feet and the stool, Felicity reeled in the tether tied to a bleating goat.

"You're not going to get milk out of that goat."

Of course it was Rye.

"The gentleman who sold me this goat told me it is a good producer."

"If that goat gives you any milk, I'll offer to buy it from you for twice what you paid."

Felicity tipped the stool back on two legs. "Is it a rare breed? It looks like any goat in the fields back home."

"I'd sell tickets to get my investment back. The fact is, ma'am, that's a billy goat."

Seeing Felicity's raised eyebrow, Rye continued. "The only thing it's gonna produce is more goats, given the right circumstances."

The goat knocked over the bucket and bounded to the end of its tether.

Aunt Agnes swatted her leg and cackled. "Told her a goat was goin' to be nothin' but trouble. How are ya, Rye?"

"Fine ma'am. How are you getting along?"

"Aside from the goat, Felicity is doin' the work of two

men."

"That so?"

Felicity itched to throw the bucket at him, but not in front of Aunt Agnes and Hannah's crying baby.

"Come with me." Rye grasped her elbow, lifting Felicity to her feet. She pulled away and rubbed her elbow.

"I'm trying to get breakfast started."

"What are you feeding the baby?"

"That's what the goat was for."

"Thought that was the problem. Grab that wailing banshee and follow me."

Rye marched Felicity and the baby through the campsite to the McHenry wagon where three small children played in the dirt. "Maggie, me darling, be ye at home?"

"Why, if it isn't young Doc Jones 'imself, comin' to call. And since when have ye taken to torturin' the young?"

Doc Jones, Felicity scowled. Make that Doctor Jones.

And I lamented the lack of a medical man.

"Can you guess?"

"Give the lad over." Maggie McHenry nodded to Felicity. "How are you, dearie?"

Rye pulled up a keg for Maggie to sit on. She drew the shawl over her shoulder and unpinned the bodice of her homespun gown.

"There, now, take a good long drink, laddie." She jumped as the baby latched on. "You're a hungry scamp, aren't you?"

Felicity stared at Mrs. McHenry. One never appeared in a drawing room with their bodice undone beneath a shawl, with a man in the room. Ever. But the woman's kindness moved her. What interest did Mrs. McHenry have vested in the baby at her breast? Yet she did not refuse the baby's hunger.

"Let's give Maggie some breathing room."

Rye led Felicity to a bench beside the ferry that served Pappin's Crossing. A raft, lashed on top of two canoes, dipped as the Cavanaugh wagon rolled on board. Butterflies flickered in Felicity's stomach. The Kansas River, two hundred yards wide, rippled and bucked a wicked current.

Swimming, not a skill she possessed.

"You're different than what I thought you'd be." Rye picked through a stand of dried rushes.

"Expected me to be more like my father?"

"Yes. I've known your father ... you must be more like your mother."

Felicity stared at the river. Shivered.

"Heard your folks were from New York."

"Originally."

"Well here's your chance to hire a guide and go home."

"I'm not going home."

"So why are you on the trail?"

"This wasn't my first choice. Why do you care whether I stay or go?"

"It's Aggie I'm worried about. If you haven't noticed, she is failing. And I might as well start digging a grave for the baby."

"That's cruel."

"The trail isn't a place for an old woman and a newborn who just lost his mother. That's cruelty."

His sun browned fingers wove the rushes in and out. "What makes Territory life so appealing? Debutantes and garden parties aren't the fashion in the Cascades."

The man is right, but I'm not giving him the pleasure of hearing that he is right.

"Returning to my former home is not possible."

The rushes took on a bowl shape. "Wouldn't you rather give up this fool notion and return to city life? Surely you have other family or friends who could take you in."

What remained? Almstead House was gone, the ball gowns were in the window at a second hand clothiers shop, and Sally Munston was likely the Ormond family's choice as a daughter-in-law. No other family, no friends. None that would admit to knowing her much less admit a Sinclair across their thresholds.

"Aunt Agnes wishes to settle in the Oregon Territory so I have to keep going."

"This isn't a tea party, ma'am, and I don't have time to watch over someone who spends her time trying to milk a billy goat."

"Don't trouble yourself on my part."

"You don't know when to quit, do you?"

Felicity's fingertips brushed the knuckle where the Tiffany, Young and Ellis ring once sparkled. "I was forced to quit on someone, once. Against my will and against my wishes. I'm not making that mistake again."

Rye cupped her chin in his rough hand. His square jaw and grey eyes unyielding. He studied her as if looking into her soul.

The contact with his hand shook Felicity. She wasn't sure what he was searching for. Resilience, perhaps?

He pressed a bonnet, woven of the dried rushes, into her hands.

"You're getting freckled. This will keep the sun off your face better than the one you have on."

The bonnet only needed a ribbon to keep from blowing off her head in the prairie winds.

"Th ... thank you, Dr. Jones."

"I want one!" Ulna Radnor bounded through the rushes on the river's edge to Rye's side. The fifteen year old whispered to Felicity over a shared campfire that she yearned to be his wife, but didn't have a chance since Rye's wife lived somewhere back East.

Clutching the bonnet, Felicity stood. "I'll just go see how Mrs. McHenry is coming along."

Leaving Rye to the mercy of Ulna, Felicity walked back to take the sleeping baby from Mrs. McHenry's arms.

"My sincere thanks," Felicity whispered.

"Ye find me whenever he needs a feedin'. I'm producin' enough for 'im and my girl. And Yetta Daniels has a young 'un as well. I'll introduce ye to 'er and I wudn't be t'all be surprised if she's a' willin' to 'elp nurse yer boy."

"How … how often?"

"Oh, dearie. When they're this wee, every few hours."

"During the day?"

"And the night. This yer first?"

"The only one I've ever spent any considerable time around."

"Didn't yer Mam teach ye the care of the young?"

"I am afraid that would have disrupted her day and given the nannies and the governesses much less to do."

"Well, then, we'll be seein' a lot o' each other. An' if ye 'ave any questions, ye be sure ta' ask. Don't be a shy miss."

As Aunt Agnes predicted, a solution was found.

Carrying the rush bonnet in one hand, Felicity propped the baby against her shoulder. He snuggled into her arms, eyes closed.

Strolling back to the wagon, Felicity caught the smell of baking biscuits. Her stomach growled. Cradling the baby in the crook of her arm, Felicity followed the smell into the structure serving Pappin's Ferry as hotel and dram house.

It was easy to pass by the whiskey and beer. Food was her indulgence. She waited to pay for fresh out of the oven biscuits, letting the clerk tuck the buttery treats in the bottom of the rush bonnet to keep from waking the baby.

She glanced up at the hand lettered sign above a stack of boots.

"Pardon me, but is that sign correct? This is a post office?"

Half running back to the wagon, Felicity slowed down to pass the cooling biscuits up to Aunt Agnes on the drover's box. Settling the baby into his blanket lined box in the wagon, she pulled off the back of a pamphlet.

"Dear Edmund" she wrote, tapping the pencil against her lips when she ran out of words. Hopefully Edmund would overlook her choice of stationery.

Against her father's wishes and without his knowledge,

Felicity wrote to Edmund before leaving New York, begging him to save her from the wilderness. She waited, but Edmund did not appear. She wrote again from Independence. Pleading. Begging. No rider swept across the plains to rescue her.

"What's that you're perched on?"

The pencil did not waver at Rye's voice. "My father's law books." In the few lines of copperplate script, Felicity did not to mention her father's death or Hannah's baby.

"You should get rid of them."

The baby fussed.

Dropping the pencil, Felicity grabbed a diaper from the stack above the flour barrel and spread a small quilt on the floor of the wagon. Lifting the baby out of his makeshift crib, she laid him on the quilt. The baby curled up his fists and whimpered.

"Here's your money from the goat. Monsieur François won't be selling off any more of his herd this afternoon." Rye's palm held more coins from the sale of the goat than what she paid out in the morning.

"You didn't have to do that." Unpinning the wet diaper, she peeled it open.

"I know. It's my chance to make it up to you for being so abrupt. How is your charge doing now that he's been fed?" Rye held up a shiny coin for the baby to play with, tucking the remainder under the quilt.

"I think he's –"

Pee squirted from the baby to the front of her apricot striped dress.

Rye snorted and snatched the clean diaper from her shoulder. "Here, cover him up like this when you change him and you won't get hit."

She brushed the droplets from her dress and wished the Kansas River closed over her head. Or Rye's head.

"Here, allow me." Rye dabbed at the wet blotch on her bodice with his bandana.

"I'll do that, thank you."

Felicity diapered the baby and she sensed Rye watched her from under his hat brim. His grey eyes were gentle, as if he enjoyed the domestic scene.

His looks are handsome for all his wildness. But what happened to his wife? Probably scared her off.

Curiosity got the better of her. "Your wife isn't traveling with you?"

"Get your wagon ready. You're next." The terse words were all Rye's tight lips allowed. The fury in the man churned as surely as the muddy water at the ferry landing. He brushed down his hat and shoulders hunched, lurched off to the Mueller wagon.

Ulna, a woven rush bonnet twisting in her hands, leaned against the wagon wheel. How much did the girl overhear?

"Ulna, could I beg a favor of you?"

"What do you want?" Ulna sulked, caught doing something unsavory.

"We're next in line for the crossing. Here's a dollar and a letter. Could you post it for me? If you need more money, let me know."

"Sure. I'll take it."

"Thank you." The dollar was more than generous, but Felicity gave it hoping Ulna wouldn't inquire about the name Edmund Ormond or the address in New York.

WANDERING AWAY FROM Felicity, Ulna examined the neat handwriting on the envelope. Spitting on the letters, she rubbed out the address.

But that wasn't enough. Tearing the letter into pieces, she scattered the bits into the Kansas River and pocketed the dollar.

APRIL BLURRED INTO May.

Felicity grew into some aspects of trail life, other aspects she did not embrace. She could not, would not call Aunt Agnes by the name 'Aggie' and she did not see the sense in keeping up Uncle Jasper's temperature journal. An amateur scientist, he started and concluded each day's journey with a temperature reading. Aunt Agnes expected Felicity to keep up with the journal as her eyes could not make out the degree markings.

Aunt Agnes held the baby while Felicity stumbled through a circuit of cooking, washing, packing and unpacking the wagon. Feeding. Diapering. Sleeping in spurts.

With the advice and counsel of Maggie McHenry and Yetta Daniels, Felicity's cooking skills improved. But the biscuits refused to rise.

The burned lumps reminded Felicity of the buffalo sign along the trail.

"Must be the dent in the lid." Aunt Agnes croaked.

After Pappin's Ferry, Rye brought Aunt Agnes fresh game and in turn she invited him to return to their campfire around supper time. For the most part, he talked with her aunt, continuing his study of Felicity in the firelight. She held the baby wrapped in a quilt against the night air.

He never spoke of a wife or family and Felicity tucked away her curiosity.

Felicity was baffled by Rye's thoughtfulness. True, she and Aunt Agnes were on their own with an infant, but for a man who stated he did not want them on the trail, why did he provide food? Was he acting out of Christian charity?

Rye set aside the biscuits from his supper, taking them when he left the campfire. Around Alcove Spring, Felicity watched him limp to the river bank beyond the wagons. It wasn't that she was following him; she timed her last check on the oxen to meet with him. The man stirred her curiosity, but she did not know why.

He was so different from any of the gentlemen in her acquaintance in the East.

Under the cover of thunderclouds, Rye bent down, offering Dodge the biscuits in his hand.

Dodge bit a biscuit. Lips curled, he dropped the biscuit. Dug with his paws to bury the biscuit. This from the dog known to eat frogs. This verdict was proof the dent in the Dutch oven was not at fault.

Rye pitched the biscuits into a patch of cottonwoods.

The man hid proof of her bad cooking where she wouldn't stumble across the evidence.

Considering the reason why kept her awake in the nest of quilts under the wagon.

CHAPTER 10

*The Narrows
May 2, 1851*

Felicity shifted barrels and shook out quilts in the back of the wagon. Switching the fussing baby to her other arm, she pried open the cedar chest filled with Hannah's clothes. She tucked the lace of a dark wool dress under a linen sheet.

"Looking for something?" Rye leaned on the tailgate of the wagon.

Felicity slammed the lid and brushed her hair back from her cheeks. "I've lost Uncle Jasper's temperature gauge."

"I'm sure it will turn up."

"I hope so." Felicity flicked a gaze at her aunt nodding beside the campfire in a scavenged rocking chair. "It's the one connection to Uncle Jasper that she hasn't had to leave on the trail."

Rye sniffed. "What do you have cooking?"

"Stew. Mrs. McHenry taught me her recipe." Felicity switched the crying baby to her other shoulder.

"Smells good."

"Will you join us?" The question was unnecessary, as the answer was unchanged these many weeks.

"Thank you, yes, I would." Rye smiled up at her.

It was a smile that lit up his squared features, a smile that warmed her heart. It pleased her, to please him with the simple act of providing a meal.

"Why don't you hand that young man over and I'll see if I can get him to settle."

Felicity passed the baby to Rye. "It's close to his supper time. I wanted to give Mrs. Daniels a chance to feed her brood before I walked him over."

Felicity shook out the embroidered tablecloth and set out the tin plates and the remains of her mother's silverware. Rye never chided her for the table setting ritual.

Putting the baby over his shoulder, Rye rubbed the infant's back. The boy whimpered when his tiny fist passed over his mouth.

Aggie stirred and held her arms out for her fussing grandson.

"I could make some biscuits," Felicity offered, straight faced.

"No!" Rye and Aunt Agnes answered in unison.

"Don't go to all that trouble." Rye grinned.

"I heard the baby. Is he well?" Ulna Radnor appeared in the shadows beyond the campfire. Wherever Rye went, Ulna was sure to follow.

"He's getting ready to pay a visit to Mrs. Daniels."

"Oh, let me. I'll take him," Ulna stroked the baby's head.

Aggie nudged Felicity. "Let the girl take the lad for a while. It'll give ya a break and he'll be happier with a full belly."

Ulna reminded Felicity of the gossipy debutantes in New York, but without the benefit of boarding school or governesses. Mrs. McHenry and Mrs. Daniels confirmed her suspicions since the crossing at Pappin's Ferry. Ulna spread the word that Felicity walked out after dark with men. Different men, every night. Having survived worse, Felicity ignored the jabs. But Aunt Agnes treated the girl with compassion, hoping Ulna would gentle her ways. Older, perhaps wiser, she understood pining for a suitor's approval.

"I'll take him straight to her, I promise."

The thought of a break tempted Felicity. The late night

changing and feeding cycle wore her thin.

"Please, please let me take him."

"Fine. But bring him right back as soon as he's done."

Felicity untied her apron, hung it on a peg on the side of the wagon and reached for the ladle and bowls.

Rye tasted the stew and raised his eyebrows. He glanced over at Aggie, who also raised her eyebrows.

"What's wrong with it?" The stew was thick and the buffalo meat gave it good flavor.

"Nothin', nothin' at all. That's the welcome surprise of it. How did ya learn to make this?"

"Maggie McHenry taught me how to use the dried vegetables we have."

The baby's crying stopped.

Felicity stood up and stumbled a few steps in the direction of the Daniels wagon. She stopped, looked at her aunt for guidance, torn between taking the child from Ulna and waiting for Ulna to return. Felicity thought of him as "the baby" and held off giving the boy a name. Afraid of what would happen if he did not survive. With such thin limbs, she feared he wasn't thriving.

"Maybe she should have made some of those biscuits," Rye whispered.

Felicity grinned and stayed where she was. Was his arm wearing out from the distance he pitched her biscuit experiments?

Aggie snorted. "Oh, go on with ya. She's workin' hard enough as it is."

"I was thinking that the gravy in this stew would cover a multitude of sins."

"Ya mean a multitude of wickedly bad biscuits."

"You know, you have something there."

"She's gettin' better."

"Those biscuits have a ways to go."

"Maybe by the time we reach the Blue Mountains they'll be

edible. Whereabouts are we?"

"The Narrows are behind us and the Platte River has got to be close by. Maybe a day or so away."

The campfire burned to coals and the twilight softened the edges of the grassland. Across the campground, Philippe Patelle tuned his violin.

Aggie yawned and tossed her spoon into the empty bowl in her lap. "I have to say this sure is fine dinin'. No roof to block the stars and the flowers are in the grass, not stuck on fine china or in some fancy wallpaper."

The crickets chirped and droned.

Felicity bolted upright.

When did it get so dark?

"Where's the baby?"

"I ONLY GAVE her the baby 'cause she asked," Ulna wailed and clung to Rye at the Landers' campfire. "She was taking him back, that's what she kept saying." Her cries roused the Robertson and Mueller families camped nearby.

Horace Mueller's daughter took Felicity aside. "I saw her … Mrs. Landers, that is. She was wrapped up in a blanket, walking around the campground in circles."

Ulna dropped to her knees and wept tears worthy of footlights and a stage.

Rye strapped his rifle in the scabbard on the saddle. He cupped Felicity's white face with his rough palms.

Felicity clung to his wrists, giving up to the force of loss. Courseless. A ship without a rudder, sails ripped, lines snapped. Mast shattered.

Broken.

"Have faith," he pressed his lips to her forehead.

Whistling for Dodge, he kicked the mare into a gallop and disappeared into the night prairie.

"Bring my baby back to me," Felicity croaked.

SOAPY FORKS AND cups slipped through her fingers. Rewashing made the water so dirty it didn't matter if the plates went unwashed or went into the dust. A lone clean plate leaned on the kindling to drain and dry.

Felicity tossed Aggie's shawl around her shoulders and wasted five sulfur matches trying to light the lantern.

"I'm going out there. I'm mucking up the dishes and I can't remember if I fed Right and Left."

"Yer doin' plenty. Like stayin' put and not gettin' lost. Rye doesn't need any more trouble than what he already has."

Crabbe Landon slumped beside her aunt. The New England seaman got up on shaky legs and captured Felicity's hand in his. "Miss Sinclair, I am so sorry."

"I shouldn't have let Ulna take the child."

"If I'd kept a closer watch, perhaps. Ulna didn't know my Phoebe's grieving."

He coughed. "Miss Sinclair, I am so sorry."

If Crabbe said that one more time with his dry voice Felicity would punch him. To keep him from harm, she kicked a log onto the campfire and stared out into the darkness, trying to will Rye's shape to appear.

"You must excuse my niece. I believe the cattle must be wantin' their grain."

How she envied her aunt's social grace. Felicity slipped off the shawl and wrapped it around her aunt's bony shoulders, pressing her cheek to the silver threaded locks for a second. They both suffered losses, but this one would break them.

Faith, Rye whispered to her.

She was adrift on a great, boundless sea of grass. A horizon so great she expected to see the curve of the earth.

How am I to have faith in this God forsaken land?

I can't fight against the wildness. No one possesses the strength. If we do not reach a settlement soon the emptiness will drive me mad.

I will lose my mind if ever left behind.

When she held the baby in her arms she would never let go. He would be thirty and getting married and she would carry him down the aisle to his bride. Who cared what folks said over that?

She wanted her boy, unharmed.

THE SUN CLEARED the tips of the grasses when Crabbe shook her shoulder. "Our prayers are answered, Miss Sinclair."

It was Rye.

Rye with his hesitant gait leading his mare with Phoebe Landon slumped in the saddle. Rye with a blanket slung over his shoulder.

Felicity blinked.

Rye escorted by five braves. They were tall, with blankets wrapped around their shoulders and fringed leggings. Pamphlet phrases on the dangers of Indian attack flooded her memory, but she flicked those thoughts aside.

Hoisting up her skirts, Felicity sprinted over the grass.

No movement beneath the blanket.

No crying.

No need to get the shovel, please, God.

"Is he ..." Felicity choked.

Rye held out his bundle to her. "He's wet. And he's all yours."

She grabbed the bundle and peeled back the blanket. The baby opened his eyes and yawned.

Hugging the baby to her chest so tightly he squeaked, she stretched up to plant a kiss on Rye's stubble cheek.

"Thank you," she whispered. Rye was no longer a provider

of fresh meat or a reluctant doctor to Felicity. It took heart to go into the darkness of the prairie and bring her child back to her.

"I wasn't about to let him stay out there." Rye rubbed his cheek, smiling down at her. He nodded to the braves. "The credit goes to these gentlemen. They found Mrs. Landon and were leading her back to us. Seems they were out hunting and came across our wanderers."

Felicity held out her hand in friendship to the tallest Indian in the hunting party. Not understanding her intentions, the Indians spoke something in their language and backed away. She did not understand the Indians' words, and they did not speak English, but there was an understanding of family and belonging.

"I think they're afraid yer gonna kiss them too." Aggie wheezed, hobbling up with Mr. Landon.

"Would they like some biscuits as a token of thanks?" Felicity's eyes sparkled over the baby's head.

Rye Jones blushed. Hard. "Offer them bacon instead for a future meal."

"After all, we'd like to stay on friendly terms with these kind gentlemen," Aggie snorted.

The hunting party departed with their side of bacon and Crabbe Landon took Phoebe back to their campsite.

Cuddling the baby up against her throat, Felicity hummed a ditty off tune beside the campfire. Her eyes closed.

I don't know why, but this child is changing my life. Rye is right. We have to hurry to beat the snow.

"You gonna name the boy now that you have him back?" Rye lifted his bandaged leg to the side and lowered himself onto a keg.

She blinked.

Pushing the blanket back, she pressed her cheek against the babe's head. "Does he feel warm to you?"

"Wrapped up like that in this humidity he should ignite."

He waved away her alarmed look. "He's fine. I looked him over when I found him. No trauma from his adventure on the prairie."

"Why didn't you tell anyone that you are a doctor?"

"How did you know?"

"Maggie called you 'Doc Jones … and, well, Ulna told me."

"Figures. She's the town crier. What other tall tales she tell you?"

Felicity didn't want to pry. But there was no putting it off. Not if this supper routine and half way friendship of his was to continue. "That you are married … that you have a wife back East."

"Had. She died." The glacial tone could freeze the Platte River.

"I'm sorry." The same paltry words Crabbe Landon used. But she meant it. Sorry she asked. Sorry his wife died. Sorry for his loss. Sorry she pricked the pain of his loss.

Sorry their peaceful unity splintered.

"Some things are best left where they are. In the past. I don't ask you about your history. Have the same courtesy about mine. That way you won't have to apologize."

Crabbe Landon coughed on the other side of the campfire. "Pardon me, folks, for interrupting."

Felicity stood and turned away from the flames, dabbing at her stinging eyes. "How is your wife?" And winced because that was the worst thing to say after Rye's bitter words.

"That's what I'm here for. I just wanted to let you all know that I'll be … that we'll be returning to Independence in the morning. Phoebe's mind ain't what it should be for the journey and I can't help but blame myself for pushing her to keep going."

"It was a pure accident, nothing else. I hope she gets a chance to heal."

"Thanks for the kind words, ma'am. Phoebe knows she did wrong and is real sorry about it."

Swaying with the baby balanced on her chest, Felicity closed her eyes and rested her lips on his warm head, breathing in the smell of his hair. This child, so trusting, was her child.

"I wanted to offer a place with us if you decided to return to the East."

Felicity's eyes flew open.

I don't have to wake Aunt Agnes. I can guess the woman's response.

"Thank you for your kind offer, but we will continue on."

"Dr. Jones," Felicity called out. He stood with his back to her, but turned a degree in her direction, the planes of his face sharp. Eyes bitter, burnt out. Drained.

"Looks like you have us for the long haul, Dr. Jones."

"So it appears, Miss Sinclair. So it appears."

Pappin's Ferry
May 15, 1851

"Suh?" The trail guide spat on the ground.

Edmund Ormond stepped back, mindful of his riding boots. The guide picked up in Independence wasn't his first choice and traveling companions.

"Yes, Miller. Any sign of the Sinclairs?"

"No, but dat ole man at the counter tells me dat one of their party came here not more'n a handful of days ago."

"Lucid speech, man. They've turned around? We've missed them?"

"These folks turned ... dat young miss and her Pa aren't wid' 'em. 'Jes a man packin' 'is wife home 'cause she's gone simple in the mind. Screamin' and kickin', I heard her out back."

"They are here?"

"Camped out back behind dat store."

"Can they tell us how far we are from the Sinclairs?"

"Maybe so."

"What do you mean, maybe? May I remind you of the bonus you'll receive if we find the Sinclairs sooner rather than later?"

"Might be further on down the trail than these folks think. 'Pends on their luck. Always room fer trouble on dis' here trail."

CHAPTER 11

O'Fallon's Bluff
May 22, 1851

Left and Right became her fellow travelers, bound by discomfort and inconvenience. Hannah was right. The notches on Right and Left helped her tell them apart, especially when one eye was closed in the morning.

"Get up there, Right. Come on, Left."

The narrow trail at O'Fallon's Bluff forced Felicity ahead of the cattle, mindful that Right didn't tread on the back of her heels. One step forward in the deep sand to slide back three steps. Sand filled Hannah's old boots through the cracks in the sole and rubbed their new wearer's slimmer ankles and heels raw through two pairs of wool socks.

Tugging her bonnet down, Felicity trudged forward and tried not to laugh out loud at Ulna. The girl perched herself on the tailgate of the Radnor wagon where Felicity would be certain see the fifteen year old flutter a lacquered fan. Pity for the girl kept Felicity from pulling the black curls from Ulna's head.

Sadie Cavanaugh confided in Felicity one evening that men in the wagon train were taking advantage of Ulna's favors. The fan was a gift from one of the girl's walking-out admirers.

Rye's name was linked to Ulna, but Felicity did not put much faith in that gossip. Ulna did her best to flirt and prove herself fit to be Rye's wife. Rye kept his distance from the girl.

Felicity understood the rise and fall of yearning. At the last campsite before O'Fallon's Bluff, she found a place where other emigrants carved their names and messages into rocks and tree trunks. Using handle of a tin fork, she scratched "D. Ormond – Miss you. F. Sinclair. May 22." The copperplate script was more out of habit, than the belief that Edmund would read it any more than he read her letters.

Did Ulna mail the letter I wrote to Edmund? Felicity pondered, worried over the waste of a perfectly good dollar.

The trail rose with the bluff and narrowed with more rock, less sand. The river, deep and swift, eddied beyond the bottom land below. Felicity put one boot in front of the other, using her sleeve to soak up the sweat from her forehead before it ran down into her eyes.

A crackle like a sapling splitting came from behind the oxen. Left spooked and Felicity lurched in front of Right to keep from being crushed.

When the team halted, she bent over, hands on her knees and took a couple of deep breaths. The last breath caught and held in her chest. The wagon was sitting at an odd angle on the trail. The kingpin held, the front wheels were straight, but the back wheels tilted inward.

A long thin splinter of fresh wood hung from the back axle. With a crack and a lurch, axle shattered.

Left panicked, surging backward against the yoke. A rear wheel spun in a lazy circle, dangling off the edge of the trail.

Felicity grabbed Left's halter and threw her body weight to tug him forward.

Up on the drover's box, Aggie did not scream but clutched the baby tight, ready to throw him overboard like a watermelon if the wagon crashed over the edge.

Ripping the bonnet off her head, Felicity beat at the oxen.

Right kicked out and connected with Left's ribs. The oxen dragged the broken wagon onto the trail.

Felicity bent over and braced a hand on Right's muscled

neck, doing her best to breathe in and out.

"You alright?" Rye's voice put steel in her spine. It was the first time he'd spoken to her since the Landers departed. He provided fresh game, but he did not accept invitations from Aggie or Felicity to stay for dinner. Felicity quit asking. Aggie kept trying.

Dodge licked Felicity's chin. Rubbing her face, she straightened her back and smoothed the apricot striped gown and pulled the rush bonnet back into place.

"We're fine, thank you."

Rye swung down from Cosmos with a grunt and flung the mare's reins to Felicity. He crouched to peer underneath the wagon. "Your wagon is less than fine."

"Are we on speaking terms now?"

"Didn't know we weren't."

"Tell me what to do." Her hands shook holding the reins and she pressed them to her chest to keep Rye from seeing that she was less than steady.

"Do you have an axle?"

"Yes, but as you can see it prefers to masquerade as firewood."

"So you don't have a spare axle?" Grey eyes squinted up at her without humor.

"Yes, I have a spare. I have to unload the wagon to get to it."

Rye limped to the back of the wagon. "I'll block the wheels. Help Aggie get up on Cosmos with the baby."

Aggie passed the baby down to Felicity. She crooned and chuckled when he pulled on the strings of her bonnet.

"How's my little man?"

"Happy to be on solid ground, like his Granma Aggie will be."

"Hold on, let me give you a hand." Felicity tucked the boy on her hip and balanced her aunt as the older woman felt for the foothold on the side of the wagon.

"I'll send Helmut back down the trail to ya," Aggie promised, settling her grandson before her on the saddle.

Rye muttered under his breath at the back of the wagon.

Felicity rolled up her sleeves. "Load the wagon. Unload the wagon. I can't wait to be done with this wagon. When I get settled and have the money, I'm buying a wagon with springs that comes with a driver."

The replacement axle was found. Shoving the planter's hat to the back of his head, Rye rubbed the stubble on his jaw. "It's too long."

"What is?"

"The axle. It must have been made for another wagon. We'll have to cut it down to fit."

A smiling Helmut Schneider's knocked on the side of the wagon. Philippe Patelle nodded over the top of a tool box he clutched in his arms.

"Miss Felicity."

"Mr. Schneider, Mr. Patelle."

Helmut studied the shattered axle. "I know, I know. Wait no more than one day. I'll have Marta look after Aggie."

"And the baby."

"Of course the baby. Marta is especially fond of your son."

Felicity swallowed, hard. It was the first time anyone referred to the baby as her child.

"My thanks."

"No worries."

Rye worked the lathe back and forth to shape the axle. Felicity organized the contents of the wagon strewn across the trail. She arched her back in a stretch and eased onto a barrel.

The canvas covered wagons topped a rise further up the trail.

"We are always playing catch up with the others."

"Yep."

Felicity settled in for a round of one word answers from the man.

They test fitted the axle. Still too long.

Ten minutes and a nicked thumb later, Rye tossed a lathe into the tool box and wiped his bandana across his forehead. He kicked the crate of law books with his boot. "I thought I told you to get rid of those books."

"You did. But they had a mind of their own and ended up back in the wagon."

"See if you can talk sense into them this time and impress upon them the pleasant aspect to be seen from the river bottom."

Another fitting of the axle found Felicity sitting on the crate of books and handing tools to Rye under the wagon. She remembered pulling books from the shelves and handing them to her father as he worked on contracts in the Almstead House library. It was a lifetime ago, when the sole discomfort in her life came from the prick of the dressmaker's pins buried in the seam of her wedding dress. Before her old life became railroad stock certificates good for stuffing cracks in an attic.

The wagon shifted.

"Felicity!"

The wagon listed off the twisting jack.

What to do? What to grab?

She put her weight behind the crate of books and shoved.

The jack slipped. The wagon bed dropped onto the crate. The crate creaked under the weight, but the wagon steadied.

"Dr. Jones?"

No answer.

Dodge barked at her heels and bit at her frayed hem. She shushed him.

"Rye!"

His legs didn't twitch when she tapped his boots.

Oh, God. Please don't let him be dead.

She hitched up her skirt and crawled under the wagon.

"Hello?"

Rye raised the brim of his hat and peered down his sweaty

nose at her. "Just wanted to see if you'd care."

Her head hit the dusty planks. "I care! I care all right. I need help reloading this ... wagon." Felicity kept herself from saying the expletive she wanted to say.

"Just don't go caring too much. My intentions may not be in your best interest."

"Who says I'm caring? I just need to get this wagon back on the trail."

Rye wriggled out from under the wagon and helped her stand, dusting off the back of her skirts with a broad palm.

"Stop that."

"You had a bit of dirt back there." Rye grinned, thumping Dodge's ribs.

She grinned back at him, surprised by his good humor.

"You're bleeding —"

"I bruised my shoulder but good and ripped my shirt. But it was in pursuit of a worthy cause. You professed to care about my welfare."

Words failed Felicity. A young lady did not admit to having emotions for a gentleman. Particularly stubborn men who resorted to sulking and speaking in monosyllables for weeks.

"Glad you didn't get rid of those books. You would've been burying me."

Felicity sobered. "Don't talk about any more burials. As for the books, they've earned their place in the wagon."

"For now. Or at least until you need to lighten the load somewhere down the trail."

WHEN AUNT AGNES issued an invitation to join them for supper, Rye accepted. He came back the next evening, and every evening when he wasn't on watch duty.

Felicity pulled out the curling tongs and forced her hair into ringlets. Aunt Agnes took over, combing and coaxing

Felicity's straight hair into curls. Working on the last strand, the smell of burning hair caught both of them by surprise.

Aunt Agnes released the tong, crisping a lock.

"Want me to cut it off?"

A woman's hair was her glory. Felicity's mother raised her daughter on that sentiment.

"Oh my, no. I ... I couldn't."

"It's just hair. It'll grow back." Aggie flicked the ringlets. "Long time since I've seen ya fussin' over yer hair. Ya miss him?"

"With every other step." Her father was an affectionate parent. He saved the roasted potatoes for her from his dinner plate. Her mother disapproved, flavoring the potatoes with a condiment tastier than butter.

"Why'd yer pa break it off?"

"I thought we were talking about Father."

"I know ya miss yer pa. Talkin' 'bout yer beau."

"Does it ... show?"

"I got eyes. And ears. That and yer Uncle Jasper told me."

"Out of fairness to Edmund ... to keep the burden from him. I was no longer in a position to be a credit to him."

"Ya need to quit thinkin' 'bout him and let that heart of yers heal. Happened to me, ya know. I was set to marry Harlan Seevers. My folks objected somethin' fierce. Almost ran off with him."

"What stopped you?"

"My pa. That and it appeared there was another potential Mrs. Seevers in the next valley. Several in town, if I recall. Seemed he had a talent for startin' a fine romance, just not finishin' up."

"What happened?"

"My Pa wouldn't let the scamp on the front porch."

"Did you think about him?"

"Cried myself dry. I figure t'was God's way to keep me from makin' the same mistake. Protectin' me when Pa wasn't there to remind me."

Felicity rolled the crisp tendril of hair between her fingers.

"Work on that heart, girl. Jasper was the love of my life. If I hadn't listened to my Pa, I'd be Aggie Seevers. Probably one of a harem."

AFTER SUPPER, FELICITY resumed the search for Uncle Jasper's temperature gauge. The birds darted and swooped, catching bugs in the twilight. The light lasted longer each day and Felicity lit the lantern later each night.

"I have no idea where it is."

"Sure ya didn't just chuck it in the river?"

"What? For the amusement of the trout?"

"Look again."

Felicity climbed back into the wagon. It was useless to search for the gauge. She was certain it was part of a prairie dog den.

Aunt Agnes stacked the tin plates. "It's always in the last place ya look."

"Thanks Ag – Aunt Agnes, for that bit of advice." Felicity choked on her reply. Aggie was her uncle's pet name for her aunt. Felicity's upbringing prompted her to use a formal address.

At the Patelle wagon, Philippe plucked the strings on his violin. Walt Anderson's guitar added deep tones. Another violin joined. The amateur musicians with the company played country dances for the amusement and scattering of applause. Some nights coyotes or wolves howled with them, adding a not so reassuring quality.

"What must the Indians think listening to that?" Aggie draped a towel over the dish box.

Glancing at the herd of cattle, Felicity took a quick look for Right and Left.

Where was the pair with the familiar red splotches on white hide?

She scanned the herd again. Mueller, Watson, Robertson, Crandall ... she went through the rest of the names, accounting for every family in the company.

Every family but her own.

No notched horns.

Chest tight, Felicity jammed her bare feet into Hannah's old boots and grabbed the ebony walking stick.

"Find it?"

"No. I have to go check on something."

"What's wrong?"

"Nothing, I want to be certain about something."

No cattle, no way to move their possessions. Everything packed in the wagon would be left behind.

Felicity stood at the edge of the herd and counted the cattle.

Right and Left were missing.

She checked the leather hobbles on the oxen's stout legs before turning Right and Left out with the herd. The hobbles ensured the cattle did not stray.

Could it be Indians? Indians traded with the wagon company or watched the emigrants pass on the trail from a distance. And it didn't make sense to Felicity that they would take an interest in their two oxen. There were stouter cattle in the herd. And mules. And horses.

Could she convince one of the families to take Aunt Agnes and the baby to the next fort or settlement? Accustomed to the daily miles, Felicity could carry the baby, but Aggie weakened while her cough grew stronger. Her aunt's coin jar held money to pay tolls and supplies, but replacing the oxen would deplete those funds and keep them from reaching Oregon City with the rest of the company.

No other family suffered a loss.

This was personal.

Deliberate.

"What's afoot?" Coughing into a balled up handkerchief, Aunt Agnes met her at the edge of the encampment.

"Us, for the time being. Right and Left have wandered off."

"I thought you hobbled 'em."

"So did I."

"Want me to come with you?"

"Stay here. They can't have gone far."

Felicity beat the high grass with her walking stick, leading reins over her shoulder.

I can hear the snakes.

I just can't see the snakes.

Seems only fair I give them plenty of warning.

She came to the edge of a gully that ran a short course and died out. Right and Left were below her, tails swishing and heads down, ripping and chewing grass. She slid down the bank and trudged through the weeds to Right. Rubbing a sore on his ribs, she figured a few minutes of grassy paradise for the hard working pair would be fair.

Relief at finding the cattle was replaced with the worry that she was out on the prairie without a rifle. She still couldn't shoot Uncle Jasper rifle with any accuracy and if she did, the shot would scare the oxen and she would be in for a longer walk.

Justin McHenry's accordion joined the violins and guitar. The rustic beat of the music begged for a few dance steps, but she was too tired to prance around in the wildflowers.

She rested her forearms on Right's back. The grass bent and rippled before the wind.

What would I plant if this was my land claim?

She snorted.

Some lady farmer she'd make, having never potted such much as an orchid. Flowers arrived in white boxes tied with wide satin ribbons, the colors coordinated to match the seasons with carefully scribed Latin text. Or at least, that was in New York.

Fireflies dipped and swirled over the grass tips. She hooked the leading rein on Right's halter and reached for Left. He took a step away from her, his usual game. She followed, brushing away mosquitoes.

His ears flicked back.

She reached down for his halter.

Left's head shot up and with a wild bellow, he bolted. Right, wide eyed, spun to follow his yoke mate.

Palms burned trying to hold the lead rope. She let go, for fear of losing her fingers. "Come back, you … you …" Felicity searched for a name that was ladylike.

A chuckle drifted down from the rim of the gully. Rye stood with his rifle cradled across his arms. Dodge lay with his muzzle on Rye's boots.

"You spooked my cattle."

"Nice night for a stroll out onto the prairie."

"I'm not strolling. Someone set Right and Left loose and I know who."

"I was with the Schneiders."

"I didn't say it was you."

"You didn't say it wasn't me."

"I'm pretty sure it was your shadow. And no, I don't mean Dodge."

"You see her do it?"

"No. But isn't it odd that Right and Left would wander but no other cattle are missing?"

"Trail justice is harsh. Be sure of the facts before you go around making accusations."

Felicity pushed the sleeves of her apricot striped gown down against the sting of the mosquitoes. "What are you doing out here?"

"Thought I'd stretch my legs a bit before settling in for the night."

"You came to check on me." His concern warmed her. It pleased her, and she wasn't sure why.

"Just curious to see if you were quitting on me."

"I told you before, I don't quit."

Rye tipped his hat back. "Well, I hope you can walk fast."

"Are you threatening to leave me out here?"

"Why no, ma'am. But your cattle are making for that rise and I can't say for certain what's on the other side."

"I'll see you back at camp."

"I'll wait."

Felicity whacked the tips of the grass with the walking stick. Rye whistled and Dodge streaked by her, low to the ground.

With chirps and commands, Rye directed Dodge in herding the cattle.

"How does Dodge know to do that?"

Rye reached out and unhooked the lead rope from Right's halter. "We both had a long enough walk today. I figured it would save wear and tear on the cattle and our own boot leather if Dodge was to hurry them along."

"Thoughtful of you. My thanks." Felicity swept a graceful curtsey worthy of a debutante posed in a Godey's Lady's Book illustration.

Rye swept his arm to indicate the smoke from the campfires. "After you, ma'am."

One of the violins squealed in the distance and Felicity applauded.

"What were you laughing at when I showed up?" Rye broke off the tasseled head of a long stalk of grass.

"Flowers," she smiled. "Hot house flowers, not like these."

"From a beau?"

"No, from my father. From a florist he represented in his early days as a trial attorney. The flowers were in exchange for services rendered."

Right and Left trotted towards camp. "Dodge isn't biting them, is he?"

"They're fine. But I fail to understand your humor."

"It was the card the flowers came with. I wasn't allowed to arrange the flowers until I deciphered Papa's note."

"Bad handwriting?"

"No, he wrote it in Latin, sometimes Greek. Usually a play on words ... something clever."

"So you are a scholar."

Mother was ever telling her that eligible gentlemen did not like educated girls.

Farming. That was a safe topic. "What can you plant here?"

"Us, if we don't get back to camp before dark." Rye relented. "Corn or wheat would be my guess. Let's get you back before the gossips put their heads together."

Striding toward the rustic music, Felicity slowed her steps to match Rye's gait. At the edge of the picket lines, he winced and stopped to rub his bandaged thigh.

"These your hobbles?" Rye frowned and used the muzzle of the rifle to lift the branches of a bush. The hobbles were rolled up and stuffed underneath.

"Yes."

"Any idea about how they got there?"

"Bolting oxen don't pause to unbuckle and stash hobbles."

"I'll check the herd later tonight in case another pair goes for a stroll."

A scream ricocheted through the encampment like a Minie ball. The violins paused, the accordion playing a few bars. Felicity froze in place, looking to Rye for direction.

"Now what?" Rye pulled his planter's hat low over his forehead.

Shouting came from the Radnor campsite. Rye and Felicity followed the others running, some with rifles, Yetta Daniels with a cast iron lid, Vivienne Patelle with a butcher's knife, and others with whatever was close at hand.

"Who did you say did this to you?" Johann Radnor's bellowed, short tempered as a bull and with a neck and shoulders suited for a plowshare in Putnam County.

Ulna, torn dress and dirt streaked face, sobbed in her mother's arms. "It was Rye. Rye Jones."

Thomas Cavanaugh, Lane Crandall, and Lucas Robertson wrestled with Rye and took his rifle from him. Horace Mueller and Pug Anderson grabbed Rye and twisted his arms up behind his back.

"That's a lie."

Seeing Helmut Schneider at the back of the crowd, Felicity clutched his hand, but he shook her off. Surely he would ensure that Rye was heard. Was it her imagination or was sweat dripping down Helmut's sideburns?

"Let me go, boys." Rye wasn't amused.

Helmut stepped into the light of the campfire. "I hate to admit it ... but I did see Rye leave the camp."

Felicity picked up her skirts above her knees and ran to find her aunt.

Aggie was standing on the drover's box. She tossed Uncle Jasper's flintlock rifle to Felicity. "Run, girl, before they string him up."

Panting with fear, Felicity climbed onto the tailgate of the Radnor wagon.

Radnor jabbed his fist against Rye's ribs with a meaty thud.

Rye groaned. "Never ... woulda treated 'er ... like that."

"Hold it right there, Radnor." Felicity waved the rifle in her arms.

Is it loaded?

How do I tell?

Will I pull the trigger?

Hope I don't have to answer that.

Hope Radnor isn't any surer of that than I am.

"Dr. Jones is telling the truth and your daughter knows it. Your daughter cut my oxen loose from the herd. Ask Aggie, she sent him out to make sure I came back."

Ulna buried her face in her mother's lap and wailed.

Felicity put the rifle up to her shoulder and lined up Johann Radnor's chest with the end of the barrel. "Rye was out on the prairie with me."

Radnor's friends released Rye's arms. He staggered, but stayed upright.

Radnor grabbed his daughter's long black hair and yanked her upwards. "Talk daughter. Tell the truth, if there be an honest bone in that body of yours."

Ulna mumbled a name.

"Louder. I can't hear you."

"It wasn't him!" Ulna screamed at her father. He raised his bloody fist.

Gripping the rifle with sweating palms, Felicity raised the rifle to her shoulder. "Let her be."

Radnor swung his head like a buffalo bull in Felicity's direction.

"What's it to you?"

"Nothing. But if she bears a mark from your hand I believe these good people will cast you out of the company."

Shoving his daughter aside, Radnor spat on the ground in front of Felicity and plowed his way through the crowd.

Rye raised his hand. "Put the gun down, Miss Sinclair."

Felicity tossed the rifle to Rye and held onto his broad hand to climb down from the Radnor's tailgate.

Holding his chin up to the light of the campfire, she dabbed at a cut on his cheek with the tail of her apron.

Brushing away her hand, Rye held his ripped and bloodied shirt away from his chest. "This is the second shirt I've torn in your service."

"Are you hurt bad?"

"I'll heal. This is a case of physician, heal thyself. But it is my turn."

"For what?"

"To say 'thanks' ... I mean it. I'd never touch a child like that."

"She has a *tendre* for you."

"A what?"

"She's sweet on you. Can't you see it?"

"Frankly, no. She's a child."

"She is a young woman experiencing powerful emotions."

"And did you possess powerful emotions at her age?"

Felicity winced. "I did. They were the source of some truly awful poetry."

"And?"

"And nothing. Like you say, 'that's the past' and not what is ahead of me."

"Philosopher."

"Blind man. Watch your back in case she decides to set upon you again."

"I'll just get Dodge to send her in the right direction."

"And what direction might that be?"

"Back to her mother until she is old enough to know better."

Felicity raised her eyebrows. "No one would ever accuse you of being romantic."

"Now there you're wrong."

"Really?"

"Care for a demonstration?" Rye caught her wrist and pulled her close.

Silver eyes glistened above his bruised lips. The spin of emotions caught Felicity unprepared.

Rye shouldn't be the one to kiss me. It should be Edmund. Blue eyes like the prairie sky, not grey eyes like a storm tossed Atlantic.

Yet she wanted it to be Rye. She was free to be natural around him, not bound up in rules of white gloves and cotillion politics. He was natural and real in his desires, yet there was a refined mind. There was more to the man than buckskins.

"What? I'm not good enough company for you?" He

cupped her chin in his hand.

"Too good, actually. Why do you make an effort to speak to me at all?"

"Would you like to walk out on the prairie with me tonight and I will confess all? I can fetch your shawl from Aggie."

Letting Rye into my heart means Edmund is truly gone from my life.

"I'm ... I should turn in. Good night."

Rye released his grip on her wrist. Clapping his hat on the back of his head, he limped away in the darkness.

She stood in the moonlight, listening to the crickets, wishing she had been kissed.

CHAPTER 12

Ash Hollow
June 9, 1851

The baby clapped his hands in his bath water, splashing the front of Felicity's apricot striped gown with soapy water.

"Baby and I can likely squeeze into that dress of yer's with ya," Aggie called from the feather bed in the back of the wagon. She coughed into her handkerchief.

Blushing, Felicity pulled up the neck of the gown. The corset, abandoned back around Plum Creek, and the petticoats, buried in a ditch out of view of the sentries at Fort Kearny, left just the tattered chemise and pantalets patched and pleated to take up the excess fabric.

The dress, her talisman.

She wasn't ready to give it up. Not yet.

The baby nuzzled Felicity's neck as she dried and diapered him. Stew bubbled in a pot on the coals of the campfire and she was pressed to get the plates and silverware arranged before Rye came for supper.

"Miss Felicity?"

Startled, Felicity buttoned the bodice all the way up to her throat.

Ezra Mueller held two rabbits and stared down her bodice where it was wet against her breast.

"I brought hares for supper. They're skinned, gutted and spitted."

"Thoughtful of you. Would you like to stay and eat with us?"

"Actually, Ma'am, there's something I wanted to ask you about." Ezra puffed out his chest like a prairie dog. "Miss Felicity, you need a man in your life."

Felicity bit her lip to keep the laughter from bursting out. "I have Baby."

"I mean a grown man ... and ... and I propose to be that man."

"Aren't you a little young to be contemplating marriage? I am older than you, you know. And I have a child." She wagered that the peach fuzz on his cheeks never met with a razor.

"I'm young, but I can provide for you and your son. I've got my own wagon ... it has grooved planks that I planed and fitted myself ... and my own stock of supplies. Dried fruits, even. And my Pa says I'm as good a blacksmith as he is."

The rabbits were a betrothal gift.

Felicity tucked the baby onto her hip and bent down to the Dutch oven and lifted the lid with a cloth.

"My Mam says you're a fine woman and my Pa ... well, both of them approves of the match. That baby of yours is a good start to a family as we're gonna need many hands to homestead claim. And if we're married we can get a bigger land claim than what I can get on my own. You know, 'cause of the wife's portion and all."

She was at a loss for words.

"So, can I fetch the preacher? I already talked to Pastor Lane. He'd do a credible job."

"I need to stir this a minute so it doesn't burn." Tasting the bubbling stew, she was careful not to let Baby grab the steaming spoon. Her hand shook.

"Well? I'm waiting."

Falling back on her mother's instruction on handling a proposal from an unwanted *parti*, she bent her head in a modest pose. "Thank you for your declaration of admiration, but after consideration I must decline your offer."

"Decline? You mean you're saying no?"

"You are correct. It wouldn't be fair to marry you."

"My folks are good with it. And you need a man if you're gonna to file a claim when you get to Oregon City. You can't make a claim on your own because you're a lady."

Ezra's point jabbed Felicity's tired brain. Why hadn't she spent more time on planning for the end of the trail? She had the time at night when she walked the perimeter of the campground, passing other mothers with fussy babies.

There wasn't going to be peace unless she attended to Ezra. "I admire your desire to start a family and provide for them, but I am too old for you. Why don't you marry a young lady closer to your age? I'm sure that Ulna would make you a good wife."

"That jilt? She's been with every man in the wagon train. She lures them out onto the prairie and lets them put their hands all over her. She kisses them and everything. I've heard her say she's done it with your precious Rye Jones."

That hurt. That hurt to the core. "That's his business, not mine."

Please let it be a lie, she prayed.

Gravy splattered hissing into the coals. Felicity brushed her hair back and bent down to move the pot away from the coals.

Ezra jerked her arm. "I don't think you should answer – "

"Don't do that. I might drop the baby."

"I think you need to spend some time thinking about it, that's all. This is a fine proposition – I mean proposal – for both of us." Ezra seized her forearm but she twisted away.

The frayed apricot silk tore and Ezra held the left sleeve and the upper part of a bodice in his hand.

Clutching the baby to her chest, Felicity grabbed the tea pot for a club.

"Everything all right?" Rye leaned on his rifle next to

Helmut Schneider. An antelope was slung across Cosmos' saddle.

Ezra struck a ten cent novel pose. "Why don't you just keep on riding to your campfire? Miss Sinclair here and I are having a private discussion."

Rye glanced from Felicity's grip on the tea pot to the fabric in Ezra's hand.

Ezra dropped the silk.

"Son, I think you're about done."

"Don't tell me what to do." Ezra raised his fists.

Rye turned to Felicity with a raised brow and a crooked smile. The scab on his cheek from Johann Radnor's fist cracked open.

"An ardent admirer of yours?"

Felicity lowered the tea pot. "I believe Ezra was just leaving."

"You owe Miss Sinclair an apology."

"You just want her for yourself. I've seen how you look at her."

"Gentlemen, let's call this discussion a draw. I have folks to feed. Everyone get on about your own business. I'm not marrying anyone tonight or any night."

Aggie poked her head out from the back of the wagon. Her bonnet was askew, her voice heavy from sleep. "Ya gettin' married?" She peered at Felicity, then at Rye.

Something strummed in Felicity's heart at Aggie's mistake. But Rye wasn't the one proposing marriage. And she was certain he never would.

Rye cleared his throat. "Ezra here just proposed."

"If that ain't something. Did she say yes?"

Rye grinned, wide.

Felicity raised the tea pot.

Aggie hooted. "Well just don't stand there gawkin'. Fetch the preacher, boy, I'm in the mood for a wedding."

"I would, ma'am, but she won't have me."

"Well, if that don't beat all. Tell ya what. I like yer looks. Why, ya remind me of a young buck that was sweet on me in Hardin County. Besides, ya really don't want to hitch yer wagon to Miss Felicity. She's still moonin' over the highbrow politician she left back East."

Rye raised his eyebrows and glanced at Felicity.

Helmut wrapped his coat around Felicity's shoulders. "Ezra do that to you?"

Felicity pressed her hand against the gaping bodice. "It was an accident."

Helmut's brow furrowed. "Rye, isn't that what Ulna Radnor's dress was like when she accused you?" He grabbed Ezra and lifted him onto the toes of his boots.

"Boy, let's go have a talk with your Pa."

TRAIL JUSTICE WAS swift.

"Choose. Exile or a hanging."

Words a parent never expects to hear directed at his child. Ezra's mother her wiped tears with her apron.

After the trial, Felicity held a lantern. Rye drew a map on an old grain invoice.

"Joe Larkin's wagon train is a few days' ride away. He's a good man and will look after you."

"Thanks. And thanks for stopping them from hanging me."

"I know what it's like to be falsely accused. Here's the map. No shortcuts. Stay on the trail and don't get lost. Be sure to rest your cattle."

"I got it."

"No shortcuts. Remember."

Felicity pressed a bundle into Ezra's hands. "Here's supper for you. I hope you don't mind … I fixed you something to eat on the trail. After all, you caught and skinned them."

"That was an act of faith as I figured I'd be meeting my Maker." Ezra climbed onto his wagon seat. "Don't you worry. I'll be wintering on Abernethy Green before you get over the Cascades. I'm going to settle into a prime land claim and you're going to wish you'd traded in the name Sinclair for Mueller."

"Good fortune."

"Good luck, ma'am."

FELICITY STARED UP at the planks of the wagon above her head, listening to the canvas flap in the dawn wind. Baby reached out in his sleep for her. She turned on her side and curled around him, tucking the blanket over his feet.

That was the second marriage invitation offered. And the second one that came to nothing.

The child's eyelids fluttered. Baby needed to grow to be able to take care of himself. But at the same time, she wished he stayed an infant, innocent of the world's hurt. Never to know mean spirited people. People who broke their promises. People that picked up and left when the times turned hard.

What if Ezra is right? What if I marry but Baby isn't wanted? If this was New York, and if this was Edmund's child, he would sleep in a nursery. Nannies would force those first steps, correct the first lisped words. Cut his hair. Choose his clothes.

I don't want to hand him off to some other woman to raise.

But some things in life I can't teach him.

Manly things.

Baby needs a father, which means a husband for me.

CHAPTER 13

Chimney Rock
June 23, 1851

"These will dry back at the wagon." Fran Watson rolled her laundry into a bundle. "Are you joining for the sermon?"

"Aggie's going for both of us." Felicity waited for it, but there was no pang at missing Lane Crandall's sermon. Not when her hands ached in the cold water of the stream.

Rinse, scrub with soap flakes, rinse.

Patelle's violin picked up a hymn and she hummed the tune. Perhaps if she sat through the sermon with Aggie and the others, she wouldn't feel like such a hothouse bloom in a wildflower field.

Edmund escorted her and Maragon Ormond to the last church service at St. Paul's Chapel before the article on the scandal went to press.

The familiar stab of thinking of Edmund was blunted.

Wasn't she in mourning for her old life? Aggie's advice to quit turning over the memories in her mind like compost every other step must be working.

The diaper she was washing floated downstream. She splashed over river rocks and scooped it up.

Not ten feet from her bare feet, a snake basked in the July heat, curled around the base of a boulder. The color of its scales blended into hues of the rock.

I'm not going to bother it and it isn't going to bother me.

Forcing herself to breathe, she splashed up the stream to her soap flakes and laundry piles.

"Look at you, all alone, doing your washing." Ulna taunted from the stream bank.

Felicity kept the rhythm. Rinse, soap, rinse.

Ulna stumbled down the bank of the stream. "I want you to go away. I want you to just disappear."

"I'm just doing my laundry. Why don't you go have a seat and listen to Mr. Crandall's sermon?"

"You don't go because nobody wants you sit next to them. The bad luck on you will wear off on them."

"Go tell your tales to someone else. I'm busy. I've still got washing to get done."

"D'ya hear me? You're not wanted here. You've been nothing but a curse on us since the beginning. Your Pa gave everyone cholera. And Ezra had to leave because of you."

"Ezra caused his own mischief –"

"And you put a spell on Rye so that he won't look at another woman."

Felicity leaned back to wring out the diaper. "So that's the problem. You want Rye and you don't care how you get him. That's why you lied to your folks –"

Ulna kicked Felicity's rib cage.

Felicity mashed the wet diaper in Ulna's nose and mouth.

The Radnor girl shoved Felicity to the piles of laundry. Pain exploded in Felicity's shoulder and her head hit the streambed with a meaty thud. Red trimmed boots kicked again and again. Arms caught up in wet linen, Felicity curled up to protect her ribs and bear the blows.

"You ... need ... to ... leave," Ulna grunted with each kick.

The cottonwood fluff whirled overhead and the bottle blue water tugged at Felicity's skirt and bare feet.

It's snowing, it's snowing.

FELICITY TOOK A sugared almond from a tray in the Almstead House conservatory. Trays of pan au chocolate. A cheese soufflé steamed on the sideboard beside a silver bowl of pears.

Comice pears.

Rows of pear trees, staggered to let the sun dapple the orchard. Red blush on pale yellow, speckled brown.

Bees humming in a hive by a fence line.

Stinging her cheek.

Hard.

"Wake up, sweetling, open your eyes."

The panic in Rye's voice roused Felicity. She opened her eyes a crack. Rye's strained face and his dark grey eyes were the same as the night Phoebe Landers stole Baby out on the prairie. The scab on his cheek was gone, replaced by a red line where the skin healed.

Rye slapped her cheek.

Hard.

"Quit that."

"Do you know who I am?"

"My tormentor?" Why was she wrapped in a quilt in Rye's arms? And why was Dodge laying at her feet? Her head ached and her shoulder throbbed with each breath. Her ribs were on fire.

"How'd I get here? I don't remember …"

Rye smiled at a pale Aggie. "She'll live."

"Of course I will. Where's Baby?" Felicity glared at Rye.

"You slipped and fell. Aggie got worried when you didn't come back and fetched me. I found you half in the water. Do you remember falling?"

The question hurt her head. Felicity closed her eyes, fingers brushing shiny leaves. Pears. Beautiful pears.

"Hey, wake up. No sleeping until I inspect that shoulder."

"Don't touch me."

"You don't have a choice. Either I fix that shoulder or –"

"Fine. You may probe and be done."

His hands were gentle, but thorough. "You've dislocated your collar bone."

"Do we need to shoot her?" Aggie nudged Rye and winked. Felicity wasn't entirely sure if her aunt was joking.

"Only if her biscuits don't improve."

"Maybe I should just go back to sleep," Felicity closed her eyes.

"No sleeping for a while. My guess is that you smacked your head on a rock."

"Is that the medical explanation?"

"Concussion would be the appropriate term."

Aggie coughed. "Sure we can't shoot her? She's been awful onery lately."

"Lately?" Rye grinned.

"I'm not dead yet. Can you pick apart my carcass on another occasion or do I have to be present?"

"Where's your laudanum?" Rye flicked the question to Aggie.

Felicity rubbed her scalp. Blood dried in her hair and it itched. "In the wagon. The medicine box. Next to the flour."

"I'm old, but I see just fine," Aggie stomped onto the crate of books and rattled things around in the back of the wagon.

"And we need something for a sling."

Aggie tossed the laudanum to Rye. He clenched the vial in his hand and it took him a full minute to relax his fingers. Muttering, he poured a dose of the dark liquid into a cup of tea. Holding his breath, he screwed the lid tight and gave the vial back to Aggie.

Rye passed the mixture to Felicity. "Drink. All of it."

Handing the empty cup to Aggie, he stood behind Felicity. "This will hurt."

There was a popping and a click. "Ouch! Do that again and

I'll –"

"Cook? You won't be doing anything for a while with that shoulder. You need to rest it or it will pop out again."

"Rest? Who is going to do –"

"I said rest."

"Fine."

"You're welcome."

"Your bedside rapport with your patients is rusty."

"Are you suggesting that I hover at your bedside?"

"No."

"If you need anything during the night –"

"Aggie will be right beside me." Felicity replied.

"If you can bear the pain, save the laudanum. There's no telling what you may need it for later down the trail."

"Rye?"

He crouched beside the feather tick, his bandaged leg angled to the side.

She sorted through her feelings like a laundress looking for a match for a stocking. There was no match. She couldn't explain her feelings to herself much less anyone else.

"Dr. Foster could not have done a finer job."

Rye squeezed Felicity's hand. "Come on Dodge. Let's let the ladies retire for the evening."

THE ACHE IN her shoulder kept Felicity awake and laying on the feather bed in the back of the wagon brought images of her father and Hannah. The lack of memory; the gap between walking down the stream bank with a bundle of dirty linen and waking up wrapped in a quilt troubled her.

In the candlelight, Felicity sorted through her memory. Didn't she watch where she put her feet? A snake. Boulder. Diaper. Did she run from the snake? And here she was trying to cure her fear of snakes.

Tea might help. Setting aside the pages in her lap, she put the tea tin between her knees and pried open the lid. The last of the loose leaves went into the tea pot. She blew into the tin to get the leaf pieces out of the crevices. Two purple smudges above what she supposed to be her lips reflected in the polished bottom. The candle flame was not bright and the tin too coarse for a true image.

"What are ya doin' up?"

Felicity jumped at Aggie's voice. The pain bit at her shoulder.

"Didn't mean to wake you."

"I don't sleep much these days. Must be my age. What's got ya up at this time of night? Shoulder gettin' at ya?"

"I was reading." Felicity scooted aside to make room on the feather tick for Aggie. "Ezra Mueller is going to be disappointed when he reaches the Willamette Valley."

"Ya still worried about that boy? What he did to ya and Ulna and probably a bunch of womenfolk back in the states wasn't anyone's fault but his own."

"I'm not so sure that he hurt Ulna."

"That remains to be seen."

"His poor mother. I was thinking about his plans for starting a homestead."

"How so?"

"He's just seventeen years of age."

"How is that disappointin'? I wouldn't mind being seventeen again knowin' what I know."

"It's the plans he laid out. He can't file for a land claim, married or not. He's too young. According to this, you have to be twenty-one years old or older."

"So what's that yer readin'?"

"It's the Donation Land Act. Father kept a copy of it. He wanted to be sure to follow the letter of the law when it came to claiming a homestead."

"Sounds just like yer father. Too bad he didn't do more of

it. What's young Ezra got to do with all that? Ya change yer mind about marryin' that young scamp?"

"Ezra got me to worrying about what we're going to do when we reach the Territory. I've been so focused on getting from day to day that I haven't really given much thought to what happens when we get into Oregon City. But I can understand his point in getting married. A single man can claim 160 acres for himself but a married couple can claim an additional 160 acres for the wife to hold in her own right."

"Yer over twenty-one … can't ya claim a parcel for yerself?"

"I am the right age, the right skin color … but not the right sex. The Act states that a married woman can claim acres as her husband can file the claim, but what I don't see is a provision for an unmarried woman making a claim in her own name."

"So what ya need is a husband."

"What I need is to get us to Oregon. Then I can worry about finding a husband."

"And just how are ya goin' to get us over the trail that with a bum shoulder?"

"I don't know."

"Ya can't yoke the team with yer arm in that sling."

"It isn't fair."

"Honey, life isn't fair. Ya know what yer Uncle Jasper told me when yer Pa joined up with us …"

"'Fair is where you ride rides and look at pigs.'"

"That's right. And there ain't that many pigs out here on the prairie so my advice is to change yer perspective. Too bad ya didn't hang onto Ezra. He'd be a right big help."

"He was so young I'd have been tempted to diaper him right along with Baby."

"Honey, that little accident ya had doin' the washin' should have taught ya at least one thing. For all yer dreams of what to plant where, ya can't so much as break out a plow until ya can get a homestead started. And ya can't do that if ya can't file a land claim without a husband to do the filin'."

"It's not like men are lining up outside the wagon."

"Look, girl ... yer doin' the work of three men. But I won't be here forever to tell ya what to do. Ya need to use both yer hands to find yer backbone and act like ya have the sense God gave a goat. Yer politician isn't going to ride over that rise to sweep ya up and take ya back to New York. So get off yer duff and get to survivin'. Find one that will take ya, a baby and an old woman. There's one man who'd do the job credit. He just needs a shove."

"Who?"

"Rye Jones, that's who. Of course, I may have done a little bit of that when ya were nappin' in his arms."

"What have you done?"

O'Fallon's Bluff
June 26, 1851

"F. Sinclair ..."

Edmund traced the grooves of the etched river bank with a gloved fingertip. Felicity's handwriting flowed with the rounded curves of perfect copperplate even in sandstone.

She was here. She stood where he was standing to leave him a message, knowing he would follow. That he would find her. That he wasn't the type of man to give up. Not while he still breathed.

Edmund turned to the guide. "This is dated May 22nd. How far ahead are they, Miller?"

"At the pace yer settin', by the time it's the nation's birthday, we should be able to see their campfire at night, suh."

CHAPTER 14

Beyond Fort Laramie
July 3, 1851

Francois Patelle hitched Right and Left to the wagon at dawn. Angus Mueller grained the team when the wagon company nooned. Greta Mueller cooked more cornbread than her family ate at one sitting and Emma Robertson found room in her wash tub for the tin dishes. Sadie Cavanaugh took dirty clothes from Aggie and returned wet clothes for hanging on the line. Johann Radnor greased the wagon hub caps with his own mixture of pork fat and tar.

Most of the families helped Felicity and her aunt in their own fashion. With a third of the journey behind them, no telling when they might need a hand.

Repaying the families by tending to their children or passing messages from wagon to wagon on the trail, she couldn't in good conscience continue to receive charity. Three days outside of Fort Laramie, Aggie rubbed yellow ointment into her niece's shoulder. Felicity willed herself not to flinch.

"That ought to keep ya for a while." Aggie wiped the ointment from her gnarled hands. "Smell alone ought to cure ya."

Felicity wrinkled her nose. "Or at least speed the healing. Does it smell as bad as I think it does?"

"Let's just say I can tell when ya walk into camp."

"Do you think it is Rye's idea of a joke?"

"If it is, he's got ya good."

Buttoning the patched apricot silk bodice with one hand, Felicity waved away the sling.

"I am going to try a day without it," Felicity bent and lifted Baby with her good arm. Pain rippled along her jaw and down through her ribs.

"Quick, grab him!"

"Come here, sweet pea. Come see what Granma Aggie has for ya." Tucking the infant into her shawl, Aggie held up the sling. "And look what I have fer ya, missy. Put it on. Left ain't as stubborn as yer bein'."

"Baby must be growing. He's heavier than I recall."

"Think that yoke over there's any lighter? 'Bout all ya can handle is dressin' yerself. And that's with one hand. Tryin' to do too much will just set ya back and then where will we be? I'll tell ya. At the end of the trail with a bum shoulder and no help in sight. These fine folks won't be on the homestead with us. They'll have their own crops and livestock and families to tend to."

"Fine. Help me with the sling."

OUT ON THE trail, wheel ruts caught Felicity's toes when the Donation Act phrase "…three hundred and twenty acres, one half to the husband and the other half to the wife in her own right …" tumbled in her thoughts.

To save the wear and tear on her shoulder, she leaned on the walking stick and waited beside the trail for the wagons to creak past her.

She could open a store.

But with no capital and no goods there was no point.

She could teach.

But with no training and no references she could not apply to a school board with a clear conscience.

She could be a companion.

But with no experience and no mention of such a position among the postings at Fort Laramie there was no hope.

No one would dare hire Miss Felicity Sinclair, lately of Almstead House.

She could marry. Marry now, or marry later in the Territory.

At least one gentleman above reproach and a boy with skinned rabbits believed her capable of the task of wife.

But who? If now, her choices were limited. The Territory, sparsely populated, would have bachelors motivated by the Donation Land Act to marry. But she had to marry with care.

Felicity caught up with Aggie and their unloaded wagon at the evening site beside the Platte River. Johann Radnor never took his attention from greasing the wagon hubcaps, but his scowl sparked a memory. But Radnor's features did not fit the flickering image of river rocks, water and silver green leaves.

"Where'd ya take off to?" Aggie coughed into a gingham square.

"Did you try the vinegar and honey mixture?" Felicity avoided her aunt's question like it was a snake.

"Tastes awful funny, if you ask me. I'm just glad ya didn't find the cod liver oil. No tellin' what ya would do with that."

"The pamphlet said it should help clear the dust out of your lungs."

"Ain't the dust I'm worried about. It's that collar bone of yers."

Felicity squared her shoulders. The pain in her shoulder crackled. "I'll be back in a while."

"Helmut already saw to the cattle."

"Something else I need to do."

RYE WASN'T HARD for Felicity to find. He was at the

Schneider campsite, filing Cosmos' hoof with a rasp in the light of a lantern.

Dodge thumped his tail.

At least Rye's dog is glad to see me. And thank goodness, no Ulna. I don't need a witness if this goes badly.

Bending down to the lantern, Felicity turned up the wick for more light.

The file rasped, shaping the mare's hoof in Rye's broad palm. "Thanks. How's that shoulder?"

Cold sweat beaded on Felicity's forehead in the humid evening air. A moth flew up to the corner of her mouth. She flicked it away.

"Marry me."

Rye picked up a knife and pared away a black spot.

"Pardon?"

"Aggie is in the mindset that I need a husband." Did Edmund have butterflies in his chest when he asked her to marry him?

"That's so?"

"Don't feel so flattered. It was either you or old Angus Mueller."

Releasing the mare's hoof, Rye straightened and rested a forearm along the mare's back. "My patients aren't usually so thankful. Sure that head injury didn't cause any damage to your sensitive nature?"

"I'm not having a case of the vapors, if that's what you mean. Do you want to marry me or not?"

"And what has put you in the mind for domestic bliss?"

"Practicality."

"Not something I would think of in terms of you, but I'll bite. How is a marriage between us practical?"

"Ever read the Donation Land Act in any detail?"

"Yes."

"Then you know that I can't file a land claim."

"Yes."

"And with my arm in a sling, I can't hitch the team or carry firewood. I've come close to dropping Baby. Aggie's doing everything that she can to help, even braiding my hair, but she still doesn't have her strength back."

"Yes."

"And Baby needs a father. I can teach him to read, to do figures, I can teach him table manners or to find a city on a globe but I can't teach him how to do … well, you know … do manly things."

"Yes."

"So you see my need for a companion of sorts."

Rye bent and picked up Cosmos' forefoot. "Bring that lantern closer."

Felicity picked up the lantern. Her hand shook. Did Queen Victoria have this much anxiety when she asked Prince Albert to marry her?

"You may want to put that down before you drop it."

"Well, don't leave me hanging. Am I that unsuitable?"

"Just how far are you willing to take this being married?"

"Meaning?"

"Is this a scheme to get a homestead started or are you looking for someone to sweep you off your feet?"

"I'm looking for a comfortable home and someone that I can stand to talk with. Someone who has some sense of manners and is clean. Someone who understands that this life is new to me and that I am still learning to cook and care for a child. Someone who –"

"Not asking for much, are you?"

"If you want a partner in chores and building a new life in the Territory, I'm your girl. If you want hearts and violins, that is up to you. I don't harbor any romantic notions at this point in my life. I did at one time, but that's over and done with."

"What about your former fiancé?"

The lantern rattled in Felicity's hand. Sadness, true, but not the open wounds from the trail head in Independence. The scabs turned to scars somewhere between Scott's Bluff and Alcove Spring.

"How do you know about ... that?"

"Aggie mentioned you were mourning his loss."

"Aggie talks too much."

Rye paused. The grey eyes appraised her, waiting for her to continue.

"She was wrong. Dead wrong. That life died with my father and is buried under the sod back in Lone Elm. I couldn't find what remains of that girl if I tried. I've come too far to go back."

"What are you gonna do when he comes a'riding over a hill after you some day?"

"He isn't coming after me, nor is he likely to." Edmund Ormond was not coming to sweep her up in his arms and take her back to her former life. There was no White Knight. Just a leggings clad man in a homespun shirt to carry her forward.

"Wouldn't you rather have the kind of life he can give you?"

That perfect life flickered in her mind, the images as remote as fanning a stack of postcards from Mars or the moon.

"I used to believe it was all that I wanted. Being his wife was my life's ambition."

"So what changed all that?"

"My father died. Baby came along. I learned to make decisions for myself. I grew up."

"Hand that to me, will you?"

Felicity put down the lantern and picked up a jar, sniffing at the open top before passing the container to him. She picked up the lantern and sniffed at her shoulder.

"Is that the same liniment that you used on my shoulder?"

Rye scooped out a glob and rubbed the yellow ointment around the folds of the frog on Cosmos' hoof. "Wanted to make sure you didn't pick up a case of thrush when you were stretched out and taking your nap along the river."

"I may not remember what happened, but I wasn't napping. I fell."

Rye snorted. "What caused you two to part?"

She squared her shoulders and pressed her hand against the sling rather than show pain. "Like you've said, that's something in the past and not the here and now. I don't expect to see or hear from him again. His pride won't allow it. And if I know his family at all, his mother has a new bride to pin her hopes on hearing addressed as 'First Lady' and they are all well on their way to wedded bliss. They did not approve of my family's social standing after ... there was a ..." She choked. "The match was no longer in his best interest."

"So you weren't socially acceptable to his family. Is that why he didn't marry you?"

"No. There was more to it."

The shame. The closed doors. The humiliation of not being received. Debutantes whispering behind lace fans, speculating on how she dared appear in public. Her future mother-in-law leaving New York for Paris to avoid speaking of her.

Her mother's choice.

Felicity set the lantern on the ground.

"Sorry to have troubled you with my problems."

"Hold on. We're not through talking."

"I know what you're going to say. You don't need to humiliate me further."

"You've already quit on one fiancé. How do I know you won't quit on me at the first sign of trouble?"

"I haven't quit on you yet, have I?"

Rye stared long and hard at her. He wiped his hands on a rag.

"You were just about to."

Felicity spread her hands. "The truth is ... my father ... he wasn't the man I thought he was. I know that now ..."

"Least we have something in common between the two of

us."

"What's that?"

"Seems we've had someone we've loved cut out of our lives, and not by our own choosing."

Rye untied the mare's lead rope and vaulted onto Cosmos' back. He whistled to Dodge.

"Where are you going?"

"I'm off to fetch the minister. I'm in the mood to marry."

CHAPTER 15

Scott's Bluff
July 4, 1851

Helmut Schneider campaigned for a layover.

The menfolk voted to rest the livestock for the day, giving the ladies time between chores to prepare for the company's first wedding. Pug Watson's children were sent to pick wildflowers for a bouquet and the Muellers and Robertsons gathered cottonwood branches for a bonfire.

In the back of the wagon, Felicity lifted Castile soap and sacks of Aggie's precious sugar from a trunk beneath the feather bed. A gutta-percha wrapped bundle was on the bottom. She peeled back the tarp.

Maison Gagelin glowed in gold embossed letters beneath a film of trail dust. Corners crumpled, the white cardboard box was not stained from stream crossings or rain storms.

Holding her breath, Felicity pulled off the cardboard lid and brushed aside the gilt tissue.

The dress was clean as if stored in the wardrobe at Almstead House, which was a blessing to Felicity. The French lace bordering the tiers of ruffles was not hardy enough to wash in the Platte River and they had no pressing iron.

The creases in the layers of cream satin were expected, but when she slipped the *point d'aplique* gown over her head she snatched the shoulders to keep the dress from hitting the floor of the wagon. Felicity grabbed handfuls of satin on each side of her waist.

The dress will lace up with Baby inside. And this is the dress that Mother couldn't close with the restraint of a corset in New York.

Such a waste.

The hours spent in fitting the dress, carrying a sample of the cream satin in her reticule in the search for roses to match. The raging debates with her mother on the edge trim for the tulle veil. If seed pearls sewn on the neckline were less than classic.

Never a worry whether she was marrying the right man. Her father chose Edmund Ormond for her. Of course he was perfection.

But Rye was her choice. She hoped that the fit of the wedding gown was a sign.

Maybe Alice Watson will exchange chores with me for help in cutting the gown down to size.

Do we have enough time to stitch the lace overlay pieces together?

What do we do with the ruffles? They run from waist to hemline.

The apricot gown crumped on the floor was Felicity's other choice. It was clean, but corset string and patches on the reverse side held the frayed silk together.

Rye isn't likely to care what I wear, but I'd like to appear clean and pretty for my wedding.

Maybe Marta Schneider has a dress she'll lend me.

Aggie peered over the tailgate. "Looks like ya got room in there for me."

"It grew since we left Independence. The veil is the only thing that fits."

"Yer the one that's grown. Which got me to thinkin'. I got somethin' that ya might like better than that apricot dress you've worn to threads."

The bundle tucked under Aggie's elbow was a dress.

"This was my weddin' dress. Hannah wore it when she married Tom. And I don't think she'd mind if ya wore it."

Tears pricked in Felicity's eyes. "I'd be proud to wear it."

Aggie sniffed. "It just wasn't right to just leave it on the trail fer someone to pick up."

The dark blue wool and the severity of the style suited Felicity. After Aggie fastened the hooks of the wool gown, she pressed a shawl into Felicity's hands. The crocheted silk smelled of the cedar trunk kept under the drover's seat.

"I thought ya could use this as a sling," Aggie coughed into a gingham handkerchief. "It's somethin' yer father sent me after his Grand Tour."

"Thank you. And thank you for the dress."

"Got those curlin' tongs of yers?"

"Think I'm going to keep things simple. Would you mind rolling it up like the other day. Do you think Rye will like simple?"

Aggie pinned Felicity's hair into place. "Sorry yer folks ain't here?"

"I'm glad you are. I wouldn't change things for the world."

"Ya know this is a good choice. Rye is the kind of man that will bid without an ace, but only because he knows what's in everyone else's hand. He'll take care of ya and Baby."

"Father was right in telling me to follow your lead. Something good can come out of all this."

"Are you ready?"

Rye's voice sent a warm rush to her cheeks. The sight of him caused her to gasp.

The leggings and leather vest were gone. In their place were the linen trousers and cutaway morning coat of a Southern gentleman, dressed for church. How was it possible that the man knew how to handle a four-in-hand necktie?

Aggie nudged Felicity. "I changed my mind, gal."

"What do you mean?"

Aggie's eyes sparkled. "I think I'm the one he should be

marryin', not ya."

Rye winked at his bride to be, his eyes the pearl grey before dawn.

Felicity accepted Rye's hand and his help down from the tailgate. "Then you shouldn't have talked me into proposing."

THE FAMILIES GATHERED on the bank of the Platte River, washed in the copper rays of the setting sun. Helmut stood beside Rye, and Aggie served in place of Gerald Sinclair. Felicity stared down at the wildflower bouquet, concentrating on the warm hand placing a borrowed gold band on her left hand. Before Pastor Lane Crandall and God, Felicity Sinclair pledged her troth and became Mrs. Peyton Randolph Daniel Jones.

Twice.

Lane Crandall lost his place in the service and she repeated her vows.

Easing Aggie's ring from her finger, Felicity pressed the gold band into her aunt's palm.

"Put this back where it belongs."

"Why don't ya keep it? I'm too old to be sportin' a weddin' ring."

"Says the woman who thought she should be marrying tonight." Felicity closed her aunt's fingers over the ring. "Uncle Jasper would have a thing or two to say about it."

Aggie slipped the ring over her swollen knuckles. "Funny how this was easier to put back on than it was to get it off."

After the well-wishers kissed the bride and clapped the groom on his back, Philippe Patelle picked up his bow and couples formed to dance a reel before the crackling bonfire.

Pulling Felicity aside from Emma Robertson and the family's gift of a silver bowl found at Plum Creek, Rye pressed a pair of buffalo hide moccasins into Felicity's hands. "These are for you. They're good for snow travel. Helps the blood circulate. Thought you'd like to wear them around the campground at night ... sort of a comfort to you after a long walk on the trail."

She flexed the dark leather and ran the tips of her fingers over the quill and bead embroidery.

Felicity winced at her lack of manners. "I have to admit that I do not have a wedding gift for you."

"You're mistaken. It isn't every day that I gain a bride ... a very beautiful bride ... and a son."

The perfect gift occurred to her. One he could appreciate. "I'll make you an offer."

"What's that?"

"You sound suspicious."

"I am. What's your offer?"

"My father's law books. When we break camp in the morning, I'll set them aside on the trail, just for you."

He whistled. "That's the second best offer you've made me in the last day or so."

She blushed all the way to the roots of her braids. "Father would understand."

"Keep the books. Who knows, they may yet be handy for fire starting. Not that I am in favor of book burning, but we may run shy of fuel at some point. Besides, they were your father's books and he bade you to keep them. He must've had his reasons."

"Can you see Aggie?"

Aggie laughed, passing from dancing partner to dancing partner across the crushed prairie grass serving as a dance floor. "You'd think that she was the one getting married."

"She's happy for you," Rye smiled.

"She's happy she got her way."

"You're onto something. Pardon me while I go ask our matchmaker to save a place for me on her dance card."

"You ... dance?"

"My mother insisted that I learn all the social niceties. Save a waltz for me?"

Felicity curtseyed with mock formality and he bowed before limping away.

Wandering away from the bonfire, the stars reflected in the wide river reminded Felicity of eating Christmas cookies, when powdered sugar spilled on her black velvet skirt.

This wedding is unlike any she attended in New York. She bit into the chunk of wedding cake in the linen napkin she held. A cake made with prairie hen eggs and frosting made from the Cavanaugh's butter and Aggie's sugar. It tasted finer than the wedding cake she planned with the cook at Almstead House.

Rye waltzed with Aggie.

My husband, not a term I never thought to apply to Rye. Who knew that his given name was Peyton Randolph Daniel Jones?

She could not imagine calling him anything other than Rye.

PHILIPPE PICKED UP a country dance and Aggie grabbed Rye's hand.

"Come on, me fine bucko. Don't tell me yer givin' up?" Aggie danced a turn with Rye and stopped to catch her breath. She coughed. Clearing her throat, she took a few more steps in the dance. She choked and lurched away from the dancers holding her side.

Waving Rye away, she coughed into her handkerchief.

"Go dance with yer wife," Aggie wheezed.

Rye upended a barrel for Aggie to sit on. "My wife …"

A howl and a shriek echoed. A coyote must have caught something out in the darkness. Rye took a quick inventory of the dancers, counting the familiar faces to make certain no one strayed from the bonfire. Felicity stood beyond the bonfire, her back to the flames. Was she regretting her choice? Was she thinking of her politician?

"Yer lovely bride. She doesn't know it yet, but she's more than half in love with ya."

"I'm finding it hard to believe you."

"She didn't ask ya to marry her just 'cause yer the only way out of a dire place. Felicity didn't have to marry ya to get ya to help us out on the trail. Yer the kind of man that would've done that anyhow, and have been since we buried our menfolk. Jes' remember that a woman always has a choice. And she chose ya because yer a kind man and will make for a good father for that young'un she packs around. She's been a good mother to that boy, and like a good daughter to me, so I'd place a strong bet that ya'll find she's a darn good wife to ya."

Aggie drew a deep breath and coughed into her handkerchief. "She didn't choose this life, it chose her."

"Her father and I had quite a talk about that."

Folding her arms across her thin chest, Aggie stared him down. Rye eased his collar open.

"I know some of yer history from Helmut."

"He's got a loose tongue."

"Can't hold her responsible for her father. Everyone else tried. Even me. I didn't let my Jasper invest, no matter how hard he fought me. But that girl. Did ya know that she stood in the driveway of that palace they called home and gave what she could to those poor folks that came by? Everythin' her pa had went to pay off investors where they could. She ain't got more than toll money left."

Aggie coughed. Shuddered. "And she wasn't the one that broke off that other weddin'. That was all Gerald. As for her former beau, my guess is his family found out what happened and couldn't face the scandal of havin' one of their own marry the daughter of a swindler.

"My fool brother-in-law made his bed and she's had to

wash the sheets ever since. If she knew the truth about all that happened she'd probably have dug a hole right next to him and climbed in and pulled the dirt over her head."

Aggie coughed into the handkerchief. She glanced at it and balled it up.

"I haven't said anythin' to her about it 'cause I figured it was yer choice to share or not share about what all happened to ya and yer family. If I was ya, I'd think long and hard about keepin' the past in the past and just work out what yer goin' ta plant on that homestead of yers. She's got her heart fixed on pear trees, although I'm not entirely sure why. Doesn't make a lot of sense to me."

Aggie coughed again and wiped her mouth with the handkerchief.

Rye grabbed her hand. He pried her fingers away from the fabric. Dark splotches of blood colored the squares of gingham. "Prolonged fever? Night sweats?"

"She doesn't know about that either. I suggest that ya keep that bit of news to yerself."

"So marrying me was your idea?"

"Ya both needed a push and since I'm not goin' to be around forever, I done got tired of waitin' for ya to make up yer mind."

Rye pecked Aggie on the cheek. "If she is half the woman you are —"

"Ya'll be a dang lucky man. Scat, youngster, and let an old woman get her breath back."

WALT ANDERSON STRUMMED his guitar and picked up the melody from Philippe's violin. A ragged Scottish folk dance drifted into the prairie.

Felicity's foot tapped in time with the music. She turned to Maggie McHenry and blew kisses at Baby nestled in a small quilt in Maggie's arms, playing hide and seek with her veil. Baby reached out and patted Felicity with sticky hands.

Rye lifted the infant from Maggie's arms and bowed before Felicity, hand placed on his vest like a courtier. "Mrs. Jones, may we have this dance?"

"Why Dr. Jones, I believe I have room on my dance card for the two of you."

Rye held Baby in one arm and bent his head towards hers. He taught her the steps to the dance, careful not to jostle the crocheted shawl.

Felicity leaned back, enjoying the strength in his arm wrapped around her waist.

"You are a mysterious man, husband."

"How so?" He spun her away from him, and pulled her back against his chest.

"I've never seen you dance."

"Seemed like a good idea at the time. Are you tired? Is this too much for you?" He drew her to the edge of the crushed grass.

She caught his hand and placed it on her waist. "I'm not quitting."

"You know that Philippe will play until we drop."

"Or until he has to hitch his team."

Rye wiped the sweat from his temples. "Good point. Shall we talk, instead?"

Felicity peeked at Baby's sleepy face. Rye shifted the nodding infant to his other shoulder and limped away from the bonfire.

A fish jumped in the river, a flash of silver. She pointed. "Kind of like a shooting star, isn't it?"

"If you want a lesson on astronomy, you'd have to consult Helmut."

"How about if we could talk of the mystery of your many names. How did you end up with Rye?"

"Some folks figured a short cut was needed."

"Was that what your family called you?"

Rye bit his lip. He tucked the edges of the quilt around Baby.

"Is he too heavy?"

"No, he's fine." Rye relaxed his grip on the child. "I can't divulge all my secrets on a single night, Mrs. Jones. Wintering over on Abernethy Green is still a ways off. We need a few stories to tell over the rest of the trail. How about a trade?"

"We're negotiating?"

"We should talk about the future."

She caught her breath. "I've been thinking a lot about what to do when we reach Oregon City."

"I understand that pear trees are involved."

"Perhaps."

"Well, it's a good thing that I like pears." He smiled down at her, and pressed his lips to Baby's nodding head.

A healing peacefulness filled Felicity's heart and she wanted to throw her arms out and spin lazy circles beneath the cloudless sky.

Here was the family she craved.

Here was the promise of love.

A shriek.

And another scream, rising at the end.

Philippe's bow screeched across the strings of his violin. No coyote cried out like that. Rye passed the baby to Felicity and limped to the campfire. She followed a step behind him.

The peace of the moment chased the notes onto the dark prairie. Ulna stumbled into the light of the bonfire and collapsed on the feet of Greta Mueller. Black hair falling around her shoulders from her loose braid, Ulna clawed at Mrs. Mueller's skirts. "It wasn't your boy."

Felicity's stomach churned. "I wondered where your shadow had gotten to."

Helmut grabbed Ulna by the elbow. "Here now, what's all this fuss about? Are ye drunk?"

"You have to tell the truth." The girl's bruised mouth quivered. Ulna's bodice gapped open, revealing a ripped chemise.

Elise Radnor knelt beside her shaking daughter to pull the bodice edges together. But it would not close. The hooks were torn off.

This was no act, Felicity believed.

Ulna's mother pulled at her daughter's hands. "Child, whatever has come over you?"

"Ezra never hurt me."

The madness, the anger in Ulna struck a memory for Felicity. Enough of a memory for her to step in front of Rye and Baby.

Helmut pulled Ulna up from the ground and gave her a little shake.

"You don't know what you're saying. Ezra got what he deserved."

"You mean what you deserved. And you. And you." Ulna batted at Helmut's hands, twisting away. You've all looked at me, wanted me –"

"Come, Ulna. You aren't yourself." Mrs. Radnor grabbed her daughter's hand but the girl lunged away.

Ulna swayed in front of Felicity. It was the girl's eyes. Johann Radnor's madness burned on his daughter's face.

Forcing down the cold spreading in the pit of her stomach, Felicity took a deep breath. "You're hurt. Sit and let Dr. Jones take a look at you."

"Don't you want to know what kind of a man you married? Huh? Don't you know what he does to women? Don't you think he's already had a look at me?"

Ulna's words, worse than the red trimmed boots, smashing into her ribs.

I can't breathe. Like before, at Scott's Bluff.

"I know you, Ulna Radnor. I know what you are capable of." Felicity reached for Rye but his arm wrapped across her waist, pulling her backwards away from Ulna. "And I know that Rye would never do this to you, or any woman."

"You don't know that. You don't know nuthin', Miss Fancy Pants. Ha! Make that Mrs. Fancy Pants."

"Call me whatever names you want, but I am 'Mrs. Jones' to you. I knew exactly what kind of a man Rye was when I asked to be his wife –"

"Ha – can't get a man to want you for yourself!"

"– and there isn't anything you can do or say to make me change my mind about him."

Ulna spat on the dark blue wool dress.

Felicity's fingers closed into a fist and her arm came out of the sling. Stepping back, she forced her fist to relax. Brawling in public, no matter the insult, was not done in polite society. She would settle with Ulna, in her own time, in private.

Helmet grabbed Ulna and wrenched her away from the bonfire. The girl kicked his shins and scratched his arms.

Mrs. Radnor dabbed at Felicity's dress with her apron. "I'm so sorry, Mrs. Jones. And on your wedding day."

Felicity grabbed the older woman's hand. "It's all right. See to Ulna."

Philippe packed his violin into its case and the minister ended the evening with a prayer for the nation on Independence Day. The remains of the bonfire crackled and popped, the coals burnt to a dull red. The families drifted to their own campfires, sitting up for a last cup of coffee before turning in.

"About Ulna," Rye did not look away or look ashamed. His grey eyes were calm.

"You were with me tonight, as you were the last time she accused you. And you've never … you wouldn't … it's not in your nature to harm a person, no matter what they've done to you. You're far too kind."

"Maybe so."

Rye settled Baby into the nest of quilts spread under the

wagon. Felicity reddened and kissed the top of Baby's head. The baby's warmth reminded her that the blankets beneath the wagon would be shared with Rye.

Rye tucked the quilts around her and Baby. "I'll stay at the Schneider's site. No need on shuffling everyone tonight."

"It is your choice."

"I'll be here early to hitch the team and get you on the road."

"Until the morning, then." Felicity smiled, appreciating his sensitivity in letting her become accustomed to the role of being his wife.

Felicity curled up on her side around Baby and waited. It didn't take long.

"Where'd that groom of yer's get to? Change his mind?" Aggie whispered from the feather tick in the back of the wagon.

"Not yet. Maybe he's waiting to see if I'm going to run out on him."

"Fool man. Well, don't stay up puttin' more hollows under those eyes of yer's. I'm getting' some sleep while I can as that young rascal of our's will be up an' needin' changin' at some point."

THE DAWN WIND ruffled Felicity's hair. A string of thunderstorms chased across the prairie and hail glittered in the crushed grass.

Rye poured coffee over a crumbled lump of sugar in Felicity's tea cup and stirred it with his finger. "Here, try this."

The smell of the coffee appealed to Felicity. She took a sip of the steaming brew and wrinkled her nose at the bitter taste.

"Keep sipping. You'll get used to it."

"I'm not sure about that."

"Trust me?" Rye brushed the wisps of hair back from

Felicity's face. She trusted Rye, trusted him with her life and the lives of everyone in the company.

"Of course," she gulped the coffee. "How far will we get today? Right and Left should be frisky after a whole day off."

"Mornin' to you." Elise Radnor tapped the toe of her boot at the remains of the bonfire, hands twisting in her apron.

Rye stood and offered his place on a barrel to Ulna's mother. "Come, sit with us."

"I just came to tell you that Ulna's missing. She took a mule and headed off sometime in the night."

Felicity placed her hand in Rye's. He spent the night at the Schneider's campsite. This time Johann Radnor better duck if she had to defend Rye.

"My husband thinks she isn't worth worrying over, but …" Mrs. Radnor's voice faded. "She's my daughter and I'm sorry for any trouble that she may have caused you and Mrs. Jones."

"Helmut and I are hunting this morning, ma'am. I'm sure we can pick up her tracks and talk sense into her coming back with us."

THE MULE'S TRACKS melted into the prairie like the hail. Rye couldn't pick up the trail in the wet grass and Dodge was too busy chasing rabbits to be of any use.

"Let's leave off, Rye." Helmut squinted. The wind gusted and he clamped his hat down on his head. "We're not gonna find her out here."

"If that was your girl out there, what would you do?"

"My girl wouldn't be out there. She'd be with her mother and me. Where she's supposed to be."

"Let's just head over to that rise."

"My guess is if we were to race a day or so down the trail to Joe Larkin's outfit we'd find her."

"Think she went after Ezra?"

"Must of. Can't imagine where else she was headin'."

"I hate to tell her mother we can't find her."

"Her father isn't goin' to be too put off that we couldn't find her. Think Radnor buried his daughter on the prairie? An evil thought, but not outside the realm of possibility."

Rye stood up in his stirrups. Using the brim of his hat to cut the glare, he scanned the prairie. The canvas topped wagons jolted along over the trail. Felicity was a slender figure, striding with one hand clenched on her skirts to keep them down in the wind.

He set Cosmos at a trot away from the trail.

No one was to be left behind. Not a shadow. Only footprints and wheel ruts.

Helmut kicked his gelding into a trot. "My advice is to ride on back to your wife and give her a spell from the oxen."

"'Your wife' sounds strange."

"Time you had a wife to look after you. Lord knows I was gettin' tired of it."

Rye grinned at Helmut. "I admit you make a fair nurse."

"I've seen you through too much and know you all too well. Marta and I wish you all the best in this marriage."

"I know. It'll just take time to get used to being married again."

"At least she's a pretty woman."

"I've noticed."

"And the trail has improved her. Remember how whiny she was? Always complaining about this thing or that thing? I figured she would have turned tail and headed back East."

"She's gotten over that."

"Have you gotten over the fact that she's Gerald Sinclair's daughter? The man you tracked all the way from New York to make sure that he roasted in Hell's fires?"

Rye pulled up Cosmos. "Watching him die of cholera cured me of that. And while I hunted him down, it was God that reminded me that it's his will, his justice to carry out. It's not up to me to punish the man."

"How much does the new Mrs. Jones' know about her father's activities?" Helmut loosened the reins to let his gelding graze.

Rye flicked his thumb over a frayed strand of leather in Cosmos' reins. "We don't talk about the past. What happened to Serena and our boy wasn't Felicity's fault. Can't hold her responsible for something she didn't know about or cause."

"You're a more forgiving man than I am."

"Her father is gone, so is Serena and our boy. I remember when my boy was born. Serena was wiped out, but I couldn't sleep at all that night. I just stayed up and counted toes and fingers, making plans. And then we lost it all."

Rye's jaw locked, but relaxed after a moment. "Gerald Sinclair didn't entice me in. He didn't know me. There isn't a thing I can do to bring them back or change what happened. We just need to go forward."

"Well, before you get too far, I've got something for you. Might call it a wedding present, in an odd way."

"You've got my curiosity going."

"Here." Helmut stood in his stirrups and worked a linen bag with red embroidery from the pocket of his trousers. Leaning from his saddle, he passed the bag to Rye.

Rye whistled, low. "This what I think it is?"

"Thought it was time it made its way back to the owner."

"How'd you get it?"

"Get that mare of yours trotting and I'll tell you the story."

CHAPTER 16

Willow Springs
July 14, 1851

Marriage did not change Felicity's day to day life on the trail. She did not see any more or any less of Rye. He slept at the edge of the encampment with Dodge at his side; Felicity slept under the wagon with Baby. Aggie curled up in the wagon on the feather tick. But the women in the company joined Maggie McHenry when she came to the campfire to nurse Baby, offering advice and gossip. Marriage made her an equal, and without Ulna underfoot the women bonded over talk of their menfolk and children.

Cooking lessons with Maggie McHenry continued. Felicity approached cooking like a lawyer preparing for trial. Scribbled notes testified to what worked and what failed when combining dried parsnips with root vegetables from the prairie and the fresh game Rye provided.

Near Fort Kasper, Felicity held a blanket over the fire ring to keep the rain from putting out the coals for her biscuit experiment.

The results pleased her and the court of opinion.

"Not half bad." Rye bit into the flaky biscuit, pulling apart the steaming layers to reveal bits of bacon.

"Either the dent in the Dutch oven is getting smaller or my cooking skills are getting better."

"I'd say that dent is filling in some."

Felicity laughed and tapped his backside with the ladle. "Get, husband. Don't you have a rifle to clean or a grouse to shoot?"

"I'm a gettin'. But how about one more of those biscuits to tide me over until supper?"

Felicity bit the inside of her mouth to keep from smiling. Rye wasn't pitching her efforts into the prairie. "Here. And here's one for Dodge."

"Don't think he'll be getting any today. He'll have to wait until I see if this is a permanent change or a fluke of metal expansion."

"That's it. Go hunting."

Rye picked up his rifle and limped away from camp.

Dodge pawed at Felicity's apron.

"Get, both of you."

Dodge cocked his ears and whined.

Breaking off a chunk of her biscuit, Felicity held the flaky treat out to the dog. "Okay, here, but don't tell on me."

Dodge took the biscuit chunk from her hand and jogged off after Rye.

But marriage changed the way Rye and Felicity behaved towards each other. A warmth, more than friendliness, grew between the two. They leaned into each other. It was the closeness that came from unity of purpose, a common goal.

It was a closeness that came up between a man and a woman when they had a life together.

A future together. That they made a family, together.

Before crossing at Willow Springs, Felicity sealed cracks in the wagon with a pitch mixture. The cold water and gritty mud rubbed into the calluses on her bare feet.

The mixture ran from a gap and she put the paint brush handle in her mouth to free her hand to push the pitch between the boards. The bitter, piney taste of the pitch made her gag. She spat, wiping the back of her hand across her mouth.

"How is my artist coming along?" Rye splashed through the shallows at the crossing on Cosmos.

"When you asked me if I could paint, I should have clarified that I'm accustomed to painting on a stretched canvas or watercolor paper."

"I like to call this work 'Pitch on Wagon Bed' or 'Keeping the Provisions Dry.'"

Felicity dipped the brush into the pitch. "How about calling it –"

"Kind words, wife, kind words only today."

"Why today?"

Pushing his hat back, Rye smiled down at her. "Because it is my birthday and I would have it so."

Felicity blushed. She didn't know where Rye was born. Or his parents' names. But surely as his wife she should know his birth date.

"I can see that you're thinking. Would you like help with that calculation?" Rye leaned back in his saddle and held up both hands.

"There's a lot about you that I don't know."

"Like how old I am?"

"That would do for starters."

"How old do you think I am?"

"Older than me, younger than Aggie."

"Thanks for the wide spread, I think. How does thirty-one sound?"

"Like you are ten years older than me."

"That's right, sprout. Get to sealing those cracks so that we stand a chance of floating the wagon rather than sinking it."

"Ten whole years."

"Paint."

"I'm working on it."

Rye turned Cosmos and trotted the mare over to the McHenry wagon, dismounting to help the McHenry boys raise the bed of the empty wagon. Paul McHenry tapped a wood block in at each corner between the rockers and the bottom of the wagon.

Wagon secure, Maggie bundled up her skirts and took her place at the head of a doubled team of oxen. Tugging the lead rope, she led the oxen across the stream with the McHenry boys ready with whips to coax the oxen along.

Felicity dipped the brush into the pitch and painted Rye's profile on the wagon planks. Dipping the brush again, she added her face. Aggie's face, and Baby.

Holding the brush steady, the empty space on the side of the wagon provided room for additional children. To Felicity, painting more little faces on the wagon bed implied a true marriage, and not a convenient partnership.

Rye splashed across the stream on Cosmos leading two oxen from the earlier doubled team. "Fancy artwork won't get us across, Mrs. Jones. What are you painting?"

"I guess you could say our family."

"Well, leave some room."

"For what?" She tipped her head back, bonnet falling into the reeds.

He winked. "More family. We'll need more than Baby to see us through our elder years."

With the McHenry wagon clear of the crossing, Felicity knotted her skirt hem around her hips and took Right's halter. Two oxen from the Cavanaugh outfit were hitched behind her team. The water went up to her hips. Joints aching and bare feet slipping on algae coated boulders, she pressed against the current, relying on Right to keep Left in place. Making faces at Baby, slung over Rye's shoulder, Felicity forced her numb legs to move until she staggered out to leave the oxen clear of the water.

The pitch coating held. The double canvas sacks of flour were dry and the crate of law books safe in the raised bed of the wagon.

"Guess what I found?" Felicity's voice carried across to

Aggie, waiting on the other bank for the Schneider wagon to clear the stream with the added help of Right and Left.

"Another box of books?"

Felicity held up Uncle Jasper's temperature gauge.

"I thought ya lost that back around the Narrows." Aggie crowed.

"It was stuck under the flour sacks."

"Helmut!" Marta's scream caught Felicity's attention. A drenched Helmut, waist deep, grabbed Right's halter but slipped on the rocky bottom and went under again.

Helmut bobbed up and waved off Rye's help.

"Just had a quick bath, that's all," Helmut slapped his wet hat back on his head.

Felicity shivered. Her feet were blue from the crossing, the blood prickling, tickling at the surface of her skin in the hot July sun.

One of the Schneider's oxen slipped and plunged in the stream, dragging Left over. Helmut grabbed the halter of the ox, hauling upwards. The wagon teetered on two wheels, canvas top catching loose items.

The load shifted and the wagon crashed into the stream.

Hauling her skirts up, Felicity started across the stream. If Right and Left were to drown they would be in sorry shape.

But Rye waved her off. "Catch what you can!"

Felicity stood on the edge of the stream and used her walking stick to snag clothing floating by. Rye and other men of the company righted the wagon and got the four oxen moving to shore.

One of Marta's embroidered pillowcases slipped downstream and Felicity hitched up her skirts and plunged into the stream. But the pillowcase eluded her, dancing away from her fingers like a kite cut lose.

A misstep into a hole at the base of willow trees sent water over Felicity's head. She gasped in icy surprise, snatched out of the water when a fist grabbed the back of her dress.

Helmut pulled her out of the water. "Let it go. It's not worth it."

"I almost had it," she gasped.

"And Rye almost lost you."

A pale Rye, blue with cold, splashed across the stream on Cosmos. "Are you okay?"

Helmut pounded Felicity's back. "She got her bath earlier than expected."

"Thanks for catching my little fish."

"No worries, friend."

Felicity's teeth chattered, hair hanging down her back in knotted clumps. She was a dripping mess, but couldn't figure out why Rye looked at her with that light in his eyes. The light that warmed her to the core, clammy clothes and all.

"Better get those wet things off before you get a chill."

Thankful that the pitch held and the cedar trunk of Hannah's old clothes made the crossing high and dry, she smiled up at her husband.

"Good thing we aren't swimming to the Oregon Territory."

By midday, the wagons made the Willow Springs crossing and lumbered down the trail with Lane Crandall in the lead. Felicity sent Aggie and Baby ahead with the McHenry outfit. She stayed behind with Rye and the Schneider family to salvage supplies and dry out clothing on the stream bank.

Felicity wrapped a quilt around Rye's bare shoulders. She took his wet shirt and spread it on a bush to dry near the small campfire she built to make coffee.

"Thanks." His lips were bluish. He hunched over a cup of coffee, long legs dangling over the tailgate of their wagon.

"Trousers?"

"Pardon?"

"Hand them over."

Rye shuddered and wrapped his hands around the coffee cup. "Forward, aren't we?"

"We're married. And I can't afford to lose you to

pneumonia. I know how cold that water is. I had a quick dip compared to your morning of ferrying teams. Besides, you'll probably want to change the bandage on your knee."

"This when the nagging begins?"

"I didn't take you for being shy, Mr. Jones."

Rye ducked his head, smiling up at her with a crooked grin. "Hardly ever, Mrs. Jones."

Felicity blushed. "Then I suggest you remove your trousers so that they can join your shirt on yonder bush."

Passing her the tin cup, Rye eased himself off the tailgate. Hand on his waistband, he held her gaze and unbuckled the clinging buckskins.

Felicity reached for the coffee pot on the coals, cheeks a blazing cherry.

A rifle shot followed by Marta Schneider's screams broke the calm.

Felicity straightened and gasped.

Raiders?

Indians?

The two wagons left behind at the crossing were vulnerable.

Rye whipped off the blanket and grabbed his rifle. He hobbled to the Schneider wagon down at the stream bed, Felicity following at his heels.

A tearful Marta grabbed Rye's arm.

"Helmut's gone and shot himself."

Helmut twisted on the ground, clutching his stomach behind his family's wagon. Rye dropped to the ground beside his friend. Blood seeped from under the clenched hands.

Pulling aside Helmut's hands and shirt, Rye assessed the wound.

"What were you doing?" Rye pressed his hand over the wound.

"Figured my rifle got wet when the wagon went over," Helmut grunted. "Figured it needed cleaning so it wouldn't rust."

Marta sank to her knees beside her husband. "He pulled it out muzzle first. It must've caught on something in the back of the wagon."

"How bad is it?" Felicity whispered, bile rising at the blood seeping between Rye's fingers.

"Not good." Rye's voice, ragged.

Helmut groaned. "Hasn't Felicity taught you any better bedside manners?"

Rye turned to Felicity. "Run get my bag, the laudanum and anything we can use for bandaging."

Felicity picked up her skirts and ran.

The bag, where's the bag?

Thank goodness that's not Rye.

Laudanum, check.

Blanket for bandaging.

Felicity ran to the Schneider wagon with Rye's medical bag under her good arm and the blanket over her sling.

Marta ripped a strip of linen from a lace edged sheet.

Helmut coughed. "Darling, those were your mother's sheets. Leave them be."

"I'm not giving up on you." Marta hit a join in the sheet and it would not split. Felicity grabbed the edge of the fabric and helped Marta tear the rest of the sheet.

"You always were stubborn," Helmut groaned.

Rye pressed the sheet scraps to Helmut's stomach but the blood soaked the material through Rye's fingers.

"What can I do? How can I help?" Felicity whispered to Rye. Please, God, please never let this be Rye.

Helmut raised his hand but it flopped to his chest, palm up. "Just bring the shovel, lass. Get Marta and the children back on the trail. Keep 'em moving. Don't … let 'em come back here."

Marta scrambled to Helmut's side. "Felicity can go. I'm staying."

"For once in our marriage, woman, do what I'm telling you to do."

Felicity tried to read Rye. Did he want her to go? Did he want her to stay? What should she do?

"Watch over Marta for me." Helmut's voice, weaker.

Rye bowed his head. "I'll follow as soon as I can." His voice shook.

"I'll be looking for you."

THE DUST FROM the two wagons hung in the humid air after the creaking wheels and Marta's dry sobs faded. A thin line of smoke spiraled over the spent campfire.

"Felicity will be waitin' ... for you," Helmut panted.

"I'm not leaving you." Rye's hand shook and he dropped the cap from the laudanum vial into a tin cup of coffee.

"Have to at ... some point."

Rye fished the cap out of the lukewarm coffee and held the cup to Helmut's grey lips. "When that comes, that's when I'll go. Until then, drink this."

Helmut gulped a mouthful, spilling most of it down his chin. "Never thought somethin' this ... stupid would get me. Figured I'd be old and ornery."

"Who says you aren't ornery ... or old?"

Helmut grimaced, a trace of his broad smile. "Need you to do something for me."

"Marta and the boys won't starve." Rye held Helmut's chin and pressed the rim of the cup to his friend's mouth.

Helmet turned away from Rye. "Figured. You're that kind of a man. Kind of man wish I'd been."

"Who's to say? You didn't think less of me when I couldn't get enough laudanum or whiskey." Rye set the cup of coffee on the ground beside Helmut and picked up the laudanum vial. "There was a time when I couldn't hold this in my hand.

Needing to taste it, letting it take me over. Drawing out the pain. I still can't keep it around me."

"You had good reason."

A fly landed on Helmut's cheek. Rye brushed it away. "Should've been stronger. Prayed more."

"Used to watch you and Serena ... always laughin' ... touchin' ..." Helmut's voice rasped.

"You and Marta are happy."

"Not like the two of you. Marta and I don't ... after she had Samuel, we didn't keep company anymore."

"That's not unusual. It's a kindness. That last pregnancy was hard on her."

"There was a young woman I kept down along River Road ... not much older than Ulna."

"There's no need to talk about –"

"Out here there were nights when I just couldn't settle ... into the life of ... husband." Helmut choked. "Can't breathe ..."

Rye cradled his hunting partner. "Better?"

"Ulna ... not lyin'." Helmut's eyelids closed, lashes wet. "Not proud ..."

"So when I was accused ..."

Against Rye's chest, Helmut's heart fluttered, a dying sprint. "Tell her Ma..."

"Can you tell me where Ulna has gone off to?"

Forty minutes later, Rye tamped the last shovelful of river sand over Helmut's grave. Reaching into his vest pocked, he pulled out the laudanum vial. It rolled over his palm. His thumb caressed the ridges of the cap.

Cosmos dozed in the twilight, ears twitching. Swifts flitted, chasing gnats over the stream.

He should be in the saddle, on the trail.

But he licked his lips, eyes tracking the sloshing dark liquid. It would be so easy to unscrew the vial, to pour the muddy liquid into the cold coffee. To let the brown liquids meld together, a murky tide to sweep him away. A gritty flood to wash out the white hot brand of the past pressed into his heart.

He unscrewed the lid to the vial, inhaling the bitter smell. A Siren's song, beckoning him to wreck on the shore of oblivion.

"Felicity," he breathed her name like a prayer to keep the tide from cresting his resistance. His heart raced, sweat breaking out on his forehead.

He closed his eyes, tears welling, conjuring up images of her. Images of her sun browned hands mixing dough, her tongue pressed against her upper lip in concentration. Her hand, passing a rasp to him. Buckling Right's hobble.

Baby splashing in his bath. Chewing on the ties of Aggie's apron.

The wisps of hair escaping Felicity's braids.

Rye stared into the open vial in his shaking hand.

FELICITY SLUMPED ON the upturned wash tub and poked the embers of the campfire, not ready to crawl under the wagon beside Baby. Aggie coughed in her sleep on the feather tick in the back of the wagon. The wind came up and ashes floated above her.

A red line on the horizon turned orange, pink tones coloring the clouds.

Clank. Clank. Clank.

Felicity pressed her palms against her skirts.

That's the point of a shovel, driven into the soil.

He's back.

Alone.

Rye propped the handle of the shovel against the wagon bed. "Hope we don't have to use that again for a while."

"I'm so sorry." Felicity's voice quavered.

"Shhh, my little love." Rye opened his arms and Felicity

burrowed against him, but leaned back when her cheek bumped up against an unfamiliar bulge. She poked her finger around the object in the pocket of his leather vest.

"What's this?"

"The laudanum." Rye pressed the vial into Felicity's hand, closing her fingers around the ridged glass. "Put it back in the medicine chest. Let's hope it is as lonely as the shovel."

"Did he suffer?"

"How about if I tell you that story another time?"

"Sure."

Rye gripped her hand, twining his fingers around her fingers. "It's not that I don't want to tell you, it's that it is hard to say."

"I see."

He kissed her brow. "Anything for supper?"

"How do you feel about cold stew? If you give me a few minutes, I can get the fire going again."

"Best offer I've had all day. Marta?"

"I thought I would spend time with her this morning. I know that she has her brother and her older boys to watch after her, but she might need help."

"I have to talk to the Radnors for a few moments. I should be back in a while."

"Ulna's parents? Did you find her?"

"No. It's not that."

"Something you'd rather talk about later?"

Rye took her in his arms. "Much later."

"I'll join you at the Schneiders."

He ground his lips into her hair. "You're a good woman."

She wrapped her arms around him and rested her head on his chest. "You're a good man."

CHAPTER 17

Three Crossings
July 18, 1851

Buffalo herds and signs of the great herds passing were as advertised in Felicity's pamphlets. Marauding bands of Indians were described down to the feather in the pages, so Felicity was surprised that with half of the journey behind her, the Indians she encountered were small bands of hunters or blanket wrapped families trading at the forts. When the wagon train stopped at Fort Casper for supplies, she studied their bronze faces from beneath the edge of her bonnet.

Near Three Crossings, the company rested the livestock and took on water and scavenged for firewood for the evening camp. Rye sighted a group of antelope and rode off with Dodge to hunt.

Felicity stopped kneading dough to help Aggie down from the wagon. The older woman froze, clutching Baby in her thin arms.

"If ya scream, so help me I'll slap ya into the next world."

Twisting to see what Aggie was going on about, Felicity's jaw clenched, teeth gritted. A band of eighteen Indians on painted horses cantered towards the wagon encampment.

The men did not have time to pick up their rifles.

"War party?" Aggie whispered.

Can I get Baby and Aggie to safety?

Fort Casper is days behind us, Fort Bridger is weeks ahead.

Where's Rye when we need him?

She was ashamed of the question. At least he was spared whatever was to come.

Aggie pinched the back of Felicity's flour covered hand. The sting got Felicity breathing.

Philippe Patelle spoke French with one of the braves that slid down from his horse, a single rein looped over his arm. The French spoken at the *Theatre de l'Academie Royale de Musique* was not the dialect of the prairie. She understood every other phrase.

Felicity's gaze flitted from one tired face to the next. "They've been buffalo hunting. Ran into raiders and were attacked."

Crusted wounds wrapped with leather bindings oozed and bruises darkened the warriors' skin. Coats stiff with sweat and blood, their horses fed, ripping at the scrubby grass.

A warrior stared over Aggie's head at Felicity. He lifted his arm in a sling and jerked his chin at her.

She plucked at the muslin sling.

He's not much older than me.

Why, they are as tired and footsore as we are.

Wiping the flour from her hand onto her apron, Felicity picked up a flat basket, tossing in the cornbread, dried apples and bacon intended for the noon meal. Sidling around the mounted Indians, she offered the basket with her good arm. One brave kicked his horse to move away from her, but others leaned down to tear off a chunk of bread or grab a handful of dried fruit. Maggie McHenry joined Felicity with a dipper and bucket of water, and Emma Robertson passed bandage materials to the injured.

After the band trotted over the ridge above the encampment, Felicity slumped on the tongue of the wagon. Thankful they met a hunting party, she had a hard time reconciling pamphlet descriptions of wagon train slaughter with this social visit.

She remembered the herd of antelope.

The basket fell to the ground. Dried fruit scattered.

"Do you think Rye ran into the others? The raiders …"

Her aunt brushed the dust off a handful of dried fruit and tossed it back into Felicity's basket. "Quit yer frettin'," Aggie coughed. "He always comes in before the wagons pull out. Why don't ya put some of that nervous energy to use and go take a gander from up there."

Felicity followed the hoof prints of the Indian horses and climbed the ridge. Shading her face with a sun browned hand, no riders disturbed the grass under the July haze. Sweat ran down her arm to her elbow.

She folded her hands, hoping God wouldn't mind dirty fingernails. Perhaps a few words would help.

This is my chance to practice faith.

But the words weren't there. No feelings of peace.

Willow Springs slipped into her mind, only Rye slumped against the wagon wheel, gut shot, not Helmut.

He might be bleeding under sagebrush.

Or face down in a creek.

She picked up her skirts and scrambled down the ridge to the encampment to escape her dark thoughts.

But Aggie was right.

The wagons pulled out onto the trail and met Rye returning with an antelope slung across Cosmos' haunches. When Aggie told Rye how his wife distributed refreshments to the warriors like they were at a fancy garden party, Rye rumpled Felicity's hair.

"Good thing your New York manners are intact. Hopefully they'll return the favor if we meet up with them again."

"Good thing I stopped short of dispensing your 'special' ointment to the wounded."

AT THE EVENING encampment, Felicity clamped a drawer between her knees from a marquetry table Aggie salvaged from the trail. With her good arm, she worked the dovetailed front piece back and forth. She should have used the noon break to scavenge for kindling.

Adding the drawer front to kindling in the fire ring, she lit a match. Fire caught, held. The shellac curled into downy ash and float away with the smoke.

"Try cooking with this."

Rye dropped a load of dirt clods beside the fire ring. But the grass stems in the clumps meant these were not dirt clods.

Felicity straightened and nudged the pile with her boot. "Is that …"

"*Bois de vache.*" Rye flicked the brim of his planter's hat. "We couldn't have passed so many herds of buffalo without you seeing their calling cards."

Felicity picked up her skirts and backed away. "Dung? You want me to cook with dung?" The McHenrys and the Watsons burned the droppings for fuel, but Felicity held out.

"Consider them as glorified grass clippings if it pleases you, my lady."

Aggie slapped her thigh and laughed, but the bark of laughter turned into a hacking cough she muffled with a gingham handkerchief. "Give 'er a try," she gasped. "Why, there ain't a tree to be had anywhere near here anyways. What can it hurt?"

"But it is dung," Felicity used a corner of her apron to pick up a piece.

"Yes, I see that. But I bet it burns just fine."

Aggie was right again. The dried buffalo droppings gave off a steady heat like charcoal.

Leaving Rye to hitch Right and Left in the morning, Felicity went out on the prairie, picking up dried buffalo dung and dropping it into her flat basket.

"What are you doing, wife?" Rye slung Baby over his

shoulder and tickled the infant's toes.

Felicity smiled up at him. "I'm gathering chips for your evening meal."

"Aren't you getting ahead of yourself? We won't be stopping for camp until late this afternoon."

"I know that. But the chips are here and who knows what we will find when we stop for camp. Since we passed Fort Laramie, there's been fewer buffalo."

"Based on the amount of buffalo we've seen over the last few days, I'm fairly certain that there will be a generous supply of fuel when we stop for the night."

"Well, one never knows."

"Trust me."

"I do."

Rye tickled Baby's toes.

I want to freeze this image in my mind forever. If moments like this could stand still until I came back to it when time spared.

"Well then, let's get moving. We have a lot of trail to cover before anyone gets around to making a fire."

"I CAN'T SEE Right and Left's horns," Aggie complained from the drover's box.

Dust scritched between Felicity's teeth when she clenched her jaw. She stumbled over a clump of sagebrush and steered Right towards the flapping canvas of the McHenry wagon ahead on the trail. The dust sucked into the cracks in Hannah's old boots, chafing Felicity's ankles.

What she wouldn't give for cobblestones to pave over the trail. Or a thunderstorm. At least a body could scrape mud off wet boots.

Lane Crandall trotted up on his plow horse. "Rye says it's flat enough to spread out. Take a side trail."

Steering the team onto a side trail cut through the brush by last season's wagon trains gave Felicity a chance to blow her nose on her apron and dig the crusted dust out of the corner of her eyes. She stopped Right and Left to wipe dust out of their eyes and nostrils. At least the flies weren't bothersome.

She shook out her skirts and coughed up a wad of what she was sure was pure mud. She spat it out on the ground, wiping her mouth with the back of her hand. Taking a dipper of water from the barrel on the side of the wagon, she handed it up to Aggie.

"Drink?"

Aggie took the dipper, splashing water on a corner of her apron. She wiped Baby's nose and chin.

"How is he?"

"Sleepin'," Aggie croaked. "Jealous?"

Felicity smiled and winced, cracking her dry lips. She took a deep drink from the dipper. The sun warmed water tasted like the oak barrel.

"Want yer walkin' stick?"

"Keep it handy. I can see far enough out in front of me."

Felicity took up the lead rope. Right followed her through the brush, Left hanging back and not pulling his share of the load.

Taking her arm out of the muslin sling, Felicity rotated her shoulder. Sore, but bearable.

Rye trotted up on Cosmos, the mare's hooves kicking up puffs of dust.

"Ready to give up the sling?"

"Just tired of being poked and prodded. I admit that I have developed a sensitivity for Right and Left's plight in this life."

"I haven't been all that bad, have I?"

"Let's just say that you are a fine healer." Felicity grinned and split her lips further. "Don't worry so much."

"I wouldn't if all my patients would follow my orders. Keep that arm in the sling for a few more days."

"Aye, aye, captain," Felicity saluted with her good arm.

Rye cocked his head to the side. "Do I look like a military man to you?"

"It is your commanding presence."

"Then get to marching, soldier, and quit your sassing."

"Yes, sir, sirrah."

Rye saluted in return. "You make an unlikely soldier, marching along with your apron and that bonnet on the back of your head."

"I admit this isn't much of a Pennsylvania Avenue parade."

"True, but I'd back you against any army, any day."

Felicity blushed. "Get along there, recruit, we have miles to go before you get fed."

"Yes, ma'am. As you wish ma'am." Rye trotted Cosmos down the side trail, kicking up dust. "Is this fast enough to suit you, ma'am?" he called over his shoulder.

Felicity picked up a dirt clod and chucked it at Rye's back, hitting his shoulder. She pressed her lips together to keep from splitting them further.

Wheeling the mare around, Rye galloped back to Felicity and tried to scoop her up.

Ducking under his hand, Felicity dodged away. "Careful there, recruit. My husband will not approve of your fondling his wife."

"I'll mind my manners, ma'am, if you will mind yours."

"My manners?" She raised her nose and sidestepped sagebrush with her gown in hand. "I have impeccable manners."

"What would the ladies in New York say about your behavior? Is this how a debutante acts? Throwing dirt clods at gentlemen?"

"I'm sorry, I must have missed. Where's that gentleman?"

"That does it." Rye set his heels to Cosmos and caught Felicity up under her arms, laying her across the saddle. He tickled her ribs.

"Put me down! What are you doing?"

"Trying to move you down the trail a little faster."

She grabbed her elbow and held it tight to her side.

"Did I undo all your healing?"

"Nope. Seems to be holding up just fine."

Rye dropped the reins and turned her so that she faced Cosmos' ears. She leaned against his chest and he slid his arm around her waist.

The pair of us must make a dusty sight, she thought.

Felicity's stomach tingled when Rye pressed his lips on the nape of her sweaty neck.

"You taste salty."

"You two gonna make eyes at each other all day or are we gonna move along?" Aggie crowed from the drover's box.

Rye tightened his arm around Felicity's waist and nudged Cosmos into a trot. "I'm moving, old woman, I'm moving."

"See to then, bucko." Aggie coughed into her handkerchief.

Felicity turned in Rye's arms. Her aunt balled up the square of material. Trail dust deepened the wrinkles on Aggie's face. But the dust has nothing to do with the pallor of Aggie's skin.

Aggie's thinness worried at her. Though Felicity put the tender pieces on Aggie's plate, her aunt did not have much of an appetite and complained that her teeth bothered her. She would try making softer food in case that was the truth. But Felicity thought it was more than bad teeth, although her own jaw bothered her from grinding her teeth at night.

Aggie's handkerchiefs never made it her way for laundering. And if she wasn't mistaken, there was blood.

Out of respect for Aggie, she doesn't mention the bloody cloth. Out of fear of losing Aggie, she tried not to dwell on her aunt's frailty.

Rye rested his chin on Felicity's head.

Leaning into him, there was comfort in his embrace. Rye would be with her when it came time to let Aggie go.

She hoped they got to the Oregon Territory soon enough

for Aggie.

THE SACK OF cornmeal purchased at Fort Bridger leaked at a corner seam. With a foot under the bottom of the sack, Felicity used her good arm to shift the sack to the left.

With luck and Aggie's quilting thread, the corner can be mended.

That is, if I can find the package of Aggie's quilting needles.

At least the cornmeal stopped leaking for the moment. Problem was, the minute the wagon hit a hole in the trail, the sack opened further.

Felicity spread a pillowcase on the crate of law books and dumped the contents of Aggie's sewing basket. Scissors, thimbles, scraps of fabric, pins, and ribbon that snagged on a hangnail.

No needles.

A quilt flapped on the back of the neighboring wagon. The Zenger family left their company when the leaders voted to go southwest on the Mormon trail. They joined the Jones wagon train at Fort Bridger.

Aggie admired Eudora Zenger's quilts.

Quilts meant a stash of needles.

At the Zenger campsite, Effie Zenger was on her knees, using a spoon to dig trenches.

"Digging for dinosaur bones?" Felicity leaned over the child to admire the neat piles of dirt.

"Yep."

"Are you an archeologist?"

Effie frowned. "No, silly. I'm a paleontologist."

Felicity blushed. "Of course. My pardon. What have you got there?"

"Pretties."

Felicity peered over Effie's braids. The white and red beads in Effie's hand were familiar to Felicity. She swallowed, hard. The beads decorating the hunting party from Three Crossings were the same color and size.

"Who gave those to you?" Did they miss sign of Indians? After the nooning incident, the company voted to set up a watch detail.

"Just found 'em."

Aggie dozed next to the wagon with Baby in her arms.

No Rye. No Dodge. And that hammer clanging on the anvil means he's still helping Marta's boys shoe a mule.

No sign of alarm.

It might be nothing.

"Where did you find these? Can you show me?"

Dusting off her smock, Effie stuffed the beads in her pocket and trotted through the camp to a creek bed. Away from the campsite, the creek bed dipped and flowed around the base of a hill. Splashing across the creek, Effie climbed the hill. Felicity followed the child, careful not to slip on the wet rocks and injure her other shoulder.

"Wait for me."

At the top of the hill, a vulture flew off a platform lashed to poles eight feet in the air.

Nothing in her pamphlet reading prepared Felicity for this.

Three platforms shared the hill.

Buffalo robes on top of the platform were ripped open. Beads and shells were scattered beneath the platform.

An Indian burial site.

"Is this where you found the beads?"

"Yes. See? There's more over here." Effie pushed back the dried grass, picking up beads.

Would she ever get used to seeing graves? On the other side of Fort Bridger, the wagon company passed five graves laid in a row after pulling aside to rest the livestock. Later in the day, a cross marked a grave on the rise above the evening campsite. The spokes of a spinning wheel, knotted together with lace, marked the head of the grave.

I remember the blocks of sod laid over Father's grave to hide it from raiders. He has Tom and Uncle Jasper beside him. At least whoever is on this hill is not alone.

No daughter wants their father's grave disturbed. It did not matter if the bundle on the platform died of illness, age or at the hand of an enemy.

Grabbing Effie's wrist, Felicity pried open the girl's fingers. Beads dropped into the dried grass.

"Give 'em back!"

Flipping the girl's pockets inside out, Felicity scraped the seams with her thumb. "These aren't for us to take."

"Mine!"

Felicity held the child's hand with a firm grip. "We're going back to camp to tell Dr. Jones that we need to be moving on."

GUNFIRE CRACKLED.

Jerked upright out of sleep, Felicity rammed her forehead on a rear wheel. She peered out of the shawl wrapped around her head. Her legs ached after the steep trail on Big Hill yesterday. Still too early to stir.

Two rifle shots in succession. A third echoed.

Too early for a hunter with bad aim to waste bullets.

Tucking the quilt around Baby, Felicity held her injured arm to her side and crawled out from beneath the wagon. She stood in bare feet listening to the night sounds of the encampment. Wind rustled laundry on the line at the Mueller campsite. Two wagons down, one of the Patelle boys snored.

Felicity knelt beside the cold fire ring.

Rye's blanket, rumpled in a heap, was warm to her palm.

The saddle and Dodge, missing.

In the purple shadows near the livestock, Rye slipped a bridle over Cosmos' head. The mare was saddled, rifle in the scabbard.

Dodge whined, ears pricked to the west.

Rye held out his arm and Felicity curled against his ribs, wishing she wore her boots. "What is it?"

"Too dark to tell. Go back to sleep. If it's anything I'll wake you."

"Ready for coffee?"

"Not sleepy?"

She yawned, rubbing the knot on her forehead. "Not now. I'll get a fire started."

"What's that from?"

"A wheel kissed me until I woke up."

Rye pressed warm lips to her bruise, breathing in the scent of her. "Better?"

"I think I have another bruise for you to heal."

He pecked her cheek. "I'm going to ride up that next rise and see if there's any game afoot."

"Something tells me it is two legged game."

"Might be."

"Be careful."

He kissed the red mark on her forehead, his stubbly chin scraping her nose. "Always."

Families fed, the women put out the morning campfires, rolled up blankets and tents. The men hitched the teams, checking buckles and tightening cinches.

Rye limped into camp, his rifle in his hand, not in the scabbard on the saddle.

Knotting Baby's diaper and tickling the child laying on his back on the tailgate, she smiled at Rye, but he avoided her gaze. Baby waved his fists, kicking his legs.

Instead he picked up the coffee pot and shook it. Coffee splashed out the spout. He propped the rifle against the tailgate out of the infant's reach and poured coffee into a tin cup, drinking it down. He stared into the bottom of the cup.

"Find anything?" Rye never ignored Baby. A prickle like

ants crawling up her neck made Felicity shiver.

Taking the cup from his hand, Felicity looked up at Rye. Avoiding her gaze, he gathered her in his arms, crushing her against his chest, the muslin sling an awkward bulge between them.

"Can't breathe down here," she gasped.

Rye relaxed his grip, but did not release her. Two minutes passed, Felicity clutching a tin cup, Rye with Felicity in his arms.

He cleared his throat and slid his hands down her arms, taking the cup from her hand.

"Time we were moving along."

"I'll wake Aggie."

"She's not up yet?"

"She coughed until late last night." Felicity hesitated, seeing the guarded look in Rye's face. She hadn't seen that look since she was bundled in a quilt and wrapped in his arms after Ulna's attack.

"I need a few moments with the Muellers and the Radnors."

RYE LED THE Watson wagon off the trail to avoid the burnt sagebrush and smoking ribs from a wagon undercarriage. The McHenry wagon and the other families followed, lips pressed and eyes focused on the tailgate in front of them. Broken harness and torn clothing from the Larkin wagon train lay across the trail. Shattered dessert plates glittered in the sun, painted roses and gold rim ground into the dirt.

Did the company members fight each other? The Radnors camped apart from the Muellers and the Muellers refused to follow the Radnors on the trail.

No arrows. No sign of an Indian attack.

"Pick up those boots, quick, before anyone else grabs 'em."

Aggie pointed at a blackened trunk.

The red trim on the top of the boots made Felicity sweat. "I know those boots."

"Pick 'em up anyway. You'll be needin' 'em afore too long. Those moccasins Rye gave ya are fine fer around a campfire and to give yer walkin' boots a rest, but they won't do ya any favors on the trail."

The thought of sliding her feet into those boots made Felicity's gut heave. "I can't do that."

"And why ever not, princess? The girl who wore 'em ain't wearin' them now."

"They belong to Ulna."

"So? She left them on the trail. Anythin' left on the trail is fair pickin' for those that follow."

"Won't Ezra want them?"

"I don't think young Ezra will be needin' 'em. Ain't that his wagon over there?"

The wagon, on its side, the grooved and fitted planks split apart. Torn canvas. Metal wheel parts, hacked off at the hub, in a pile.

"Like I said. Pick up the boots. It's plain Ezra's not in a position to care who wears Ulna's boots."

Picking up the boots by the laces, Felicity tossed them into the wagon.

"Good girl. No sense wastin' a good set of boots 'cause of delicacy."

Felicity stuffed the boots next to the crate of law books.

I've come a long way, in that I would pick up a dead girl's boots because it is practical.

CHAPTER 18

Soda Springs
July 30, 1851

A geyser erupted at Soda Springs and Pug Watson threw the reins to his wife and scampered down to the springs. When the Muellers and the McHenrys joined Pug, Rye called a halt. The wagons were left where they stopped as their owners followed Pug's route to the geysers.

Felicity stayed at the wagon, not willing to wake or leave a sleeping Aggie. Rye checked the metal rims of the wheels and tightened the spokes where he could.

A prairie dog den sprawled across the trail where the wagon company pulled off and Dodge ran until his sides heaved, herding the furry prey from hole to hole. Felicity laughed when another prairie dog popped out of a burrow yards away, barking at Dodge, only to duck down and pop up at another burrow.

Rye shoved Dodge in the back of the wagon next to a sleeping Aggie with a terse command.

"Stay."

"I was getting worried Dodge was going to collapse in the heat." Propping Baby on her lap, Felicity let him play with the ties of her sunbonnet.

"Where were we?" Rye tipped her chin up and pressed a kiss below her ear.

"Prodding my shoulder."

Rye pressed his thumbs around the lump on her collarbone. "You have a souvenir from the journey."

"Will it go away?"

"Perhaps. Once you get a little flesh on your bones you won't even notice it."

"I am a mite bit thin."

"The way you're feeding me I'll have to walk twenty miles a day once we settle our land claim or I won't fit through the cabin door."

She glanced up at Rye. "There is one souvenir I don't mind from this trip."

"What's that?"

"It's a who."

"Who, then? Me?"

A blush burned up from her chest to her cheeks. "No, but yes."

"Regretting your generous offer of marriage?"

"No regrets. The who is Baby." Tiring of the sunbonnet ties, the infant patted his chubby hands against Felicity's lips.

"When are you going to get around to naming that boy? When he gets older he isn't going to appreciate that name as much as you would like him to."

"I've been meaning to ask you about that."

"How so?"

"I'd ... I'd like to name him after you."

"Not Thomas, for his father?"

It occurred to Felicity that Rye may have children in the East.

"Unless the name is taken ... you are, after all, the only father figure he knows."

Rye cupped her chin, rubbing his thumb over her lips. "I'm touched." He bent his head and kissed her lips. She clutched Baby so she wouldn't drop him.

"I thought you were, taking the three of us on like you have," she mumbled against his lips.

"I didn't mean touched in the head, but touched, here." He slid his hand down to press against her heart. Her heart beat fast. Rye had to feel how it raced beneath his broad palm. Dodge wasn't the only one who would collapse if this kept up. She'd have to lie down next to Aggie in the back of the wagon.

She cleared her throat. "I thought we could name him 'Daniel' as that is one of your many names."

Rye smiled. His eyes were grey like the high overhead clouds.

She scuffed the toe of Hannah's old boot in the dust. "It does leave the rest of the names available."

"True, especially if we pick up more souvenirs along the trail."

Felicity opened her mouth to reply, but snapped it shut. At Willow Springs, Rye mentioned children, but Felicity slept under the wagon with Baby and Rye rolled up in a blanket next to the campfire with Dodge. Rather than address certain aspects of married life, Felicity chose to focus on the child on her lap.

"Do you know the meaning behind Daniel?"

"Tell me, scholar wife."

"It means 'God is my Judge'."

"That's so? Well, maybe he'll have a career as a judge like his Uncle Ransome."

"Uncle who?"

"My brother."

"I ... didn't know you had a brother." At least she knew Rye's birthday and his age. Family was a topic he avoided and she was careful not to pry. Not after the iciness when she asked about the first Mrs. Jones. It wasn't anger, she supposed, but agony. Getting to know the man was a like handling a prickly artichoke, peeling one leaf at a time.

I need patience to get to the heart of him.

And if Aggie knows Rye's background, she's not sharing.

"We'll save that story for when we are snowed in for a

week or so."

"I can't wait."

"You'll see. Being stuck inside a well chinked cabin during a howling snow storm will be … an adventure."

"The thought of living under a roof again is so remote. I've gotten used to falling asleep looking up at the bottom of the wagon."

"If you have trouble sleeping, I'll suspend the wagon over our bed."

The blush when straight to the roots of her hair. "Our bed?"

The grey eyes did not waver. "Yes, our bed. In our home, in the Willamette Valley."

She swallowed. "I see."

"Does that cause you distress?"

"Being in Oregon or having a wagon hung over my head?"

"The sharing of a bed."

"No. We've never talked about it, much less done anything about it."

"I thought I'd let you get accustomed to the idea of being a wife. We married in a hurry, and at a time when you were in a bad patch of luck. Saying the words in a marriage service is one thing, acting on them is another."

"So you gave me room to run."

Rye grinned down at her. "Pretty much."

"I didn't run."

"So I see."

Felicity bit the inside of her cheek.

This is territory I don't have a map for, or a pamphlet.

I'm not sure if he is suggesting what I think he is suggesting.

"But I can set you free."

"What do you mean?" Her stomach tightened.

"Dig a hole and bury that sling wherever you'd like. I figure that's a souvenir you'd rather not keep."

She laughed. He meant the sling. "And no more stinky yellow stuff?"

"Only if you want to smell like Cosmos."

Felicity folded her arms around her ribs, holding herself together. Time to peel the artichoke. "Were you suggesting a change to our arrangements?"

"Maybe."

"Maybe? How maybe?"

"Thought I'd see how you'd react to the idea."

Putting her free hand on his cheek, she pulled his face down. Hesitant, she kissed him on the lips, tasting the salt of his sweat.

His arms wrapped around her and Baby, molding her to him. He slanted his mouth across her lips.

This is no chaste peck goodnight. Edmund never …

Baby squeaked at being crushed.

Breathing hard, Felicity pulled away and placed the child on her hip. "I wondered what that would be like."

"And?"

"I think I need to explore that further."

Rye dipped his head and met her lips again, until she braced a hand on his chest. "Oh, my …"

"Suitable?"

She flicked a finger against his vest buttons. "It'll do."

He captured her hand. The light in his grey eyes took whatever breath left in her lungs. Bending down, he whispered against her ear. "If you'd like to, we could spend a bit of time together after everyone settles in for the evening. Just you and me."

"Good thing Daniel is sleeping through the night."

"Good training on your part. Let's hope Aggie is as deep a sleeper or we will never hear the end of it."

Felicity rested her head on Rye's chest and listened to the rock steady beat of his heart. "She planned this match from the beginning."

"She's a wise woman."

"And don't you two go fergettin' it." Aggie croaked from the back of the wagon.

Felicity blushed. Rye tipped his hat and whistled for Dodge.

"I'm off to round up our fellow travelers. They can come back to see the geysers on their own. Wake up the oxen, darling, we've got miles yet to go today."

AFTER SHE TUCKED the baby beside Aggie on the feather bed, Felicity strolled to the edge of the wagons.

It is a marvel, this life of mine.

Here I am, skirts blowing in a July wind watching water spurt out of the ground, miles from New York.

July. She would have been Mrs. Edmund Ormond, of the New York Ormonds, for over a year. The date for the wedding that never happened came and went, lost in the constant refrain of hitching Right and Left, unloading the wagon, changing diapers, searching for firewood.

Where was June? Spent somewhere between Ash Hollow and Chimney Rock.

She tripped over a weathered shoulder blade, a bone large enough to have come from a buffalo and one of the few bones not taken over by the Bone Express. No note from a loved one or message of water holes or Indian sign scrawled on the gray surface.

Perfect.

"What are ya doin', girl?" Aggie's voice made Felicity pause in her search for a pencil and the envelope she kept tucked under her pamphlet collection.

"Getting something."

"Well something's wet if ya get my drift."

"I'll change him in a minute. There's something that I've

got to take care of."

"If it involves ice and lemons, count me in."

Felicity chuckled and tucked the pencil behind her ear, the envelope in her apron pocket.

Dragging the shoulder blade out from the sagebrush, she slid it closer to the trail where it would be seen. Crouching in the thin grass, she brushed dust off the rough bone with her apron.

Felicity tapped the pencil against her nose. The wood smell took her back to the Almstead House library. Right to the box of freshly sharpened pencils on her father's desk. He preferred writing drafts in pencil, removing whole sections with a gum eraser that he let her play with.

That was her past. A life she no longer wanted to live. A hothouse she was thrown out of, broken windows and all.

Gerald Sinclair's former library did not have sufficient shelves to hold a record of everything that weathered her since leaving Independence. But her choice of stationery fit these words:

> To Edmund Ormond –
> No need to follow.
> Wish you a good life.
> – Felicity Jones,
> nee Sinclair

She propped the daguerreotype Edmund gave her against the buffalo bone. The slim features of the serious young man in grey and black tones were a shadow. She hoped her father would take her leaving the portrait on the trail as a way to make up for the letters that she sent to Edmund, begging him to rescue her.

It was silly to waste the pencil lead, but the thick black letters meant she moved on down the trail, souvenirs and all. Other feet beat down the prairie grass, as her boots left a path for the ones behind to follow.

If other people can survive this, I can.

If someone tells me that I can't, I will go out of my way to show them that I can.

If Edmund came riding down the trail, I'd turn him away.

I am Oregon bound.

UNDER THE STARS, a coyote squealed, cries pitching up at the end. A second cry joined, and another. A pack hunted at the base of Sheep Rock.

Rye turned on his side and tucked his arm under Felicity's neck. "Uncomfortable?"

"No."

"Not too cold?" He pulled the quilt over her bare shoulders.

"No."

"Not too hot?"

"No."

He ran his finger along her jawline. "Do you have any other words than 'no'?"

"No."

"Funny squirrel."

"Squirrel?"

"Yes, squirrel. Like a squirrel peeking up out of a nest."

The cries of the coyotes faded and rose, carried on the night wind.

"Rye?"

"Yes, wife?"

"That was nice."

"Yes, that was."

"Rye?"

"Yes?"

"Am I going to be … with child?"

"I thought you wanted children. Was I wrong to – "

Felicity tapped her fingertips on his lips. "No. It was good to wait, to let me adjust to being Mrs. Peyton Randolph Daniel Jones. But having seen what Hannah went through, I have to admit I'm afraid of ..."

"... having a baby?" Rye finished her words.

She ducked her head, letting the sun streaked hair fall to cover her face.

Rye brushed back her hair, kissing her forehead. "It doesn't always go like that. She buried her husband and your uncle. She went into labor on the trail, in the open ... without proper tools or medications."

Felicity remembered Daniel's birth. The lantern burning low, Hannah struggling, losing. Hopefully finding Tom in her own grassy heaven.

"The other reason I held off from introducing you to this part of married life is that if you did carry our child, we would be further along the trail and you would not be at risk of delivering a baby in the back of a wagon."

"That's just like you. Looking out for me."

"More like looking out for me. Two children not yet out of diapers would be a handful."

Felicity snorted. "I see your point."

This manner of talk was new between her and Rye. Uncomfortable at first, but she was gradually learning that the relationship between a man and a woman was bound by the rules they set. It made her free to speak her mind.

Well, about most things. Curious of how he got his thigh wound, she wanted him to tell her without her asking.

"Rye?"

"Yes, wife?"

"There's something I'd like to tell you."

"You'd like to do that again?"

"Yes ... no ... that's not what I wanted to tell you." She thumped him on the chest with the back of her hand.

"Something about your life in New York? We don't have to talk about that."

"No. About my present."

"What's that?"

She rolled onto her elbow and pushed back the sweep of hair that fell over his forehead. His eyes glowed like moonstones in the August night. She trusted the resilience in those eyes. "I love you. I am certain that I love you. I don't know when it happened, but I do."

"Maybe it was when I hollered at you for setting the whole prairie on fire."

"It wasn't the whole prairie, just my corner of it."

"And your skirt."

"Yes. Although at the time I didn't appreciate your putting the grass fire out first and then my dress."

"I have something that might make up for that."

"What?"

Rye tousled her hair. "A moment, impatient one."

"I thought I was a squirrel a minute ago."

"You still are. Hold on, I'll be right back." Rye slipped on his moccasins and limped to Cosmos. He threw back the flap of a saddlebag.

Felicity rolled onto her back and pulled the quilt up to her chin.

He didn't exactly say he loved me.

And why did Rye ask if there was something I wanted to share about New York?

Aggie wouldn't say anything to him. Did he overhear gossip at one of the forts? Should I tell him why Father forced us to leave?

She chewed on a hangnail on her thumb, tearing at the loose skin.

Rye tossed a small linen bag embroidered with red thread onto her stomach.

She sat up, pinning the quilt under her arms, the night air

cool on her bare back. "What is it?"

"Open it."

Felicity picked at the knot with her broken fingernails. Rye sighed.

"Here, allow me." He opened the bag and dumped a ring into her calloused palm. Creamy pearls clustered around a sapphire like petals and engraved leaves twined down to a simple gold band.

"There is a locket on the bottom side. My grandmother kept a lock of my father's hair in it at some time. And don't worry, it isn't there now."

Turning the ring in her hand, she admired the stone's flash in the moonlight. Tears welled. She never expected to have a wedding ring.

"Do you like it? It may not be as fancy as some rings, but it's a family piece."

Not at all the diamond Tiffany, Young and Ellis ring I left on the Ormond's doorstep.

Why, this ring's yellow gold is warm like the sun. "Reminds me of the wildflowers that we've walked through since leaving Independence."

"The edges of the stone are worn, but maybe we'll find a jeweler to fix that."

"It's lovely."

Rye slipped the ring on her finger. "I hoped you'd like it. The color of the center stone reminds me of the color of your eyes.

"Serena, my wife …" Rye cleared his throat. "My first wife, that is, never wore this ring because she felt it was too fancy for her. She had small hands and preferred a plain band."

Serena.

Her name was Serena.

What was she like?

Curiosity burned. She saved her questions for another night. Not tonight.

"This was the one thing that I didn't lose because Serena gave it to Helmut for safekeeping. I lost my farm, my medical practice, my son, my wife." He paused, his voice cracking. "In that order. I made a poor choice of investments. When the stock failed, I couldn't get my investment back." He stared down at the ring on her hand.

She shivered. "What did you invest in?"

"Railroad stocks."

Felicity listened, but Rye's words were drowned out by the thrumming in her ears. Gerald Sinclair's part in the swindle caused this good man's farm and medical practice to be taken. His three year old son and his wife dead of cholera in a boarding house. Everything lost, because he trusted in her father's scam. Alone, adrift on a sea of laudanum and rye whiskey.

"Serena and our son are buried near St. Luke's church, in Virginia. Helmut and Marta got me back on my feet. Dried me out."

"So that is how you came to be on the trail?" she whispered, throat tight.

Tears dripped from her chin onto his hair.

Rye brushed her tears with the heel of his hand. "That's enough history for one night. And I am out of jewelry to tempt you with."

"There is something you should know –"

"Are you going to keep talking or are you going to curl up beside me? I have a new life. Give me time to heal, just as I gave your shoulder time to heal. I was pretty well broken, but you and Daniel helped put me back together."

"But –"

"Felicity, I promise you a good life." He kissed her palm.

She curled up in a ball on her side.

The blasted Garrety-Brown Railroad. Am I to be punished with this for the rest of my life?

I could tell Rye what I know of my father, all of it and risk that this fragile new life will crumble.

I could put down the baggage I've carried all this way. Sort of a cleansing. Leave my old identity on the side of the trail like other emigrants left broken chairs and side tables.

My choice? Drag my prior life along with me or lighten my load.

I've been rejected by everyone I knew in New York. If Rye abandons us, Daniel and I will not survive on the trail alone.

I can't tell him about Father. I can't. I can't see that any good will come of talking. I cannot change history.

But would he leave? Or would he take out his anger on me?

All I can do is be a good wife and work hard beside him to provide for our family.

Rye propped his chin on her shoulder. "Where did you go? You disappeared there for a moment."

"Thinking about something that a wise man told me once."

"What's that?"

"The past is the past."

"A fount of wisdom."

"I like to think so. So when will we reach Fort Hall?"

CHAPTER 19

Fort Hall
August 3, 1851

"We've got company," Rye pulled up Cosmos and dropped the mare's reins, leaning over in the saddle to loosen his leg bandage.

Twelve wagons took shelter outside the main gate to Fort Hall under grey clouds. A white haired woman trimmed the scorched edge of a canvas top and two teenage boys plugged splintered holes in another wagon bed. A wheel with raw wood spokes leaned against the fort's adobe walls, missing a metal band. The clanging of a hammer on an anvil inside the fort stopped. And started again.

"Is it the Larkin party?" Felicity halted Right, thankful Uncle Jasper won the argument in Independence to split from the Larkin wagon train.

"That's Joe Larkin's dairy herd. Or what's left of it." Rye dismounted, catching himself on the fender of the saddle. He rested the toe of his left boot on the ground and waved to the McHenry wagon behind them. "We'll camp here. That way we won't crowd the fort all at once."

Felicity set the brake lever on the wagon. "I hope they have a doctor. I'd like someone to look at that leg of yours."

"I'm a doctor and it doesn't need looking at."

"And I am the doctor's wife. Do you mind if I have a differing opinion? I notice you can't put your full weight on it."

"You worry too much."

Felicity snorted and unbuckled Right's harness.

Rye shaded his eyes. "Well, I'll be ..."

"Something wrong?" Felicity glanced at the fort, oxbow pin in her hand.

Dust rose up from the hooves of a trotting mule, the lanky man riding bareback, sitting like a soldier, back straight, shoulders square. Felicity figured the red haired man's outfit, a buckskin shirt over cavalry trousers or the spotted mule bred from an Appaloosa, made Rye pause. An odd mix for what she took to be a trapper.

The trapper dismounted and flipped the reins over his mule's head when he reached Pug Watson's wagon and glanced inside the canvas top. He sauntered around the McHenry outfit.

Felicity shook out her skirts and tied the strings of her bonnet. His eyes studied her from bonnet to hemline, his cold stare a reminder of when she first met Rye.

Her husband whistled a command to Dodge. The dog streaked by her and raced around the trapper, nipping at his hands and jumping on the man, paws leaving dusty prints on the dark blue trousers.

Felicity grabbed the dog by the scruff of the neck. "Get down! I am so sorry, sir."

"That Dodge?" The trapper slapped the dust from his trousers.

"How do you know ...?"

The trapper saluted Rye. "Captain Jones, I heard you were coming this way."

Rye pushed his planter's hat back and extended a hand to the trapper. "Lieutenant Cade Braedon."

Braedon laughed, clasping Rye's hand. "That's Captain Braedon to you, recruit."

Felicity released Dodge. Rye failed to mention his military

background. It accounted for knowing the brief words to the burial service he used over the course of the trail. And it explained the cavalry trousers on his acquaintance.

"What kind of uniform is the army issuing these days?" Rye tugged on the fringe of the Braedon's buckskin shirt. "Dodge, get down."

"Dropped the Captain part when the cantonment closed and the military and I separated. I turned trapper for Hudson Bay."

"That's quite a career change for you."

"Just following your lead."

"You don't look all that surprised to see me."

"I heard you were out this way. The wagon train camped here said you were a few days behind. Fellow named Larkin told me."

"We were worried about them. Came across what looked like a battlefield around Big Hill."

"They had a young couple join their group. Brought nothing but trouble with them."

"We figured they might be the pair that left us around Scott's Bluff."

"They won't be bothering anyone, any more."

Rye glanced at Felicity. "Their families are still traveling with us."

"My condolences, if the families are anything like their offspring. But I have to say that I'm not surprised you found your way out here. You never were someone to stay in one place for too long."

"It was time for a change."

Cool eyes appraised Felicity standing beside the wagon. "That your rig?"

"Yes. And my wife, Felicity. We were married about a month ago."

Her cheeks flushed at Rye's words. This was the first time Rye introduced her as his wife and she did not expect the rush

~ 188 ~

of warmth at the simple words. The pride in his voice made her chest light. Anyone hearing that voice could tell she was cherished. Felicity tucked the oxbow pin in the pocket of her apron and walked up to Cade, extending her grubby hand.

"It is a pleasure to meet you, Captain Braedon."

He shook her hand. "Welcome to Fort Hall, Mrs. Jones." Captain Braedon jabbed Rye in the shoulder. "Trust Peyton to find a pretty girl to marry."

That was the first time anyone called her husband by his given name, Peyton. "Please, call me Felicity."

"With pleasure, ma'am."

Daniel fussed in the back of the wagon. Aggie poked her head above the drover's seat.

"And a family?"

Rye grinned and tucked Felicity under his arm. "Long story, my friend."

There was something she liked in Captain Braedon's answering smile. "Captain Braedon – "

"Just 'Cade', ma'am. I confess that the 'Captain' part was just showing off for Peyton."

"Cade, it is. Please join us for dinner if you are available. I believe my husband would enjoy the opportunity to visit with you."

"I accept your invitation, madam, and look forward to our engagement this evening."

THE RAIN CLOUDS over Fort Hall burned into wispy trails long before nightfall. Campfire smoke hung in the humid air, dulling the stars.

"So your wife was pretty surprised to find out you'd been a cavalry sawbones."

"We're still in the honeymoon phase. I don't want to give out all my secrets at once like someone else I know."

"Surprised you didn't tell her about the Twisted Creek skirmish." Cade leaned back and pointed the tin cup in his hand at the bundle of quilts under the wagon. "You did well. I like your Mrs. Jones. And Daniel is quite the lad."

"She's a strong woman. I didn't believe that once, but she proved me wrong." Rye tapped his fingers against the bottom of his empty cup. "And watch out for Aggie. She's a matchmaker just waiting for a sweet, unsuspecting bachelor like you to come along."

"Both hands and all ten fingers are still burnt from getting singed ... I'm staying clear of damsels and their distresses for the time being."

"That bad, huh?"

"Just don't do what I did ... stay away from anything wearing a corset claiming she's not married. Her husband is likely to disagree." Cade tossed the remains of his coffee into the fire. "I ... uh ... didn't think it right to mention the prior Mrs. Jones in front of the current Mrs. Jones."

"I appreciate that."

"Does she know what all happened?"

"You might say that the Garrety-Brown Railroad is something we have in common."

"All those folks should have been strung up."

Rye loosened the edges of the dusty bandage wrapped around his knee. Yellow crust from the day's ride stained the buckskins. "Felicity's father was Gerald Sinclair."

Cade whistled. "That's a wild card. Did you know that before you went and married her?"

"Cholera hit the train early on and took Sinclair with it. If I could have buried him alive with my bare hands, I would have. But he asked me to watch over Felicity."

"I see that you took his words to heart."

"Wasn't planned that way. Just happened."

"Didn't she know what her father did for a living?"

Rye plucked the edges of the bandage. The buckskins stuck

to the wound and the pulling ripped the scabs. "Can't say. And I can't blame her for something that she didn't have a hand in."

"Probably best to let it go."

"Best thing we can do is get ourselves to Oregon and get a land claim filed." Rye gritted his teeth and pulled the buckskins back, glad that the dark hid the shriveled skin around his wound. "Sure is muggy out tonight."

"The Shoshone guides say there is a storm brewing. But I gotta tell you that they've got to be off in their predictions. Never rains here in August. Hasn't rained in months."

"Hopefully we'll be down the trail before it hits."

"Larkin tell you why he's here?"

"Figured their wagon repairs delayed them."

"This is their second pass through Hall."

Rye soaped and rinsed the wound over a basin. "How so?"

"They opted to take the Sweetwater Trail. It's a shortcut through to south of Fort Boise on the Snake ... 'la riviere boisee' to the trappers in the area."

"They run into trouble?"

"They ignored their guide's expert advice and took a game trail that goes to a lot of nowhere. They chose poorly. Lost a lot of livestock and members of their party."

"You were the expert guide?"

"Yep."

"Why'd they take the cutoff in the first place?" Rye wrapped a linen bandage around his knee, tucking in the ends.

"It shaves off about two to three weeks of travel time."

"Unless you turn around." Rye threw the dirty bandage into the campfire.

"Well, there is that. But an old army man like yourself should be able to navigate without any problem."

"Who you calling old?" Rye waved away smoke that drifted up to him.

Cade held up his hands. "No offense meant ... but there is

one more thing. The Blalock brothers."

"Friends of yours?"

"Not particularly. Their folks died a year or so back, caught between here and the Snake. Cholera. They're a couple of youngsters who went into a more lucrative trade."

"What would that be?"

"Stealing from the Shoshone ... scavenging what they can from wagon trains. Marcus and his brother Pete can be a couple of bottom feeding raiders when they are liquored up. I tried getting them to sign on with Hudson Bay, but the pace of trapping wasn't fast enough for them. The idea of waiting a season to get paid, versus picking up what they can off the trail and stealing in the winter months ... well, I thought you should be aware. I didn't see them when I was out with the Larkin outfit, but that doesn't mean they didn't see us."

Rye rubbed the stubble on his chin. "I'm not in favor of shortcuts. There is too much that can go wrong ... and luck has been with us as far as raiders go. But I owe it to the company to put it to a vote."

Rye coughed, choking on the smoke. "Now I'm sounding like Aggie. I'll turn in before I get around to dabbling in matchmaking."

AFTER BREAKFAST, FELICITY cut the knot on the bandage around Rye's knee and eased the linen layers apart, rolling the dirty material into a loose ball. Each layer revealed a yellow stain. She poured a dipper of water mixed with carbolic acid on the layer next to his skin to loosen the crust that formed overnight.

Rye inhaled, sweat breaking out on the back of his brown hands.

Felicity chewed the inside of her cheek. The coffee she drank with breakfast roiled in her stomach. She pulled the last bit of linen away. Ridges stood out on his knee where the bandage layers crossed. She dipped the edge of a rag in the acid mixture and cleaned the pus on the edges of the wound.

"Rye?"

He bit his lip. "Yes, love?"

"Does your family call you Peyton?"

"Yes."

"What if I called you Peyton?"

"Sounds kind of funny coming from you."

Because I am a stranger, not family.

Not true family.

Just a marriage of convenience to help a fellow traveler out of a bad place. A woman who didn't know anything personal about the man she married on the prairie.

"You should take Cade's advice and have Dr. Barton take a look at this before we leave the fort."

"I know what he'll say."

"Are you a mind reader as well as a physician?"

"That would have come in handy with some of my former patients."

"What would Dr. Barton tell you?"

"That I have a caring wife who enjoys hovering."

"Did your first wife call you Peyton?"

He peered up at her but she couldn't return his gaze. "Does it matter?"

It mattered. The intimacy, that knowledge of a personal history of the man she married mattered to her. Simple facts, like his birthday, the names of his family members. Where he went to school. When he first knew he wanted to be a doctor.

"Yes, but I don't know why."

"Does my being married to Serena long before you ever thought of leaving New York make you uncomfortable?"

"No," she glanced away, took a breath, and met his gaze. "Yes. I don't know. It's that I know so little about you."

"We did go about our marriage in reverse. Wedding vows,

then the courting."

"Do you have any regrets?"

"About marrying you? Not a one. It's easier to get you started on the trail on time."

She snorted. "Not funny, Dr. Jones."

"I find it pleasing to see that our wagon is the first one ready for the day." Rye wrapped his arms around Felicity and pressed her to his ribs, kissing her eyebrows, her nose. "As for Serena, she was my first love, not my last love."

Felicity's tight shoulders eased. She touched the bandage on his thigh.

"So what would Dr. Barton have to say about this?"

"I wouldn't like hearing what he had to say."

"Could we try one of the remedies I read about?"

"Would you hover less?"

"Only if you promised to give it a solid try."

"And do you have this magic elixir hidden on you?"

Felicity reached into her apron pocket and pulled out a small tin with "Chocolat de Vouvrais" on the label.

Rye lifted the lid and clamped the lid down. "It reeks."

"So does your 'special' liniment but Cosmos and I put up with the stench. Aunt Aggie swears this will work."

"It would take the pitch off the side of the wagon."

"Please?" Felicity batted her lashes in an exaggerated flirtation.

"I'll take the matter under advisement, Mrs. Jones."

She smiled up at him. "And I'll follow up with you to see that you do."

"There you go, hovering."

"But you are so nice to fuss over."

Felicity dried the wound and wrapped a fresh bandage around Rye's knee. He took the ends of the bandage from her hands and tied the knot. He kissed the creases from her forehead.

"What about your former beau? Any regrets?"

She waited for the ache in her chest to surge. All that remained of the madness of that first love was a scar, a raised welt on her heart to remind her that life changed course in a single moment.

"My feelings for him are kind of like the clothes I started out with. They don't fit me anymore. Can't cook in them without ruining the fabric. One spark – "

"And the whole prairie is on fire."

"And I never could joke with Edmund like I do with you. I doubt that he would have lasted this long on the trail without a butler and a stack of pressed neck clothes."

"Bit of a dandy?"

Felicity smiled. "He kept his tailor well employed."

"Not a wearer of buckskins, I'd wager."

"You'd be correct. But it takes a special man to make buckskins an item of high fashion."

CLOUDS FORMED OVER the range to the north of Fort Hall. Rain fell in grey sheets, but the droplets evaporated before hitting the ground.

The sooner the company was on the trail, the better Felicity would feel. The nightmare that woke her before dawn haunted her.

Felicity crouched under Right to check the gall under his harness. A whiff of tobacco smoke meant that the men returned from the meeting at the Crandall wagon. She grabbed Right's harness and pulled herself up, startling a grey haired woman with a pipe.

"I recognize those boots, missy." The woman's deep set wrinkles around her mouth kept the pipe balanced on her thin lower lip.

"Pardon?"

"I knew their owner. She was mighty proud of that red

trim. A pretty young thing, younger than you. I wager you're a heck of a lot sweeter, though. I liked her husband, but it was a shame what happened to him. At least her boots will see Oregon and I have to say that is a comfort to me."

"Were you in the Larkin company?"

"Still am. I'm Mrs. Larkin."

Aggie poked her head through the canvas flap. She sniffed. "Smells like Tennessee."

"Aggie Sinclair, that you?"

"Sure as the day is long." Aggie coughed, catching her breath.

"I thought we would have missed you folks by now. Figured you were already out on the trail this morning."

Felicity reached up to take Daniel from Aggie. "We took a few days to rest the livestock."

"Well, rest them while you can and while you still got them."

"Will you and the other families be joining our company?"

"No, dearie. We're taking the trail to the south, to California. Ran into foul water that hit the company hard. Buried about half of the company, including my son-in-law. Lost most of the stock. Even with fewer folks, we're plumb near out of supplies and the money to replace them. The tolls for ferry crossings and what not that we've paid so far was more than what we were told they were going to be. I'm guessing that we have enough money left to get us to San Francisco where we'll sell the wagons and the oxen."

Felicity pressed a cloth doll into Daniel's grubby hands.

Aggie took a deep breath, holding her hand to her chest. "We came across sign of one of yer campsites around Big Hill."

"We had trouble with that young couple that your Mr. Jones sent to us. I was just telling this sweet young thing about the wife. They're gone. I heard tell that the young feller had folks with your group. If you don't mind pointing them out to me, I'd like to talk with them and let them know what happened."

"Were you attacked? We didn't see any Indian sign."

"Wasn't Indians. One of the young bucks in our company took a liking to Mr. Mueller's wife and it ended badly, for everyone involved."

Felicity kissed Daniel's forehead to hide the tears that rimmed her eyes. Ezra's plans for a homestead were buried with him.

"Can you tell us about the cutoff ahead?" Aggie leaned forward.

"I can tell you to avoid taking it."

Felicity rested her chin on Daniel's head. "Aren't we taking the main road?"

"For bein' married to the trail leader and all, you'd think she'd be better informed. That's what the meeting at the Crandall wagon is all about. They're putting it to a vote."

An icy prickle started between Felicity's shoulder blades. "So the shortcut is real?"

"Our group was the second company to try the route this season. If my recollection is correct, it was recommended in Hinckley's pamphlet and was supposed to save us weeks of travel ... instead it nearly cost us the trip. Cholera hit and it just spread like it was fire. Then we had the enlightened idea of trying to make the shortcut even shorter by taking a turn that led us into a canyon. All that way with thirsty cattle and we ended up boxed in with sand up to our axles. We were just too smart for ourselves."

"Mrs. Larkin, I was hoping you'd get a chance to meet my wife before we departed." Rye limped to Felicity's side and took Daniel in his arms.

"I hear you were putting Sweetwater to a vote."

"We did. Against my one vote, the company chose to take the shorter route."

Felicity's shoulders tightened at the news.

Rye took Felicity's hand in his. "From your expression I see there would have been two votes against the shortcut."

"Up to now we've stayed together and on the trail."

"Cade and I stayed up talking last night after you went to sleep. The route follows the edge of lava fields. Cade says we can't miss them. It's an old route used by the Shoshone and comes out north of Tea Pot Dome, south of Fort Boise on the Snake River. Must be a real pretty spot, and a welcome one. Trappers call it 'la riviere boisee'."

"'The wooded river' …"

"We should be able to make it over the trail in about two weeks."

Daniel fussed and Felicity rubbed the infant's back. Aggie tickled the boy's feet to get him to smile.

Felicity turned to Mrs. Larkin. "What's the drawback? Seems like more folks would take a cutoff like that to save time."

"Not much water. And what water is to be found, ain't drinkable. It's hard going on man and beast."

"Rye. It's too risky. Not with Daniel and Aggie."

Aggie elbowed Felicity's ribs. "What are ya afraid of? Not bein' able to bathe?" She hacked into her handkerchief. "If anything this trail would have taught ya, is that the folks who'd take the easy trail never left their farms. Ya been talkin' 'bout gettin' to the Territory as quick as a beetle. I say we take the hard path and save us time."

Folding her arms around her ribs, Felicity glanced up at Rye. He squared his shoulders. The deep lines around Rye's mouth were more than trail fatigue.

"The men in the company voted thinking it's worth the risk if it shaves time off the trail."

"But the main trail has water and feed for the livestock. And there are other companies on the trail if we need help."

Mrs. Larkin knocked her pipe and against the sole of her boot. "I'll let you three talk it out. I've got to help get my daughter's family fed this morning."

"Safe travels, ma'am." Rye flicked the brim of his hat.

Felicity clamped her lips tight to hold her words until Mrs. Larkin departed. "Rye, darling, we need to stay on the trail. All along you've said 'no shortcuts.'"

"Your concern is valid. If it was up to me, we'd take the main trail. But I can't leave the company to navigate on their own. Crandall has plenty of good sense, but I'm responsible for getting the group through to the Territory." Rye tipped his planter's hat back of his head and rubbed his neck. "I just wish Larkin hadn't changed his mind about heading to Oregon. I could've sent you, Daniel and Aggie with them while I took our company through the cutoff."

"You wouldn't want us with you?" Felicity tried to keep the quaver of emotion out of her voice. She tamped down the panic in her chest.

"Don't look like that, sensitive girl. Of course I want you with me. Always. But I'd rest easier if I knew you were safe." Rye's grey eyes were warm, reassuring. He ran his hands up her arms and kissed her forehead.

She pulled away. "I wouldn't go with the Larkins. What if something happened to you and I couldn't get to you?" The prospect of a life without Rye barren, like the land around Fort Hall.

"I wouldn't take us on a wild goose chase if I didn't think there was a goose to be caught at the end of the game."

"But we may get caught. Not in a snow drift in the mountains, but out in the heat without water." The prickle between Felicity's shoulder blades became an ache. She rolled her shoulders to shake off the tension.

Rye turned her to face the range of hills to the north. "See those clouds? The Indians are certain of rain. That means water on the trail for us."

"But what if they are wrong?"

"We have to make up time that we lost at the start of the

trip."

"You mean because of my father and Hannah."

"Because things happen on the trail that no one can predict."

"I want to hurry. I do. I have these nightmares about trying to carry Daniel through snow drifts. I keep slipping and falling into the snow and then I lose him."

"I know because you've been talking in your sleep. I see the strain of the trip on your face and it pains me. Trust me that this decision is the right one for us. We've been safe this long."

"I trust your judgment, but we are safer on the trail."

"Daniel isn't the only one I think about. I worry over Aggie as well. The sooner we get everyone to Oregon the less I'll worry."

"I trust you. But the next two weeks won't pass fast enough for my liking."

"I promise that once you get to the Willamette Valley you will have all the water you want."

"I'll hold you to that promise."

Soda Springs
August 4, 1851

"I thought it looked like you, sir."

Trumbo, a survivor of a cholera attack that wiped out most of the members of a wagon company, replaced Miller after the guide abandoned Edmund at Fort Bridger. A lanky man with a lazy eye, he was raised in service and serving Edmund gave him a taste of the old life from Boston. A life conducted indoors, arranging trays of bourbon and cigars for a Mr. Barton and picking up books from the library for a Mrs. Barton, with the occasional horse race on a day off.

Edmund blew off the dust on the daguerreotype, a portrait taken at Smith & Son studio, given to Miss Sinclair after their engagement.

Why did Felicity leave it on the trail?

"There's writing, too."

"Show me."

The block letters in pencil on the shoulder blade were not in Felicity's copperplate. Edmund brushed the dust from the bone, smearing the letters.

Words written under duress, no doubt. Untrue words, words meant to put him off the hunt.

"Is it her writing, sir?"

"Can you read, Trumbo?"

"No, sir, never have."

"Then 'tis a good thing that I can."

CHAPTER 20

The Sweetwater Trail
August 5, 1851

The noontide sun, absorbed by the lava flows on the Sweetwater cutoff, flared back at the wagon company. The trail skirting the lava beds forced the wagons into a single file. The wheel tracks from the Larkin company passage were eroded by wind, but dried manure and scattered housewares like the jelly mold Maggie McHenry snatched up marked the way.

Rye rode ahead on Cosmos to guide the company, with Cade's map fluttering in his hand.

The lava fields surrounded Felicity, covering the landscape. The bare flows and dried grasses were like the flesh stripped bones and tattered hide of a buffalo carcass left to weather on the prairie.

Felicity tried to imagine the degree of heat to turn rocks to liquid, flowing from the cinder cones. It couldn't be far off the day's temperature. She feared to take Uncle Jasper's gauge out of the velvet box, certain the heat exceeded the marks at the tip.

The creaking wagons did not drown out the slosh of water in the bucket on the side of the wagon. She wanted a long, cool drink out of a stream. The back of her throat dry like a rasp. Perspiration stained the armpits of her gown and dried on the back of her neck.

Pug and his boys stopped their wagon to load a samovar into their wagon. Stuck behind the Watsons, Felicity picked up a tarnished ladle and tossed it up to Aggie. She didn't pause to read the initials or test the quality of the silver. It would replace the wooden spoon with the cracked handle.

Focusing on the swinging ties of the canvas top in front of her, Felicity tugged on Right's halter and put one red trimmed boot in front of the other.

On the first quarter moon, the men of the company voted to travel at night to spare the livestock. Wagons were hitched when the black rock cooled after sunset. Lane Crandall left off Sunday services, and ministered the families in the shade of the wagons during the day. His wife walked with their oxen. He slept when he could in the back of the jolting wagon.

Dry country meant no crickets to fall asleep to during the day. Philippe Patel's violin stayed in its velvet lined case. After the soundboard split on Walt Anderson's guitar, he handed the instrument to his wife for firewood. Falling asleep at dawn came easy to the children; their parents stared at the dry rocks and dust and prayed for water.

Felicity stumbled over her boots in the twilight behind the Crandall wagon. She bit her tongue and tasted blood. Right and Left were thirsty. The cattle came first. And Cosmos. Daniel, Aggie and Felicity after the livestock. Rye drank a mouthful from the dipper, sharing his ration with Dodge.

AT DAWN, RYE halted the company at the base of a steep ridge. The single track followed the line of the ridge, but the wheel marks from the Larkin wagons turned right, down a slope to a muddy creek bed. The cracked mud preserved the ruts of the wagons and hoof and boot marks.

Felicity rubbed a wad of lard on her lips. Mud meant water.

Water meant relief from the dry scales on the back of her throat.

Dropping Cosmos' reins to the ground, Rye spread Cade's map out on a boulder. The men in the wagon train gathered around the map. Lane Crandall put on his glasses and checked a compass, wrote a notation on the paper.

Rye joined Aggie and Felicity in the shade of the wagon. "The vote is to keep to the migration route." He took off his hat and wiped the back of his sleeve across his forehead. He blew his nose on a bandana. "I see why Larkin wanted to take that turn off. They were desperate to get their livestock to water."

"Mrs. Larkin was right about the water." Felicity's voice cracked at the end.

"There isn't any."

Aggie traced a finger along Daniel's eyebrows. The baby, silent in her lap, lay listless in the heat. "For a trail named Sweetwater, I hoped to see more of it. I'd wager the water only shows up in the spring."

"Let's hope that's not true." Rye stared at the fierce blue sky. No clouds, not a whiff of white.

Felicity pushed herself away from the warped boards of the wagon. "Will you take a look at Left? He's hanging back in the traces more than usual. Right's doing most of the work but I'm not sure how he's got the strength to do it."

Picking up one of Left's hind feet, Rye pulled out a thorn wedged between the cleats with a pair of pliers. "The cracks in their heels are better. Keep up with greasing them."

"The Radnor's lost another mule today." Felicity took the edge of her apron and wiped the dried tears and dust from her eyes.

"That so?"

She rubbed the ridge between Right's horns. "Anything on Cade's map about finding water?"

Rye ducked his head and pulled down the brim of his hat.

"Dump anything out of the wagon that you don't need. You'll need to pile it up on the rocks so it doesn't block the Zenger's wagon behind you."

"What's left to dump? We cut our load back at the cutoff from the main trail."

"Do it, don't argue woman." The echoes from Lone Elm Grove in his voice stung her.

Tears pricked her eyes. "Fine."

"Hold on. I'm sorry. It's the heat talking."

"And it's the heat that's making me cry."

"Hush, darling. Don't waste the water on tears."

"I'm too tired to care."

He kissed the tears from her cheeks. "A few days more."

"You said that a few days ago."

"And we're that much closer to water."

"I can't bear to hear Daniel cry like last night."

"It's colic and the heat, nothing more serious. As soon as we reach the Snake River he'll be fine."

"I'm learning to swim so I can jump in."

"That's my girl. Go through the wagon and weed out what you can do without out. Anything that isn't used for survival needs to be left behind. That means your father's books."

"But I promised my father —"

"If he were with us, he'd make you dump them."

"Fine."

"So we're back to 'fine'?"

"Yes."

"You'll do it?"

"Fine."

"I'm sorry darling, but those books are an anchor you're dragging. Leave it behind on the trail. You won't need be needing law books in the Oregon Territory."

She jerked away to hide her tears. "Let me get to work."

Rye cupped her chin with a gritty palm. "Right will thank you for it."

Aggie stayed in the shade of the wagon and held Daniel. Felicity sorted. The linseed oil for waterproofing the canvas, flour sacks and Dutch oven stayed in the wagon. Rancid bacon sat next to the campfire. Hannah's empty cedar trunk went bouncing onto the rocks. The silver ladle took the wooden spoon's place on the hook in the wagon. The silver bowl, the wedding gift from the Robertsons, was next to go. Then curling tongs. Aggie's glass punch bowl was propped on the rocking chair scavenged from the trail around Soda Springs.

"Shame to see your chair stay behind." Felicity liked the way Aggie's thin face softened when rocking Daniel to sleep at night beside the campfire.

Felicity put the rancid bacon in a pot over the coals. It was so far gone that Dodge avoided the barrel. The wheat bran the bacon was packed in didn't protect it from the heat. When cooked down, the grease could be used for the wheel hubs.

"Could be worse." Aggie wheezed. Every breath she took was like breathing through a cotton wad.

"How so?"

"Ya could be leavin' me behind in it."

Aggie might not fear death, but Felicity feared Aggie's death. "Quit thinking like that. Do like Rye tells me … imagine dipping your feet into a snow fed lake."

"Just my feet? I'm goin' in, bonnet and all. Wouldn't even take time to take off my boots."

"Why not?"

"Don't want to scare the fish with this skinny old body. While we're at it, I'm imaginin' that this lake is also full of good eatin' fish."

Felicity snorted in reply.

The box of law books on the tailgate was too heavy for her arms to lift. Lacking the will to take volumes out one by one to toss on the rocks, she slumped next to the crate. Not without help. She heard Rye's voice on the other side of the Zenger wagon, but she couldn't see him and Dodge. Aggie nodded over the baby, eyes closed.

Picking at a long splinter on the inside of the wagon, Felicity sighed. The dried wood made the gaps between the planks wider.

If Rye returns, the crate stays on the trail.

If Rye doesn't return, the crate stays in the wagon.

Rye did not return. When the Crandall wagon lurched forward, she shoved the box of books under the flour sacks and took up Right's leading rein.

Perhaps they would find water today.

Perhaps the thunderclouds would let loose.

"One boot in front of the other," she whispered.

ON THE DAY of the fourth dry camp, Felicity dropped the dipper into the barrel when they nooned. The pewter dipper banged against the band holding the wood staves together. Each time the wagon lurched on the trail, the metal clanged a warning. Low water, no water.

No sign of water on that day.

The clouds promising rain in the morning took back their offer in the heat of the day.

In the grey light of the morning of the fifth dry camp in the lava fields, Left wouldn't get up from where he bedded down overnight. Fetlocks swollen, he laid his head in the dust and lowed. Puffs of dust rose with each exhalation. Right stood with his feet splayed, swaying beside his yoke mate at his place in front of the wagon.

Felicity's empty stomach churned. She ate nothing at breakfast, giving her share of spoon bread to Daniel to chew on after sneaking a handful to Dodge. The baby smelled ripe and they were short of clean diapers.

Palms sweating, Felicity tightened the halter on Left and pulled on the leading rein. He raised his nose, snorting a wad of dirty mucus.

"Get up there, Left. Come on, boy." She dropped the rein and grabbed his halter. If she could have pulled him up on her own, she would have. When that didn't work, she got a handful of grain from the back of the wagon. She held it under his nose, out of his reach.

Left eased forward and she let him eat a share of the grain from her hand.

Aggie steadied herself against the front wheel, gasping for breath in the heat. "Rye will have yer hide if we're not ready to move."

"I can't get Left up off the ground."

"Make him get up, girl."

"He's trying."

"Tryin' isn't enough. Use yer whip on him."

"I think he just needs more rest."

"There's no restin'. We gotta get him movin' or he'll die right where he's layin'. And so will we. Either ya use that whip on him or I'll use it on ya."

Felicity pulled on the halter, throwing her weight back on her heels. Her shoulder throbbed with the strain.

"Get up, you mule." Sweat ran down to drip off her elbows.

Left shifted and clambered up to stand on three legs, unwilling to put pressure on his fourth leg.

"That's my girl," Aggie wheezed and shuffled to the back of the wagon where Daniel cried.

Felicity packed the cracked heel with a mix of grease and turpentine. She wobbled to her feet and rested her head against Left's red and white splotched ribs. If she did not get out of the sun, she would run mad, her sanity cracking like the fissures in the rocks; her skin withering and crackling, curling in on itself like Left's halter.

Would Aggie take a whip to her when she couldn't rise from the quilts under the wagon?

Not wanting to test her aunt, she jerked her bonnet into place and picked up the yoke.

ON THE EVENING of the fifth camp without water, too hot to sleep under a sheet, Felicity lay on her side facing away from the dry night wind. With a start, she woke to Rye crawling under the wagon to join her and Daniel on top of the quilt.

The shadows under Rye's grey eyes were dark as the night sky. He rolled onto his back with an arm folded under his head.

"Sorry for the stink."

"No one smells all that sweet," she whispered. "Not even Daniel."

"Map says we're close to water. Maybe not enough for a bath, but at least enough to fill the barrel and water the livestock."

"I hope so. That barrel gets lighter every day."

"Soon, love," Rye rubbed her shoulders, thumbs gliding over her shoulder blades.

Felicity yawned, rubbing her eyes. "Let's see that leg."

"Aren't you too tired to be hovering? You walked a fair piece today."

"So did you. What did you wrap around Cosmos' feet?"

"Buffalo leather. I've been saving it, thinking I'd use it for harness repairs. The rocks are hard on her feet and she'll go lame on me if I'm not careful."

"That crack Left's got isn't healing like it should."

Rye grunted, closing his eyes. He shivered and rolled on his side.

Felicity plucked at the side lacing on his buckskins.

"Madam? May I help you?"

"Bandage time."

"Still trying to hover?"

She unlaced the buckskins further. "Still resisting?"

"I'm too done in to fight. Have your way with me."

"Shhh. Aggie will hear you."

"Guessing by the snoring going on above our heads, she's too far gone in sleep to hear us."

Felicity rubbed her hands together. "Excellent. Buckskins, please."

"Fine."

"That's my line."

Rye stripped the buckskins away from the wound. The smell of the dirty bandage reminded Felicity of rotting cheese on Uncle Jasper's farm.

"When was the last time you changed the dressing? Fort Hall?"

"Not long ago."

"Define that, please."

"We don't have water to waste on it."

"We do unless you want to change your nickname to 'Peg Leg' Jones."

"It's all right." Rye reached down to pull up the dusty buckskins.

"Hold it right there, Dr. Jones. I know what to do."

Felicity fished around in the satchel she used for a pillow. Clean linen in her lap, she unwrapped the caked on bandage, wincing as she tugged it apart. Balling up the used bandage, she tossed it from under the wagon. Holding her breath, she opened a small tin with "Chocolat de Vouvrais" on the label.

"That smells worse than me, Daniel and you put together."

"It will work until we get to water for a proper washing. And just so you are prepared, we will be repeating this process as per the instructions in the pamphlet I got the recipe out of." She worked the salve over the sloughing edges of the wound and over the black scab. With the cleanest linen she found, Felicity wrapped a bandage around his knee. Rye loosened and retied the knot.

He lay beside her, arm curled under his head.

"Rye?"

"Yes, love?"

"You're awfully quiet."

"It is a quiet night."

"No fooling. You could hear an ant crawl. I've never been away from the sound of frogs and crickets for so long."

"Must be the lack of water."

"Could be."

Rye rolled onto his side and rubbed his stubble chin on her shoulder. "I'm thinking we should turn back."

"What?"

"I'm thinking – "

"I heard you the first time. We're not turning back. We're not the Larkins. We didn't come all this way just to turn tail and retreat."

"You sound like Cade."

"No, I sound like you. We have got to this point. According to the map we should be almost half way. Can't be all that much left to go."

"Suppose this has been a mistake. I can't have you and Daniel dying in the desert. We should put it to a vote of the company before it is too late to head back to Fort Hall."

"I'm not dying anytime soon. I promise you that. I'm not quitting. If you want to go back to Fort Hall, be my guest. But I'm pointed towards Fort Boise."

"I'm too tired to argue."

"You're too tired to try to make sense out of all this. You're carrying the responsibility for all the families on your shoulders. Turn in early tonight and we'll push harder tomorrow."

"I think I've finally got you figured out. It's not that you won't quit, it's just that you don't know when to quit."

"I know when to quit, I just won't quit. Not on you, not on us. We'll make it, but only if we keep going."

He folded her into his embrace and kissed the top of her head.

"I love you," she murmured against his throat.

"You have me, heart and soul. No room for doubt."

Rye's pale skin beneath the crust of grime worried her. She put the back of her hand against his forehead and his lean cheek. She pressed her hand on her cheek.

"You feel warm to me."

"Really? I'm feeling kind of chilled. Must be the heat. Should have spent more time in the saddle and less time on the trail." He took her hand in his, raising it to his mouth. He blew air against her palm, making a gassy sound like Daniel moving from breast milk to soft foods. "Can you stand to have me sleep beside you, stench and all?"

"I can't imagine why not. Can you stand me in all my grimy glory?"

Rye wrapped his arm around her ribs and pulled her against his side. "With pleasure, my love. With pleasure."

The Dutch oven thumped on the floor of the wagon above their heads. "Would ya two lovebirds go to bed so this old lady can get some sleep?"

"Aggie's rules." Felicity snorted.

"Let's turn in for the night. I'm ready to curl up in our quilt and shut my eyes until sunset."

Long after Rye closed his eyes and his breathing slowed, Felicity rolled on her side, staring out at the crumpled bandage glowing in the sun. If it burst into flame, it wouldn't surprise her.

The thirst, the dirt, the fear choked her, squeezing her throat, cutting off her air. She took deep breaths, forcing air into her lungs. The tight band around her ribs ached, her heart clanking in time like the pewter dipper in the barrel.

Daniel's chest rose and fell. She focused on that exchange of air, letting it calm her.

She brushed the damp hair from Rye's forehead. Her

fingertips registered the heat and sweat. The wound beneath the linen bandage was infected, she was certain.

And yet this man curled around Daniel would give his life for a child that was not his, for a wife he barely knew, and for an old woman who spent her days on a feather bed in the back of the wagon.

What man loved like that? Certainly no one she knew in New York.

What man agreed to a marriage like theirs? A marriage nothing like the one she expected to have with Edmund Ormond. With Rye, she pulled her own load. Meek and obliging was not practical on the trail and she suspected in the Oregon Territory as well. That she did not have to hide her education was a gift. Critical thinking and a quick mind were valued.

Who knew that she would love Rye? Or that he would love her? Aggie was certain of it long before Felicity considered him with affection beyond gratitude for supplying fresh game.

Rye twitched in his sleep.

What did he dream of? Was it water?

The lack of water ate at him. The worry consumed him, drop by drop. The clouds gathered and she was certain he cursed them under his breath when they withered, withholding the rain. Holding each precious droplet away from him, like a bully teasing a weaker boy.

"Serena," he murmured.

She scraped her teeth over the cracked skin of her lips, tongue tasting the salt from her sweat.

Of course he would have dreams of his earlier life.

It is natural.

He was married to Serena, had a son with her.

Buried them.

Because of Father.

I've got to get a handle on myself. If I go to pieces like Phoebe Landon did back at the Narrows, Rye won't be able to deal with it.

She curled on her side, tucking her fist in Rye's palm.

AT DAWN ON the sixth day without finding water along the trail, Rye limped into camp and a smell burned Felicity's sinus passages and brought tears to her eyes. She dropped the shovel and clapped her hand over her nose and mouth.

"Oh, Rye, what is that stench?"

"Haven't you ever smelled a skunk?" He held up the black and white striped carcass. "Surely there's one or two to be found in the great state of New York."

Dodge hobbled into the shadow of the wagon. He lay in the dust and licked his bleeding paws.

"You'll have to excuse Dodge. He called on the local skunks on a regular basis back home."

The dog stayed clear of the skunk.

"Can't say I'd fault Dodge … I have no idea how to cook a skunk."

"Doubt this is in your repertoire and God willing this is the last time we have to resort to eating one."

"You skin it, I'll figure out what to do with it."

He nudged the shovel handle on the ground. "Burying it isn't an option."

"I was digging a trench with the hopes of keeping a campfire lit in this wind. Didn't know about your prize until you came down wind."

"At least we wouldn't have to worry about Dodge digging it up."

"Being that it's the first fresh game we've had since the fort, we might as well be thankful for what we have and make a feast of it."

"That's my girl." Rye placed a pouch filled with fat leaves in her hand. "I found these while Dodge and I were scrambling around on the flows. They taste about as I figure the skunk is going to taste, bitter as all get out, but it gets liquid into your body. Make sure Aggie chews a few these as well."

"She's asleep."

"She was sleeping when we pulled out last night."

Felicity put a leaf in her mouth and chewed. Tart juice filled her mouth and making her pucker. She spat out the leafy remains and popped another leaf in her mouth. "Rye, how long do you suppose she has with us?"

"I can't say for certain. This part of the trail has been hard on her ... hard on everyone."

"She's got a touch of a fever today."

"I'm not surprised. Keep her out of the sun as much as possible, and like I said, make sure she chews those leaves. Best we can do is to keep her comfortable."

"Too bad Cade Braedon isn't around to spark a round of matchmaking for her. Ever since she was successful with us, she's wanted to try her luck again."

"Try to convince her to work her charms again when Daniel is a little older."

Felicity smiled, picturing Daniel courting a young lady. "Should we tell his potential bride that for the first several months of his life we called him 'Baby'?"

"Aren't you glad you named him?"

The skunk tasted like dirt and the smell hung around the campsite. Rye burned his shirt to get the scent off of him.

After supper, Rye leaned on his rifle at the edge of the encampment. The lava beds spread out and over the edge of the horizon. He folded his hands, bowed his head. The thunderheads failed to build in the morning. Not a high cloud or ripple of wind.

Felicity rubbed the lump where her collarbone mended, reminded of Hannah watching over the prairie, listening to a voice that only she heard.

Did Rye listen for Serena's voice when he prayed for water?

IT WAS THE dream.

She punched down the instinct to run away, run far away from what was caged behind the door and turned the knob.

It was her mother's bedroom in Almstead House. The pee soaked rugs, ocher wallpaper on the walls, the cracked Delft tile on the fireplace proved it.

Faith Millicent Sinclair twisted around in a wicker chair to face her, a Pekinese pup asleep in her lap. Put a frame around her and she was the portrait of motherhood.

I will survive this, I will survive this, Felicity chanted to herself.

"You dare to come in here?" Her mother's mouth a tight line. Sparks exploded from her eyes.

Felicity's heart beat like she was two gasps from drowning in the Hudson River.

Faith Sinclair burst into flames, crushing Felicity against the ocher papered walls. A burning scream caught fire in her throat.

Her mother was killing her, killing her.

"Sweetheart, wake up." Rye's voice, his arms wrapped around her hips.

Felicity dug her nails into Rye's hands.

"Easy girl." He used the same tone to calm Cosmos after a bad spook. "Breathe. Catch your breath."

She inhaled to the limit her lungs allowed.

"Better?"

"Fine."

"What brought that on?"

Fear.

Fear I am like Mother.

Fear you are still in love with Serena.

Fear you blamed Father for her death.

Fear you chose the Sweetwater trail to punish me in place of Father.

"Nothing." She curled away from him, facing into the dawn wind with the hope it blew away her pain.

"Was it the skunk?"

"It's the heat. It's baking my brain."

"Have faith. We'll find water soon."

The embers in Felicity's chest flickered.

"Go back to sleep. I'm fine."

AT DAWN ON the eighth dry camp, Daniel laid in a wet diaper on a quilt in the shade of the wagon. He waved his fists, hungry and needing a change. Felicity worked water into flour to make spoon bread. Maggie's breast milk slowed under strain, but she nursed Daniel whenever Felicity asked. Felicity caught herself staring at the chest bones on her friend when Daniel fed.

Dodge barked at the rocks next to the campsite, yanking on the rope that tied him to a wagon wheel.

"Hush!" Felicity kept kneading the dough, not looking up to see what Dodge was after. Rye left camp to hunt for water, leaving Dodge behind. The dog's paws were raw from the lava rubble.

"He's steppin' all over Daniel," Aggie wheezed, slumped on a barrel.

"Morning, ladies," Lane Crandall called. He leaned his rifle against the side of the wagon and pulled up a crate next to Aggie, the last stop on his daily prayer route.

He took her wrinkled hands in his and kissed the bony ridges with cracked lips. "How's my favorite parishioner today?"

"I'll get Daniel fed and changed so you two have some peace." No fresh diapers, no way to wash the dirty ones. She turned the dried diapers to the outside so the cleanest fabric was closest to the baby. If they did not get to "la riviere boisee" soon, she planned to cut up one of Hannah's old dresses.

I'm not going to call the Snake River by its name. But I can't wait to see that tree lined river at the end of the cutoff.

"Can't ya get that beast to –" Aggie coughed and couldn't catch her breath.

A rattlesnake sounded a staccato warning.

Felicity's head whipped up. Coiled beyond the edge of the quilt, a small rattlesnake flicked its tongue. Daniel's fists waved, and the snake shook its tail.

Dodge lunged, the rope cutting into his neck.

Felicity grabbed the quilt border with doughy hands and scooped Daniel and the quilt into her arms.

The snake struck, thumping against Felicity's skirts.

Shoving Daniel into Lane's arms, Felicity kicked the snake with her red trimmed boots. Lane yanked her backwards and she shrugged away, picking up a drawer front in the campfire but dropped it when the brass hardware seared her hand.

Lane groped with his free hand for his rifle, struggling with a wailing Daniel. The rifle slid down the side of the wagon, pointed at Felicity. She caught the muzzle before the rifle hit the dust.

Felicity froze, hand on the muzzle.

"Use the dang gun!" Aggie croaked.

Felicity whipped the rifle up to her cheek and put the writhing snake between the sights.

She jerked the trigger. The rifle butt smacked her cheek.

Hard.

Pieces of snake peppered the rock.

"That's my girl!" Aggie crowed. "Did he get ya? Pull up yer skirts and check."

Gripping the rifle with shaking hands, Felicity bent over and vomited.

Rye hallowed, hobbling over the blocks of lava and into the campsite. He glanced at the snake bits and his wife clutching Lane's rifle.

Rye put his palm up and limped to Felicity. "Serena, put down the rifle."

Her heart pounded in her ears, buzzing from the shot. His words rang clear. The name hurt worse than the rifle butt smacking her cheek.

Rye wrapped his fingers around the barrel of the rifle and pulled it from her sweating hands.

"I'm not Serena."

"What?"

"You called me Serena."

He stared down at her, grey eyes clouded with pain. He shook his head to clear his head. "Are you sure?"

"Why would I lie about something like that?"

"My head is half fried in this heat. It's seeing you, with a rifle in your hands …"

Sobs broke free of her chest. "I didn't see it. It could have got Daniel."

The pain in the grey eyes above her was too much. She leaned her head against Rye's chest, and he wrapped his arms around her, crushing her against his chest.

He passed the rifle to Lane, who held a screaming Daniel. "My thanks, Lane. We'll be voting tonight. Keep going or turn back."

"Good shooting, Mrs. Jones." Lane passed the boy to Rye. He pressed Aggie's hand and strode away to find his campsite.

"I'm sorry I wasn't here. Good thing Aggie's praying more these days or you'd have been without a rifle."

She wiped her eyes and straightened her apron. "Did you find water?"

"No."

Aggie lurched to her feet and picked at the ties holding the shovel to the side of the wagon.

Felicity pulled the shovel off the wagon. "Diggin' a well for all of us?"

"Need to bury the snake's head. But if I strike water, I'll bathe first and let ya know after."

"You rest." Rye took the shovel from Felicity. "I'll do it. I should have been here."

"Guess its fittin' since yer wife shot it," Aggie grinned. "At least she didn't go puttin' a new dent in the Dutch oven."

Felicity caught Rye's sleeve and he swung the shovel up to his shoulder.

"There's a vote?"

"Seems only fair."

"Mind sharing which way the election will go?"

"We haven't voted yet."

"I've got to get Daniel to water."

Rye's grey eyes were granite hard. "Are you saying you want to go back to Fort Hall?

"I'm saying we need to get to water. Whether that water is in the form of a creek, lake or snow, we need water. I know there are snakes all along the main trail. But there is water. What good are two or three weeks of time saved if we're dead from thirst?"

"If we go back to Fort Hall, we will hit snow over Mt. Hood."

Felicity pulled her hand back from Rye's sleeve. "Then we go forward. That would be my vote."

FELICITY KNEELED BESIDE a leather wrapped trunk and inhaled the spice scent. The varnish was scratched, the dovetailed joints loose. Two dresses, a prayer book covered with her grandmother's embroidery, and a stack of letters piled on her knee.

Her father's walking stick, splintered on the bottom but

serviceable. She set it aside.

Serena. He called me Serena.

Did he long for his first wife? He did not have much time to mourn her loss before joining the wagon company. Did he yearn for Serena because she was taken from him? Her cheeks burned. Rejected, this time for a girl she never met.

Oh, she was married to Rye, but would they ever have a chance to be free if both were anchored to the past? The wedding ring slid over her knuckle. She made a fist to keep it in place. Perhaps it would be safer to return it to Rye.

"Anything else coming out?" Rye's cheeks were grooved, etched by dryness and exhaustion. What drove him to stay in the saddle? She would have turned back days ago. But he kept everyone moving forward.

"I'm done." Felicity wiped the sweat from her eyes. The canvas covering kept the heat in the back of the wagon like a lid over a boiling pot.

She passed the walking stick to Rye. "This is for you."

"It was your father's, wasn't it?" He did not move to take it from her hands.

"It's not a snake, it won't bite you." Felicity's voice faltered. "Better you use it than your rifle as a crutch. I don't want end up like Marta Schneider."

Rye cupped her chin. The kiss pulled at the splits in her lips, but the gesture warmed her. Perhaps he did care for her; perhaps Serena's name an accident.

She slipped a hand between his shirt and skin, burrowing into him. "I miss this."

Rye snorted. "I'm sure this will be more popular after a proper bath."

"Before, after, does it matter?"

The arms around her tightened. Listening to the thump of Rye's heart, she didn't care if the buttons on his shirt left round marks on her cheek. Peace, for a moment from her heat addled thoughts.

Rye picked up a painted fan. "What's this?"

"Something silly I kept." Edmund presented her with the fan on a country outing. He said it was to keep the bees from landing on her sweet lips or some nonsense like that.

"You kept this after I told you to dump what wasn't necessary?"

She tossed the fan out the back of the wagon. "Happy?"

"Very."

"Then here, maybe you should keep this as well." She slipped the wedding ring off her hand. "It's pretty, not practical. Just like me."

Rye slipped the ring back on her finger and kissed the sapphire. "I'm sorry. I'm a … well I can't think of the bad enough word. I'll leave that up to your imagination."

He slid the ring back and forth over her knuckle. Breaking a string off his buckskins, he slipped the ring off her finger and wound the leather three times around the thinnest part of the band and tied a knot. He bit off the long ends. "This is more than a fan, isn't it? It's because I slipped and called Serena, isn't it?"

Felicity pulled back, but he tightened his fingers and pushed the ring back on her finger.

"It's not the first time you've said her name."

Rye traced the bones on the back of her hand, waiting for her to speak.

"You called out her name in your sleep."

"Listen, my love. You are my wife. I love you beyond all others. Beyond Serena. Perhaps I've done you a disservice by not sharing more of my history with you."

Felicity gulped. She wasn't prepared for a history lesson on the Garrety-Brown Railroad scandal.

"Where do you think the wound on my knee came from?"

"I assumed after meeting Cade that it came from your military service." She smiled a crooked grin.

"Serena shot me after our boy died. She was distraught,

blaming me – and rightly so – and you had that same pain in your eyes."

Felicity choked. In her imaginings, Serena was good and pure not at all the type to pick up a gun and fire it at Rye.

"Oh."

"I'm just lucky. Her aim was worse than yours."

"Here." Felicity laid the walking stick in Rye's hand. "I'll let you throw Father's cane. Bet you can't hit that boulder."

"Which one?"

"The black one."

"Darling, they're mostly all black."

"I know. I'm letting you know how much I appreciate your aim."

"Come here, squirrel."

CHAPTER 21

Lost
August 14, 1851

On the evening of the tenth dry camp, the Jones' wagon was the first in line. The lava beds were behind them, but the heat was constant. Felicity stumbled beside Right with her bonnet banging against her shoulder blades. The bonnet trapped heat against her skull, and she could have sworn she wore the Dutch oven on her head.

To pass the time, she made up recipes. Cherry cobbler. Lamb stew. Roast chicken. Might need a rotisserie in the new house. Apple cider. Need to get a press.

Cosmos picked up the pace, trotting forward with ears pricked.

Right lowed, cracked nostrils flaring. Left shook his horns, picking up the slack in the harness.

Striding as far as her skirts allowed, Felicity repeated one plea; let water be ahead of us.

At an outcropping rising off the trail, Rye stood up in the stirrups and pulled up the mare, pushing his planter's hat back on his head. He dismounted, dragging his bandaged knee over the cantle of the saddle. He eased his foot onto the gravel.

Lane Crandall sidled to Felicity's elbow, curious to see why the wagon company stopped in the middle of the trail. Felicity shoved the leading rein into his hand.

Lurching over the field of boulders that separated the

outcropping from the trail, Rye rested his hand against the red streaked rock outcropping and grinned back at Felicity.

Water.

"He did it," she whispered.

Lane let out a whoop. "Thanks to you, all merciful God, for leading …"

Word spread. The wagons emptied.

Felicity didn't stay to hear the rest of Lane's words and grabbed the silver ladle from Aggie. Pulling her skirts up over her knees, she stumbled through the boulders to Rye.

She didn't bother to listen for snakes, the buzzing of the wagon train behind her blotted out the wind rattling the dry glasses and the rocks rolling out from her red trimmed boots.

This must be the cave.

This meant five days to the Snake River. Five more days and they were safe.

A grey pool reflected the outcropping above it. Enough water to refill the barrels, to spell the cattle. To bathe in, but that would be a waste.

They would have to set up a bucket chain over the rocks to move the water from the pool to the trail.

Everyone would drink their fill of water tonight, and for the days to come.

"I can't kneel. Fill the ladle, my love." Rye's voice cracked with relief.

"Is it a spring?"

The overhanging rock hid the pool from the sun's drying rays during daylight. She braced herself on the ledge and filled the ladle to the brim, passing it up to Rye. Drops splashed on her palm and she wiped her face with the droplets, not caring if she made mud.

Rye closed his eyes, raising the ladle to his mouth.

Grey eyes flicked open. He sniffed. He considered the red streaked outcropping. Scraped his boot against the white rim above the water level.

He sipped, swishing the mouthful. He spat it out, dropping the ladle, not caring where it landed.

Rye wiped his lips on his sleeve, and Felicity wasn't sure if tears weren't in his eyes.

"Keep the cattle moving," he croaked.

She picked up the ladle and dipped it into the water. The stars reflected in the bowl of the ladle.

Rye slapped the ladle to the rocks, water splashing her wrists and boots.

"Rye! What's wrong with you?"

"The water is foul." His voice broke.

She expected to see a deer carcass or something rotting in the water. "Can't we boil it?"

"It's alkaline. It will kill us and the livestock faster than going thirsty will. Keep them moving."

"You can't mean that. It's cruel."

"Better to be thirsty than to be dead. Just a little while longer, darling, and you can drink all that you want."

"Are you sure this isn't the cave? Do you want me to get the map?"

He thrust the ladle at her. "Get back to the wagon and move on."

She turned the ladle over, savoring the water on her hands. Was it better to die of thirst or gamble on foul water?

"But Rye –"

"Do as I say, woman!"

The buzzing at the wagons stopped like crickets. One voice started, and another picked up. Lane Crandall clasped his hands in prayer again.

She dropped the ladle into the rocks and stumbled back to the wagon, the rocks scraping her shins. Taking the leading rein from Lane's hand, she waited for Rye to give the command to move forward, ready to beat Right and Left from the water. No cattle, no way to move their supplies.

"Don't cry, Mrs. Jones. He'll guide us to water."

She wasn't sure if he meant Rye or God.

Felicity followed Cosmos and the ladle clanking against the silver rosettes on the saddle, forcing each step toward the Oregon Territory and away from the pool. She imagined a tree lined river, the burble of water, the pebble bottom pressing against cold numbed feet.

A handful of miles away from the outcropping the wagons passed three graves, a bleached ribbon fluttered at the join in a cross wedged into a mound of rocks. An hour later, they filed past the weathered corpse of a pack mule, the pack still strapped around the ribs, bones poking through the strips of hide like driftwood in the moonlight.

Felicity turned to watch the wagons strung out behind her. The red streaks across the horizon meant dawn.

Another dry camp.

Another day to hope for water.

NO CLOUDS THAT day, no clouds the following night. The storm the Indians predicted and Rye relied on failed to arrive.

Felicity chewed a broken thumbnail. The wagon train halted twenty minutes ago and no word passed back from the front.

Must be a wheel off or an ox dead in its traces. Can't tell whose it is.

Johann Radnor stalked past his wagon and brushed by Felicity.

"Mr. Radnor, will you tell me –"

Radnor ignored her and strode back to the Cavanaugh rig. Five minutes later, the men from the wagons behind her walked to the front of the line, single file. None of the men met her gaze, studying their boots or the rocks or the moon.

She waved to Sadie Cavanaugh.

"May I borrow Grady to keep hold of Right?"

Felicity picked up her skirts. Trotting and walking quickly when her ears rang, she confirmed that the Radnor, Watson and Anderson outfits had intact wheels. The livestock stood head down, eyes sunken, alive.

The men gathered around Rye and Cosmos. A flutter in her chest made her start forward, but she stopped. He found water. It had to be. One inch remained in the barrel. Not enough to keep the oxen alive much longer.

Cracked hands held Cade's map spread on the ground, a lantern added to the moonlight. The dry wind teased the edges of the map.

"How do you vote, Rye?" Pug Watson leaned over the rock. "This is your friend's map. You get us out of this."

Rye rubbed the back of his neck and tilted his planter's hat forward. "I vote we keep going. I'll ride ahead and mark the way."

Felicity slunk back to the wagon, trailing her fingers along the rough rocks.

Grady sat cross legged in the trail with Right's leading rein wrapped around his thin wrist. She knelt in the dust, and gripped the twelve year old's shoulder. He wasn't much taller than Felicity.

"Thanks," she choked out.

"My pleasure, ma'am."

Rye grasped her elbow and steadied her. The bleak grey eyes confirmed her worry.

They were lost.

"Grease the hubs and check Left's hind foot when Lane calls the next halt."

Felicity nodded, staring at the puffs of dust the wind kicked up. Aggie coughed in the back of the wagon, breaking Felicity's stare.

"Let me take a look at your leg."

"No need to fuss, love."

"It will just take me a few minutes. Sit."

Salve applied and bandage changed, Rye ran his fingers through a strand of Felicity's hair. "The curl has gone out of it."

"And to think I tossed those curling irons out of the wagon miles ago." She held his hand, kissed his knuckles. "How bad is it?"

"We should have turned back when we had the chance." His voice cracked.

He spread the map on her lap, making a copy of it on the end page of Aggie's bible.

"This is for you. Lane has Cade's drawing. I want you to be looking for a rock cairn."

"The rocks look alike to me ... red streaked, greys, black –"

"Cade told me it's like a pillar. It means that a slot cave with water is nearby. Should be about 500 feet off the trail. To the north. If ..."

"I know, you've told me. Once we find the cave, it is five days travel to the Snake River. Mark the way so that we can find you in the dark."

"And don't forget what I told you about the Blalock brothers. It's anyone's guess if they are tailing us."

"Marcus and Pete. I feel bad for them if they meet up with Aggie. She'll set those boys straight."

Rye crushed her to his chest. "I swear we will get out of this."

"What is it that you are always telling me? Have faith, Rye. Have faith."

"I have that in you."

"SHEEP SHEARS? WHAT about my embroidery scissors? Seems they might be a bit more suitin' ... why, I jes might lop off an ear."

"Your choice. Just do it before I change my mind."

"Are ya sure, girl?"

"If you want me to ask Marta to cut it off, I will."

"Just makin' sure ya not drunk on heat."

"Cut it all off. As close as you dare without nicking my ears."

"I'll have you know I sheared sheep right alongside Jasper and never once spoiled a fleece."

"Yes, but what happened to the sheep's ears?"

Aggie worked the shears over Felicity's head. Long sun streaked clumps fell into the dust.

"Got to say, it ain't bad. Ya might be settin' a new fashion." Aggie slapped her thigh.

Felicity ran her hand through the shortened locks. Greasy, but with the weight removed it had a wave of its own.

"Good thing I got rid of the curling tongs when I did. Probably wouldn't have had the courage to do it."

Splat.

"Did you hear that?"

"What?"

"That sound. Like something dripping."

They were quiet for a moment. Felicity brushed prickly hairs from the back of her neck. "Guess I'm hearing things."

"What do ya think Rye will say 'bout yer hair?"

"Not sure, but I'd guess he'd say it's practical."

It was practical. She packed Left's hind foot with grease and wiped her hands on her apron without having to tuck a strand of hair behind her ear.

At least the grease is helping to heal my hands.

But the linen apron with the deep ruffle at the hem could surely stand on its own, the starch a mash of dried food and grease.

Splat.

Splat.

Am I losing my mind? I swear I hear water dripping on the other side of the wagon.

Do the rocks hide a spring?

Splat. Splat. Splat.

She pulled the pamphlet cover from her bodice and turned the penciled map so it pointed west to the sunset.

No stone cairn. The twelfth dry camp. One more sunset before she allowed herself to expect Rye to return.

Or I calculated wrong. It could happen.

My math skills are wanting.

If this is the spring, where is Rye?

Splat. Splat.

She lunged to the other side of the wagon.

The water barrel lost a droplet of stale water.

The wood staves had shrunk and cracked, allowing the drops to escape.

Tearing a strip from her apron, Felicity jammed the fabric into the gap. She dipped her hands into the grease bucket and rubbed the mixture over the barrel staves.

I can't bear to open the lid.

How long the barrel leaked was a question she couldn't answer on a dare. She swallowed, her throat raw. She would worry over the leak later.

Later, after they found Rye and water.

Splat.

Another leak. More cloth. More grease.

"Ready?" Aggie leaned on the back wheel, watching, silver mixed in with the raven black hair. How those silver hairs dared to grow at Aggie's temples was a wonder to Felicity. Aggie's body may be failing, but the older woman's eyes were alert.

She rubbed grease from the bucket into the chapped skin around her aunt's mouth and kissed the wrinkled cheek. No use talking about the barrel.

"Ready."

ON THE SECOND day of travel after Rye left, Felicity belched into the back of her hand. She chewed a bit of spoon bread. It served as breakfast, or was it dinner? With the nighttime travel and the daytime sleeping, Felicity wasn't sure if she should call it a morning meal or supper.

Whatever it was, it stuck in her throat. Dropping her plate she whirled and made it to the brush outside the wagon.

Her hands shook. Bile burned the back of her dry throat. She smelled it, tasted it. Holding her skirts out of the way, she leaned over and vomited into the brush. She waited, hunched over, and vomited again.

"Here, girl, take this."

Felicity wiped her mouth with Aggie's crusty handkerchief. Shuddered. Braced for another round. Her empty stomach heaved, but nothing came up.

"How far along are ya?"

A flash of Hannah's face in labor sprang up. Felicity tamped it down, not wanting to relive the details of Daniel's birth. The preparations Hannah made for the birth of her son. The swaddling clothes and diapers from earlier "disappointments" filling a wicker chest.

"I'm not ... with child."

"Are ya sure?"

"No."

"Does Rye know?"

"What? That I walk out of camp to deposit my dinner in the weeds? I hope not. And don't you go telling any tales on me, Aggie Sinclair. I don't want to add to his worries."

"If he's half the doctor I figure him to be, I'm sure he's got it figured out."

"I just don't think a ... another baby, right now, would be the thing for us."

"Bound to start a family at some point, Missy. Can't go on bein' afraid of bein' a mother."

"Who says I'm afraid?"

"Now, don't go gettin' yer bloomers in a bunch. Ya done for Daniel as good as his own mother would have done, had she lived. Ain't anyone else in this troop who would've cared for him as well as ya have. But don't ya see? Ya beat yer demons."

"Speak plain, Aggie. What are you going on about?"

"Yer mother."

"We don't talk about her. Ever." Felicity twisted the handkerchief around her fingers. She tightened the fabric, cutting into her dry hands.

"I think yer afraid yer just like her."

"Am not. Are we through?"

"Not a chance. Can't ya see yer nothin' like her? Ya may look a little like her, and frankly that's a blessing ya didn't take after yer father's side in looks, but ya got yer father's heart."

"And look where that's got us."

"Don't be bitter, young lady. Yer father loved ya as much as any father ever loved their child. It's just that sometimes a parent can't help but make a bad choice when it comes to their child. He thought he was providin' for ya, he just didn't go about it in the most lawful of ways."

"Like Rye is doing for us now. Out there, somewhere. Why he chose to honor the company's vote and take this God forsaken route."

"God hasn't forsaken us, darlin'. He's testin' to see if our faith is with us."

"Mine got tossed out somewhere on the trail."

"Nah, it's there. Otherwise ya wouldn't be wearin' out yer boot leather. Ya may not be ready fer it, but it will jump up when ya need it most."

"And don't you think now would be a good time?"

"In time, darlin', just ya wait and see if yer old Aunt Aggie ain't right."

Felicity shook her head. "I'm not sure who is more

stubborn, you or me."

"Both of us. We're of the same stock, ya and I. When yer wanderin' boy comes back, ya need to tell him about gettin' sick."

"I'll think about it."

"It might inspire him to get us to the Snake River a little faster."

"The inspiration is there." Felicity stuffed her cropped hair under her bonnet and tied the ribbons. "Just wish I knew where Rye is."

"He'll be back. With water, if I'm a bettin' woman."

"My worrying over Rye is what's making me sick. His leg doesn't seem to be getting any better, and he's on his own ..."

Aggie's gnarled fingers undid the button at the top of her bodice. Felicity blinked at the bones thrusting up under the wrinkled skin.

How could Aggie be so gaunt and still draw breath?

"Help me with this," Aggie coughed. She held a carved ivory cross on a gold chain in her hand. "I can't get to the clasp in the back."

After Felicity undid the clasp, she laid the chain and cross in Aggie's creased palm. Her aunt kissed the yellowed ivory, and pressed the piece into Felicity's hand.

"I'd like ya to have this. My grandmother gave it to me when I married yer Uncle Jasper, just as her grandmother gave it to her when she married her Mr. Peterson in Bannockburn. I don't have a granddaughter to share it with, and I'd be honored if ya would wear it in memory of me."

"Oh, Aggie. It is lovely."

"If you hold still, I'll help you with the clasp."

The chain and cross were warm against Felicity's skin. Too bad the hand mirror rested on the lava fields.

"Fits you just right. Like it was made for you."

"I'll treasure it, and pass it along to Daniel's bride when the time comes."

"Kind of fun thinkin' about our little scrapper gettin' hitched one day, ain't it? It's like us goin' on into time, through generations of family yet to come."

"You're in a deep mood tonight."

"I'm tired. I'm ready to sleep for a long time."

"Well, let's get you tucked into the back of the wagon. Mr. Crandall will have us on the move before the sun sets."

"He's a fine man, darlin'."

"Lane? I know you like him."

Aggie nudged Felicity's shoulder with the back of her hand. "I'm talkin' 'bout the man ya went and married. I'm right glad ya took my advice and took him up. 'Bout time ya had someone good happen along in yer life."

"It seems to be working out. But then I have a feeling you knew it would."

"When ya get as old as I am, my dear, ya find that ya was right about a lot of things."

"Sleep well, Aggie."

"That's my plan."

FELICITY HELPED AGGIE climb into the back of the wagon and waited for the older woman settle onto the feather bed.

She took the red trimmed boots off, peeling her socks down and stretched out beside Daniel. She twitched her pale toes in the sun. She was a patchwork of color like one of the Indian horses on the plains; some parts white, some parts browned by the sun.

The baby scrunched up his legs and kicked, fist wrapped in the yarn hair of the plaid doll with blue stitched eyes. She loved a doll like this, so unlike the figurines with porcelain molded lips and starched pinafores in the Chinoiserie chest. The doll her mother swore to burn. Felicity tucked the doll, wrapped in white tissue, between the rafters in the attic of the

Almstead House. And like that doll, Felicity hid in the attic when her mother was angry.

Daniel let go of the doll to tug on the gold chain around Felicity's neck. He put the cross in his fist and into his mouth. Felicity pulled it out of his wet hand, tucking the ivory into her bodice.

The boy screeched and she propped the plaid doll on her stomach, making it dance a jig with the hope of Daniel's eyes closing.

Felicity envied his innocent sleep. No worries about the next meal, no worries over finding water or shelter. What did he dream of, in that infant world? Clean diapers? She reached down to check his diaper. Wet. Daniel cried, face red.

Getting to water wasn't about her thirst.

She changed the diaper, but he did not settle. The diaper fit him loosely. He was thin, but not to the point of Aggie or herself.

"Hungry little man?" she crooned. Felicity reached for her boots.

Hopefully Maggie McHenry can't sleep either.

Felicity pressed Daniel to her chest. She patted his back, singing a song with jumping cows and the moon. She wandered to where she could watch the herd.

Her stomach rumbled.

Am I with child?

I remember Daniel's birth. The blood. The pain. Hannah's passing. But what if the child doesn't love me or what if under the strain of two children I turn out to be more like Mother than I care to be? Could I hurt a child, the way Mother hurt me? Could I hate a child, withholding my affection? Is it in me to shun a child's love?

She shuddered, pushing the thoughts of her mother away like a rotted trout. No good will come from these thoughts, she mused.

She missed Rye's lanky body on the quilt. He calmed her

mind, gave her peace. If she carried a new life, the child came of a loving union. Surely any child would be welcomed by Rye, on the trail or in a cabin somewhere in the Willamette Valley.

She traced the lines Rye marked on the rock pile beside the McHenry wagon. The chalk arrow meant go straight. Before he rode out of the encampment, Rye told her when she saw three white slashes next to the chalk arrow, it meant he loved her and Daniel, and he was thinking of them on the trail.

She strolled away from the herd, following a single track of hoof prints. They had to be Cosmos' tracks.

No movement ahead on the trail. Scrub brush and rocks and burning daylight.

If anyone could find water on this trail, Rye could.

She wasn't giving up on him, any more than he was giving up on her.

A BREATH TICKLED her eyelashes.

She flinched. Must be dreaming.

A warm breath brushed her ear lobe. Her eyes flicked open.

"Rye!" she squeaked.

"Expecting someone else?" The grey eyes glowed like moonstones above her. She blinked. The deep grooves of his cheeks showed washing. And shaving.

Dodge nuzzled her neck. She pushed the wet nose aside, groggy in the heat.

Rye ducked his head and grinned. "Brought you a souvenir."

A full metal canteen.

She coughed, inhaling the water. Her lungs burned. The sun warmed water lapped at the edge of her thirst.

"Slow down, darling. More where that came from."

THE CAVE RAN underground beyond the reach of daylight. The game trail in and out of the cave was broad, but not wide enough for a wagon. Johann Radnor organized a bucket brigade, and Philippe Patelle danced a polka up and down the lines with his violin playing "One Day While Working on my Plough" to keep the buckets moving.

Felicity sang off key, the blisters building under calloused on her palms worth the water passing by her to fill the barrels.

The men voted to rest the company until the evening of August 17th. September would find them on the trail from Fort Boise to the Cascades; hopefully they would reach Oregon City by early October.

Aggie clamped her bony arms around Daniel. Both napped. The cave didn't interest her and she stayed at the wagon. Felicity got an earful when she took a linen towel and soap to her aunt's thin limbs. When it came to more intimate areas, Felicity handed the washcloth over and stepped away.

With clean diapers drying in the wind, Felicity curled up next to Rye. He played with a strand of her fresh washed hair.

"I like it. I wasn't sure at first, but it's practical."

Felicity snorted a laugh. "I told Aggie that's what you'd say."

"It has a curl to it, not being weighed down."

"Or forced to curl. I know, it's more natural."

Rye closed his eyes, fingers rubbing the nape of her neck. Finding a knot, pressing and nudging it to release.

"Doctor Jones, how do you know when a patient is with child?"

"Depends on the patient. You thinking Johann is beginning to show?"

Felicity ducked her head to keep from laughing. "The man puts away the meals of three men." She nudged his leg. "Let me change that bandage for you."

"Someone come to you and ask?"

"About your wound?"

"Child bearing, Squirrel."

"No."

Rye's face tightened. "Is this a personal inquiry, Mrs. Jones?"

"I want to know the signs."

"Have you been reading your pamphlets again? What makes you ask?"

"The pamphlets do not contain much on the subject. I believe the writers did their best to protect the delicate sensibilities of their lady readers."

"Keep talking."

"Aggie will tell you anyway if I don't …"

"Already has."

"Well, aren't you the rascal for making me go through all this?"

"I want you to feel comfortable that we can talk about anything. Anything at all. There will be times when we might not feel like talking, just like there will be times that we can just look at each other and know what the other one is thinking."

"Can you tell what I'm thinking?"

"Maybe, after everyone is asleep." He pulled her close. "Know what I'm thinking?"

"You married a woman with no clue that being a mind reader was a requirement?"

"I was thinking I worried you more by leaving than if I had stayed with the company."

"You found the cave. The barrels are filled. Right and Left are sloshing."

"Should have kept closer."

"I didn't know your being gone would affect me like that."

"Missed me a little?"

"We've been together since April. Every day. The landscape around us changed, but you've been a constant. Like the north star."

"And I always will be. I promise." He kissed her and passed her the canteen. "Thirsty?"

"No. Just tired."

Rye kissed her eyelids. "Sleep. We're a handful of days away from the river."

"Rye?"

"Yes, Squirrel?"

"What is the chance …"

"You'll appreciate the scientific approach. I observed your habits and determined from a timing perspective there wasn't much of a chance you'd get with child. We're still adjusting to each other as husband and wife. We can wait to give Daniel a brother or sister after we get a cabin raised. Then you can have as many offspring as is healthy for you."

"Rye?"

"Hmmm?"

"Do you think …" her voice failed.

"Yes?"

"Do you think I'd make a good mother? For our children?"

Rye propped himself up. "We never talk about your mother."

"No need."

"Want to talk about her?"

"No." She shuddered.

"When you're ready, then. Only then. But from what I've observed, again, falling back on science, you have been a mother to Daniel when you could have chosen to relinquish that position to some other woman. You've kept him fed, reasonably clean until lately," Rye nodded his head toward the drying diapers. "And loved. Remember when Mrs. Landon took him out onto the prairie? I brought that boy back to his mother, not his caretaker, nanny or some responsible party. I brought him back to his mother. The woman who was at his birth and has cared for him, protected him, when she could have handed him over and headed back East."

"That wasn't a choice – "

"You always have a choice. You picked the tougher of the bunch and I haven't seen you slack off. So if you want my opinion, there it is. You're a good mother to Daniel, and you will be a good mother to our children, should we be blessed to have them."

Felicity blushed. He raised her chin with a finger and made her meet his gaze. "You are a good mother, Felicity Jones, no matter where you have come from, what you have experienced, whatever you endured. You are not your mother."

Tears burned and she buried her face in his shirt. He wrapped his arms around her, letting her cry it out. They slept, the salty drops splattered on his shirt drying in the dry wind.

"WAKE UP, LOVE."

Rye's face was gray and drawn in the afternoon light. The deep lines around his eyes weren't from fatigue. It was pain, plain and simple.

She reached out. Daniel, beside her on the quilt, flushed and warm. Safe.

"What is it? Did I oversleep?"

The grayness in Rye's skin and his bloodshot eyes sent brought back a memory of her father showing signs of cholera.

"Are you well?" she croaked.

"Why?"

"You just seem so … tired."

"You'll get wrinkles if you worry like that." The tone of his voice warned her.

"I'm not hovering. I'm worrying."

She listened for Aggie's cough.

Silence.

"Did Aggie walk up to the cave?"

"No, darling."

She buttoned her bodice, tearing off a button. "Is she all right? Did she fall?"

He grabbed her wrist. "She died sometime last night."

Felicity clenched the button. Pulling the loose thread from her bodice, she rolled the cotton strands into a tight ball between her thumb and finger. "Just like Aggie, to pass without being a fuss to anyone."

"Lane Crandall will miss his sparring partner." Was that her voice, so controlled?

Aggie appreciated theatrics on the stage, not in her niece. No crying, no wringing of hands. Leave that to the Sarah Siddons of the world, she'd say.

Rye gathered her hands in his. His fingers were hot, dry.

"I'll find a place for her …" The shovel was propped against the wheel. Another grave, another service. Another family member left behind on the trail.

She kissed his cheek. "Aggie would tell you to find a place—"

"Out of the sun, so she would be comfortable."

"She'd also tell you to hurry, not to waste time. That we have a wagon company to get on the road. That you need to get us to the Snake River. If you see to the others, I'd like to spend time with Aggie." She dug her fingernails into her palms, hoping the pain kept her from bawling. "I didn't get to say goodbye."

Rye fingered the ivory cross on the chain around Felicity's neck. "Seems to me Aggie told you everything she had to say."

Felicity washed Aggie's slight body and wrapped her in a linen sheet, tucking sagebrush in the folds.

The menfolk scraped a shallow grave in the red dirt and piled rocks on the sheet wrapped bundle to keep animals out. The wind picked up and the mourners kept one hand on their bonnets and the other pressed to their hearts in prayer. After Lane Crandall's brief words, Felicity propped Uncle Jasper's temperature gauge under the cross at the foot of the rock mound.

The families trudged back to pack the wagons. Maggie McHenry lingered. She pressed Felicity's wet cheek to her broad bosom. "You come talk to me when you want a break from your menfolk."

"Thanks for being here, for Aggie." Felicity stood, rooted to the red dirt.

This is the last time I'll be with you, Aggie.

Leaving you is harder than walking behind the wagon when leaving the Father at Lone Elm.

All alone, nothing but sagebrush for company.

Nothing but a pile of rocks to mark your place in my life.

"She was a sweet woman, yer auntie."

"She gave me an appreciation for family I never had." *That family is everything. That all the money in the world doesn't add up to much. That you can lose everything, and still be rich.*

"I'd bet 'er matchmakin' brought more than Doc Jones and you together."

"It was a good thing she went into midwifery." Felicity sniffed, and pressed her palms to her cheeks.

I will not cry, she promised, concentrating on the lace fluttering on the back of Maggie's bonnet. *I'm not that girl crying in the prairie, leaving her father under the grass. That girl, rationing tea leaves and pining for fancy dress ballrooms, cut glass punch cups and fans. That girl needed a boot in the rear.*

The frayed edge of the feather bed poked out. Felicity rolled a rock into place with the toe of her red trimmed boot.

Aggie was right about everything. From boots to matchmaking.

The wagons behind them in the campsite would be loaded and the livestock harnessed. The Oregon Territory was down that trail. A good life awaited her. The man she bet her life on stood beside her, holding her son slung over a shoulder.

"Shh, darling, all will be well." Rye's arm came around her, broad hand pressing her head to his chest. Daniel patted her with a sticky hand.

She took the baby in her arms and nuzzled the curls on his head. Tears welled.

"Daniel and I are all that is left. She was the last connection to my father. And she's all alone out here. Wherever here is on a map."

"Knowing Aggie, she'll enjoy the peace and quiet."

Felicity sniffed. "She did come from a large family."

"And if she were here, she'd tell you to dry your eyes, pack your wagon and get on the trail."

"True enough. I hate leaving her here."

"I'm sure if she had the choice, she'd be leaving with us. But that isn't possible, so we will have to carry on for her. Let's get packed and on down the trail."

She saluted him, palm facing her shoulder. "Aye, aye, Admiral Jones."

"Silly Squirrel. Wrong branch of the military."

"Seeing I didn't know about your military experience, I figured I would cover all the options."

"That's one you can rule out."

She cuddled Daniel against her neck. "Come, family, let us depart. We have miles yet to go before we can call it a day. Or a night. This travel schedule has me turned around."

"Just march, recruit. Right is giving me the squint eye like I've kept you from his company long enough."

Rye stumbled over a rut and wrenched his leg. He bit off a curse and grabbed Felicity's shoulder.

"Rye!"

"Ripped it … open … there's blood."

"Mr. Watson! I need help!" Felicity shoved her shoulder under Rye's armpit.

"I'm not a cripple. I can walk."

Rye took a step and crumpled.

"Thought you had a fever. Stubborn man."

"Gotta get the wagons – "

"We're getting you back to the wagon and if I have to tie you down, I'm getting a sight of what's under that bandage."

"Bossy wench. Sound just like your aunt."

Pug Watson and his son Peter carried Rye and eased him onto the tailgate of the Jones' wagon.

"Sorry Rye. Wife's orders."

The wound bled. But it wasn't the blood that made Felicity blanch. Pus and red streaks radiated around the wound like a stylized sun burst.

"Doctor Jones, what do I do with this?"

"Wrap it up and finish getting the cattle hitched."

"Try a different answer. If that knee was Left's hock, and I didn't want to leave the wagon behind, what would you prescribe?"

"Cutting away the black flesh, dressing the wound. Rest. There's not a cure for –"

"Kind words only, husband."

Rye hissed, shifting his weight on the tailgate.

"It's bad, isn't it?" Felicity helped to steady his leg.

"It's not good. Not by a long shot."

"I'm not joking."

"I might be losing my leg, I'm not losing my humor."

"You're about as good humored as Left."

"That's it. Medical lecture is over." Rye slid off the tailgate and braced an arm against the wagon. "Look. It's fine. I can ride."

"Pug?"

"Aye, Mrs. Jones?"

"Fetch Mr. Crandall for me, please."

"What are you about, Mrs. Jones?" Rye with a heavy dose of suspicion in his voice.

"I'm doing what you would be inclined to do ... I'm putting it to a vote."

"You're not serious."

"Watch me."

"What do you want out of all of this? To prove yourself right? Well, you're right. It's infected. I let it go too long. My fault. This is all on me."

"It's on us. And we're not moving until you talk me through what I need to do. I didn't request Mr. Crandall's presence just for his vote. I asked for him because I can't do this alone."

"Do what?"

"You're about to make me the second finest surgeon this company has."

Felicity wrote the instructions Rye gave her so she would know what to do if he passed out.

The last thing he fought her on was the laudanum. He wouldn't take the vial from her no matter how hard she pressed him.

"I can handle the pain. Do not give laudanum to me, no matter how I beg."

She cut away the dead flesh, Lane holding the lantern and Pug's hands steadying Rye's leg. She avoided watching Rye's hands clenching the top of his thigh, looking up only when the grip slackened.

Lane's hand shook and the light wavered. "He's out, Mrs. Jones. Get a move on."

After midnight, Rye twitched in his sleep.

"He's coming around," Marta Schneider shook Felicity's shoulder.

Rye's eye lids cracked open.

"Darling?"

Rye reached down to pat the edge of the bandage around his knee. His toes flexed. "Thought you took it off."

"You have a souvenir."

Felicity pressed a metal ball into his palm.

Rye blinked and held it up.

"It practically popped out on its own."

"You took this out?"

"You'll heal better without it."

"Any other miracles you'd like to perform? You couldn't surprise me any more than you have."

"Told you before, my love, I'm not a quitter."

THE FAMILIES WAITED Rye's signal to move out. Philippe Patelle plucked at his violin. The children played a game of tag, running wild through the sagebrush. Their elders watched from drover's boxes and horseback, letting their offspring have a chance at play.

For the first time since they were married, the Jones wagon was not packed. Daniel needed feeding and a wet diaper changed.

Life goes on. Through births and deaths, work needs to be done. On the trail or off the trail.

"Well, wife, we're back to where we met. We're late packing up." Rye steadied himself on the tailgate of the wagon.

"Bet I can be ready before –"

"Halloo! I say, halloo!"

Rye turned and shaded his eyes with his planter's hat.

Three men on lathered horses leading a string of pack mules and a flashy chestnut horse came up the trail from the east.

Lane strode up to stand beside Rye. "I thought we were the only company on this spur."

"Who is it?" Felicity shook out her skirts. "Some of the Larkin party?"

Rye pulled the brim of his hat lower. "Could be trappers. They're travelling fast. Nine mules. No wagons."

Felicity squinted. One of the riders rode straight backed.

"Isn't that Captain Braedon?"

"Cade was heading up north to Canada. Fetch me the rifle."

Lane grabbed Rye's arm. "Maybe it's the Blalock brothers out for a lark."

Felicity slipped away to the back of the wagon and pulled on the butt end of the rifle. The muzzle caught in the scabbard, and she stopped. Not wanting to cause a panic if it went off, she turned to Rye to ask for his help.

One of the riders was Cade Braedon.

I recognize him from the way that man rides, shoulders back, legs dangling off that Appaloosa crossed mule.

Looking like he could spend the day and into the evening in the saddle.

Then ride more.

"The rifle?" Rye's voice, terse, snapped her out of her reverie.

But the other rider. The dark hair, the hands gloved on a hundred degree day.

"Oh, my ..."

PART III

The Trial

1851

CHAPTER 22

Found
August 18, 1851

A rattlesnake buzzing in her head warned her. Felicity left the rifle part way out of the scabbard and yanked the brim of her bonnet down, wanting to melt into sagebrush like a rabbit.

Dust flew up from the arrivals, carried on the east wind.

"We forget something back at the fort?" Rye's voice cool, neutral.

"I see you can still follow a map. Good to see you."

All Felicity could see from a quick glance was the back of a tall man climbing down from a thoroughbred and throwing the reins to Rye. Dressed in a hunt jacket, the hat on his head would not keep him warm or keep the rain off his face.

Marta Schneider craned her neck to stare at the handsome stranger and what appeared to be a servant. Felicity stepped behind Marta.

"I'm searching for a Mr. Gerald Sinclair and his daughter, late of New York. My guide, Braedon here, indicated they are travelling with your company."

That voice, once desired above all others. It meant sidewalks, buildings, plate glass windows. Civilization. Her skin prickled, her hands icy.

"Felicity?" Rye's voice crackled.

Marta took Felicity by the wrist and towed her forward.

Felicity flinched at the polished toes in her field of vision under the bonnet. A kidskin gloved finger tipped her chin back to examine her features. He might as well be inspecting a broodmare. Flat eyes matched the daguerreotype she left at Soda Springs.

He ripped the ties at her chin and tossed the sunbonnet to the ground. "Filly? Is it you?"

Of course he used the hated name from boarding school. The name shared with all of the young ladies and gents by Sally Munston who branded her with the nickname because Felicity was taller, more awkward than the well-fed pups of New York aristocracy. When she ate to fill herself out like a Clydesdale, the name stuck.

"It is you. Oh my sweet love, I've stopped every wagon train between here and Independence looking for you."

Fingers dug into her scalp. He kissed her, not the gentle buss one might steal at the Drayson's garden party, but a demanding kiss that stung her split lips like a cut lemon.

The bayberry scent he wore burned her nostrils. The scent of spoiled daydreams, ripped pages from her day journal where she scrawled her wedding name to be, mold on a wedding cake.

Felicity ripped her lips from his and wiped her mouth with her apron. Snatching up her sunbonnet, she knotted the ribbons tight under her chin.

"Whatever are you doing out here?"

"My God, woman! What happened to your hair?"

Did he think I'd been scalped?

It was just hair.

"Rye, this is Edmund Ormond. He is ..."

"I know who he is." Terse. Words bitten off.

"Edmund, this is – "

"I was half mad with fear when I couldn't find you and your father. You left so quickly. I stood outside your home after the fire. Mother was certain you had gone to Europe with your father to recover until your letter appeared."

"What letter?" Rye, curt. Grey eyes assessed Edmund's every gesture.

"Trumbo. The case." A leather portfolio of papers fell open, a grimy letter with copperplate script removed.

The letter from Independence. Written at Mawbry's boarding house. Dated March 3, 1851. Before Rye signed on to lead the company.

Edmund handed Rye the letter. She reached for the pages, but he shrugged away from her, reading ink blotched pages.

She remembered the phrases. "Save me from the savages." "This life is repugnant." "How can decent women survive this squalor?" "Buckskin wearing men no better than animals."

Father said she would regret further communication with Edmund. He was right.

Edmund pressed her hand. The comb marks in his hair were perfect grooves, unaffected by the wind. How he maintained his New York polish was a curiosity. Perhaps when one travelled with staff, one's appearance could be attended to.

"How ... did you find me?"

"I purchased the services of guides. I travelled light, with only Trumbo to attend to me since Fort Bridger. I was so desperate to find you that I promised the guides triple the pay if we found you within a month. We found sign that you passed along on the trail, but it took longer than expected. But I never gave up on finding you. A lesser man, perhaps, someone who didn't feel for you as I do, would have turned around. My good fortune came at Fort Hall when I met with Captain Braedon. He assured me that you were on the Sweetwater Trail."

"But I don't understand why you are here. I mean ... I wrote that letter, but ..." She didn't trust herself to speak.

What to do about Edmund?

Invite him to stay?

Welcome him to join the company and a life in the Willamette Valley?

Felicity peeked at Rye's tight eyes. He wasn't a man that took to a stranger kissing his wife.

Rye shoved the pages at Trumbo. "Perhaps you and Mr. Ormond would like to have a few moments in private to greet each other."

She took Rye's hand and pressed her lips to the sun browned knuckles. "I don't have anything to say to Mr. Ormond that you can't hear."

Rye spread his fingers and let their contact drop. He lurched over to the back of the wagon and shoved the rifle into the scabbard.

Her shoulders lowered. He wasn't pointing the rifle at their guests. All would be well.

"Lane can take the company on ahead." Rye's voice, the southern accent pronounced. That happened only when exhausted. "Watson outfit has the lead today."

Rye turned to Edmund. "Why don't you and Mr. Trumbo join us for supper before your guide takes you back to the fort?"

"Cade, there's coffee in that pot."

Cade glanced at Edmund, avoiding eye contact with Felicity. "Water for the stock first, coffee later. Come on, Trumbo."

Trumbo and Cade stripped the packs off of the mules, stringing the baggage along the trail. Dodge nipped heels and barked, driving the livestock towards the cave.

Edmund offered Felicity his arm. "May I escort you to a place where we can converse in private?"

"Rye, can you watch over Daniel?"

At Rye's nod, Felicity laid her hand on Edmund's sleeve and let him pull her away from the campsite.

"My sweet girl ... have you suffered? You are so thin."

"Walking twenty miles a day will do that to a body."

"You father never should have embarked on this folly. Where is your father? I need to speak to him and then the company's minister, if there is one, in that order. This isn't St. Paul's Chapel, but I'm here to make you my wife before we return to New York."

"You are too late. Didn't Cade – Mr. Braedon, that is – tell you …"

Edmund kissed her wrist, the thin lips cool. "Surely you can find the words to forgive me. I should have fought for you. But I'm here. I pray that you do not let pride stand in the way of our happiness, our marriage. And anyone who slights the wife of Edmund Ormond may go to the Devil himself. I have the appointment. The seat is mine. You will be the wife of a Senator. A man on the rise. Someone of your own class, your background. Surely Gerald will not object to our marrying?"

"My father is buried at Lone Elm Grove."

"He … has passed?" Edmund rubbed his forehead. "He's dead?"

"Quite."

"Then, may I ask, why did you not return to wait for me in Independence? Surely you knew I would respond to your letter?"

"I had no right to wait for you. Plenty of hope, but no claim on you. Aggie … that is, my Aunt Agnes, chose to continue the journey. She was weakened by the cholera attack that took Father. I chose to travel with her."

"My sympathies, my darling. I did not realize you travelled with family other than your father."

She pressed her thumb over the pearls and sapphire, taking comfort in the worn edges of the stone.

"Even if my father were alive to give that consent, I cannot marry you."

"Why ever not?"

She held up her left hand. The pearls surrounding the sapphire ring glowed. "I am married."

He bowed his head for a moment. "To that buckskinned

ruffian? Is that the reason you didn't you wait for me? Surely you knew I would come for you. You were to be my wife, for God's sake."

"It was clear that I was an unwelcome *parti*. Your mother made her position known."

"But never unwelcome to me. We could have travelled abroad until people stopped talking."

"No one will easily forget the names Sinclair or Garrety-Brown. I don't know why your mother ever allowed the match. Father's money made me acceptable, but there wasn't ever enough money to make me more than barely passable. And that was before the Evening Post editorials."

"We are right together, you and I. You know that in your heart. You weren't raised for this life. Look at you." Edmund grabbed her wrist and pried her fingers open. "This used to be the hand of a lady."

"It still is."

Broken nails on one side, callouses on the other. These hands cooked, sewed, washed. These hands caressed a baby's head, a husband's cheek. Perhaps Edmund was right. The cracked skin belonged to a laborer, not a lady.

"That's not what I mean. You should be cared for, not made a drudge for a yokel."

Anger shot up her spine. Rye was more of a man than the well fed skunk before her. Felicity pulled back but Edmund changed his grip to above her elbow.

"I'm not finished."

"I am and we are, Edmund. Let me go."

"You have to come back with me." He twisted her arm, holding her close. To anyone watching, it would look like a loving embrace.

"I have a husband who will say otherwise. And we have a child to raise."

"A child?"

The Watson wagon pulled out onto the trail, Pug Watson at

the head of his oxen. Lane trotted forward to take the lead, the Robertson wagon swaying into the line.

"I have to pack the wagon."

Edmund laced his fingers through her fingers and they stood, palm to palm. "Come back with me, Felicity. I can make you happy. Just like before. We will marry as we planned. It will be as if none of this ever existed."

He leaned down to her, breathing words of devotion she did not believe. She stared up at Edmund.

How did I ever care for him? His eyes are nothing like the prairie sky, but a blue washed out in the daylight.

How did I ever yearn for polite society and a life where clipped hedges passed for scenery and life was measured by the number of calling cards on a silver tray or pleats in a cravat?

"I am married to a gentleman. And just so there is no misunderstanding on your part, Mr. Ormond, I love my husband and my child. Everything I do for them comes from that love. I have a happy life. Oh, there are hard times, but the good outweighs anything the trail can throw at us."

His fingers tightened. "You loved me, once."

"I did. And that feels like a century ago. For the life of me I can't say what happened to that girl. When Father forced me to leave, I didn't understand why he wanted to punish me. I hadn't done anything wrong. But what life would I have had there? No one received me. We had no money, no position. We left boarding houses without paying for our stay, so we had money enough to pay the tolls to Missouri. Where were you then, Edmund? In an armchair in your club? Rejoicing in your escape from the tar brush?"

"Looking for you. Searching. I hired investigators to locate you."

"You did?" He released her fingers, but stayed close, his knee brushing against her knee. The stance that anyone would see as possession.

"At Mother's suggestion. She loves you like a daughter. No one has ever touched her heart like you."

"There was a time when I would have given my left arm to hear that …"

"You'll see. With Mother's help, you can recover that life. I'll be at your side. No one ever dares to refuse her. The doors to society will swing wide for you. No one will whisper a word against us."

"We had a chance, once. That time is over. I'm sorry you wasted the shoe leather getting here."

"What are you saying? Are you refusing me?"

"Yes, Edmund. In plain terms, I would rather raise my child in a cabin in the wilderness with the … what did you call him? The 'buckskin ruffian' than return to New York with you."

"Then I must congratulate your husband on his good fortune." He bowed with the formality of society.

Felicity's shoulders unknotted. Even if she were not wed to Rye, the Edmund of her memory did not measure up the living and breathing Edmund. She remembered his eyes as Meissen porcelain blue. But the prairie sky proved more intense.

"Returning to your father, my condolences. I know that you were quite fond of him. Did Gerald discuss with your husband the matter that separated us?"

But she did not hear the conversation and Rye did not share what her father said to him. "I … cannot say, for certain." It was not a lie. She did not hear the conversation at Lone Elm Grove and Rye did not share what her father said to him. It was between patient and doctor.

Edmund caught her elbow. "Does the gentleman know of your father's infamy?"

"My husband is a private man, and respects my privacy as well."

"But what if the matter were to be known? Have you

thought of that? I ask, of course, as a friend."

"As a friend I can reply that we would discuss the topic. Thoroughly. Do you think he'd abandon us? Never. My father is dead and buried. There's nothing left but a lot of heartbreak."

"Are you certain that your father did not leave behind any papers? Anything that gave the details of the matter?"

"What is it that you want? Aside from declaring your undying love for me, of course. What is the true reason for chasing after Father?"

"There is an investigation. A committee has been formed. Because of our engagement, I stand accused of involvement with the railroad."

"But our engagement was broken off. Months ago."

"The taint lingers on. And the other board members are not available for comment."

"Of the eight members, you can't persuade someone to make a statement on your behalf? What of Messrs. Garrety and Brown?"

"In London. Unavailable and not likely to venture to the United States to testify on anyone's behalf."

"What about Mr. Wilkerson?"

"I regret to inform you that Mr. Wilkerson has passed."

She gasped.

"Mr. Samuels?"

"He is buried at Hearton Manor."

"Demarais?"

"Deceased. Influenza."

"Waite?"

"Suicide."

"What about his brother?"

"His wife has not seen him since before Christmas. It is assumed he joined his brother. Your father is ... was, the last member of the board who could testify on my behalf."

How can it be that they were all gone, the men who dined

at the long table set with her mother's silver at Almstead House. Dead. Gone. Buried. And yet their victims lived with the board's mismanagement.

"In lieu of your father, your testimony is necessary."

"Why my testimony? I did not know the extent of his dealings. What of the other families? Mrs. Waite is quite fond of you."

"Your father was the secretary. He wrote the contracts, made the stock offerings."

"What about an affidavit affirming to the best of my knowledge you were not involved with Father? Aside from our engagement, that is. I would write that for you. We can have it witnessed."

"That is a generous offer, but not enough. I must produce you, on a witness stand, before the fall term starts. The committee will not accept anything less. Mother has her heart set on being there when I am sworn into office."

"We have to be in Oregon City by October. I didn't come all this way to turn around. I doubt that my word will carry any weight in an investigation. I am not my father."

"You know the censure I face, and not from the committee. My family will not be received by anyone of note. Mother will not fare well in such an existence. She's not bred for that life, if that can be called living."

"You'll find that you can endure. That acceptance doesn't mean what you think. I used to think that way. That wearing the latest hat style or receiving an invitation to the Lordston's ball was living. It is not. This is living … making something of myself."

"You could have that in New York. Remember how we talked of the house we would build, the children we would raise?"

"How you talked. I listened. I fell in love with an illusion of what I thought I was supposed to do. What I thought I should be. What was normal. I wanted it badly. To fit in with polite society. Blend in, be one of the hostesses that everyone craved an invitation from. The one that Mrs. Overton would whisper about, saying to your mother 'I had no idea your daughter-in-law was so accomplished.' And your mother, proud of her daughter-in-law. I wanted to be a good daughter, I wanted her to love me like a mother. To have tender moments."

"You can. It is all there. In New York."

"There is nothing there for me. I don't know how much more plainly I can put it."

"There is nothing I can say to sway you to consider my needs? Out of the feelings you once had for me? You can be made presentable, if you are embarrassed. You hair will grow, your hands will heal."

The Zenger wagon pulled out, the last of the company, canvas billowing and dust blowing.

"I have a wagon to pack and a meal to pull together."

Edmund caught her elbow and jerked her to his side.

She dug her elbow into his vest and pried herself loose.

"I'm no dog to be checked with a leash."

Edmund stepped back, blue eyes wide.

"You stated your case." She held her hand out in farewell. "I wish you a safe trip, Edmund."

RYE LURCHED TO his feet. He squinted down at her. "Daniel's sleeping. I'll see how Cade's getting along with the mules."

"I'll get supper ready, if that is what you still want." Felicity rolled up her sleeves, tied her apron with a square knot. Why ever did Rye offered a meal to Edmund? Out of politeness?

"I won't be long." Rye limped away unable or unwilling to meet her eyes.

She reached into the back of the wagon and pulled out the Dutch oven with its dented lid. Trumbo took the iron pot from her, turning it over, scraping the outside rim with his thumbnail. "Please, ma'am, if you don't mind."

Edmund took her elbow and pulled her towards the campfire. "My dear, Trumbo will prepare our meal. That is his purpose."

"I'm accustomed to cooking. I enjoy it."

What's Trumbo's penalty if I do not comply with his master's wishes?

She pleated the front of Aggie's apron. The red and white squares offered no comfort. Aggie would have sized up Edmund and sent him on his way.

"I promise not to press you on the matter further. Let us have a final meal as true friends."

She pulled the end of her apron ties and hung the apron on a peg on the side of the wagon.

"If you insist."

"Rest, he is doing what he was acquired to do."

"And what is that?"

"Serve me." Edmund patted the seat of an upholstered folding chair before a roaring campfire. "Sit, here, my dear."

She dragged the chair back from the heat and smoke. One chair for her, one chair for Edmund. Trumbo must be accustomed to standing or sitting on the ground.

"Did your mules pack in firewood?"

"Mr. Braedon made it understood that firewood was scarce on this portion of the trail."

"I see."

"Sugar for your tea? I remember how you like it. I'm afraid cream does not travel well without ice to cool it." The samovar on the folding camp table put Pug Watson's find on the trail to shame.

I bet the man has a pack mule dedicated to carrying ice to cool his dairy supplies.

Felicity's lips twitched. "No dairy herd?"

"Too slow. I had the guide release the one beast we

acquired into the prairie. I'm sure it found its way into some farmer's herd."

The waste. The unholy waste of a good dairy cow. What she wouldn't have done for one around Pappin's Ferry. The wolves surely made a grand meal of it.

She sipped her tea. The black brew did not soothe her. This from the young woman who counted out tea leaves. She preferred coffee, but did not want to offend Edmund.

Her fingers traced the brass nail heads on the chair. "You travel very comfortably."

"It was the best I could do on short notice."

Trumbo opened a case. Rows of silver knives, peelers, graters and measuring spoons glittered in the sun. The next case opened contained a bone china service. Gold rimmed. Linen napkins, pressed. That meant an iron somewhere in the baggage.

"No candelabra?"

"The candles melted in the case. I gave the set as a thank you to a gentleman ... Trumbo, what was his name? We met him near one of the ferry crossings."

"A Mr. Landers, sir."

"That's right. He said that you had been kind to his wife."

Felicity's cup and saucer rattled. Setting the cup and saucer aside on a marquetry table, she smoothed her skirts. "Yes, his wife was not well. They turned back. Was she ill when you met them?"

"Who, his wife? I assume so. I did not inquire."

"The gift was thoughtful of you, Edmund."

"I'm pleased that you are pleased."

Trumbo rinsed a sauté pan. The water tossed to the ground made a red slurry.

"Your husband cannot provide a staff for you?"

"I do all the cooking, washing and light chores."

"And you care for the child by yourself?"

"The women in the company have been very kind. I can't

nurse Daniel, but no woman with a child at her breast refused the baby nourishment."

Edmund stared at his tea cup.

She waited, eyes steady.

He shifted in his chair. Tapped his spoon on his knee.

"Forgive me, but I am surprised by your frankness. Where is that blushing maiden I remember trying on hats and worrying if Clarice DuBois used the same ribbon to trim her chapeau?"

Trumbo filled the tea cup at her elbow. The service, unexpected, startled her. The silence of good service forgotten. She didn't remember their names, the names of the Almstead house staff. There was Poole, and Cranston. Just last names, no first names. Only the uniforms of the upstairs maids stayed in her memory. Pointed lace on black cuffs. She stared at that lace in the mirror when Anvelle dressed my hair. Miss Anvelle or Mrs. Anvelle? The brush laid on a shelf in the wagon, Anvelle's hands reflected in another woman's mirror.

"Shall I tell you news of our friends? Sally Munston married."

"Oh?"

"A judge. In New Jersey."

"I see."

"And Burton Langley —"

"Let me offer you my congratulations on the outcome of your election."

The last thing I need is a recitation of former acquaintances.

If he hopes to change my mind by reminiscing, he is in for disappointment.

Better to listen to him prattle on the necktie he wore to his election and the refreshments served at the reception.

"Appointment, actually. But Mother has such plans. She has presidential aspirations."

"For you or for herself?"

"While a formidable woman, she has no plans for herself. She is quite dedicated to my political career. Just as she was to Father's career."

"And she supported your travel plans?"

"How surprised Mother would be at your transformation." Edmund sipped his tea. "Which reminds me. She sent you a gift."

"For me?"

"Of course. I told her of my plans to marry you immediately upon receiving your father's blessings. Trumbo – my Mother's valise."

"That was kind of her, but under the circumstances, I –"

"She would expect you to accept it. I told you, she loves you as a daughter."

"But we are not ... that is, conditions are not as you ... expected."

Trumbo placed the valise at Edmund's feet and flicked open the latches. Edmund waved the servant off and bent on one knee to open the case.

"Mother, and indeed myself, would be disappointed if you rejected her gift. Think of it as a token of our esteem, our friendship."

The pleated satin gleamed. Edmund caressed the smooth material. "It was to be worn on our wedding day."

"I can't, I just can't." She flattened her skirt against her shins, tucking her boots beneath the upholstered chair.

"Wearing the gown would let me view the Felicity Sinclair I knew in New York. The one that I proposed to in your mother's drawing room, in front of your family and my parents. Do you remember that day?"

"She disappeared many, many miles ago. My life is different, here. I've changed to embrace it."

"Of course. But do put on the dress ... for Mother's sake."

Perhaps compliance would convince him to pack his folding chairs and leave. Or at least order Trumbo to pack the folding chairs. If they tarried longer, an arrow in the side of the wagon or a missing mule might influence Edmund to depart.

"As you wish."

"I do."

"I'll be just a moment."

"And you are certain your father did not leave any papers with you?"

"There is a crate of my father's books in the wagon. From his practice. You are welcome to look through the box after I change."

UNFOLDING THE SATIN dress, dried rose petals fell onto the wagon floor. *Maison Gagelin* glowed in gold letters on the white carton. The box smelled like violet and roses, fresh from the hothouse. A pair of slippers with lace ribbons completed the ensemble.

The polished threads in the pink satin, so unlike the homespun threads of Hannah's wool dress.

She buttoned the pearl buttons on the front of the chemise. Settled the whalebone corset above her hips and pulled the laces tight, wrapping the ties around her waist to keep the corset from sliding over her hips. On went the under-petticoat, hoop petticoat, over-petticoat, and the satin dress.

Sweat beaded between her breasts under the weight of the garments and the heat trapped by the layers. Why didn't Edmund sweat? Buttoned, with cravat, starched cuffs. No sign of his body reacting to the heat.

The satin dress hung on her. She hunched forward and glimpsed the cracked boards of the wagon floor between the folds of material.

Perhaps I can get help to cut the gown down to fit once we get settled.

But I gave my word to Edmund.

Eating supper in satin is the least I can do for a man crazy enough to cross most of the country to find me.

And Rye gets to see me in something pretty. Something other than a creek washed dress.

"Soon as they eat, we're hitting the trail." Rye limped past the wagon. Her wide skirt rustled, knocking against the shovel. She caught the handle before it scraped the flour barrel.

Cade glanced up, nudging Rye in the ribs.

Rye gripped the tailgate, "I haven't seen that on you before."

"No, you haven't."

"I told you to get rid of anything that wasn't necessary for survival."

"But I – "

"Is that dress worth killing the cattle for? Or were you saving it for your Mr. Ormond? Hoping that he would come a riding up and sweep you away? To save you from your life of hardship?"

Cade whistled off key and wandered towards the picket line. The mules stood with lowered heads in the sun. He scratched the ears of a black jenny.

Thankful the hoop petticoat caused the skirt to bell and hide the crate of law books behind her in the wagon, Felicity waited until Cade walked out of earshot. "You're bleeding."

"Not your concern."

"You are my concern. My dearest concern."

"Sure about that?"

"I love my life. I love you. There is no other life for me."

"I'm sure he'd take you back, no questions asked."

"I don't want him. I don't want that life. I don't want to lose you."

"How long are we expecting to enjoy his company?"

"I don't know. Come. Eat something."

"You eat. I'm not hungry."

Rye pulled the leather satchel with his initials printed on it to the tailgate. "Where's the laudanum?"

"In Aggie's chest."

"Get it."

"Are you in pain?"

Rye glared at her, grey eyes rimmed with red. "Any other reason you can think of that I'd be asking?"

"You've said that I'm not to give it to you."

"Well, I changed my mind. Haven't you ever had the occasion to change your mind?"

She flushed. Edmund watched their exchange from the folding seat before the campfire, the flames bright orange in the dusk. He turned attention to Trumbo.

Felicity held up the vial. "Here. Would you like me to mix it into some coffee for you?"

"No." He rubbed the band of the sapphire ring on her hand.

"Hurts bad?"

"Doesn't hurt good."

Tears stung her eyes.

"Don't waste any water. Not over this."

"Help me down and I'll get the coffee. It will hide the taste."

"About the dress ... he brought that to you?"

"A gift, from his mother."

The coffee pot rattled against the rim of the tin cup. She passed the cup to Rye. "There is something that we need to talk about."

"This?" Rye held up the laudanum.

"No. It starts with that letter you read."

"Your correspondence was on the dramatic side. What makes you think I'm interested in your old love letters? Got another one you don't want me to read?"

"It affects my future, with you." Felicity ran her thumbnail along the wood grain of the tailgate.

"I'm listening."

"My father was not just an attorney."

"What was he? A butcher? A baker?"

"He was the member of a board of directors."

"Not unusual."

"There were ... irregularities. Misrepresentation of available cash. There wasn't any due diligence. The principals told investors if they didn't like the progress of the construction, to take their money and invest elsewhere. But no one did. Not a one. The initial investors convinced other people to throw their money into the scheme.

"It got so bad that Father wrote to his friends, begging them to withdraw their funding. But they thought he was trying to keep them out of a sure thing. They saw our house, the way we maintained our living.

"You see, he came from wealth ... but his father couldn't hold onto it. So he grew up knowing what money bought. More wealth. Through marriage. He wanted me to have security."

Rye held up the laudanum. "The money was a drug to him."

"Once he started, Father couldn't keep himself from taking more."

"And Mr. Ormond?"

She twisted her wedding ring. "He was my Father's choice. I accepted his wishes."

"Before the engagement was announced, I thought Father had a seizure of some sort. He never left Almstead House. He forgot to bathe, to put on clean clothes. When my maid asked me for her wages, Papa told me it was a misunderstanding with the housekeeper.

"Then I called at the Graydens. Their butler advised me that Mrs. Grayden was out. I went to the Langstons. Then the Van Der Hoffs. No one received me. I asked to see Miss Van Gelder. She was not at home. I asked for Mrs. Ormond ... her carriage was in the drive. She was not in the residence. I asked to wait for Miss Van Gelder. I was told waiting was not convenient. Not that day. Not any day."

At Rye's silence, she plucked the folds of the dress.

"Uncle Jasper was my father's last chance at salvation. I was so desperately unhappy. Against Father's wishes, I left a letter for Edmund, with my apologies and the engagement ring he gave me. I wrote again, after we travelled out of New York, begging him to rescue me from Missouri. The trip to the jumping off point wasn't what Uncle Jasper's pamphlets said it would be. While the family waited for my cousin Hannah to give birth, I waited for Edmund, but he did not come. That was months ago, before we left Independence ... I sent another at Pappin's Ferry, but he must have left New York by the time it arrived."

"And?"

"All my life, my father was hailed as a brilliant legal mind. An ethical man, of highest principles. Sought after for his opinions. But the contracts my father wrote were all lies ... all of five miles of track were laid by the Garrety-Brown Railroad Company. You know the rest. My father is the reason you lost everything that mattered to you."

"I am the reason anything was lost. I chose to invest. No one forced me."

"I am so ashamed."

"And your mother? You never talk about her."

"No."

"Is she – "

"Don't."

Rye held her hand against his heart. He cleared his throat. "Your father and I had an enlightening discussion before he died."

"So you knew?"

"Pretty much everything."

"And you still married me?"

"I told you once, months ago, that I was a bad choice for

you, that nothing good could come of it. I followed your father, with the intent of ending my suffering. I felt that his death, that the revenge I could take for what I had lost, would cure me of the pain. But the end of his life didn't heal a thing. I prayed. I talked to God and prayed all the more. And then there was you. You complicated the heck out of everything. I didn't have it in me to harm you ... I knew what it was to lose a child. I couldn't in good conscience take your father from you. It was apparent that you wouldn't last five minutes on the trail without someone to watch over you."

"Proved you wrong."

"Sure did ... and then some. I didn't have the right or the power to take revenge for what your father did. If he had known me, he would have tried to talk me into taking my funds out. I wouldn't have listened to him any more than his friends did. I'd still be in the same place."

"But maybe – "

"I healed. Just like you are doing. Look how brave you are, talking to me like this. Putting down your baggage. It gets heavy after carrying it for so long by yourself."

"I figured you would run ... or hate me for being my father's offspring."

"Figured wrong, didn't you? You're not your father. You are Felicity Jones. Daniel's mother. My wife. A wife of my choosing. I even took you on before you learned how to cook."

Felicity wiped her eyes and blew her nose. "I knew then it was true love on your part. Or a healthy constitution."

"Like I've said all along, the past is the past. There is nothing you can do to change what happened."

Rye tipped his head towards Edmund sitting by the campfire. "And he can't change the present any more than we let him."

"MY DEAR, I would like a word with your ... Mr. Jones."

"Rye?" Felicity did not trust Edmund to treat Rye with respect, although her former betrothed's elocution fit the polite tones of meeting an acquaintance at Niblo's Garden.

Rye put the yoke on the ground. "It's all right. I'll speak with Mr. Ormond."

Cade took the water bucket from the back of the wagon and grasped Felicity's elbow. "Why don't we go top off the water barrel? We're looking at days without water."

"We? Are you planning to join us?"

"In a manner of speaking, you might say that." Cade helped Felicity up the path to the cave.

Edmund tucked a portfolio under his arm and grasped his poie de soi lapel. All he needed was a podium on the floor of the Senate. "Thank you for this opportunity to –"

"Speak your piece and be done with it." Rye dumped another dose of laudanum into the tin cup. Stirred the hot brown liquid into the coffee with his finger.

"A direct man. I like that."

"Don't have time for speeches. Not today." Tipping back the cup, Rye drained it.

Felicity picked up the satin skirt and turned to look back at him.

Is she trying to tell me something?

The laudanum is making it so I can't think straight.

"I will be plain. I am returning to New York with Felicity. I am prepared to offer you a substantial sum of money for you to forget you ever met her, much less exchanged vows with her. I assume that this sham marriage was entered into for convenience's sake due to the death of her father and has not been consummated."

"Didn't think you'd be telling me you were joining the company. But Felicity is clear in her intentions. She's not leaving with you."

"She doesn't belong out here. Felicity is a creature for a drawing room in the Capital rather than a crudely made cabin. She deserves the best that life can give her ... that I am in a position to give her. Why keep her in homespun when she is so lovely in satin and lace? I saw you, watching her. She was raised to manage a household, not be a maid servant in her own home. Free to take her proper place in life."

Rye examined the rivets on the tin cup.

"I ... ah ... have the means to make a fair settlement for her time with you."

"What?"

"I'll pay you a fair amount for you to forget you ever met Mrs. Edmund Ormond."

Rye threw the cup against the side of the wagon. "I've heard just enough, you milk fed weasel. No man is paying me money for my wife. You can stuff it up your –

"I believe Felicity confessed our past challenges."

"What brought you out here? Surely not just the affection you feel for my wife."

"My wife, you mean."

"Pardon?"

"Surely she told you – "

"That you were engaged at one time. She broke it off."

"The truth is Felicity left me to face the brunt of the scandal her father caused. That is the word of a gentleman and future Senator. Do you require proof that she is my wife, not yours?"

Rye crossed his arms.

Edmund opened his coat and withdrew a small blue box. "This is the ring I gave her. The ring she left behind." A ring no homesteader could afford.

"Good one, Ormond. You had me there for a moment."

"I dislike causing distress, but here ..." Edmund opened the leather portfolio and pulled out a newspaper. He held it out to Rye.

"It is the New York Post dated June 1, 1850."

"So?"

"Oh. My pardon. You do read, do you not?"

"I read just fine. What is it that I'm looking for?"

"Halfway down the page ... you can't miss it."

Rye flattened the paper against his thigh and scanned the page.

Married

Last evening, by the Rev. Dr. Wintre,

Edmund Charles Ormond, Esq.,

to Felicity Sinclair, daughter of

Gerald Augustus Sinclair,

all of this City

Rye crumpled the paper in his fist.

Burning the page in the campfire wouldn't take the words from his memory.

Edmund held his hand out for the paper. "If her father were alive, he could attest to arranging our engagement. He was very involved with the planning of the wedding as Felicity's mother ... was ... indisposed. As for additional proof, will a copy of the marriage certificate suffice? The original was duly filed with the county clerk."

"What's your game?"

Edmund held up a receipt from the Fairview Hotel and Hot Springs. "This is a receipt from the hotel where we spent our honeymoon."

"And how was the view?"

"What do you want me to say? That I came this way because Gerald Sinclair had something that I wanted? How ridiculous. What man wouldn't pursue a beloved wife?"

Rye took a step backwards.

Edmund opened the portfolio.

"Do you want to see a certificate?"

A black bordered certificate. The names blurred.

"Do you want to read it?"

Rye rolled his head back, loosening his tense shoulders.

She lied.

I can't stand to touch the certificate. No need to read the names.

Just like her father.

Disappointment bitter, like the laudanum. There weren't enough vials to dull the rage, the pain.

As much as he wanted to, he couldn't kill Edmund. He'd learned that lesson with Gerald Sinclair.

Felicity had to live with what she had done to both men. And Edmund was her best ticket for survival. She should live the affluent life she was raised in and think about the independent life she forfeited.

Cade returned, bucket sloshing. Felicity looked to Rye, concern puckering her brow. The hovering look. The satin glowed in the light of the campfire. The color was lovely with her skin. Out of place on the trail, but right for a drawing room.

He turned away. When he glanced up, Felicity joined Trumbo at the folding table and examined a boning knife under lamp light.

"And the boy?"

Edmund snapped the portfolio closed. "Your son?"

"Yes, Daniel. You'll take Daniel?"

"If that is the only way that I will get Felicity, well … then, yes. We can perhaps leave it with someone on the trail. They can raise it for a laborer. Surely she will become accustomed to its loss."

"Don't try to separate them. She would never forgive you."

Rye cleared his tight throat. "Cade. Join us."

Cade walked up to Rye. He took the laudanum vial from

Rye's hand and held it up to the light. "Leg botherin' you?"

Edmund glanced from Rye to Cade. "Our witness?"

"What all am I witnessing?"

Edmund shoved his hand at Rye. "Agreed, then? Felicity and the child return to New York."

"Wait ... hold on here," Cade grabbed Rye's arm. "Your head clear enough for this?"

Rye stared at Edmund's soft hand with buffed and trimmed nails.

Those hands, caressing Felicity's back, clutching her, pleasing her ...

He spat on the ground. "Agreed."

"As I mentioned, I am prepared to make a generous settlement with you."

Rye grabbed the vial from Cade's hand. He took a swig straight from the laudanum vial. "I don't want your money."

"You jest? Or is this just your way to extort a high settlement?"

"No. I don't want it. Give it to Felicity. Or better yet, give it to the victims of the Garrety-Brown Railroad."

Edmund grabbed Rye's arm. "Are you mad?"

"Just sick."

"Is it cholera?" Edmund backed away from Rye, wiping his hands on his vest.

"Don't worry, you can't catch what I have." Rye turned to Cade. "I need to you do something for me."

RYE CLAPPED THE saddle on Cosmos. The mare shied, crashing into the wagon. He tightened the girth with a savage pull. The mare kicked out.

"Rye?" Crouched in the nest of quilts under the wagon, Felicity braced a hand on the wagon box. "Daniel's sleeping."

The bit, jammed into the mare's mouth, pinched the

sensitive lips. Cosmos threw her head in the air, rearing away from Rye.

"What's wrong?" Felicity crawled out from beneath the wagon, shaking out the satin skirts. Cosmos shied away from the rustle, wild eyed.

Rye shook out the bridle, draping the reins over his shoulder.

He inhaled, deep. Took another breath. Let the air hiss out between his teeth.

Cosmos calmed.

Felicity waited, hands twisted. Palms sweating.

Rye braced his hands on the saddle. "Why didn't you just tell me the truth?"

"I ... I did."

"The entire truth?"

"Y-yes."

"What kind of man do you think I am? The kind that would steal from another man?"

"What?"

"Did you take me for a wife stealer?"

Felicity gawked at him.

"Get that stupid look off your face. You can't twist your way out of thish'."

"Whose wife? I'm married to you."

"Not any longer. Seems you had a prior commitment."

"You knew I was engaged."

"Mrs. Edmund Ormond have a familiar sound? Things get rough in New York and you decided to run away? You are your father's daughter. Spittin' image of him from where I'm standin'."

"What?"

"What do they do in New York? Pull you aside and teach you society folks how to be crooks? Or ish' it somethin' borne in you? Daniel's got a right prideful life to look forward to."

"You aren't making any sense."

Rye swayed and caught the saddle horn. "No? What about the marriage certificate your beloved Edmund flashed in my face? Got a good story on how that came about?"

"What certificate? We were never married!"

"Why would anyone other than a husband come all thish' way after you?"

"You aren't making sense." She grabbed Rye's hand.

He twisted away from her grasp. Raised his hand. "Doan' touch me."

"He wants me to testify for him. In court. That he was never involved with my father. How much laudanum –"

"Not enough to blot out the sound of your voice." Rye sucked the laudanum vial dry and pitched the bottle into the sagebrush. "You're going back with your Edmun' in the mornin'."

Felicity grabbed his arm and hauled him around to face her. "No, I won't. My place is here with you."

"Your place is at a cotillion. Or shoppin' for gowns. Or whatever it 'ish you society women do. You're takin' Daniel and leavin' in the morning."

She reached for the girth on the saddle but he shoved her hands away.

"I'm not –"

"You'll do ash' I say and that's the end of it. I … I deserve a clean break. You owe me that mush'."

"You are my life."

"Forget you evah' met me."

"You are my husband. The only one I've ever had."

Rye spread his arms. Cosmos and Felicity flinched. "I releash' you."

"You can't just ride off because Edmund showed up, uninvited."

"You invited 'im. You deal with 'im. He's your 'responshibility."

"I can't believe we're arguing over this. We promised until

death do us part. Far as I can tell —"

"It wash' a bad idea from the beginning. We aren't suited for each other. You said so yourself. I'm just a buckskin wearin' rube."

"How can you hurt me like this?"

"You're 'jes hurting yourshelf. Over nothin'."

"Don't you feel anything for me? Was it all a lie?"

Rye tightened the girth on the saddle. She tugged his arm to turn him to her but she might as well been pulling Left away from an open sack of grain.

"With Aggie dying and Edmund showing up, everything is a jumble. You're slurring your words. You're in no condition to ride."

"And you're in no 'poshition to tell me what to do, Mrs. Ormond."

"Quit calling me that."

"Get used to it. 'Ish a title you wanted more than anythin' you once told me."

"That was before."

"Then 'ish your misfortune."

"Let's just get on the trail and talk it through in the morning."

"You 'woan be here. Heck. I can start all over again … this time with someone I know mush better. Marta Schneider needs lookin' after. She can cook. Proven breeder an' a fine mother. I know she doesn't have a husband alive to chase after 'er."

"Rye!"

"Have a pleasant journey, Mrs. Ormond."

"I'm begging you."

"We're done. Get that through your head, Mrs. Ormond."

"You … hate me?" Felicity stepped back. She needed something to grab, something to keep her upright.

"Ish' all I can hold onto. The only thing that stays with me."

"Rye!"

Rye snatched the rife, slinging the leather scabbard over his shoulder. Hauled himself onto the saddle. Warbled a whistle for Dodge.

"Please, oh please, don't do this to us."

Rye glared down at her. His eyes grey glacier ice.

Spurring Cosmos onto the trail of wheel tracks, Rye bent over the mare's neck. Dodge raced after his master.

Bunching up the layers of her dress, Felicity ran after the sound of hoof beats. Breathing in the dry wind, she forced herself pick up her knees and lengthen her stride.

If I can get him to stop.

To stop and think.

To talk.

The slipper ribbons cut into her calves, the soles fraying against the stones.

She pressed her fists on her knees to take longer strides.

Tripped, fell. Got up again. Ran.

Felicity stopped to get her bearings. Was she still on the trail? The hard packed dirt, scrubbed by the wind, did not show hoof prints or wheel ruts.

Feet bleeding, chest heaving, she sank to her knees.

Wrapping her arms around her ribs, she vomited.

"Please, come back to me."

A whisper.

A plea.

A prayer.

Midnight
August 18, 1851

"Quick, man. Get that crate open."

Trumbo pried the lid back and removed each book, stacking them on a square of canvas on the dirt. Feeling each panel of the crate, he rapped on the sides and the bottom of the wood.

"No false bottom, no sliding panels that I can find."

"Any contracts, anything of interest?"

"Just this, sir."

Edmund flipped through the pages of the Donation Land Act and held the pages up to the lamplight. No hidden text showed through the paper fibers. He licked his fingers and tried to separate the paper edge, but it rolled and frayed. A single piece of paper, not two pages glued together. No hidden words, no word gram or puzzle.

Nothing hidden.

He tossed the pages into the campfire ring. The page browned and flames punched a hole in the upper corner. The edges curled.

Felicity's dreams of the Oregon Territory turned into ash and floated on the heat current.

"And the rest?"

"Just books, sir."

Edmund inspected a book, checked the lining the binding, the end notes. He picked up another book, inspected the lining. No notes in the margins. The pages, crisp, flipped under his thumb. Pages uncut.

Nothing between the stiff pages. Nothing in the spine.

He tossed the volume back into the crate. Picked up another. Flipped through the pages. Five books inspected, Edmund dusted his hands on his trousers.

"He must have been thinking of opening a practice in the Oregon Territory."

"What shall I do with the books, sir?"

"Burn them."

"Sir, if I may," Trumbo waited for his employer's nod before proceeding. "Do you not think Mrs. Ormond would notice their loss?"

Edmund tapped the crate with a polished toe of his boot.

"Repack the crate. They will serve as a memento of her adventures on the trail. A reminder of the life I saved her from."

CHAPTER 23

East
August 19, 1851

Crumpled on the trail, satin skirts twisted awry, she dug her fingers into her scalp. Discarded, set aside like a hand painted set of dishes too frivolous to stay with the wagon. Who needs bone china when pottery will serve the same purpose?

Rye never left anyone on the trail. Was this the revenge he wanted on Gerald Sinclair's daughter? To change her life, and take pleasure destroying any trust she would ever have?

It had to be the laudanum.

Strong hands grabbed her shoulders and help her to stand.

"Steady, there."

The wrong hands, the wrong voice.

Felicity swayed, feet burning. She gulped, forcing air into her lungs.

"Cade, please. Go after him. He's not well."

"Can you walk?"

"He's still bleeding. You have to help him."

"He's his own man."

"But he is not himself."

"Shhh."

"Why aren't you listening to me?"

"Calm down, Mrs. Ormond."

A wildfire streak of anger straightened her spine and she shoved him away. "That's 'Mrs. Jones,' to you."

"According to Rye, there's a piece of paper that says otherwise."

"Edmund and I were never, ever married. Just ask him. I am married to Rye and was married to the man before God and a whole wagon company. My father —"

"If he were here, I'm sure your father would testify to that. But he's not. And I'm not sure what stock Rye would put in your father's statement. Rye made me swear to see you and Daniel through to New York."

The anger in her turned to ashes. "He did what?"

Cade bent and swept her up into his arms. He flattened the folds of her gown to see over the mound of lace and satin.

"Put me down."

"Not until you can be sensible. Rye charged me with looking after you, so this is me, looking after you."

"I'm going after Rye. I'll steal a mule if I have to."

"And what am I going to do with your child?"

Daniel. Caught up in Rye's fury, she forgot her son. Forgot her duty to Daniel. A reminder that her decisions were not solely about her life.

"Thought that would make you come back to sense."

"I'm not going back. I'm not going anywhere with Edmund."

"I'll tie you to the drover's box if I have to."

"Lay a hand on me and Rye will kill you."

"What are you going to do? Chase down a man who doesn't want you?"

"He's got to see reason."

"We don't know each other very well, but I know Rye through and through. He's hurt. Bad. Go to New York. Leave the man in peace."

Felicity's head bounced against Cade's shoulder.

There has to be a way back to Rye.

If I take the sling for Daniel, a mule and enough supplies to catch up with the wagon train, Rye can surely be made to see the truth.

He has to believe me.

"Felicity, my dear, are you injured?" Edmund met Cade at the edge of the campsite.

Cade set Felicity on her feet.

"Well, Mr. Ormond, Felicity and I were just reaching a mutual understanding regarding our travel plans."

Edmund pressed a handkerchief into Felicity's fist.

She threw the silk square at him and wiped her tears on her sleeve. "Don't touch me. Don't ever touch me."

"Trumbo, tea, please. Mr. Braedon, will you see that everything is in order for an early departure in the morning?"

Cade looked from Felicity to Edmund. He pulled on the brim of his hat and strode into the dark.

"I don't want any stupid tea. You need to order Cade to ride out after Rye."

"I would my dear, but I don't think there is much we can say to Mr. Jones will be of any help. He is quite determined. Calm yourself."

"It is 'Doctor' Jones." Felicity batted away the tea cup Trumbo offered. "I want to see this proof that you have."

"Pardon?"

"You have something that says we are man and wife."

Edmund's eyebrows shot up. He pressed a hand to his cravat. "My darling, while my hope is to be united with you in marriage, I ... possess no such document. You are welcome to look through my personal papers if you wish."

"But Rye said —"

"I'm sure he said a lot of things, unpleasant things —"

"Rye doesn't lie, if that's what you're inferring."

"Far be it for me to paint a false picture of your alleged husband."

"Meaning?"

"Do you have a certificate of your marriage to Mr. Jones?"

No piece of paper to document the night out on the

crushed prairie grass. Aggie in the light of the bonfire. Rye teaching her the steps to a dance, holding Daniel. Whispering in her ear. Walt Anderson's guitar, the sound board whole. Philippe Patelle's violin.

"Were there witnesses to the wedding?"

"Yes. The wagon company."

"A company that may, or may not, survive to rejoin the main trail to the Oregon Territory."

"Edmund, where is this going?"

"I'm trying to illustrate for you that I likely saved your life, and the life of your cousin's child."

"My son."

"Call it what you will."

"His name is Daniel."

"As you wish. But your Mr. Jones, if he survives, will be a wealthy man landowner."

"Rye isn't a wealthy man."

"He is now."

Felicity stepped back. "What have you done?"

"I've said too much."

"Explain yourself."

"Mr. Jones requested compensation for his expenses and care of you during your passage on the trail. In return for a substantial sum, he pledged his word to forget he ever met you, much less exchanged vows with you."

Her stomach felt like Left kicked her, hard. Breath short, heart sticking to her ribs. Not beating right.

"I don't believe you."

"No? Should I summon Mr. Braedon, who was witness to our arrangement?"

Edmund waited, hands spread.

Daniel stirred on the quilt under the wagon.

Breathe in, breathe out. Listen to the crackle of the fire.

"Wait. I need to understand."

"If I make the request, I am certain Mr. Braedon will affix

his signature to an affidavit confirming the arrangement."

Rye took money from Edmund. He sold her to Edmund. To a life with Edmund.

"He was not heartless, my dear. There are provisions."

"What?"

"The child. He was most adamant that I accept the boy as my own family member."

Daniel, unwanted as well.

It was a lie.

It was all a lie.

He lied to her.

Rye lied.

Right and Left waited for their grain.

"Let Mr. Braedon alone. His statement is unnecessary. I'll get the team settled for the night."

"Rest, darling. Mr. Braedon will see to it."

"Fine."

CHAPTER 24

*Leave Taking
August 19, 1851*

Felicity found the smooth apricot striped silk stitched into the quilt under the wagon. Aggie joined the last triangle at Sheep Rock.

Darling Aggie. She would approve of the bundle and the canteen under the bedding.

Daniel stirred, whimpering in his sleep, kicking his thin legs.

Kissing the baby awake, she tucked him into the sling with the canteen hanging between their bodies. Enough water to keep them going until she reached the wagon company.

Daniel cried. Felicity crawled out from the quilts and slid the bundle of food and Aggie's bible into the sling on top of Daniel.

Cade rolled over and flipped the blanket over his head next to the wheels of the wagon. Too bad the wagon was too heavy to roll or she might have pinned the man to the rocky ground with it.

No light from Edmund's tent. Trumbo slept on a folding cot outside the tent, ready to serve.

Whatever proof of marriage Edmund possessed had to stay behind.

She walked the perimeter of the camp two times, the picture of an innocent young mother soothing a restless babe.

She stepped around Cade.

His boots, next to his head, tempting her.

I just can't steal the man's boots. Even with him believing Edmund over me.

But I can trade him for something more practical.

Felicity found Right with his nose to the ground, his breath stirring the dirt. She rubbed the sweat marks from his ribs and wiped the crust from his eyes. She kissed the oxen on the withers, breathing in his smell for the last time.

"I can't risk taking you." It cracked open her heart to leave him behind, the sturdy trail companion who never failed her.

The wagon, the supplies, the oxen had to be left. In the morning when he learned she was gone, Edmund could take out his anger on the wagon, probably shooting holes in it with a dueling pistol. Felicity relied on Cade's instinct not to waste good livestock. The oxen would fetch a good return at Fort Hall after time off with good feed.

Taking a bridle and the flashy chestnut mare's side saddle and girth, Felicity shuffled to the picket line of mules and horses. Which mount to choose? Something to make time with so Edmund had less of a chance to run them to ground on Zeus. The thoroughbred stallion lost his sleek look and short cropped mane from his racing days but retained the long stride that put his owner in the money every time.

She needed a sturdier mount than the chestnut mare with the white socks and blaze Edmund purchased for her. The lack of water and sharp pace set by Edmund wore the mare to a sour state.

At the Appaloosa crossed mule, Felicity dropped the saddle and bridle.

Two oxen in exchange for one mule is a fair bargain. It was better than stealing his boots.

She put the coarse woven saddle cloth on the mule, then lifted the saddle into place. It fit, rising above the mule's withers. Probably the first time the beast wore a lady's saddle.

At least he didn't kick me.

Girth buckled to the point straps on the far side, Felicity stepped around the mule to buckle the other side. She reached for the girth under the belly of the mule and pulled, but the girth stopped three to four inches shy of the saddle flap.

Okay, so no saddle.

Just a bridle.

Dumping the saddle and blanket, she shook out the bridle and slipped the halter off, buckling it around the mule's neck. The mule accepted the bit, but she couldn't pull the bridle over the beast's long ears and no adjustment of the cheek pieces could make it fit the mule's large head.

Felicity dumped the bridle on the ground.

Okay, so no bridle.

The mule's halter and lead rope would make do.

But how to get on the beast with Daniel and without stirrups?

Keeping the canteen between herself and Daniel, Felicity shoved the handkerchief wrapped cornbread into the pocket of her apron. She could go without a meal, but Daniel could not. She held Aggie's bible, the gold stamped letters flaking off the cover and the gilt edges worn grubby from use.

I can't leave this. Aggie's hand was never far from this bible, and she's got favorite passages marked that she always turned to.

I've hauled a crate of law books this far; I can ride with one book.

Felicity walked the mule away from the picket line.

Please, oh please do not call to your mates and announce our departure.

A boulder served as her mounting block. Settled astride, Felicity nestled Daniel against her ribs, and he curled into her, sucking his fist.

"Walk on," she whispered.

The mule twitched his ears back. She tapped his sides with

her boots.

The beast snorted, planting all four hooves as if posing for the mule version of the Bamberg Horseman.

Wrapping her fingers in the sparse mane, Felicity dug her heels into the spotted sides.

The mule crow hopped, turning back to the campsite. Felicity pulled the lead rope, yanking the mule's head away from the picket line and kicked the mule with legs hardened from miles of walking next to Right.

The mule bolted down the trail, narrow hooves beating out a trot. Wrapping an arm around the baby, Felicity clung like a jockey to the mule.

She glanced over her shoulder. No sign of pursuit.

"We're free," she whispered to Daniel.

CADE LISTENED TO the fading staccato beat of the mule's hooves. He whipped back his blanket and reached for his boots.

CHAPTER 25

Stubborn
August 20, 1851

One boot in front of the other. Don't think about the canteen. Let the sweat run down my back. Don't think about chafed knees from riding that spotted bottlebrush of a mule.

Just keep walking. To the West. To Rye. Keep up the pace.

Felicity shifted the sling with the sleeping Daniel over to her other shoulder. The shoulder barely mended from her fall at Chimney Rock. The shoulder Rye healed.

Just walk. To Rye. Think about what to say when I find him.

The mule spooked to the right and wrenched her arm.

"There's nothing out here but sagebrush."

She pulled on the lead rope. The mule leaned back.

Gritting her teeth, Felicity swung the rope and whacked his belly with the knot at the end.

The mule brayed, sounding like something between a horse's whinny and a donkey's bellow.

Felicity clamped her hands around the mule's muzzle. Sound carried in the dry air. She didn't need Cade or Edmund to notice a mule had gone missing. Not yet. Not until she put miles between her and Edmund's intentions.

Ahead on the trail, a horse whinnied. It wasn't an echo.

Felicity's heart thumped. Tears started. There was just one person who could be ahead of her on the trail.

Rye.

He must've come out of his laudanum dreams.

He came back for me. I knew he'd never leave me behind. That darling man has come to his senses.

Felicity jerked the lead rope and forced the mule into a jog, bouncing Daniel awake in his sling. She put her hand under the sling to keep the worst of the motion from making him sick. Rounding a clump of sagebrush, a horse raised its head with ears up at the sound of hooves.

"Rye? Rye darling?" Tears rolled down her chin.

The horse snorted.

It lacked Cosmos' dappled gray pattern in the moonlight.

And another horse scrambled to its feet. It wasn't Cosmos.

The young man sitting up in the bundle of blankets was not Rye.

Hauling back on the lead rope, Felicity braced her hand on the mule's chest and shoved. But the mule laid back its ears and brayed.

"Looks like we've picked up a stray."

It was not Rye's voice.

And it did not belong to Cade.

The gun barrel in the boy's hands was pointed at her and Daniel. As much as she didn't want to run into Cade on the trail, Captain Braedon's rifle would have evened things out.

A second boy with a rifle laid across his arms stepped out from behind the sagebrush. He wasn't much older than Ezra Mueller. "I'll be having that mule of yer's."

Felicity put the lead rope behind her back, but the boy reached for the halter. He pointed with the end of the rifle and she walked into their camp.

The Blalock brothers. Just as Rye described them.

One shoulder higher than the other, Marcus Blalock had the face of a lad who should be teasing a girl in a pew at St. Paul's Chapel and learning to shave. But the short boy of thirteen or fourteen in the bundle of blankets with a knife-'em-in-the-ribs-then-ask-questions look to him, was Pete Blalock.

In the moonlight, the samovar Pug Watson discarded on the trail gleamed next to a crate of silverware, a music box, and the end of an ivory fan.

Her fan. The painted fan Edmund gave her in New York.

The Blalocks had been trailing the wagon company, picking up discarded treasures.

Pete pointed the muzzle of his gun at the sling holding Daniel. "Whatcha got in that sack?"

"My son."

"Show 'im to me."

Felicity opened a slit in the sling to show Daniel curled around her chest, thumb in his mouth.

"Where'd you come from?"

"I'm with the Jones company."

"Strayed away? Or they left you behind with a kid?"

She could lie or she could tell the truth. But would the truth matter when she was left for dead on the trail and Daniel discarded or sold to some family needing more hands to tend a homestead?

"Yes, to your second question."

"Paint us lucky, Petey. We picked us up a lady."

"Looks like yer right."

"Think we oughta celebrate some, don't you?"

Felicity backed away. "I won't tell anyone I've seen you. You can just keep … the cargo you already have."

Marcus rested his arms on the muzzle of the rifle. "Sounds right charitable of you."

"Just let us pass. Please."

"Don't know, but she said please real ladylike and all." Marcus tossed his rifle to his brother. "I think we should keep her. Kind of like a pet. You can cook, can't ye? My brother's cooking doesn't do much to kill a person's appetite if his grub doesn't kill a body outright."

"Shut your trap, Marcus."

Felicity clutched Daniel to her chest. "Take my mule."

Marcus held up the lead rope. "Already have."

"Then let me go. We can't be of any value to you."

Rye. Did he know the Blalock brothers were trailing the company? At some point, they wouldn't be content with picking up cast off items. They would go after what wasn't being left behind on the trail.

Marcus grabbed her elbow. "You ain't goin' jest yet."

"Now, Marcus, you know I don't go along with harmin' a mother and a child."

Pete climbed out of the blankets. He pried Marcus' thick fingers from Felicity's elbow.

"That's my fan." Felicity picked up the fan from the crate. "And that's my mule." She yanked the rope from Marcus's hand hoping the rough fibers scraped the skin from his palm.

"An jes' what do you plan on doin' with both?" Pete asked with a crooked smile.

"Leave the two of you behind. I'm catching up with that wagon train if I have to shoot my way out." Felicity slid her hand into the sling and stuck the end of the fan out as if it were a pistol. "Gentlemen, I'll take my leave."

"Didn't you check her for a gun?" Pete whipped the stock of the rifle to his shoulder, muzzle pointed at Felicity's chest. "Show me that pistol."

"How'd I know she'd keep a gun in with the kid?"

Felicity backed the mule up and turned to face a solid chest in a buckskin shirt. A chest with two arms cradling a rifle.

"Cade!" Felicity gasped, glad she left the man his boots.

"Braedon, that you?"

"'Deed it is, boys." Cade tipped his hat to Felicity. "Fine night for moon gazing, Mrs. Ormond."

"Still 'Jones' to you."

Cade scratched a white spot on the mule's head. "I'll have to thank you properly for returning my mule when we return to camp."

Pete lowered the muzzle of his rifle. "Thought you were with that dude and all those mules."

"Yep."

"We figured you had your hands full with Mr. Fancy Pants ... we figured t'was best to leave you be."

"Right kind of you, boys."

"You know the lady?"

"Yep."

Pete lowered the rifle. "How well?"

"You might say she's under my ... protection, for the time being."

Pete gestured with the rifle to Felicity. "I don't think a woman packin' a pistol needs much in the way of protectin'."

"Now there's a truth, if I ever heard one." Cade peered inside the sling at the sleeping Daniel. "But you just never know what or who a body might run into on the trail."

Marcus took a step backwards. "She found us ... we didn't go lookin' for her. Walked straight into our camp, scaring us both awake."

"Then we'll just be letting you get on with your beauty sleep." Cade grasped Felicity's arm and marched her from the campsite.

"Don't go getting lost, boys."

CHAPTER 26

Persistent
August 21, 1851

My time of chasing the sunset is over. I will be face first into the sunrise until the day we reach New York.

One boot in front of the other. Mind the gravel, the tufts of grass. Do not look beyond the edge of the bonnet. Do not look at the landmarks I hoped never to see again.

By noon they reached the marker with the three chalk hash marks. The arrow pointed the other way, not east.

The campsite where Rye woke her up with a full canteen and the promise of safety.

Did Rye find the wagon company? The man could track an antelope on the prairie, but with an open wound and a fever anything could happen on the trail.

And if he did reach the wagon company, was he explaining to Marta and the families that Gerald Sinclair cost him another wife and child?

Marta and Rye would do well together on the money Rye extorted from Edmund. Allegedly, extorted.

"We would make better time if you rode." Edmund's voice cut in on her thoughts.

"Your mare needs time off in a pasture. Not a rider."

"She is now yours. I bought her just for you. I assure you that Daphne is for you to ride."

"There's no one to drive the oxen." Trumbo, afraid of the

oxen, and Edmund, above the role of mule skinner and drover, left Cade to manage the mules and Felicity to resume her place beside Right.

"Then whip them on."

"Not in this heat. They'll die, and I'll be the one pulling the wagon."

"Then abandon it."

Felicity looked up from her study of the trail to Edmund, mounted on Zeus.

To think she used to be afraid of that horse.

She hated riding behind Zeus' docked tail in New York, round and round the park, nodding at the same riders. It made her sweat and in a fashionable riding costume she did not make for an elegant picture on a horse. She preferred the Meringue, the name Edmund called the white carriage with the velvet upholstery her father purchased for her use for errands in the city.

"What about the supplies?"

"Take what we need, purchase the rest along the way."

"That's just wasteful."

"It's practical, my dear."

"This wagon is Daniel's inheritance." Edmund would never understand why she kept a family bible, Aggie's wedding ring and a cross for the child. Touching the ivory at her neck, Felicity took one step, and another.

"Will the lad accept a cash payment for it?"

"He does not require charity."

"Then Mr. Braedon will sell it and the cattle at Fort Hall. We'll purchase a suitable mount for you. We'll travel faster by horseback."

Right and Left to be sold.

My steady companions.

What's left for Edmund to strip from my life?

Thunderheads blew in, greenish gray and lit scarlet underneath by the sunset. Thunder rumbled, but the rain teased, evaporating into a sweaty humidity. Wind snapped at the canvas on the wagon. Felicity held the blue wool dress tight against her shins to keep from tripping.

Daniel fussed in the sling across her chest.

"Is there something wrong with that child? He keeps crying."

"He's hot. And tired. And getting hungry."

"You will need to interview for a nursemaid. Perhaps there is someone suitable we can acquire for the trip to Washington."

She glared. No one would touch her child.

"Do not frown, my dear. All will be well. You'll see."

"How do you expect to explain my sudden appearance in New York to your friends?"

"Our friends, darling. When we reach Fort Hall, I will send a message to New York of our marriage. I'm certain that we can find someone to perform a lawful and binding marriage service. As for our friends, we will merely tell them I found you in Italy. That will account for your tanned skin."

"And how do 'we' explain Daniel?"

"I think that we should stay with the story that he is adopted from your deceased cousin who travelled with you."

"How convenient. You have thought of everything."

"Yes, everything fits as it should."

"How is it that your family did not find a more suitable bride for you? I figured your mother would have contracted with a match by now."

"Mr. Ormond?" Cade trotted up on a mule. He did not look at ease, not like that first day at Fort Hall.

"Yes?"

"We'd best camp for the night. There's an area just up ahead that will give us some shelter. I don't like the look of these clouds."

"There are more miles to be gained before dark. Just remember, the sooner I get to New York, the grander the bonus you will receive."

"Bonus or not, sir, we need to seek cover. Those clouds don't give a wit about your travel plans."

THEY CAMPED ON a shelf that jutted above the desert floor. The rust colored dirt had the looks of an old stream bank. They had to be near the pool where Rye slapped the ladle from her hand.

Edmund helped Felicity into the smaller of the upholstered folding chairs. She patted her forehead with her sleeve. Spreading her knees, she flapped the hem of her skirt, fanning air underneath the petticoat.

He brushed his finger over the sapphire ring on her left hand. "That's a lovely piece. Your mother's?"

Felicity shoved her hands into the pocket of her apron. "It's a family ring." She rose to join Daniel, sleeping in the back of the wagon. Humidity mixed with heat made the child whimper. "Good night."

Edmund grabbed her arm. "You're restrained with me." Forcing her hand from the apron, he kissed the blue veins on her wrist. "After we are home, I am certain you will recover from your misadventures and all will be well."

She picked at her eyebrow, pulling several hairs.

"I do love you. I wouldn't have come all this way if I cared nothing for you."

"Then I am sorry for you."

"I suggest a different tone of voice with me. Mr. Jones rejected you. Remember that you have a relation to raise. My generosity can provide him with a life of ease."

Edmund lifted Aggie's bible on the marquetry table and pressed it into her hand. "Accustom yourself to the weight of this, Felicity. You will be holding it when I take my oath, or I'm not worthy of the title Senator Edmund Ormond."

Rain drops splatted on Felicity's dry skin, rolling down to soak into the wool dress. The drops she caught on her tongue tasted like lead.

"Take cover, Edmund. Here comes the storm."

CHAPTER 27

The Storm
August 22, 1851

The canvas top flapped, belling and straining at the ties on the wagon. Felicity covered the supplies with the gutta percha tarp, rocking the barrels back on the tip of their metal bands to tuck the edges of the tarp underneath. Heavy, watertight items went on top of the tarp.

The gold initials on Rye's satchel gleamed when she shifted a sack of corn meal. The worn case, discarded. Her fingers found the lump on her collar bone. He was right about her shoulder. Rest, a sling, a cure.

If Rye could be so right about so many things, how could he be so wrong about their marriage? For all he talked of leaving baggage, he carried his along wrapped up tight like a poncho and tied to the back of Cosmos' saddle. He shook it out and wrapped himself in it at the first chance of rain.

Felicity put the case behind her calves to keep it dry and pulled the quilt over her shoulders and Daniel.

Rain pricked the canvas like a needle picking up threads on an embroidery hoop. She snorted.

Since when did a little rain frighten Cade?

Hopefully Rye found the wagon company and shelter.

Was Rye tucked in with Marta?

Would he marry Marta out of spite?

Did he already get Lane to say the binding words in front

of the company? Did Rye teach Marta to dance under the stars?

She had to harness her thoughts. What's done, was over. Severed.

Felicity stroked Daniel's hair. The curls twined around her fingers. He clutched the rag doll and slept with a hand on her neck.

The boy needed more than a nanny and boarding school and a military life.

She didn't have a choice.

Or did she?

With Edmund fretting in his tent over the weather, could she get Right and Left hitched and on the trail? If not the wagon, a mule? Would Cade drag her back again to Edmund or let her go? If Edmund touched her once more, she was sure to vomit on his shoes.

Aggie would tell her it was time to use the sense God gave a goat to take charge of her life.

The rain sizzled like bacon in the skillet, fat popping in the coals.

Rye was her rightful and yes, stubborn, hurt husband. Their path to marriage wasn't a straight path, but she chose not to stray.

The rain slowed, dripping. She peeled the tarp back and stood up, pushing the sagging pockets of water in the canvas covering. Water splashed on the ground. Cade cursed under the wagon.

Petty, true, but a small revenge on her watch dog.

If she had to point a rifle at Cade, he was going to help her hitch the team. He owed her that much for believing Edmund's tales of marriage. Not sure what she would do when she found Rye, she would just have to figure that out on the way to the meet the company.

The air cooled and the wind picked up. The tent across the campsite flapped, the guidelines snapped and fluttered.

Sheets of rain fell. Water ran into the wagon through the seams and cracks in the wagon walls.

Lightning flashed. Thunder rolled.

Right or Left bawled in the darkness.

Lightning rode overhead. Thunder crashed. Felicity caught a whiff of sulphur. The hair on her arms stood out and her shins ached.

Felicity pounded on the floor of the wagon. No response.

Crawling out of the quilt, she hung her head over the tailgate. "Cade, you under there?"

A burst of lightning flashed a black and white image of the campsite. Runoff chewed at the edges of the picket line.

"Get in here before you float away!"

Cade tossed his hat in the wagon. "Don't have to invite me twice."

WET BACON. WET wool. Wet corn meal.

A wet and hungry Daniel. Trumbo stirred a thin gruel for the baby over a smoking fire.

The campsite crouched on the edge of a new cut stream bed. But the stream bed dried into cracked mud in the heat, the water absorbed into the gritty soil or evaporated.

Edmund nudged a slumped bag of flour. His muddy hunting boot left a dent in the side.

"We'll depart as soon as we have breakfasted."

"Surely you've noticed that we are without locomotion?"

"Where's the stock?"

"Cade is on round up duty. My guess is that Right and Left didn't get far in their hobbles."

"How long will that take?"

"I have no idea."

"What are you doing?"

"Drying supplies."

"Leave them for scavengers."

"We'd starve on the trail."

"Then I'm going hunting."

"There's not much to be had in the way of game." She grinned, recalling Dodge's reaction to the skunk.

Edmund scraped a boot on the sack. "I do look forward to the plains. I quite enjoyed hunting buffalo. In one day, I shot twenty-three of the beasts. Trumbo kept tally for me. Didn't you, Trumbo?"

"Yes, sir. Twenty-three."

She pressed her tongue to her teeth. Edmund probably left them to rot. What a waste of hide and meat.

While Trumbo fed Daniel the gruel, Felicity laid supplies from the wagon on the tarp. Steam rose from the clothing and quilts slung over a clothesline.

When Cade returned, she planned to take him aside and beg him to look the other way while she hitched the team. She would find a way to repay the money he would lose by not fulfilling his contract. Surely he saw Edmund wasn't after marriage. Or maybe he did want to marry her, but only to keep her from testifying. He needed to produce her to save his career. A career and an image he worked hard to preserve.

The crate of law books waited for her on the tailgate. Prying up the top, the wrinkled leather binding and musty odor made her want to shut the lid and leave the box for scavengers.

The books, her only legacy from Gerald Sinclair. She gave her word to keep them.

And to pray for her father. She never fulfilled that promise.

Felicity opened the cover of the first book to meet her hand. Weighed down with water, the book pressed into her lap. The wet leather and the binding separated at the spine. An absolute loss. She set the book on the muddy ground, and picked up the next.

The edges of the pages wrinkled and stuck together. She

picked at the binding, pulling at a loose thread to tighten the loops. The stitches unraveled and the binding separated. Another loss. She tossed the book to the mud and pulled up the next book on the crate.

Heavy, but not wet. Too heavy for the law books she handled in her father's library.

The paste under the end paper smeared onto the leather. Not the mark of a quality binder or pressman. She picked at the paste, exposing the long stitches under the end pages. Hand sewn stitches.

Was the entire collection flawed?

A fourth book. Same binding.

A gunshot echoed from the other side of the ridge. Edmund must have found a target.

Another shot. She prayed he wasn't using Left or Right as skeet.

A third shot.

My, the lad is busy. Is he killing all the wildlife?

Felicity pulled the tail of the thread. It broke. She picked at the stitches. The end page peeled away.

Five gold coins. Felicity stared at the coins. Not bank notes. Coins.

She blinked, peering out from the edge of her bonnet. Trumbo diapered Daniel, tickling the baby's feet.

Felicity peeled the coins off the binding and tucked them into her apron pocket.

The books in the mud at her feet yielded coins. And Latin.

No wonder the crate was heavy.

Penciled phrases written on the back side of the end pages in Gerald Sinclair's handwriting. Her eyes blurred, seeing the curve of the beloved letters. The last riddle from her father was not in the text, but in the hiding place. In precise Latin, the coins represented her dowry, inherited from her mother. Converted to gold, pasted under the binding.

She pulled all the books out, feeling for coins. Nine books

yielded coins. Coins she dropped into the pocket of her apron. The slimmer volumes had Latin phrases written in the margins. She scanned, flipping through the pages.

Details of board meetings, decisions. Members present who voted and how they voted. Garrety and Brown. Sinclair, Wilkerson, Samuels. Demarais. Waite. The other Waite.

And one name, underscored.

Ormond.

Edmund Ormond.

The ninth member.

The letter in the thick white Ormond stationery. On her father's desk, the morning he confessed his part in the railroad. Did he threaten Gerald Sinclair with exposure?

Edmund and his fine manners, writhing in and out of scandal. He changed his skin depending on who he needed to impress, coiling when threatened, striking blindly when stepped upon.

Trumbo wiped Daniel's face. Aggie's blue dress steamed beside the quilts the clothesline.

No Edmund, not yet.

Maybe he would trip on the rocks. He carried a rifle. Helmut Schneider wasn't the only emigrant to die of an accidental gunshot.

No wonder her father forced a broken engagement on her. Forced her onto the trail.

It was the only way to save her.

She ripped the pages with underscored phrases from the books, stacking the pages in order by date.

She recalled her father's words. It isn't so much the books, but what the books contained that was critical to her survival in the new country.

I thought he meant the law, the codes set down for a civilized existence.

How many times did I come close to pitching the books on the trail? And now they were going to save my life.

"Felicity?"

Cade was as tall as Rye, and he wore a familiar expression. The look that Rye wore when something was wrong. Dead wrong.

"You'd better come with me."

Tucking the pages and the apron full of coins into Daniel's chest of clothes, she waved to Trumbo. He waved back, holding up the rag doll.

She lengthened her stride to keep up with Cade and followed him and a confusion of faded hoof prints into the lava field.

Three mules, dead. She slipped on the loose rocks. A steadying hand caught her elbow and kept her from falling.

"Legs were broke. I had to put 'em down."

Felicity shook her head, unsure why Cade felt the need to show her the dead mules. Unless he needed her help to divide their load among the rest of the string.

"This way."

Some of the washed out tracks skirted the lava field, headed toward a stream bed.

The hoof prints were not mule. The tracks were made by cleft hooves.

A vulture hopped away from Left. Felicity ran forward, flapping her apron. The bird hopped, spread his wings and flew overhead.

"Looks like he got caught in the gully washer last night and drowned." Cade unbuckled the hobbles on Left's legs.

"He never did swim well." Tears welled. "Where's Right?"

"This way."

Right wasn't far from his yoke mate, resting on his chest. The dirt was kicked up around him.

"It's your decision."

The ox bawled, rolling on his side, thrashing his hobbled legs, struggling to stand, to take up the yoke. When the ox quieted, she caught and cradled Right's head in her lap and with her skirt hem cleaned out the dirt from his eyes.

Felicity rubbed the notch on his horn, as she did in the prairie, resting her elbows on his ribs at sundown.

"It's his back, isn't it?"

"Can't say for sure, ma'am. Rest might help, but I think it would be a mercy to put him down."

I wish I could tell you why you were taken out of the home pasture in New York and forced to cover thousands of miles, only to lay in the dirt in the desert.

Kissing the red flecked forehead, Felicity unbuckled the hobbles.

Cade handed her his pistol.

She aimed at the white swirl between Right's eyes. "I am so sorry, boy."

Closing her eyes, she pulled the trigger.

The shot sent the vulture soaring into the air. Other birds, circling, waiting their turn.

Cade walked a few paces and stopped. "Coming?"

"I ... I need a few minutes. To think."

"I'll come back for you if I don't see you following."

She picked up a rock, and another, stacking others around Right. The heat made her dizzy and the dry thirst pricked at the back of her throat. She tossed the rock in her hand to the dirt. On her knees, she pulled the rocks away from Right's body. The vultures and foxes and other scavengers needed to feed and it was fitting that Right fulfill his life as a creature of service.

Aggie was right.

They've been my constant companions.

And my best chance to return to Rye.

I am flat out of tears.

The vulture landed in the tree. A patient bird, waiting for her to leave. Or join the cattle.

Felicity bent her head, stretching her neck to relieve the knots along her spine.

Time to choose.

Be silent. Pocket the coins, burn the pages and regain her former life of ease. Daniel never had to know hunger or risk his life in the backwoods. If she married Edmund, as his wife she could not testify against him. His presidential aspiration may be fulfilled, publicly supported by his doting and obedient wife.

Speak the truth. If she exposed Edmund and his less than presidential actions, she had no refuge. Cast out by the men who promised to protect, love and cherish her to the end of her days. She would be alone.

Rye may not want her, but she wanted Rye. She had faith that was the right direction.

She waited for her guard. He walked up the wash, looking for her. Time to move on.

"I'll go east with you, peacefully, but no further than Fort Hall."

"Pardon?"

"I'm going after Rye. I'll wait for the next company that's headed to Oregon. I would rather die and be left to rot on the prairie that travel with Mr. Ormond."

"I made a promise to Rye – "

"As did I. In front of a whole company of witnesses. And I intend to honor that promise."

"What makes you so sure he'll take you back?"

"I'm not sure. But let me show you what I came across this afternoon. Then you can make up your mind to help me or not. Either way, I am heading west."

CHAPTER 28

Fare You Well
August 23, 1851

"My dear, you have been crying."

Edmund slumped in his folding chair, palms up, shirt collar open and vest spread wide. His skin pale, eyes bloodshot. Not the dapper man who left camp swinging a rifle at his side.

"Right and Left are dead."

"Who?"

"The cattle. We need to find a way to harness the mules to the wagon. If that doesn't work, you or Cade will have to go to Fort Hall to secure oxen."

"Abandon the wagon. You'll ride the guide's mount. We can't afford the delay."

"We need the supplies and the mules are overloaded."

"We will buy new supplies. New oxen, or mules, or whatever your fancy is ... just hurry and decide what must be salvaged. Do it quickly."

Yellow sweat stained Edmund's shirt. The humidity wrung it out of all of them.

Wasn't the man impervious to bodily functions? Must be a victim of heatstroke. That's what Rye would tell her.

"When I get to Fort Hall, I'm turning around."

"You'll do as you are told." A flash of anger, not the controlled speech he used with her.

"You don't need me to testify for you. I think that you

need to keep me from testifying against you."

"That's absurd. After the inquiry, all will be well. You'll see. I know you can do this. I saw the mob collected on your doorstep after the article in the Evening Post. You handled the rabble with grace, doling out what you could from the walls and drawers and shelves of your home. That grace you exhibited will carry you far in the Capital."

Edmund folded forward, forearms on his knees. He bit pressed a fist to his mouth. Belched.

"I heard some of your father's landscapes made their way in the hands of the crowd. I liked those paintings; they were rather well done." He grabbed his belly with both hands. "Pardon me, I must retire –"

"Are you well?"

Edmund vomited. He held up a shaking hand, skin flushed at his lack of control over his body.

Her stomach roiled. She passed him a napkin to wipe his chin.

He kicked dirt over the mess on the ground.

"Cade!"

Cade and Trumbo carried Edmund into the tent. She tossed the lap desk from the bed to the floor and flung the sheets over the footboard.

"My pardon, Felicity. I don't know what overcame me … urp … must be something in what Trumbo fixed this morning."

"I think you're overheated. Will you be alright for a minute? I need to check on Daniel."

"And I felt so much better after bathing."

Felicity turned. Did Rye miss a water source on the trail? They were a day or so from the cave. The trail was dry all the way to Fort Hall and no water to fill a canteen unless rainwater pooled. But that would have drained or evaporated by this hour. "Bathing? Where? There is no place that I recall …"

"I found a pool this morning while hunting. Surely the

former Mr. Jones had the wit to find it."

At the word "former," Felicity caught her breath.

"Rye wouldn't let us stop there. It wasn't fit for the livestock."

"Nonsense. It was most refreshing. Rather a metallic taste ... like the Fairview Springs."

"You should rest."

"I will ride in the wagon until I am recovered. Take my mount."

Edmund rose, but wracked with cramps, coiled on the sheets. He vomited into a basin, an arm wrapped around his gut. His long body rippled.

"Water ... in the pitcher ... please."

Felicity stepped from the tent, handing Daniel to Trumbo. "Keep my son in the wagon. Don't bring him anywhere near Mr. Ormond."

Vomiting, milky stool, gut pains, thirst. Rye's voice ticked off symptoms in her memory. All that was missing was milky stool.

Cholera? Rye said the pool was foul.

Edmund slept for a few hours, or passed out, she was not sure.

A foul smell came from the sheets. Felicity ticked off milky stool on the list of symptoms.

"Wagon packed?"

She startled, his wide blue eyes staring at her.

"You're too ill to be moved."

"You shouldn't see me like this. It is not proper for a lady."

"As a wife, I would be present at my husband's side."

"We must marry, and soon. My heart, I cannot wait for us to be joined."

Cade lifted his head, listening to Edmund's words. The former captain stood guard at the entry to the tent, arms folded. Turning red, he looked at the rug, then at the canvas walls, but not at her. Coughing into his fist, he backed out through the flaps. "Seems there's something I need to tend to out here."

Was he ashamed for his part in Edmund's stack of lies? He should be.

"I am bound in marriage to Rye. Even if I were free, I would never marry. I don't care what your mother wants you to do." Maragon Ormond, with her perfectionist ways, took a sweet boy and molded that child's soul into the kind of man who would tell lies and steal from the innocent to get his mother's approval.

"You are free. You are free to marry ... to marry me." His teeth chattered. "Jones took the cholera ... sent you from him. To save you and that wailing child. Oh, please, make that child silent. My head hurts so."

Felicity swayed, dizzy. Was that the reason for the laudanum?

"Rye was sick and you let him ride off?"

"I believe I am ill, my love."

"How could you leave him?"

"Leave who?"

"Rye, my husband."

"Better off without him. Fool. Refused money ..."

"What money? You told me Rye took the money."

"For you."

"You're not making sense."

Edmund closed his eyes, sinking into the mass of pillows.

"Wake up. Come on, Edmund. Open your eyes."

"Let me sleep. Go 'way."

"What have you done?"

"Thirsty."

Cade passed a cut glass tumbler. She put it in Edmund's hand, but he shook so hard the water spilled onto the sheets.

"Did he say he had cholera? Tell me about Rye." Felicity crouched on the carpet. She rocked back and forth on her heels, hands pressed to her forehead. Did Rye sent her away to keep her safe? So that she would not be made ill or left to travel the remainder of the journey with a baby and no one to protect her?

A soft life with Edmund was the best solution Rye grasped in the face of hardship.

Three hours later, Edmund argued with his mother. Felicity exchanged one wet cloth for another on his forehead.

"This is not to be borne..."

"What about Rye ... wake up." Felicity whispered, voice hoarse from hours of pleading. Was cholera the reason for Rye taking the laudanum?

Edmund died at dawn. He died, never knowing Felicity found her father's papers, and they revealed Edmund's hand in the Garrety-Brown scandal.

She gathered the spyglass, a small oval portrait of his mother, and a tie pin. At Fort Boise, she would send the items and daguerreotype to Mrs. Ormond. Her last letter to that New York address.

If something happened to Daniel, I would hope someone would be kind enough to let me know what happened to my son.

Felicity stepped into the morning wind. It was dry, familiar to her. Clean.

Cade rose from the upturned wash tub. "Begging your pardon, Mrs. Jones, but I won't be doubting your word in the future."

"Finally. Mrs. 'Jones'. Took your time."

"Let's just say I have a history with a "Miss" who was more of a "Mrs." than she let on ... and my sympathies are with her husband."

"Get me to Rye and no apology is necessary."

The vultures floated in the midmorning wind.

"There's something else we need to do. How well are you acquainted with a shovel and a burial service?"

"All too well, ma'am."

Cade and Felicity sorted through the saddlebags. A silver tea set landed in the pile to stay at the campsite. She added the satin dress. Kept the leather portfolio to sort through on the trail. The Blalock brothers had fine pickings to fight over.

But the money box with a silver lock and key, Felicity handed to Cade. "This, I believe, belongs to you."

"That's not mine."

"It's your bonus. He promised you a grand reward. You can start a farm with what's in there."

"Goes against my conscience. Never should have let Rye talk me into this fool venture."

"What are we going to do with it?"

Cade rubbed his jaw. "Trumbo? For back wages?"

"What wages?"

"Exactly that."

"Seems fitting."

"He'll think so."

The wagon was a loss without the oxen. Zeus was recovered. Daphne given to Trumbo for a mount. The mule string packed. Water distributed among the mules so that if one mule ran off, the water supply was not sacrificed.

She was ready.

Felicity turned her face to the sunset.

FELICITY BOUNCED ON Zeus's back, her backside slapping against the flat saddle. His trot was a high stepping stride and the saddle slippery. They rode past the boulder with the hash marks, refilled barrels at the cave. A fresh cut bundle of sagebrush joined the faded bouquet on Aggie's grave.

Grass shoots and the tips of wildflowers emerged. The rain drove life into the dry, scrubby land.

Two days later, the tracks of the wagon company were wind damaged, not washed out by flooding or dimpled by rain.

Felicity stood on the edge of the campsite that night, eyes wide, trying catch the glimmer of a campfire in the distance.

Three days into the trail, Cade rode ahead, marking the way for Felicity and Trumbo to follow with the string of mules. Daniel rode in the sling over her shoulder, sleeping in the heat. He was thin, too thin for her liking.

Cade trotted up the trail to Felicity. She was drowsy, the sun high overhead. The thirst returned, denied until the evening halt.

"Prepare yourself."

Shifting the reins to her left hand, she dug her heels into Zeus' ribs. The Thoroughbred shot forward, the mules trotting behind with Trumbo.

A burnt wagon, wheels buckled.

Scorched barrels and rotting bacon sides scattered in the sagebrush.

Bullet holes splintered the Robinson's drop leaf table.

Crates, bonnets, a clothing trunk and Pug Watson's scavenged samovar littered the old campsite.

The samovar she last saw at the Blalock campsite.

The boys tired of picking up scraps. They went after what folks weren't pitching out of the wagons.

A pile of stones with a wood marker. She put a hand to her throat.

Was it Rye?

She trotted forward, jumping down from Zeus. Leaving the reins trailing, she dropped to her knees at the wood marker.

No name, no date. No lettering that would have washed off in the rain. Her hand removed one rock, then another. She held the third rock in her hand, turned it over. The rock, warm from the sun, made her remember the squares of sod at Lone Elm.

She dropped the rock onto the grave. If it was Rye, she couldn't bring him back to life no matter how many rocks she pawed through.

If Rye lived, he wouldn't give the wagon company time to carve a name.

Rye can't be dead. Please, oh please God, do not let him be dead.

If not Rye, which of the families suffered a loss?

Felicity clasped her hands. As a girl, she believed in God. Believed in her father. Trusted Edmund. Believed Rye would keep his promise to always be with her.

Faith. Rye told her to believe in it.

Perhaps it was not the ending of their marriage, but the testing of their bond.

Felicity bowed her head and prayed, the words pouring out of her, washing away her doubts. Cleansing her, like the sweetest creek water. This was the peace she missed, the peace she yearned for. The comfort that comes from a true father, one that never betrayed, one that never lied.

He may test me, but He never abandoned me, even as I left Him.

"They can't be more than a few days ahead." Cade held Zeus' reins out to her.

"You were in the cavalry. Can't you ride faster? Use those spurs, man."

FELICITY PACED IN the moonlight, a shawl wrapped tight around her shoulders against the wind. No smell of smoke from a campfire, no flicker of distant flames. Cade guessed that the river was near. Crickets chirped, the first in weeks.

Rye is close, I'm sure of it.

But how do I approach him?

Edmund is dead. If he still believes I am Mrs. Ormond, that obstacle is dead and buried.

I'll just have to argue my case, using the evidence in the portfolio to prove my points to the judge and jury.

And I won't stop until I have the verdict I want.

Cade snored on his bed roll, Daniel tucked next to his side. The man needed a wife. A son or daughter of his own.

She scratched her chin. Aggie's matchmaking skills apparently rubbed off on her.

Above the click of the crickets, a rhythmic screech wailed in the distance.

Faint, but true.

Cade snorted and jumped up, reaching for his rifle.

"Indians? Sounds like they're torturing some poor soul."

"You're wrong. It's Pug Watson's bagpipes."

CHAPTER 29

La Riviere Boisee
August 30, 1851

The first wagon she recognized belonged to the Zenger family. Nudging Zeus into a trot, she stood in the stirrups searching for Maggie McHenry.

"Felicity?"

Maggie's shock melted into a broad smile and a joint grinding hug.

"Lass, I've missed ye and yer little one. Where's me boy?"

"He's missed you just as much."

"Rye said you'd left us to head back to New York."

"Changed my mind and picked up a few new members for the company. You remember Cade Braedon ... and this is Trumbo, who is a rival for you in Daniel's affections."

"That's so? Well, welcome Mr. Trumbo. Any friend of Danny's is welcome at my campfire."

"Where's Rye?"

Maggie took Daniel into her arms. "He's been stayin' outside the encampment."

"He's not staying with the Schneiders?"

"Keepin' ta 'imself, he says."

Felicity stood at Rye's lone campfire. Smoothing her gown, she wished for a mirror. And a comb. The dark wool dress needed washing and the red trimmed boots split open at the heel around start of the cutoff. Any sign of *Maison Gagelin*, scrubbed out.

Cosmos stood with one hip cocked, dozing in the sun. The saddle and blanket were in the grass, but the rifle wasn't in the scabbard.

Putting the satchel with the gold initials next to the saddle, she used her apron as a potholder to lift the lid of a pot on the coals. A savory stew simmered. Her mouth watered.

Marta's cooking?

She greased the Dutch oven, her finger dipping into the dent on the lid. Taking flour and other ingredients from Trumbo's camp kitchen, she whipped up a batch of biscuits and nestled the Dutch oven in the coals to bake.

A cold nose pushed against her palm.

"Dodge!"

"I thought I told you to get lost." Rye, haggard, a man without a full meal or a full night's sleep. Three ducks hung from a leather throng in his hand.

"I told you, I don't get lost. I may get distracted, but I don't get lost. Besides, these boots have a desire to walk into Oregon City and so do I."

"Where is your Edmund? I figured you'd be almost to Fort Hall by now. Daniel with you?"

"He's with Maggie."

"The wagon?"

"Gone. Cattle, too."

"Mules yours?"

"Ours, if you want them."

"Figured they were your husband's property."

"They are. You can name them whatever you'd like."

"So where you hiding him?"

"Who?"

"Mr. Ormond."

"You were right about not drinking from that pool."

He tossed the mallards to the ground. "So you're a widow?"

"Not as long as you're drawing a breath."

"I think you know what I mean."

"I do. And I have Cade here to help you see reason."

Felicity opened the portfolio.

Rye winced, backing away. "Come on, Dodge."

"Did you ever stop to read it?"

Rye crossed his arms. Dodge stretched out at his feet, tongue lolling.

"Exhibit One. The letter I wrote to Edmund. The letter was written on March 3, 1851. You joined the company on March 14th, after I sent the letter. I was new to trail life. I hated the dust and the death and the hardness. I hated you, for a time. But then my life changed. I changed. I am not the same girl who you met in Independence.

"Exhibit Two. The announcement in the Evening Post. This was submitted before we were married with the instructions to run the announcement on the day of our wedding. My father was thorough, but you can understand that he forgot to cancel the announcement. It ran, to the Ormond's humiliation. There was an immediate retraction, to my humiliation."

Rye grunted. Cade glared at him.

"What, you too?"

"Just listen to your wife."

"Exhibit Three. The alleged marriage certificate. While the 'certificate' bears my name embossed on it, with Edmund's name, please note the blank signature line. The lack of witness signatures. The certificate was prepared, but never executed."

Rye opened his arms.

Cade took the certificate from Felicity and nudged her towards Rye. "I think you got the verdict you wanted all along."

"I'm just glad that you didn't make Pug give up his bagpipes or I would never have found you." She laid her head against his shoulder, nestling into him.

Home. At long last.

She sniffed. He smelled like the liniment she made for him.

"Thought you'd appreciate that."

"Marta cooking for you?"

"Don't be sore about Marta. I just said that to get you mad enough to leave."

"Took up cooking while I was away?"

"When Cade and I campaigned, there were times we had to forage for ourselves. You kill it, you cook it … or you go hungry."

"All this time and you neglected to tell me you cooked?"

"You're a quick study."

"And the laudanum?"

"Gone. Never going near it again."

"Edmund said you came down with cholera."

"Just the infection. It's clearing up."

"And the grave? We passed what looked like an ambush."

"All's well. You missed a brawl. The Blalock brothers won't be harassing wagon companies in this life time."

"What happens when the next bad patch comes up? Going to send me back East?"

"About what I said to you … I figured the safest place for you was back East with Edmund rather than widowed in the Territory."

"I didn't know it, but he was the one who structured the Garrety-Brown Railway Line. I found my father's papers."

"What papers?"

"The ones you kept trying to get me to pitch overboard about every hundred miles."

"In the crate of books?"

"My father had a fine sense of humor. Tucked in the spine and between the pages he stuffed meeting notes and contracts as well as this." She dug into a pack and pulled out a bag of coins.

"We're not taking Ormond's money."

"I gave all of Edmund's cash to Trumbo for services rendered."

"Then what's all this?"

"My dowry. My father held back my mother's inheritance after her … suicide. My mother burnt down Almstead House rather than live a less than decorous life. She quit on my father and I."

"I had no idea."

"This money was never part of my father's dealings and I think it would cover the cost of a land claim and staking us for seed, stock and equipment."

"Seed, stock and equipment?"

"Yes, I've been thinking about planting fruit trees."

"Glad you didn't pitch those books. Fruit trees are expensive."

"Thought you'd be glad."

"I'm just happy you showed up this morning. I missed those biscuits of yours."

"You've run out of prairie to hide them in."

"You weren't supposed to see that."

"Course not. But where to do you think I pitched mine?"

Cade elbowed Rye in the ribs. "She's all yours, now."

Rye held out his hand to Cade. "Thanks for watching over her."

He kissed Felicity's brow. "Stay for breakfast. My wife makes the best biscuits you've ever tasted, dented pot and all."

EPILOGUE

Oregon City
October 18, 1851

Felicity pulled the quilt over Daniel. The steam off the backs of the mule team joined the mist under the gold and scarlet leaves of the maple trees on the bluff overlooking Abernethy Green. The lead jenny jerked on her bit, pulling against the collar and the harness. Felicity set the brake on the wagon. The new wagon, purchased at Fort Boise.

Rye walked with a sure step through the wet ferns, working with Cade to tighten the girths and check the harness before the descent.

The back of the wagon was packed with barrels and crates. She threw out most of what she packed along on the trail, not all of it spoiled flour, curling tongs or silver ladles. It got tiresome, hauling old baggage around. It bruised the shins, got dropped on folk's toes, and tripped her up when she needed to move ahead.

In place of what was lost, she carried a feeling of worth. Worthiness of receiving love, worthiness of giving love.

Of being a wife.

A mother.

To have faith in those unions.

To make choices with the knowledge she had the freedom to choose.

The sleeping Daniel kicked his legs in the sling she made

from Aggie's shawl. The child with the chance to grow up in a land that wasn't populated by quitters. They were free to live in this new territory, one not bound by the need to match a china service to wall paper or the colors in the brocade of a man's vest to his cravat.

Where a person was measured in stamina and courage and innovation.

She turned her face up to the sprinkle of rain drops. "Looks like the only snow we will see is what's above the timber line."

"Don't go getting comfortable, my love. There's a storm over the mountains to the south of us and we need to push on."

"Come on, Dodge. Let's go."

The snow was at their backs, on the flanks of Mt. Hood.

Oregon City was before them, drawing them on.

End Note

The story of Rye and Felicity will continue as a part of the next novel in the series, "Cornerstone", due to be released in the summer of 2013.

To understand the scope of crossing the Oregon Trail, please visit the National Parks Services site to view a topographic map of the 2,000 mile journey beginning in Missouri and ending in Oregon. The map is located at http://www.nps.gov/oreg/planyourvisit/upload/HFC%20OREG_map2007a.pdf

About the Author

N. L. Campbell lives and writes at the end of the Oregon Trail where the history of the pioneers is part of everyday life.